C0-BWY-044

TOP CRIME

TOP CRIME

The Authors' Choice

Selected and introduced by the authors themselves

compiled and edited by

Josh Pachter

St. Martin's Press
New York

 For information, address St. Martin's Press, 175 Fifth Avenue, New York, N.Y. 10010.

Library of Congress Cataloging in Publication Data
Main entry under title:

Top crime.

1. Detective and mystery stories. I. Pachter, Josh.
PN6120.95.D45T6 1984 808.83'872 83-27254
ISBN 0-312-80906-9

First Published in Great Britain in 1983 by J.M. Dent & Sons Ltd.

First U.S. Edition

10 9 8 7 6 5 4 3 2 1

For Vicki,
with love

Contents

Isaac Asimov, 'Out of Sight' 1
Michael Avallone, 'Every Litter Bit Hurts' 17
Gary Brandner, 'Parlor Game' 23
Leslie Charteris, 'The Pearls of Peace' 38
Stanley Ellin, 'The Specialty of the House' 59
Michael Gilbert, 'The Unstoppable Man' 77
Joe Gores, 'Goodbye, Pops' 87
Patricia Highsmith, 'The Terrapin' 95
Edward D. Hoch, 'The Leopold Locked Room' 108
James Holding, 'Second Talent' 126
H. R. F. Keating, 'Gup' 135
Peter Lovesey, 'The Locked Room' 149
Florence V. Mayberry, 'Woman Trouble' 163
Ed McBain, 'First Offense' 177
Patricia McGerr, 'Somebody's Telling the Truth' 195
Francis M. Nevins, Jr, 'Black Spider' 207
Josh Pachter, 'Invitation to a Murder' 223
Bill Pronzini, 'Proof of Guilt' 235
Ellery Queen, 'The Adventure of Abraham Lincoln's Clue' 245
Georges Simenon, 'Seven Little Crosses in a Notebook' 261
Henry Slesar, 'The Right Kind of a House' 316
Julian Symons, 'A Theme for Hyacinth' 324
Lawrence Treat, 'L as in Loot' 344
Janwillem van de Wetering, 'A Great Sight' 357

Contents

Introduction

In the autumn of 1981, I came up with an idea for an anthology of crime stories – literally, a superlative collection. The idea was to put together a volume of the very best contemporary detective and mystery stories, as selected, not by me, not by some distinguished panel of critics or fans, but by the authors themselves.

Egged on by my publisher, I wrote letters to some fifty of the finest living crime writers. 'What's the *best* short story you've ever written?' I asked them. 'Or, otherwise, what's your personal favourite of all the tales you have penned?' Some of the authors I contacted never replied to my letter. A few wrote back – or had their agents do so – to say that they were not interested in the project. But, on the whole, the response was overwhelming: replies came pouring in.

Several writers told me that it had been difficult or even impossible for them to select a single best or favourite story. 'Trying to pick the "very best" of the 50-odd short stories I have published,' wrote Gary Brandner, 'is rather like a parent trying to pick out the best of his children.' 'I'd probably give a different answer each time I was asked,' Ed Hoch admitted. The best comment, or, at least, *my* favourite, was Peter Lovesey's: 'I don't think of particular books or stories as favourites. I'm always more interested in what comes next than in things I wrote some time ago. It was G.J. Smith, the callous murderer of the Brides in the Baths, who was quoted as saying, "When they're dead, they're dead." The same is true of writing books. But, of course, Smith took the insurance money, and I'm only too grateful to take the royalties.'

In spite of the difficulty of choosing, Brandner, Hoch and Lovesey all eventually *did* select stories for inclusion in this collection. So did 21 other writers. Many (like Ellery Queen, Georges Simenon and Ed McBain) had no trouble at all, and unhesitatingly picked a story to send me. A few sent anywhere from two to seven stories and asked *me* to choose the one I wanted to use. Leslie Charteris narrowed the field down to five of the Saint's buccaneering adventures and had his wife make the final selection. Isaac Asimov submitted a lovely tale of the

Black Widowers, titled 'The Cross of Lorraine,' in which the solution of the mystery requires the reader to be familiar with the existence of Exxon gas stations, which can be found on every third street-corner in the United States; since Exxon stations are all called Esso stations in Europe, though, 'The Cross of Lorraine' would make little sense to European readers, and when I pointed that problem out to him, he cheerfully selected a different Black Widowers story, 'Out of Sight', as his favourite.

Along with the stories themselves, I also received letters from the various authors. Without exception, these letters were warm, encouraging, friendly – and often filled with intelligent and well-expressed explanations of the reasoning behind the writers' choices. It quickly became clear that the task of introducing all the stories in this volume was one which could best be performed by their respective authors, rather than by me.

So out went another series of letters, and back came another series of replies. One or two people declined the invitation to introduce their own stories – they declined in the kindest possible terms, though, and I've never felt so good about being said no to! The rest of the writers whose work appear in these pages graciously took time out from their hectic schedules to prepare brand-new introductory material for their stories. And so the end result is a collection of 24 excellent stories, from leading writers in England, France, Holland and (the majority) America. It would be too enormous a task to list each writer's books and stories in some kind of appendix, and in any case their collective pedigree, output and quality probably makes this unnecessary. All you – the reader – have to do is to sit back in the secure knowledge that you are in the safe hands of the supreme masters of the genre.

It's traditional for editors to extend thanks to the various people involved in the putting together of the books they edit. That's a tradition of which I wholeheartedly approve, and I'd like to begin by offering my deepest gratitude to my collaborators in the preparation of *Top Crime* – the authors whose stories you are about to read. Without their generous co-operation, the volume you now hold in your hands would be a thin one indeed.

Special thanks go to Ed Hoch, for a host of invaluable comments and suggestions, and to Stan Cohen, for providing me with many much-needed addresses. Pat Hoch, Ed's wonderful wife, also located some hard-to-track-down addresses for me. To you, too, Pat, my thanks. Vanessa Holt, of John Farquharson Limited in London, was kind enough to put me in touch with Peter Lovesey; she also ably represents Ed McBain overseas. Joyce Aitken, who works for Georges Simenon, provided me with valuable biographical information about her employer. And Barbara Bazyn of *Ellery Queen's Mystery Magazine* was helpful in arranging for the use of Isaac Asimov's 'Out of Sight'.

Thanks also to Peter Loeb, whose enthusiasm and support enabled me to turn my idea from a pipe dream into a reality. If there were more publishers like Peter, there would be fewer editors walking around with ulcers.

And finally, my thanks to you, the reader, for adding *Top Crime* to your personal library. I hope you have as good a time reading this book as I have had putting it together!

Josh Pachter
Amsterdam, January 1983

TOP CRIME

OUT OF SIGHT

Isaac Asimov

First, let me tell you something about myself.

I was born in the Soviet Union in 1920 and was brought to the United States by my parents when I was three years old. I grew up in Brooklyn, and eventually attended Columbia University, where I got my Ph.D in chemistry in 1948. I joined the faculty of the Boston University School of Medicine the next year, and I am now Professor of Biochemistry there – though I am of course a full-time writer.

My first professional writing sale was in 1938, when I sold a story called 'Marooned off Vesta' to Amazing Stories. *For eleven years I sold science-fiction stories to various magazines, mostly to* Astounding Science Fiction. *Then, in 1950, I published my first book,* Pebble in the Sky. *Now, thirty-five years later, I have published nearly 300 books, most of them non-fiction, dealing with various branches of science.*

While I am best known for my science fiction, I also write mystery stories. I have selected 'Out of Sight' for this collection because the background is authentic. I was actually on *the cruise which the story revolves around, and the people I describe were with me at the table in actual fact. Mr and Mrs Smith (if you want to know a secret) are based on myself and my wife, Janet. We are exactly as I described the characters to be.*

What's more, Janet really did have hot chocolate spilled on her, and she did *send me to the head steward to make sure the waiter didn't get into any trouble.*

Of course, there was no mystery aboard ship and no cabin was invaded and there were no spies and so on.

All that I just made up.

The monthly banquet of the Black Widowers had reached the point where little was left of the mixed grill except an occasional sausage and a markedly untouched piece of liver on the plate of writer Emmanuel

Rubin – and it was then that voices rose in Homeric combat.

Rubin, undoubtedly furious by the serving of liver at all, was saying, even more flatly than was usual for him, 'Poetry is *sound*. You don't *look* at poetry. I don't care whether a culture emphasizes rhyme, alliteration, repetition, balance, or cadence, it all comes down to sound.'

Roger Halsted, mathematician and composer of limericks, never raised his voice, but one could always tell the state of his emotions by the color of his high forehead. Right now it was a deep pink, the color extending past the line that had once marked hair. He said, 'What's the use of making generalizations, Manny? No generalization can hold generally without an airtight system of axiomatics to begin with. Literature –'

'If you're going to tell me about figurative verse,' said Rubin hotly, 'save your breath. That was Victorian nonsense.'

'What's figurative verse?' asked artist Mario Gonzalo. 'Is he making that up, Jeff?' He added a touch to the tousled hair in his careful caricature of the banquet guest, Waldemar Long, who, since the dinner had begun, had eaten in somber silence, but was obviously following every word.

'No,' said Geoffrey Avalon, the patent lawyer, 'though I wouldn't put it past Manny to make something up if that were the only way he could win an argument. Figurative verse is verse in which the words or lines are arranged typographically in such a way as to produce a visual image that reinforces the sense. "The Mouse's Tail" in *Alice in Wonderland* is perhaps the best-known example.'

Halsted's soft voice was unequal to the free-for-all and he methodically beat his spoon against a water goblet till the decibels simmered down.

He said, 'Let's be reasonable. The subject under discussion is not poetry in general, but the limerick as a verse form. My point is this – I'll repeat it, Manny – that the worth of a limerick is not dictated by its subject matter. It's a mistake to think that a limerick has to be dirty to be good. It's easier –'

James Drake, the organic chemist, stubbed out his cigarette, twitched his small grizzled mustache, and said in his hoarse voice, 'Why do you call a dirty limerick dirty? The Supreme Court will get you for that.'

Halsted said, 'Because it's a two-syllable word with a meaning you all understand. What do you want me to say? Sexual-blasphemous-and-generally-irreverent?'

Avalon said, 'Go on, Roger. Make your point and don't let them needle you.' And from under his luxuriant eyebrows he frowned austerely at the others. 'Let him talk.'

'Why?' said Rubin. 'He has nothing to – Okay, Jeff. Talk, Roger.'

'Thank you all,' said Halsted, in the wounded tone of one who has finally succeeded in having his wrongs recognized. 'The worth of a limerick rests in the unpredictability of the last line and in the cleverness of the final rhyme. In fact, off-color content may seem to have value in itself and therefore require less cleverness – but it produces a less worthwhile limerick. Now, it is possible to have the rhyme masked by the orthographical conventions.'

'The what?' said Gonzalo.

'Spelling,' said Avalon.

'And then,' said Halsted, 'in seeing the spelling and having that instant of delay in getting the sound, you intensify the enjoyment. But under those conditions you have to *see* the limerick. If you just recite it, the excellence is lost.'

'Suppose you give us an example,' said Drake.

'I know what he means,' said Rubin. 'He's going to rhyme M.A. and C.D. – Master of Arts and Caster of Darts.'

'That's an example that's been used,' admitted Halsted, 'but it's extreme. It takes too long to catch on and amusement is drowned in irritation. As it happens, I've made up a limerick while we were having the argument –'

And now for the first time Thomas Trumbull, the code expert, entered the discussion. His tanned and wrinkled face twisted into a dark scowl and he said, 'The hell you did. You made it up yesterday and you engineered this whole silly discussion just so you could recite it. If it's one of your *Iliad* limericks I'll personally –'

'It's not the *Iliad*,' said Halsted. 'I haven't been working on that recently. It's no use my reciting this one, of course. I'll write it down and pass it around.'

He wrote in large block letters on an unused napkin:

YOU CAN'T CALL THE BRITISH QUEEN MS.
'TAIN'T AS NICE AS ELIZABETH IS.
BUT I THINK THAT THE QUEEN
WOULD BE EVEN LESS KEEN
TO HAVE HERSELF MENTIONED AS LS.

Gonzalo laughed aloud when it came to him. He said, 'Sure, if you know that MS is pronounced Miz, then you pronounce LS as Liz.'

'To me,' said Drake scornfully, 'LS would have to stand for "lanuscript" if it's going to rhyme with MS.'

Avalon pursed his lips and shook his head. 'Using 'TAIN'T is a flaw. You ought to lose a syllable some other way. And to be perfectly consistent, shouldn't the rhyme word IS be spelled simply S?'

Halsted nodded. 'You're quite right, and I thought of doing that, but it wouldn't be transparent enough and the reader wouldn't get it fast enough to laugh. Secondly, it would be the cleverest part of the limerick and would make the LS anticlimactic.'

'Do you really have to waste all that fancy reasoning on a piece of nonsense like this?' asked Trumbull.

'I think I've made my point,' said Halsted. 'That humor can be visual.'

Trumbull said, 'Well, then, let's drop the subject. Since I'm host this session, that's an order. – Henry, where's the dessert?'

'It's here, sir,' said Henry softly. Unmoved by Trumbull's tone, the perennial waiter at the Black Widower banquets deftly cleared the table and dealt out the blueberry shortcake.

The coffee had already been poured, and Trumbull's guest said in a low voice, 'May I have tea, please?'

The guest had a long upper lip and a long chin. The hair on his head was shaggy but there was none on his face and he had walked with a somewhat bearlike stoop. When he was first introduced, only Rubin had registered any recognition.

Rubin had said, 'Aren't you with NASA?'

Waldemar Long had answered with a startled 'Yes,' as though he had been disturbed out of a half-resentful resignation to anonymity. He had then frowned. He was frowning now again as Henry poured the tea, then melted unobtrusively into the background.

Trumbull said, 'I think the time has come for our guest to enter the discussion and perhaps add some sense to what has been an unusually foolish evening so far.'

'No, that's all right, Tom,' said Long. 'I don't mind frivolity.' He had a deep and rather beautiful voice that had a definite note of sadness in it. He went on, 'I have no aptitude for badinage myself, but I enjoy listening to it.'

Halsted, still brooding over the limerick, said with sudden forcefulness, 'I suggest Manny *not* be the grillmaster on this occasion.'

'No?' said Rubin, his sparse beard lifting belligerently.

'No. I put it to you, Tom. If Manny questions our guest, he will surely bring up the space program since there's a NASA connection. Then we will go through the same argument we've had a hundred times. I'm sick of the whole subject of space and whether we ought or ought not to be on the moon.'

'Not half as sick of it as I am,' said Long, rather unexpectedly. 'I'd just as soon not discuss any aspect of space exploration.'

The heavy flatness of the remark seemed to dampen spirits all around. Even Halsted was momentarily at a loss for any other subject to introduce to someone connected with NASA.

Then Rubin stirred in his seat and said, 'I take it, Dr Long, that this is a recently developed attitude of yours.'

Long's head turned suddenly toward Rubin. His eyes narrowed. 'Why do you say that, Mr Rubin?'

Rubin's small face came as close to a simper as it ever did. 'Elementary, my dear Mr Long. You were on the cruise that went down to see the Apollo shot last winter. I'd been invited as a literary representative, but I couldn't go. However, I got the promotional literature and noticed you were on the cruise. You were going to lecture on some aspect of the space program, I forget which. So your disenchantment with the subject of space must have arisen in the six months since the cruise.'

Long nodded his head slightly a number of times and said, 'I seem to be more heard of in that connection than in any other in my life. The damned cruise has made me famous, too.'

'I'll go farther,' said Rubin, 'and suggest that something happened *on* the cruise that disenchanted you with space exploration, maybe to the point where you're thinking of leaving NASA and going into some other field of work altogether.'

Long's stare was fixed now. He pointed a finger at Rubin – a long finger that showed no sign of a tremor – and said, 'Don't play games.' Then, with controlled anger, he rose from his chair and said, 'I'm sorry, Tom. Thanks for the meal, but I'll go now.'

Everyone rose at once, speaking simultaneously – all but Rubin, who remained sitting with a look of stunned astonishment on his face.

Trumbull's voice rose above the rest. 'Now wait a while, Waldemar. Damn it, will all of you sit down? Waldemar, you too. What's the excitement about? Rubin, what *is* all this?'

Rubin looked down at his empty coffee cup and lifted it as though he wished there were coffee in it so that he could delay replying by taking a sip. 'I was just making like Sherlock Holmes, simply demonstrating a chain of logic. After all, I write mysteries, you know. But I seem to have touched a nerve.' Then gratefully, he said, 'Thanks, Henry,' as the cup before him sparkled black to the brim.

'What chain of logic?' demanded Trumbull.

'Okay, here it is. Dr Long said, "The damned cruise has made me famous, too." He said "too" and emphasized the word. That means it did something else for him and, since we were talking about his distaste for the whole subject of space exploration, I deduced that the something else was to supply him with that distaste. From his attitude I guessed it was sharp enough to make him want to quit his job. That's all there is to it. As I said, elementary.'

Long nodded his head again, in precisely the same slight and rapid way as before, then settled back in his seat. 'All right. I'm sorry, Mr Rubin. I jumped too soon. The fact is I *will* be leaving NASA. To all intents and purposes I *have* left it – and at the point of a shoe. That's all. – We'll change the subject. Tom, you said coming here would get me out of my dumps, but it hasn't worked that way. Rather, my mood has infected you all and I've cast a damper on the party. Forgive me, all of you.'

Avalon put a finger to his neat, graying mustache and stroked it gently. He said, 'Actually, sir, you have given us something we like above all things – the opportunity to indulge our curiosity. May we question you on this matter?'

'It's not something I'm free to talk about,' said Long guardedly.

Trumbull said, 'You needn't mention sensitive details and as far as anything else is concerned, everything said in this room is confidential. And, as I always add when I find it necessary to make that statement, the confidentiality includes our esteemed friend, Henry.'

Henry, who was standing at the sideboard, smiled briefly.

Long hesitated. Then he said, 'Actually, your curiosity is easily satisfied and I guess that Mr Rubin, at least, with his aptitude for deduction, has already filled in the details. I'm suspected of having been indiscreet, either deliberately or carelessly, and, either way, I may find myself unofficially, but very effectively, blocked from any future position in my field of competence.'

'You mean you'll be blackballed?' said Drake.

'That's a word,' said Long, 'that's never used. But that's what it will amount to.'

'I take it,' said Drake, 'you were not indiscreet.'

'On the contrary, I was.' Long shook his head. 'I haven't denied that. The trouble is they think the story is worse than I admit.'

There was another pause, and then Avalon, speaking in his most impressively austere tone, said, 'Well, sir, *what* story?'

Long passed a hand over his face, then pushed his chair away from the table so that he could lean his head back against the wall.

He said, 'It's really so undramatic. I was on this cruise, as Mr Rubin told you. I was going to give a talk on certain space projects, rather far-out ones, and planned on explaining exactly what was being done in certain fascinating directions. I can't give you *those* details. I found that out the hard way. Some of the stuff had been classified, but I had been told I could talk about it. Then, on the day before I was to give my lecture, I got a radiophone call saying it was all off. There was to be no declassification.

'I was furious. There's no use denying I have a temper and I also have very little gift for extemporaneous or impromptu lecturing. I had carefully written out my talk and had intended to read it. I know that's not a good way of giving a lecture, but it's the best I can do. Now I had nothing left to give to a group of people who had paid considerable money to listen to me. It was a most embarrassing position.'

'What did you do?' asked Avalon.

Long shook his head. 'I held a rather pathetic question-and-answer session the next day. It didn't go over at all well. It was even worse than just not giving a speech at all. By that time, you see, I knew I was in considerable trouble.'

'In what way?' said Avalon.

'If you want the story,' said Long, 'here it is. I'm not exactly talkative at meals, as you perhaps have noticed, but when I went in to dinner after getting the call, I suppose I put on a passable imitation of a corpse that had died with an angry look on its face. The rest tried to draw me into the conversation, if only, I suppose, to keep me from poisoning the atmosphere. Finally one of them said, "Well, Dr Long, what will you be talking about tomorrow?" And I blew up and said, "Nothing! Nothing at all! I've got the paper all written out and it's sitting there on the desk in my cabin and I can't give it because I just found out the material is still classified." '

'And then the paper was stolen?' said Gonzalo.

'No. Why steal anything these days? It was photographed.'

'Are you sure?'

'I was almost sure at the time. When I got back to my cabin after dinner the door was not locked and the papers had been moved. Since then it's become certain. We have proof that the information has leaked.'

There was a rather depressed silence at that. Then Trumbull said, 'Who could have done it? Who heard you?'

'Everyone at the table,' said Long despondently.

Rubin said, 'You have a voice that carries, Dr Long, and if you were as angry as I think you were, you spoke forcefully. Probably a number of people at adjoining tables heard you.'

'No,' said Long, shaking his head. 'I spoke through clenched teeth, not loudly. Besides, you don't realize what the cruise was like. The cruise was badly undersubscribed, you see – poor promotion, mostly. It was carrying only 40 percent capacity and the shipping company is supposed to have lost a packet.'

'In that case,' said Avalon, 'it must have been a dreary experience apart from your misadventure.'

'On the contrary, up to that point it was very pleasant for me, and it continued to be very pleasant for all the rest, I imagine. The crew nearly outnumbered the passengers, so the service was excellent. All the facilities were available without crowding. They scattered us through the dining room and gave us privacy. There were seven of us at our dining table. Lucky seven, someone said at the beginning.' For a moment Long's look of grimness deepened. 'None of the tables near us was occupied. I'm quite certain that nothing any of us said was heard anywhere but at our own table.'

'Then there are seven suspects,' said Gonzalo thoughtfully.

'Six, since you needn't count me,' said Long. 'I knew where the paper was and what it contained.'

'You're under suspicion, too. Or you implied that,' said Gonzalo.

'Not to myself,' said Long.

Trumbull said peevishly, 'I wish you'd come to me with this, Waldemar. I've been worrying over your obviously anxious attitude for months.'

'What would you have done if I had told you?'

Trumbull considered. 'Damn it, I'd have brought you here. – All right. Tell us about the six other people at the table. Who were they?'

'One was the ship's doctor – a good-looking Dutchman in an impressive uniform.'

Rubin said, 'He would be. The ship was one of the Holland-America liners, wasn't it?'

'Yes. The officers were Dutch and the crew – the waiters, stewards, and so on – were mostly Indonesian. They'd all had three-month cram courses in English, but we communicated mostly in sign language. I can't complain, though – they were pleasant and hard-working and all the more efficient since there were considerably less than the usual number of passengers.'

'Any reason to suspect the doctor?' asked Drake.

Long nodded. 'I suspected them all. The doctor was a silent man; he and I were the two silent ones. The other five made continuous conversation, much as you do here at this table. The doctor and I listened. What I've brooded about in connection with him was that it was he who asked me about my talk. Asking a personal question like that was not characteristic.'

'He may have been worried about you medically,' said Halsted. 'He may have been trying to draw you out.'

'Maybe,' said Long. 'I remember every detail of that dinner; I've gone over and over it in my mind. It was an ethnic dinner, so everyone was supplied with little Dutch hats made out of paper and special Indonesian dishes were served. I wore the hat but I hate curried food and the doctor asked about my speech just as a small dish of curried something-or-other was put before me as an appetizer. Between fuming over official stupidity and sickening over the smell of curry, I just burst out. If it hadn't been for the curry, perhaps –

'Anyway, after dinner I discovered that someone had been in my cabin. The contents of the paper weren't so important, classification or not, but what was important was that someone had taken action so quickly. Someone on the ship was part of a spy network and that was more important than the actual coup. Even if the present item were not important, the next one might be. It was vital to report the matter and, as a loyal citizen, I did.'

Rubin said, 'Isn't the doctor the logical suspect? He asked the question and he would be listening to the answer. The others might not have been listening. As an officer, he would be familiar with the ship, know how to get to your cabin quickly, perhaps even have a duplicate key. Did he have an opportunity to go to your cabin before you did?'

'Yes, he did,' said Long. 'I thought of all that. The trouble is this. Everyone at the table heard me, because all the rest talked about the system of classification for a while. I kept quiet myself but I remember the matter of the Pentagon Papers came up. And everyone knew where my cabin was because I had given a small party in it for the table the day before. And those locks are easy to open for anyone with a little skill at it – though it was a mistake for the spy not to lock the door again on leaving; but whoever it was had to be in a hurry. And as it happened, everyone at the table had a chance to get to my cabin during the course of the meal.'

'Who were the others, then?' asked Halsted.

'Two married couples and a single woman. The single woman – call her Miss Robinson – was pretty, a little on the plump side, had a pleasant sense of humor, but had the bad habit of smoking during meals. I rather think she took a fancy to the doctor. She sat between us – we always had the same seats.'

'When did she have a chance to visit your cabin?' asked Halsted.

'She left shortly after I made my remark. I was brooding too deeply to be aware of it at the time but of course I remembered it afterward. She came back before the fuss over the hot chocolate came up, because I remember her trying to help.'

'Where did she say she went?'

'Nobody asked her at the time. She was asked afterward and she said she had gone to her cabin to go to the bathroom. Maybe she did. But her cabin was close to mine.'

'No one saw her at all?'

'No one would. Everyone was in the dining room and, to the Indonesians, all Americans look alike.'

Avalon said, 'What's the fuss over the hot chocolate you referred to?'

Long said, 'That's where one of the married couples comes in. Call them the Smiths and the other couple the Joneses. Mr Smith was the raucous type. He reminded me, in fact, of – '

'Oh, Lord,' said Rubin. 'Don't say it.'

'All right, I won't. He was one of the lecturers – in fact, both Smith and Jones were. Smith talked fast, laughed easily, turned almost everything into a double entendre, and seemed to enjoy it all so much he had the rest of us doing it, too. He was a very odd person – the kind of fellow you can't help but take an instant dislike to and judge to be stupid. But then, as you got used to him, you found that you liked him after all and that under all his surface foolishness he was extremely intelligent. The first evening, I remember, the doctor kept staring at him as if he were a specimen, but by the end of the cruise the doctor had come to like and respect him.

'Jones was much quieter. He seemed horrified at first by Smith's outrageous comments but eventually he was matching him, I noticed – rather, I think, to Smith's discomfiture.'

Avalon asked, 'What were their fields?'

'Smith was a sociologist and Jones a biologist. The idea was that space exploration should be viewed from the light of many disciplines. It was a good concept, but there were serious flaws in the execution.

Some of the talks, though, were excellent. There was one on Mariner 9 and the new data on Mars that was superb, but that's beside the point.

'It was Mrs Smith who created the fuss. She was a moderately tall, thin girl. Not very good-looking by the usual standards but with an extraordinarily attractive personality. She was soft-spoken and clearly went through life automatically thinking of others. I believe everyone quickly grew to feel quite affectionate to her and Smith himself seemed devoted. The evening I shot my mouth off, she ordered hot chocolate. It came in a tall glass, very top-heavy and, of course, as a mistaken touch of elegance, it was brought on a tray.

'Smith, as usual, was talking animatedly and waving his arms as he did so. He used all his muscles when he talked. The ship swayed, he swayed – well, anyway, the hot chocolate went into Mrs Smith's lap.

'She jumped up. So did everyone else. Miss Robinson moved quickly toward her to help. I noticed that and that's how I know she was back by then. Mrs Smith waved help away and left in a hurry. Smith, looking suddenly confused and upset, tore off the paper Dutch hat he was wearing and followed.

'Five minutes later he was back, talking earnestly to the head steward. Then he came to the table and said that Mrs Smith had sent him down to assure the steward she was wearing nothing that couldn't be washed, she hadn't been hurt, that it wasn't anyone's fault, and that no one should be blamed.

'He wanted to assure us she was all right, too. He asked if we could stay at the table till his wife came back. She was changing clothes and wanted to join us again so that none of us would feel as though anything very terrible had happened. We agreed, of course. None of us was going anywhere.'

Avalon said, 'And that means Mrs Smith had time to go to your cabin.'

Long nodded. 'Yes. She didn't seem the type but I suppose in this game you have to disregard surface appearances.'

'And you all waited?'

'Not the doctor. He got up and said he would get some ointment from his office in case she needed it for burns, but he came back before she did by a minute or so.'

Avalon said, tapping his finger on the table slowly to lend emphasis, 'And he, too, might have gone into your cabin. And Miss Robinson might have when she left before the hot-chocolate incident.'

Rubin said, 'Where do the Joneses come in?'

Long said, 'Let me go on. When Mrs Smith came back she denied having been burned and the doctor had no need to give her the ointment, so we can't say if he even went to get it. He might have been bluffing.'

'What if she had asked for it?' said Halsted.

'Then he might have said he couldn't find what he had been looking for but if she came with him he'd do what he could. Who knows? In any case, we all sat for a while as though nothing unusual had happened and then, finally, we broke up. By that time ours was the last occupied table. Everyone left, with Mrs Jones and myself lingering behind for a while.'

'Mrs Jones?' asked Drake.

'I haven't told you about Mrs Jones. Dark hair and eyes, very vivacious. Had a penchant for sharp cheeses, always taking a bit of each off the tray when it was brought round. She had a way of looking at you when you talked that had you convinced you were the only other person in the world. I think Jones was rather a jealous type in his quiet way. At least, I never saw him more than two feet from her, except this one time. He got up and said he was going to their cabin and she said she would join him soon. Then she turned to me and said, "Can you explain why those terraced icefields on Mars are significant? I've been meaning to ask you all during dinner and didn't get a chance."

'It had been that day that we'd had the magnificent talk on Mars and I was rather flattered that she turned to me instead of to the astronomer who had given the talk. It seemed as though she were taking it for granted I knew as much as he did. So I talked to her for a while and she kept saying, "How interesting." '

Avalon said, 'And meanwhile Jones could have been in your cabin.'

'Could be. I thought of that afterward. It was certainly atypical behavior on both their parts.'

Avalon said, 'Let's summarize, then. There are four possibilities. Miss Robinson might have done it when she left before the hot-chocolate incident. The Smiths might have done it as a team after deliberately spilling the hot chocolate. Or the doctor could have done it while supposedly going for the ointment. Or the Joneses could have also done it as a team, with Jones doing the dirty work while Mrs Jones kept Dr Long out of action.'

Long nodded. 'All this was considered and by the time the ship was back in New York, security agents had begun the process of checking the backgrounds of all six. You see, in cases like this, suspicion is all you need. The only way any secret agent can remain undetected is for him or her to remain unsuspected. Once the eye of counterintelligence is on him, he must inevitably be unmasked. No cover can survive an investigation in depth.'

Drake said, 'Then which one did it prove to be?'

Long sighed. 'That's where the trouble arose. None of them. All were clean. There was no way, I understand, of showing any one of them to be anything other than what they seemed.'

Rubin said, 'Why do you say you "understand." Aren't you part of the investigation?'

'At the wrong end. The clearer those six are, the guiltier I appear to be. I told the investigators – I *had* to tell them – that those six are the only ones who could possibly have done it, and if none of them did, they must suspect me of making up a story to hide something worse.'

Trumbull said, 'Oh, hell, Waldemar. They can't think that. What would you have to gain by reporting the incident if you were responsible?'

'That's what they don't know,' said Long. 'But the information did leak and if they can't pin it on any of the six, then they're going to pin it on me. And the more my motives puzzle them, the more they think those motives must be very disturbing and important. So I'm in trouble.'

Rubin said, 'Are you sure those six are really the only possibilities? Are you sure you really didn't mention it to anyone else?'

'Quite sure,' said Long dryly.

'You might not remember having done so,' said Rubin. 'It could have been something very casual. Can you be *sure* you didn't?'

'I can be sure I didn't. The radiophone call came only a few minutes before dinner. There just wasn't time to tell anyone before dinner. And once I got away from the table I was back in my cabin before I said anything to anybody.'

'Who heard you on the phone? Maybe there were eavesdroppers.'

'There were ship's officers standing around certainly. However, my boss expressed himself Aesopically. I knew what he meant, but no one else would have understood.'

'Did you express *your*self Aesopically?' asked Halsted.

'I'll tell you exactly what I said: "Hello, Dave." Then I said, "Damn it to hell." Then I hung up. I said those six words. No more.'

Gonzalo brought his hands together in a sudden, enthusiastic clap. 'Listen, I've been thinking. Why does the job have to be so planned? It could have been spontaneous. After all, everybody knows there's this cruise and people connected with NASA are going to talk and there might be something informative going on. Someone – it could have been anyone – kept searching various rooms during the dinner hour each day and finally came across your paper – '

'No,' said Long sharply. 'It passes the bounds of plausibility to suppose that someone, by the merest chance, would find my paper just in the hour or two after I had announced that a classified lecture was sitting on my desk. Besides, there was nothing in the paper that would have given any indication of importance to the non-expert. It was only my own remark that would have told anyone it was there, and that it was important.'

Avalon said thoughtfully, 'Suppose one of the people at the table passed on the information, in perfect innocence? In the interval they were away from the table, they might have said to someone, "Did you hear about poor Dr Long? His paper was shot out from under him?" Then that someone, anyone, could have done the job.'

Long shook his head. 'I wish that could be so, but it can't. That would only happen if the particular individual at my table was innocent. If the Smiths were innocent when they left the table, the only thing on their mind would be the hot chocolate. They wouldn't stop to chat. The doctor, if innocent, would be thinking only of getting the ointment. By the time Jones left the table, assuming he was innocent, he would have forgotten about the matter; if anything, he would talk about the hot chocolate, too.'

Rubin nodded. 'All right. But what about Miss Robinson? She left before the hot-chocolate incident. The only interesting thing in her mind would have been your dilemma. She might have said something.'

'Might she?' said Long. 'If she is innocent, then she was really doing what she said she was doing – going to the bathroom in her cabin. If she had to desert the dinner table to do so, there would have had to be urgency; and no one under those conditions stops for idle chatter.'

There was silence around the table.

Long said, 'I'm sure investigation will continue and eventually the truth will come out and it will be clear that I'm guilty of no more than an unlucky indiscretion. By then, however, my career will be down the drain.'

'Dr Long?' said a soft voice. 'May I ask a question?'

Long looked up, surprised. 'A question?'

'I'm Henry, sir. The gentlemen of the Black Widowers Club occasionally allow me to participate – '

'We sure do, Henry,' said Trumbull. 'Do you see something the rest of us don't?'

'I'm not certain,' said Henry. 'I see quite plainly that Dr Long believes only the six others at the table could possibly be involved, and those investigating the matter apparently agree with him – '

'There's no one else,' said Long.

'Well, then,' said Henry, 'I am wondering if Dr Long mentioned his views on curry to the investigators.'

Long said, 'You mean that I didn't like curry?'

'Yes,' said Henry. 'Did that come up?'

Long spread his hands and then shook his head. 'No, I don't think it did. Why should it? It's irrelevant. It's just an additional excuse for my talking like a jackass. I told it to you here in order to get some sympathy, I suppose, but it certainly would mean nothing to the investigators.'

Henry remained silent for a moment, and Trumbull said, 'Does the curry have meaning to you, Henry?'

'I think it does,' said Henry. 'I think we are in rather the position Mr Halstead described earlier in the evening in connection with limericks. Some limericks to be effective must be *seen*; sound is not enough. And some scenes to be effective must be seen.'

'I don't get that,' said Long.

'Well, Dr Long,' said Henry. 'You sat there in the ship's restaurant at a table with six other people and therefore only those six other people heard you. But if we could *see* the scene instead of having you describe it to us, wouldn't we see something that you have omitted?'

'No, you wouldn't,' said Long doggedly.

'Are you sure?' asked Henry. 'You sit here with six other people at a table, too, just as you did on the ship. How many people have heard your story?'

'Six – ' began Long.

And then Gonzalo broke in, 'No, seven, counting you, Henry.'

'And was there no one serving you at the table, Dr Long? You said the doctor had asked you about the speech just as a curried dish was put before you and it was the smell of curry that annoyed you to the point where you burst out with your indiscretion. Surely, the curry didn't place itself before you of its own accord. The fact is that at the moment you made your statement, there were six people sitting at the table, and a seventh standing just behind you and out of sight.'

'The waiter,' said Long in a whisper.

Henry said, 'There's a tendency never to notice a waiter unless he annoys you. An efficient waiter is invisible, and you mentioned the excellence of the service. Might it not have been the waiter who carefully engineered the spilling of the hot chocolate to create a diversion, or perhaps took advantage of the diversion, if it were an accident. With waiters many and diners few, it might not be too noticeable if he disappeared for a while. Or he could claim to have gone to the men's room if it were noticed. He would know the location of the cabin as well as the doctor did, and be as likely to have some sort of picklock.'

Long said, 'But he was an Indonesian. He couldn't speak English.'

'Are you sure? He'd had a three-month cram course, you said. And he might have known English better than he pretended. You would be willing to suspect that Mrs Smith was not as sweet and thoughtful underneath as she was on the surface, and that Mrs Jones's vivacity was a pretense, and the doctor's respectability, and Smith's liveliness and Jones's devotion and Miss Robinson's need to go to the bathroom. Might not the waiter's ignorance of English also have been a pretense?'

'By God,' said Long, looking at his watch, 'if it weren't so late I'd call Washington now.'

Trumbull said, 'If you know some home phone numbers, *do* call now. Your career is at stake. Tell them the waiter ought to be investigated and for heaven's sake don't tell them you got the notion from someone else.'

'You mean, tell them I just thought of it? They'll ask why I didn't think of it before.'

'Ask them why *they* didn't. Why didn't *they* think a waiter goes with a table in a dining room?'

Henry said softly. 'No reason for anyone to think of it. Only very few are as interested in waiters as I am.'

EVERY LITTER BIT HURTS

Michael Avallone

'Every Litter Bit Hurts' is the short story that will probably outlive me, my only claim to a yarn that sticks in the reader's mind – along the lines of, say, Ellin's 'Specialty of the House' and Dahl's 'Lamb to the Slaughter'.

How did I get the idea? Simple: a neighbor friend, every time his children climbed into the family machine, always pronounced, 'Now, remember, don't throw anything out of the car while I'm driving', or some such. The rest is the writer, the man with a vivid imagination, a sense of drama and irony, and the ability to turn an entire life – two lives – on a simple line of dialogue.

When I wrote the story, in 1967, I drove an Impala myself and the school building with the American flag was visible from my house; the name Robert Black was my kind of mental tribute to Robert Bloch, the best man in the field for this sort of thing. Amazing, isn't it? . . . how even a short story is a mosaic of so many bits and pieces finally coming together into one whole, just like a successful crossword puzzle.

*Since its debut in the 1968 Mystery Writers of America anthology (*With Malice Towards All*, edited by the one and only Bob Fish, a treasured friend and colleague), 'Every Litter Bit Hurts' has been reprinted twenty-one times — all over the world — in newspapers, anthologies and magazines from Canada to Germany to pirated Russian collections.*

I'll tell you one thing: you will never forget it!

The Impala gleamed shiny and red on the sloping driveway. Bobby ran toward it, eyes twinkling, clapping his hands. He and Daddy were going for a ride! He paused, a bit puzzled, while his father lifted the hood and studied the engine carefully, peering at the electrical terminals of the starter to be sure no new wires had been added, wires which could connect to a dynamite bomb.

Jamison hadn't been that careful, and Jamison had been killed.

Bobby, of course, had no way of knowing the reason for his father's action, nor did the thought remain with him long. All he knew was that he and his father were going for a ride! And Daddy had strapped on his gun, even. Right under his coat in that dark leather holster.

The large man closed the hood, satisfied with his inspection, smiling at the boy.

'Remember,' Daddy was saying, 'don't ever throw anything out of the car. Understood? It's not nice. Especially when Daddy's driving fast on the highway. It just isn't *nice*, Bobby. You could hit another Daddy in the eye and cause an accident. *Do you understand?*'

Bobby nodded, tugging at the big Impala door.

'Good boy. I knew you'd understand once you knew the reason. Mommy will be proud of you when I tell her.'

Bobby smiled. The words were running around in his head like happy puppies. *Mommy. Proud. Good boy.* When you are only five years of age, those words are glowing beacons of progress and love.

But above all, progress. The march forward, the long trip toward that mysterious land of Growing Up.

'Where are we going today, Daddy? Police station again?' When Daddy took his gun, it almost always meant the police station.

'Daddy's got to go to Elmira,' Robert Black, Sr said, a funny glint in his eye. 'Part of the job, too. I have to go to the District Attorney to hand over some papers. You know. I told you. We'll meet Mommy there and then maybe we'll take in a movie. Would you like that?'

He paused, lighting a cigarette from the dashboard lighter. Bobby watched him, bursting with ride-fever and pride. He liked the sure look of the strong hands, the keen profile of his father. Sharp, like the face on a coin under a porkpie hat. Daddy had told him that once and he had remembered. What a funny name for a hat! Maybe Porky the Pig wore porkpie hats, too.

'Mommy's in town?' Bobby prodded with that unswerving curiosity of the young.

'That's right. Shopping. She took the bus. You were sleeping – '

'I miss Mommy.'

'So do I. But we'll see her soon enough.'

Daddy did some things with the dashboard and the wheel, and the car motor roared. Bobby liked that sound. It always meant going places and doing things. Though not very often with Daddy. Daddy was always away – packing bags, calling on the telephone from far-away places like Washington, D.C., and hardly ever having time to play games or go walking in the woods. Bobby wasn't too sure what

Daddy did – he didn't go to work like the fathers of his friends, or leave the house in the morning and come back the same day for supper, or play catch – no, nothing like that.

Bobby only knew that the big man's work had something to do with the shiny badge he had seen pinned inside the black wallet that was sometimes left on the bureau in the bedroom. That and that scary gun he sometimes saw when Daddy was putting on his jacket. He remembered he had once tried to pick it up, and his father had been very cross with him for it. Bobby knew he'd never do *that* again!

Robert Black, Sr patted his son affectionately on the cheek and released the emergency brake. Bobby knew what he was doing. The brake always made a funny sound when Daddy touched it with his hand.

'Now, Bobby – what is it you're going to remember?'

'Not to throw anything out of the car window.'

'Right. So if we stop for candy or gum, you'll fold up the wrappers neatly and give them to me, and I'll put them in the ashtray. Okay?'

'Okay.'

'You know last time when you tossed that paper bag out of the car window, it blew all the way back against the windshield of the car right behind us. The man couldn't see where he was going or what he was doing. He might have gotten hurt and you wouldn't want that, would you?'

'No, Daddy.'

'Good boy. Well, we're off.'

Daddy backed the Impala down the driveway. The line of trees looked so pretty in the sunlight. The big man turned the car around, heading it out toward the highway, his thick wrists relaxed, his large hands holding the wheel lightly. Bobby recognized the big school building with the American flag flying above it; next year he'd be going there like the rest of the kids.

He sank back happily against the soft seat and folded his arms. It was nice going someplace with Daddy for a change, instead of Mommy. Mommies were nice and fun, too, when they went to stores and places, but Daddies were better.

And Daddies never cried, while Mommies did. Like last night –

'Daddy, who was that man on the phone last night? The one who said something to make Mommy cry? Was it the man who got hit with the paper bag – did he want you to spank me?'

Robert Black, Sr smiled, but it was a humorless smile, a grim smile.

'No, son. It was a bad man. It was a man who thought he could keep me from doing my job if he threatened – ' Robert Black, Sr suddenly closed his mouth. 'It was just a bad man, son. Forget it.'

'Why did Mommy cry?'

'I told you to forget it, Bobby. The man wasn't very nice. Like the big bad wolf in Red Riding Hood – '

'Or in the Three Little Pigs?'

'That's right. Don't worry. He won't call any more. Not after these papers are delivered in Elmira.'

Robert Black, Sr's mind was on the road and the traffic; Robert Black, Jr was thinking of all the things he could tell Mommy that happened that morning after she left. About the loose front tooth, the striped kitten he had found wandering in the back yard, that nest of chirping sparrows in the carport.

And the wonderful breakfast of French toast with syrup that Daddy had made. Daddies could cook good, too, just like Mommies.

'Daddy?'

'Yes, son?'

'What's F.B.I. mean?'

Robert Black, Sr chuckled. 'Who told you that?'

'I was watching television with a couple of the other kids, and they said you were a F.B.I. man. Are you, Daddy?'

'Billy and Gary, I imagine. The neighborhood stool pigeons. What we need are about eight guys like them available to the Department. Well, they were telling you the truth, Bobby. I'm an F.B.I. man.'

'What's that? Some kind of policeman?'

'That's right. It means the Federal Bureau of Investigation. That's my job. You knew I was some kind of a policeman, didn't you?'

'I guess so.'

The Impala zipped ahead, going around a flying big blue car. Daddy drove like a race-car driver. Bobby beamed proudly.

'Is Mommy glad you're a F.B.I. man?'

Robert Black, Sr shook his head, amused. 'Sometimes I wonder, son.'

'She gets – *afraid*? Like last night?'

'Sometimes. Women are like that, son. But it's a man's job, you know. And somebody has to do it.'

Bobby nodded his head wisely.

'I wouldn't be afraid. I'm proud you're a F.B.I. man. Honest to Pete, I am.'

'Thanks, Bobby.'

Robert Black, Jr glowed, glanced at his father, and was surprised to see the smile on the sharp features suddenly change to a frown. His mind searched for a reason for the obvious displeasure.

'What's the matter, Daddy? I didn't throw anything out of the window.'

His father's attention returned to the highway, a smile on his lips despite himself. 'No, but you did something almost as bad. You didn't fasten your seat belt. You always said you were big enough – '

'I *am* big enough!' Bobby's voice was stout.

He pulled the buckle from its place between his father and himself and then reached down between the seat and the door for the spring-retractable tongue that wound itself up into its holder when not in use, like that turtle Gary used to have, pulling its head in whenever you touched it.

His fingers found the end of the seat belt and he tugged. It seemed to be stuck. He tugged harder without success and then leaned over, peering into the dim recess between the seat and the door.

A strange egg-shaped object was lying there where nothing had been before, apparently pulled from beneath the seat by his efforts, and now firmly wedged.

Bobby bent lower, working it loose, bringing it to his lap together with the end of the seat belt to which it was attached. He blinked at it, fascinated.

Robert Black, Sr, guiding the car along the highway at 60 miles an hour, wasn't looking anywhere but straight ahead. His profile was just like those policemen Bobby saw on television. Bobby sighed and returned his attention to the egg-shaped thing in his lap. He had never seen anything like it before.

It was made of metal and was heavy, and it had odd squarelike bumps all over it and a funny round pin in its top, held to the end of the seat belt by a thin strand of wire. He was sure Daddy would be interested, but first he had to obey his instructions. He tugged at the egg shape; it came away from the tongue of the seat belt, separating also from the little pin which now dangled comically. Bobby held the egg shape in his lap and latched the belt.

'Daddy – '

'Yes, son?' Robert Black, Sr turned his head. And stared.

His face went white.

Bobby could never remember Daddy's eyes seeming so big or so *scary*. His face was all screwed up, like he had a toothache.

The roar of the car motor drowned out something that Daddy was yelling. There were so many other cars racing by, thundering, bulleting along the highway. Bobby whimpered in sudden fright.

His father's right arm shot out, flailing. Bobby recoiled, thinking for one awful second that Daddy was going to hit him.

He hugged the egg-shaped thing to his chest and shrank against the car door to make himself smaller.

Cars were hurtling forward, zooming ahead in a race for the sun and the horizon. A car horn blasted, frightening Bobby even more.

'Bobby!' Robert Black, Sr screamed. 'Throw that thing out of the car!'

The flying trees, the ribbon of road, the thundering motors, and four vital seconds had fled.

'*Bobby!*'

'But, Daddy,' Robert Black, Jr protested, his small face crumpled in confusion, 'you said never to – '

PARLOR GAME

Gary Brandner

The private eye of fiction is, like the Knights of the Round Table and the cowboys of the Old West, a mythical figure. Unlike the knights and cowboys, though, real-life private detectives are still with us, and to a man they are eager to point out how different their real life is from the way we writers write it.

Well, so what? They're probably a lot more fun our way, and they sure make better heroes!

Stonebreaker was not my first private eye. That was a smoother character named Dukane, who operated in circles where Stonebreaker would never be invited. But when my stories took me away from the lights and glamor of the city and into its hard gritty core, I needed a hard, gritty man to write about. Stonebreaker.

'Parlor Game' was the most recent (I don't want to say last) Stonebreaker story I did. On re-reading it, I'm still pleased with the essence of Los Angeles I got into it.

People have asked, often with a knowing elbow nudge, how I handled the research for the story. I usually answer with an enigmatic smile – but near the end of the story the sharp-eyed reader may spot a sheepish character slipping out of the massage parlor as the detective enters.

Even in bright sunshine Western Avenue is not one of the beauty spots of Los Angeles. In the rain it can be downright ugly. I stood in the rain on the corner of Western and Romaine and squinted up at the window of my new office. The window was dirty and had a crack across one corner and no name on it. The name was down at the foot of the stairs in white plastic letters stuck on a black directory board. *D. Stonebreaker, Private Investigator*.

The new place was not much, but it was no worse than my old office downtown on Fifth. That building was being demolished so they could put up some future slums. It's called urban renewal.

The new neighborhood looked lively enough. Right under my office was the Erotique Massage Parlor. Next door was a movie theater advertising *Hard Core Nudies – Open All Night*. Also in my block were beer bars, pawnshops, a pool room, a Mexican lunch stand, and a Chinese laundry. And a couple of places whose business I couldn't guess.

I was getting wet. I ambled back across the street and started up the stairs. Just before I got to the landing I heard the moist smack of a fist on flesh. I went on up, and there just in front of my office a big-shouldered stud was slapping around a slim girl in cutoff jeans. She had shiny black hair that bounced away from her face every time he hit her. I walked up behind the big guy and grabbed him by the meat of his shoulder.

'You're blocking my door,' I said.

He spun around as though he was going to let me have one, too. He had a big-jawed handsome face spoiled by a pouty little mouth. When he got a look at my size and my face, which is not cheery at best, he changed his mind about hitting me.

'What's the matter, mister?' he said. 'You a hero or something?'

'Beat up your woman someplace else. You're bad for my business.'

The girl, who couldn't have weighed more than 100 pounds, looked from one of us to the other with dark frightened eyes. The left side of her face was red where the guy had smacked her.

Just so she wouldn't think he was chickening out, the tough guy said to her, 'Remember, there's more where that came from.' He walked away and down the stairs, turning to give me a fierce look when he was out of reach.

The girl was rubbing the side of her face when I turned around. 'Damn, I hope I don't get a black eye. Listen, are you the private detective who's moving in here?'

I admitted that I was.

'Can we go into your office?'

'Sure, but we can't sit down. The furniture isn't here yet.' I unlocked the door and the girl walked in ahead of me. She was wearing a lightweight shirt with the tails tied in front, exposing a whole lot of skin north and south of the navel. She glanced around the empty room without enthusiasm.

'It'll look better when I get the carpet laid and the stereo in,' I said.

She ignored the sarcasm. 'I'm Abby Deane. I work downstairs in the massage parlor.' She waited a couple of seconds to let me absorb the information. 'Does that make any difference?'

'Why should it?'

'Some people don't want to do business with a girl who works in a massage parlor.'

'Some people feel the same way about private detectives. What kind of business did you have in mind?'

'I think I'm getting in some trouble that's bigger than I can handle. I might need your help.'

'Tell me about it.'

She looked at the big colorful watch strapped to her wrist. 'Listen, I have to go now, I've got a ride home waiting for me. I've got to be back here to go to work at seven. I'll come an hour early and talk to you then. If you're going to be here.'

'I'll be here.'

She started out the door.

'Wait a minute.' I eased out past her and walked softly down the stairs. Sure enough, just inside the doorway where the rain wouldn't spoil his hair style was the tough guy with the shoulders.

'Forget something?'

He looked at me and licked his pouty little lips. 'What's it to you?'

'I don't like you in my doorway. You scare away clients.'

'What are you gonna do about it?'

'You don't really want to know, do you?'

He thought that over, measured me again with his eyes, and decided he had business somewhere else. He sauntered up the street and got into a grubby Volkswagen. From long habit I memorized the license number.

I went back upstairs and told Abby Deane it was all clear below. She hurried out and left me standing in my bare office feeling restless and depressed and listening to the rain rattle against the window.

By six o'clock the movers had all my stuff in place. When I say 'all' I mean desk and swivel chair, two straight-back chairs for clients, a pair of four-drawer file cabinets, and an elderly typewriter with matching stand. For the walls a couple of sincere landscape prints. I was lying before about the carpet and stereo.

An hour later it was dark. The rain still slapped my window and the cars going by on Western Avenue made a melancholy hissing sound. Abby Deane failed to show. I sat there for another hour trying to decide whether I liked my file cabinets on the left or should I move them over to the right. At eight o'clock I decided to leave them where they were. To hell with Abby Deane. It wasn't the first time I'd been stood up. Still, something nagged at me. It was that persistent little nag that has gotten me into more trouble than I like to think about. It couldn't hurt, I decided, to look in downstairs and see if she went to work on schedule.

I let myself out of the office and clumped down the stairs into the wet night. The entrance to the Erotique Massage Parlor was a few steps toward the corner. It is possible, I hear, to get a legitimate massage in one of these joints, but it's the optional extras that pay the rent. This one had a little anteroom with a soft carpet, all rosy lights and strawberry incense. The walls featured unlikely nudes painted on black velvet. A curtain of beads parted and a chesty blonde girl swayed up to me and flapped her eyelashes.

'Hi there,' she said. 'I'm Bunny.'

'You would be.'

'How about a nice massage tonight?' Her fingers were already busy with the buttons of my coat.

'Maybe another time,' I said. 'I just looked in to see if one of the girls showed up for work.'

'What's on your mind, fella?' The voice came from across the room where a kid of twenty or so sat behind a small desk. He had oily black hair and an uncertain complexion. One of his hands was out of sight below the desktop where he probably kept something to quiet troublesome customers.

I went over to the desk and glowered down at him. 'There's a girl named Abby Deane says she works here.'

'So?'

'Did she come in tonight?'

'You're not a cop.'

'My name is Stonebreaker.' I jerked my thumb at the ceiling. 'I'm your new neighbor.'

The kid relaxed a little, but his hand stayed out of sight. 'You say you're a friend of Abby's?'

'Just met her today. We had a business appointment couple of hours ago. She didn't show up.'

'No, she didn't come in tonight.' The kid brought his other hand back up on the desk. 'She didn't call either.'

'Did you try to call her?'

He threw a glance over his shoulder at a door somewhat hidden by a dark red drapery. The door was open a couple of inches. 'I couldn't call her because I don't know her number,' he said. 'I don't know nothing about her. All I do is work out front here.'

The door opened inward the rest of the way and a neat little man walked out to join us. He was wearing a dark suit and vest of the type you don't see any more, with a starched white shirt open at the throat. He was bald with a long skinny nose and a little excuse-me moustache.

'What's the trouble, Rick?' he asked the kid.

'No trouble. This guy was just asking about Abby.'

'Who are you?'

I told him. He was not impressed.

'My name's Otto Boatman,' he said. 'I'm the owner. What did you want with Abby?'

'Just curious. She was afraid she was in some kind of trouble.'

'It's possible. These girls don't come here straight from the convent, you know. What they do on their own time is none of my business. Yours either, as far as I can see.'

'Maybe not,' I said. 'Would you mind giving me her address?'

'Can't do it. For all I know she's freelancing, and if I steered you that would make me a panderer.'

'We wouldn't want to do that,' I said. I'd taken it as far as I'd planned to, anyway. I didn't owe Abby Deane a thing. As I started out into the rain something plucked at my sleeve.

'Come back some time,' said Bunny. She grabbed my hand and gave it a little squeeze.

I winked at her. 'Keep the table warm.' I left the massage parlor and stepped into the shelter of the stairwell to read the note she had pressed into my hand. It had Abby's name on it and an address on Willoughby over near the Desilu studios. Inside my head a small voice said, *Don't get involved*. Sound advice. I got my jalopy out of the parking lot and headed west toward Willoughby.

The apartment was one of those stucco and redwood numbers that went up all over L.A. during the building boom of the Fifties. It was a little frayed around the edges now. At one spot rainwater poured in a splattering stream over the clogged roof gutter. The squatty date palms out in front looked wretched. Los Angeles should never be seen in the rain.

I took a look at the six mailboxes. White envelopes showed through the grill of number three, which was Abby Deane's, putting her downstairs at the rear of the building. I walked along the edge of a small swimming pool to a redwood fence with a metal 3 hanging on the gate. Inside the fence was a two-by-four patio with a sliding glass door into the apartment. I pushed the button and listened to the harsh buzzing inside. Nobody came to let me in.

Okay, said my wise little voice, *you've done all you can. Let's get out of here.*

In a minute, I told the voice. Why, I wondered, if Abby Deane was on her way home when she left me this afternoon, didn't she take in the mail? I popped the door lock with no trouble and stepped into a small, cluttered living room. A quick look in the kitchenette, bath, and bedroom turned up no dead bodies. So much for the good news.

I prowled around a little, getting a feel for the girl who lived here. There was food in the refrigerator and the usual junk in the bathroom, plenty of clothes in the bedroom closet and drawers, and a matched pair of suitcases under the bed. If Abby Deane had gone on a trip, it must have come up mighty sudden. On the way out of the bedroom I stopped to admire a mounted Polaroid shot of Abby and oily-haired Rick from the massage parlor. They were standing by the pool outside her patio with their arms around each other, grinning self-consciously.

A card table was set up in one corner of the living room. Among the papers spread across the top was a pocketsize address book. I thumbed through it and glanced at the clusters of numbers inside that were almost surely names transcribed into a simple number-for-letter code. All the groupings under the *A* section began with the figure *1*, under *B* the figure *2*, and so on. It wouldn't take the CIA to crack Abby's code.

Also on the table was a sheet of lined notebook paper ruled into three columns. Entries in the first column were dates, in the other two were figures in the thousands. For every date the figure in the second column was larger than the third. The dates covered the month just past, but the figures meant nothing to me. I stuck the sheet in my pocket along with the coded address book in case it might mean something later. I went out the way I came in and clicked the lock on the sliding door back into place.

A cold wind was blowing the rain around and Western Avenue was deserted when I strolled back into the Erotique Massage Parlor. Bunny and another girl, both in shorty nightgowns, were sitting on the floor with a deck of cards telling fortunes. Rick slouched behind the desk reading a motorcycle magazine. Bunny saw me first and started to get up. I waved her back down and walked over to the desk.

'It's not nice to lie to people, Rick,' I said.

'What do you mean?'

'You told me you didn't know Abby Deane or anything about her. I just came from her place, and there was a nice picture of the two of you groping each other out by her pool.'

Bunny came over to join us. 'Is Abby all right? How come she didn't show up tonight?'

'I don't know if she's all right or not,' I said. 'She wasn't home. Why did you hold out on me, Rick?'

He jerked his head back toward the curtained door, closed tight now. 'The boss was back in the office, and he don't want me to date any of the girls. He'd fire my butt if he knew.'

I pulled out the address book and the sheet with the figures and showed them to Rick. 'These were in Abby's apartment. It looked like she'd just been working on them. Do they mean anything to you?'

Rick shook his head.

I said, 'If this book is what I think it is, your girl friend might be in as much trouble as she thinks she is.'

Beside me Bunny drew in her breath sharply. 'Can we go in the back and talk?'

I nodded and followed her through the curtain of beads. Along one wall were half a dozen stalls with what looked like padded operating tables inside. Curtains could be pulled across the front for privacy. Straight ahead was a washroom with a couple of showers. Bunny and I were the only ones back there. She took me into one of the stalls.

'I didn't want them to hear this up front,' she said.

'Something about the address book?'

She nodded. 'Abby had a little thing going on the side. When a customer came in and took a shower – everybody has to take a shower first – Abby would go through his wallet. She never took anything, just wrote down the names. The next day she'd check out the names to see if any of the johns were rich or famous or anything. If he was a nobody she'd forget it. If he was some guy with money she'd call up and see if he, um, wanted to give her a little present or whatever you call it.'

'You call it blackmail,' I said.

Bunny toyed with a bottle of scented oil from a shelf over the table. 'Abby didn't think of it like that. She never asked for a whole lot of money, and I don't think she'd have done anything about it if the john refused to pay.'

'Are you telling me the names in this book are the guys on her sucker list?'

'Maybe. She said she kept them in some kind of code.'

'Yeah, very clever of her.' I left the massage booth and rattled back out through the beads.

Rick looked up quickly from the desk. 'Are you going to try to find Abby?' he asked.

'Why should I?'

Bunny came up behind me and said, 'Because you're a detective and she came to you for help.'

'I do this for a living,' I told her. 'Helping people buys no bananas.'

She looked disappointed in me. 'How much do you charge?'

I named my daily rate.

Bunny looked over at Rick. 'I'll go half if you will.'

'I don't know, that's a lot of money.'

'After all, you did have a thing going with her.'

After a little more discussion they came up with the money. I pocketed the bills and went home, where I did the first thing a good detective will always do. I called the police.

Sgt Dave Pike of L.A. Robbery-Homicide used to be my partner before I left the force over a disagreement I had with the Supreme Court. Dave came on the line after a minute or so of clicks and buzzes.

'I've got a missing girl,' I told him. 'Age 22 or 23, five foot five, maybe a hundred pounds, long black hair. Bruise on left side of face. When I last saw her she was wearing short cutoff jeans and a shirt tied in front with a lot of bare skin showing.'

'Hang on a minute while I check with DB.'

While I waited for Dave to query the detectives on dead body detail I shook out a Pall Mall and lit up. I was down to one pack a day, but it didn't look like I would get any lower.

Dave came back on the line. 'No stiff answering that description. It's a slow night for killings.'

'Must be the rain,' I said. 'Give me a call if she turns up, will you?'

'Sure. Stonebreaker?'

'Yeah?'

'Are you sitting on anything that I ought to know?'

'I hope not, Dave, I sincerely hope not.' I hung up and scowled at the phone for a while. I didn't much like the idea of Abby Deane being dead, but little girls who play with blackmail are likely to get that way.

The next day was another dreary wet one. I ate a late breakfast at a Mexican cafe that served *menudo*, and went over to the Department of Motor Vehicles on Hope Street. I paid a small fee to the girl there and she punched out the license number of the tough guy's Volkswagen on a computer keyboard. In a couple of seconds a name and address flashed on the TV-like screen in cool blue letters. The name was Joseph

Kady, the address was up in the Silver Lake district east of Hollywood.

The place was one half of a duplex on a street of tired little houses that looked as uncomfortable in the rain as I felt. I picked my way across the muddy front lawn and knocked on the door. A washed out brunette of about thirty opened up. She had nervous, unhealthy eyes.

'I'm looking for Joseph Kady,' I said.

'What do you want with him?'

'I'm a private investigator.' I flashed my card, which the woman ignored. 'I want to ask him a couple of questions.'

'Oh my God, what's he done now?'

'I don't know that he's done anything. Is he here?'

'No, he's at work. You're not from the probation office, are you?'

'No. Where does he work?'

'He's got a job as driver for Lew Harvester.'

'The state assemblyman?'

'That's right. Joe says he's going to be governor some day.'

'That's nice. Have you got Harvester's address?'

She went away and came back with a number on Roxbury Drive in Beverly Hills. I thanked her and left. While I was driving out Sunset I got to thinking that Lew Harvester – rich, important, ambitious – was a likely candidate for blackmail. I pulled to the curb and got out Abby Deane's address book. Under *H* I found *12-5-23 8-1-18-22-5-19-20-5-18*. It didn't take a computer brain to translate that into *Lew Harvester*. The mix of letters and numbers under the name would be the Beverly Hills address. I put the book away and drove on through the rain. In the mirror I noticed that a black Buick that had stopped half a block behind me started up again when I did.

The lawn in front of Harvester's white colonial house was a little smaller than a football field and green enough to hurt the eyes. I walked up the wet flagstones leading to the front door and thumbed the button. Inside the house a set of chimes played a muted tune. While I waited I glanced over at the three-car garage. The door was raised, and inside a man in a grey uniform was peering under the hood of a Mercedes. I couldn't see his face, but I recognized the shoulders. I could talk to Joe Kady later if I had to.

The front door opened and a man in a tailored leisure suit grinned at me and stuck out his hand. He smelled of expensive cologne.

'Hi, I'm Lew Harvester. I expect you're Frank Endersbee from the citizens' committee. Come on in, Frank, and get out of the rain. Isn't this weather something else?'

'I'm not from the citizens' committee, Mr Harvester,' I said when he was through greeting me. 'My name is Stonebreaker. I'm a private investigator.'

He dropped my hand as though it had grown fur.

'Can we go inside and talk?' I said.

'Why, uh, yes. Certainly.'

Harvester led the way through a living room filled with furniture that looked too good to sit on. We went into a smaller room where there were soft leather chairs, a clean desk, and lots of books in bright new bindings. Harvester perched uncomfortably on the edge of the desk. His politician's smile had come all unstuck. He looked worried.

'I'm looking for a girl named Abby Deane,' I told him.

He made a try at looking mystified. 'Should that name mean something to me?'

'How about the Erotique Massage Parlor on Western Avenue?'

'I – I don't know what you're talking about.'

Harvester's eyes got all shifty and he started to sweat. He couldn't lie worth a damn. He would probably never make governor.

I spelled it out for him. 'Abby Deane worked at the massage parlor. She had your name in an address book as one of her customers. Yesterday your chauffeur was down there slapping her around. Today the girl is missing. What can you tell me about it?'

Harvester stood there stammering and blinking, the guiltiest man since Jack the Ripper.

There was a movement behind me, and a cool blonde woman in a tailored pant suit came into the room.

'Let me handle this, Lew,' she said to Harvester. He gave her a grateful look and hurried out.

'I'm Christine Harvester,' the blonde said when we were alone. 'I'm the one you want to deal with.'

'I do?'

'Sometimes my husband suffers a lapse in judgment. Like getting drunk at a fund-raising dinner last month and going off to that massage parlor with his so-called buddies. Trying to prove his manhood, I suppose.'

I could see where Harvester's manhood might need reinforcing, but I didn't mention it.

Christine Harvester went on, 'Then, when that little tramp came around asking for money, Lew went to pieces. I had to handle that for him, too.'

'So you sent the chauffeur out to beat up the girl.'

'Of course not. I sent Joe to pay her off. Getting rough was his own idea. He probably kept the money I gave him for himself.'

'It's tough to find good help any more,' I said.

'Joe doesn't know it yet, but he just lost his job. Now, what about you, Mr – Stonebreaker, was it? How much do you want? I don't suppose you'll take a check, so I'll have to go to the bank.'

'How much do I want for what?' I said.

'For the girl's address book. I heard you tell my husband about it. Just give me your price and let's not waste time.'

'The book is not my property,' I told her. 'And even if it was, it wouldn't be for sale. That's not my line of work.'

She gave me a look that could knock a man down. I found my own way out and across the acre of green to my car.

Driving back to Hollywood I added up the score so far, and it depressed me. It was still raining, Abby Deane was still missing, and the Buick was following me again.

At least I could do something about the last of those problems. I waited for a stoplight where the Buick pulled up behind me, then got out of my car and went back to knock on the driver's window. He rolled it down a couple of inches and I looked in at a pair of beefy individuals in expensive suits and tinted glasses.

'Hi, fellas,' I said. 'If it would make it any easier for you, I can write out a schedule of where I'll be the rest of the day. Just in case we get separated in traffic.'

The hood on the far side leaned toward me. 'Smartmouth son-of-a –'

'Shut up,' the driver cut him off. To me he said, 'Mr Giordano wants to talk to you.'

'Mr Anthony Giordano?'

'That's right.'

'What if I don't want to talk to him?'

'Mr Giordano wouldn't like that.'

We could have carried on the tough-guy dialog for a while, but I was tired of standing out in the rain. I parked my own car and got into the Buick. We drove in silence out to the gleaming high-rise island called Century City where Anthony Giordano kept a suite of offices. 'Tony John,' as he was known to his pals, had a finger into most of the illegal pies in the city, but he worked hard at keeping his name out of the papers.

We found Giordano on the twenty-first floor of one of the steel and glass towers. The layout was more like a plush apartment than an office. There were a couple of furry sofas, a free-form coffee table, built-in audio equipment, and a bar. Giordano was standing in front of a tall tinted-glass window with his hands clasped behind him. He had a beautiful health-club tan and shiny black hair that faded to a dramatic white at the temples. He got right to the point.

'I want to know what your interest is in Otto Boatman and his massage parlor.'

'Maybe I wanted a massage.'

'Or maybe you're doing a job for Boatman.'

'What if I am?'

'I'm curious. Let's say I have a certain financial interest in the operation.'

'Let's say you own it.'

'Not me personally,' said Giordano, 'but the people I represent.'

'Uh-huh. No, I'm not working for Boatman. I'm trying to find one of his girls. Abby Deane. Know her?'

'No. I don't get involved with the merchandise.'

'Good for you. You must have been watching Boatman for some reason to pick me up this fast. Are you worried about him?'

'My people like to keep an eye on their investments, that's all. Thanks for coming in, and good luck in finding the girl.'

'Sure.'

Giordano walked over and touched a button that was concealed in the arm of a sofa. The door opened immediately and the hood who drove me out stepped into the room.

'Vinnie, take our friend wherever he wants to go,' he said, and I was dismissed.

I had Vinnie take me back to my car, which was looking cleaner than it had in months after being rained on for two days. The talk with Giordano gave me something to think about as I drove back to my office. When I got there I had even more to think about. My answering service had a message for me to call Sgt Pike. I dialed the police number and got right through to Dave.

'We found your girl,' he said.

'Where?'

'Griffith Park, in the brush along the road that goes up to the observatory. A cruiser was checking out a lost child report, and there she was. White female, early twenties, black hair, dressed the way you described.'

'Dead, I suppose.'

'Sure, dead, what do you think? Strangled with a necktie still knotted around her throat so tight the coroner had to cut it off. No I.D. on the body. Who is she, Stonebreaker?'

I gave him Abby Deane's name and the address on Willoughby.

'Anything else?'

I hesitated. 'Not yet, Dave. I'll get back to you.'

'Stonebreaker, you're holding out on me.'

'Would I do that?'

'You would.'

'I'm just looking out for my client's interests, Dave. I guarantee that by tonight you'll know everything I do.'

Dave Pike started to chew me out, but before he could really get going I told him goodbye and hung up.

At about seven o'clock I strolled into the strawberry-scented anteroom of the Erotique Massage Parlor. A customer sidled out through the beads as I entered. He assumed a preoccupied look, as though he were just gathering material for a book.

I ignored the customer and walked over to the desk where Rick was looking at me worriedly. 'I've got bad news,' I said.

He shook his head and gestured toward the door behind the red drapery. The door was open a couple of inches.

'This is something your boss ought to hear, too.' I said it loud enough to make sure he did.

Otto Boatman came out of his office wearing the same dated three-piece suit as the day before. His narrow striped tie was also out of step with the current fashion. At the same time Bunny came through the bead curtain. She was wearing see-through harem pants and some spangles across her chest.

'What is it I ought to hear?' Boatman asked.

'First, Abby Deane is dead.'

It took a second for them to absorb the information. Bunny was the first to speak.

'What happened?'

'She was strangled and dumped in the weeds in Griffith Park.'

'Do they know who killed her?' Rick asked.

'Not yet, but they will soon.'

'What do you mean?' said Boatman.

'Chances are it was somebody from right here at your massage parlor.'

Bunny's eyes went wide. 'You mean one of us?'

While they all stared at me, I went on. 'When I talked to her yesterday, Abby was in a hurry to meet someone who was supposed to give her a ride home. Who but somebody she knew from here would pick this spot to meet?'

'I hope you're not including me,' said Boatman.

'I haven't seen her since night before last,' said Rick.

'I don't even own a car,' said Bunny.

'Even though she wasn't very good at it,' I went on, 'Abby was a blackmailer. It figures that she was killed by somebody she was trying to shake down. I wondered what she could have on anybody that was heavy enough to get her killed. Some people might be embarrassed to be caught going into a massage parlor, but you don't commit murder out of embarrassment. On the other hand, if you were stealing money, very dangerous money, you might go all the way to keep that quiet.'

'I don't think I like what you're getting at,' Otto Boatman said.

'No, I don't suppose you do, Otto. I had a talk with Tony John today, and he let me figure out who really owns this place. I also got the idea he doesn't quite trust you.'

Boatman whitened around the nostrils, but he kept his indignant expression in place.

'At Abby's apartment I found a sheet of paper that shows he was right.' I let Boatman have a quick look at the page with the columns of figures. 'It doesn't take an accountant to figure out that, after each date, the first figure is the money you took in and the second is what you reported to Giordano. Tony John would be very interested in this.'

'That piece of paper doesn't mean anything,' Boatman said, but there was no conviction in his voice.

'You probably met Abby here to talk about her price for keeping quiet. The price must have been too high.'

Boatman's little eyes glittered. 'You're just guessing. You don't have one real piece of evidence.'

'Gathering evidence is the D.A.'s job,' I said. 'Sure, maybe you can beat the rap. If you want to. Then again, maybe you'd rather be safely locked up than out on the street where Tony John can reach you. It's something to think about.'

Otto Boatman started to come apart then. 'If only she hadn't started snooping around in the office. She shouldn't have tried to hold me up. I didn't mean to . . . I would never have . . .'

Boatman swayed on his feet. Rick got up fast and let him drop into the chair. The little man sat there staring at the wall. His face was the color of mozzarella cheese. I picked up the phone.

After the police came and took Boatman away I stood out on Western Avenue with Rick and Bunny in front of the padlocked massage parlor. The rain had quit and people were beginning to show up on the street.

'You know,' Rick said, 'you really didn't have much to go on.' He sounded resentful, as though he had caught me cheating.

Bunny came to my rescue. 'Well, I think you were fantastic, the way you figured it all out.' Then she added, 'But you were guessing a little, weren't you?'

'Not much,' I said. 'You see, I didn't exactly tell Boatman about the most important piece of evidence.'

'What's that?' Rick asked, right on cue.

'The necktie he used to strangle Abby. I had to get a look at him tonight to make sure he usually wore one. That corny suit and vest outfit looks even worse without a tie, but last night he had his collar open.'

Bunny said, 'But why would he leave the tie behind after he . . . after he . . . ?'

'The knot was too tight for him to pull it off. He couldn't risk parking up there indefinitely wrestling with a dead body. He probably got nervous and shoved her into the brush when he heard a car coming.'

I was losing Rick's attention. He shuffled his feet and looked up at the sky, where the clouds were breaking up and stars were showing through the chinks. He said, 'At least it stopped raining. Look, man, I think I'll split.'

It was nice to know Abby Deane's death hadn't ruined his whole day.

Bunny was fidgeting, too. 'Hey, I ought to go, too, you know.'

'Go ahead.'

'I mean, I'd stick around, but the night's young and a girl has to make a living. Unless you're interested?'

'Some other time,' I told her.

Bunny gave me a farewell smile and strolled up the street in her short, tight skirt and vinyl boots. The storm was over, the people were out, and on Western Avenue it was business as usual.

THE PEARLS OF PEACE

Leslie Charteris

From a press release by the author:

Leslie Charteris was born in Singapore in 1907 . . . His first professional sale, at 11, was of a short poem to a boys' magazine . . . He sold his first adult short story to a national magazine at 17 . . . With some astonishment, he soon discovered that the publication of a few books and magazine stories was not an instant passport to the life style which he felt had been intended for him, and for several years he was forced to supplement his income with a variety of part-time jobs, some of them almost legitimate, in many different parts of the world, of which he is saving the details for his autobiography, which he has promised to write at the age of 150 . . . Starting in 1931, he experienced matrimony three times, but became hopelessly addicted on the fourth experiment, which has lasted more than 30 years . . . Now firmly addicted to the pursuit of idleness, he still manages to produce a new book occasionally, under pressure from his publishers, but without letting it distract from his more serious preoccupation, which is concerned with the relative speeds of racehorses.

About the story which follows, Leslie Charteris himself writes:

The problem of choosing my best short story is a difficult one. In trying to make a short list, I still ended up with four or five favourites which have special associations for me. So I turned the problem over to my wife, who unhesitatingly preferred 'The Pearls of Peace', from Señor Saint – *because it is quite specially different in its way. The 'special association', by the way, is that I got the idea for the story on part of our honeymoon, during which we stayed for a little while at Las Cruces, Baja California, which is near La Paz.*

Before the idea becomes too firmly established that Simon Templar (or, as it usually seems easier to call him, the Saint) never bothered to steal anything of which the value could be expressed in less than six figures, I want to tell here the story of the most trivial robbery he ever committed.

The popular conception of the meanest theft that can be committed is epitomized in the cliché of 'stealing pennies from a blind man'. Yet that, almost literally, is what the Saint once did. And he is perhaps prouder of it than of any other larceny in a list which long ago assumed the dimensions of an epic.

The Saint has been called by quite a thesaurus of romantic names, of which 'The Robin Hood of Modern Crime' and 'The Twentieth Century's Brightest Buccaneer' are probably the hardest worked. By public officials obligated to restrain his self-appointed and self-administered kind of justice, and by malefactors upon whom it had been exercised, he was described by an even more definitive glossary of terms which cannot be quoted in a publication available to the general public. To himself he was only an adventurer born in the wrong age, a cavalier cheated out of his sword, a pirate robbed of his black flag, with a few inconvenient ideals which had changed over the years in detail but never in principle. But by whatever adjectives you choose to delineate him, and with whatever you care to make of his motives, the sober arithmetical record certainly makes him, statistically, one of the greatest robbers of all time. Estimates of the total loot which at one time or another passed through his hands, as made by mathematically-minded students of these stories, vary in their net amount: his expenses were always high, and his interpretation of a tithe to charity invariably generous. But by any system of calculation, they run comfortably into the millions.

Such a result should surprise nobody. Simon Templar liked big adventures, and in big affairs there is usually big money involved, this being the sordid state of incentives in our day and age.

But the Saint's greatness was that he could be just as interested in small matters when they seemed big enough to him. And that is what the incident I am referring to was about.

This happened around the town of La Paz, which in Spanish means only 'Peace'.

La Paz lies near the southern tip of the peninsula of Baja California, 'Lower California' in English – a long narrow leg of land which stretches down from the southern border of California and the United States. On account of the peculiarly ineradicable obsession of American statesmen with abstract lines of latitude and longitude as boundaries, instead of more intelligible geographic or ideographic frontiers, which accepted the ridiculous 38th-parallel partition of Korea as naturally as the quaint geometrical shape of most American state lines, this protuberance was blandly excluded from the deal which brought California into the Union, although topographically it is as obviously a proper part of California as its name implies. There is in technical fact a link of dry land south of the border connecting Baja California with the mainland of Mexico, but there is no practical transportation across it, no civilized way from one to the other without passing through the United States: for all the rest of its length, the Gulf of Lower California, or the Sea of Cortez as the Mexicans know it, thrusts a hundred miles and more of deep water between the two.

Thus, like an almost amputated limb, Baja California hangs in the edge of the Pacific, bound to Mexico by nationality, to California by what terrestrial ligaments it has, nourished by neither and an anomaly to both. The highway artery leaps boldly across to Tijuana and contrives to keep going south to Ensenada, bearing a fair flow of tourist blood; but then almost at once it is a mere dusty trickle of an almost impassable road, navigable only to rugged venturers in jeeps, which meanders through scorched and barren waste lands for hundreds of empty miles to La Paz, which is the end of the line.

La Paz is a port of long defunct importance, seeming to survive mainly because its inhabitants have nowhere else to go. But that was not always true. Here in the fine natural harbor, once, toplofty Spanish galleons came to anchor; and bearded soldier-monks peered hungrily at the rocky shore, eager to convert the heathen with *pax vobiscums* or bonfires, but with some leaning towards the latter, and always with an eye to the mundane treasures that could be heisted from the pagans in exchange for a sizzling dose of salvation. But the gold of that region, though it was there and is still there, was too hard to extract for their voracious appetite, and they sailed on towards the richer promise of the north. Others, however, who came later and stayed, discovered treasure of another kind under the pellucid warm blue waters near by: once upon a time, the pearl fisheries of La Paz were world famous, far surpassing the product of the South Pacific oyster beds which most people think of in that connection today.

And that is what this story began to be about.

'It was the Japs,' Jocelyn Ormond said. 'They put something in the water that killed off all the oysters. They were all up and down this coast just before the war, pretending to be fishermen, but really they were taking soundings and mapping our fortifications and getting ready for all kinds of sabotage. Like that.'

'I know,' said the Saint lazily. 'And every one of them had a Leica in his pocket and an admiral's uniform in his duffel bag. Some of it's probably true. But can you tell me how destroying the Mexican pearl industry would help their war plans against the United States? Or do you think it was some weird Oriental way of putting a hex on everything connected with pearls, like for instance Pearl Harbor?'

'You're kidding,' she said sulkily. 'The oysters *did* die. You can't get away from that.'

When they were first introduced by a joint acquaintance he had had a puzzling feeling that they had met somewhere before. After a while he realized that they had – but it had never been in the flesh. She was a type. She was the half-disrobed siren on the jacket of a certain type of paper-bound fiction. She was the girl in the phoney-tough school of detective stories, the girl that the grotesque private eye with the unpaid rent and the bottle of cheap whisky in his desk drawer is always running into, who throws her thighs and breasts at him and responds like hot jelly to his simian virility. She had all the standard equipment – the auburn hair, the bedroom eyes, the fabulous mammary glands, the clothes that clung suggestively to her figure, the husky voice, the full moist lips that looked as if they would respond lecherously enough to satisfy any addict of that style of writing – although the Saint hadn't yet sampled them. He couldn't somehow make himself feel like the type of cut-rate Casanova who should have been cast opposite her. He couldn't shake off a sense of unreality about her perfect embodiment of the legendary super-floozy. But there was no doubt that she was sensational, and in a cautious way he was fascinated.

He knew that other men had been less backward. She was Mrs Ormond now, but she had discarded Ormond some time ago in Reno. Before Ormond, there had been another, a man with the earthy name of Ned Yarn. It was Ned Yarn whose resuscitated ghost was with them now, intangibly.

'I mean,' she said, 'they were all supposed to have died – until I got that letter from Ned.'

Simon went to the rail of the balcony which indiscreetly connected their rooms, and gazed out over the harbor and the ugly outlines of La Paz, softened now by the glamor of night lights. They were sitting outside to escape from the sweltering stuffiness of their rooms, the soiled shabbiness of the furniture and decoration, and the sight of the giant cockroaches which shared their tenancy. For such reasons as that, and because your chronicler does not want to be sued for libel, the hotel they were staying at must be nameless.

'Let me see it again,' he said.

She took the worn sheet of cheap paper from her purse and gave it to him, and he held it up to read it by the light from inside the room.

> Dear Joss,
>
> I know you will be surprised to hear from me now, but I had no heart to write when I could only make excuses which you wouldn't believe. You were quite right to divorce me. But now I have found the pearls I came for. I can pay everyone back, and perhaps make everything all right with you too.
>
> The only thing is, it may be delicate to handle. Say nothing to anyone, but send somebody you can trust who knows pearls and doesn't mind taking a chance. Or come yourself. Whoever comes, go to the 'Cantina de las Flores' in La Paz and ask for Consuelo. She will bring him to me. I won't let you down this time.
>
> Always your
>
> Ned

The writing was awkward and straggly, up hill and down dale, the long letters overlapping between lines.

'Is this his writing?' Simon asked.

'It wasn't always that bad. Maybe he was drunk when he wrote it. Now that we're here, I wonder why I came on this wild-goose chase.' She stared at the anemic residue in her glass. 'Fix me another slug, Saint.'

He went back into the room, fished melting ice cubes from the warming water in the pitcher, and poured Peter Dawson over them. That was how she took it, and it never seemed to affect her much. Another characteristic that was strictly from literature.

'That letter is dated over five months ago,' he said. 'Did it take all that time to reach you, or did you only just decide to do something about it?'

'Both,' she said. 'I didn't get it for a long time – I was moving around, and it was just lucky that people kept forwarding it. And when I got it, I didn't know whether to believe it, or what to do. If I hadn't met you, I mightn't ever have done anything about it. But you know about jewels.'

'And I'm notorious for taking chances.'

'And I like you.'

He smiled into her slumbrous eyes, handing her the refilled glass, and sat down again in the other chair, stretching his long legs.

'You liked Ormond when you married him, I suppose,' he said. 'What was the mistake in that?'

'He was a rich old man, but I thought he needed me. I found out that all he wanted was my body.'

'It sounds like a reasonable ambition.'

'But he wanted a bird in a gilded cage. To keep me in purdah, like a sultan. He didn't want to go places and do things. He'd give me presents, but he wouldn't let me have a penny of my own to spend.'

'An obvious square,' said the Saint. 'But you fixed him. What about Ned?'

'I was very young then, just a small-town girl trying to crash Hollywood and making doughnut money as an extra. And it was during the war, and he was young too, and strong and healthy, and that Navy uniform did something for him. It happened to a lot of girls . . . And then the war was over, and I woke up, and he was just a working diver, a sort of submerged mechanic, earning a mechanic's wages and going nowhere except under docks and bridges.'

Simon nodded, leaning back with his freebooter's profile turned up impersonally to the stars. He had heard all this before, of course, but he wanted to hear it once again, to be sure he had heard it all.

'That's all this Tiltman wanted,' she said. 'A good working diver. Percival Tiltman – what a name! I should have known he was a phoney, with that name, and his old-school-tie British accent. But he knew where the richest oyster bed of all was, and it was one that the Japs had missed somehow, and he had some real pearls to prove it . . . Of course, he needed money too – for equipment, and a boat, and bribes. Mostly for bribes. That should have been the tip-off, all by itself.'

'I don't know,' said the Saint. 'I can believe that the Mexican government might take a dim view of foreigners coming down and walking off with their pearls.'

'Well, anyway, he got it.'

'It was about $10,000, wasn't it?'

'Exactly $11,000. Most of it was from my friends – people I'd known in the studios. Ned's best friend put some in. And $2500 was my own savings, from what Ned had sent me while he was overseas.'

'And Ned and Brother Tiltman took off with it all in cash?'

'All of it. And that's the last anyone heard of them – until I got that letter.'

'How hard did you try to find him?'

'What could I do? I didn't have an address. Ned was going to write to me when he got down here. He never did.'

'There's an American vice-consul.'

'We tried that, after a while. He never heard of them.'

'How about the police?'

'I wrote to them. They took three weeks to answer, and then they just said they had no information. Perhaps some of the money *was* used for bribes, at that.'

'I mean the American police. Didn't anyone make a complaint?'

'How could I? And make myself the wife of a runaway crook? Our friends were very nice about it. They were sorry for me. I've never felt so humiliated. But it was all too obvious. Ned and Tiltman had just taken our money and run off with it. It wasn't even worth anybody's while to come down here and try to trace them. They'd had too long a start. By the time we realized what they'd done, they could have been anywhere in South America – or anywhere in the world, for that matter. I just waited till Ned had been gone a year, and divorced him as quietly as I could, for desertion.'

'But,' said the Saint, 'it looks now as if he'd been here all the time, after all.'

Mrs Ormond swished the Scotch around over the ice in her glass with a practised rotary motion, brooding over it sullenly.

'Perhaps he came back. Perhaps he spent all his share of the money, and now he thinks he can promote some more with the same gag. Who knows?'

'It was nearly ten years ago when he disappeared, wasn't it?' said the Saint. 'If he got half the loot, he's lived on less than six hundred a year. That's really making it last. If he was going to try for more, why would he leave it so long? And why did he disappear when he did, without any kind of word?'

'Don't ask me,' she said. 'You're the detective. All I know is, there's something fishy about it. That's why I wouldn't have come here alone. You'd better be careful. I hope you're smarter than he is.'

Simon raised an eyebrow.

'When this started, you gave the impression that he was almost boringly simple.'

'That's what everyone thought. But look what he did. He must have had us all fooled. You can't believe anything he says.'

'I'm not exactly notorious for buying wooden nickels – or plasticine pearls. I'll keep my guard up.'

'Do that in more ways than one. I told you, he was a very husky guy. And he could be plenty tough.'

'I can be tough too, sometimes.'

She eyed him long and appraisingly.

'Come here,' she said, in her throatiest voice.

He unfolded himself languidly and stood beside her.

'No, don't tower over me. Come down to my level.'

He squatted goodhumoredly on his heels, close to her chair.

'You look strong,' she murmured, 'in a lean leathery way. But I never found out how far it went. That's why I like you. You're different. Most men are in such a hurry to show me.'

Her hand felt his arm, sliding up under his short sleeve. Her eyes widened a little, and became soft and dreamy. The hand slid up to his shoulder, and the tip of her tongue touched her parted lips.

Simon Templar grinned, and stood up.

'I'm strong enough,' he said. 'And I'll be very careful.'

He had already located the Cantina de las Flores – had, in fact, been inside it earlier in the evening. It was a small and dingy bistro in a back street of unromantic odors, and the only flowers in its vicinity were those which were painted in garish colors on the sign over the door. An unshaven bartender in a dirty shirt had informed him that Consuelo would not be there until ten. It was only a few minutes after that hour when the Saint strolled towards it again.

He would probably have been less than human if he had not thought more about Jocelyn Ormond than about Consuelo on the way over. Consuelo was only a name; but Mrs Ormond was not easy to forget.

He tried to rationalize his reaction to her, and couldn't do it. According to all tradition, there should have been no problem. She not only had all the physical attributes, in extravagant abundance, but she knew every line in the script, in all its cereal ripeness. The dumbest private eye on the newsstands could have taken his cue and helped himself to the offering. Yet the Saint found a perverse pleasure in pretending to be blandly unconscious of the routine, in acting as if her incredible voluptuousness left him only amused. Which was an outright glandular lie.

He shook his head. Maybe he was just getting too old inside . . .

The bar, which had been drably deserted when he was there before, was now starting to jump. There were a dozen and a half cash customers, a few obviously local citizens but a majority with the heterogeneous look of seamen from visiting freighters – a sterling and salty clientele, no doubt, but somewhat less than elegant. There were also half a dozen girls, who seemed to function occasionally as waitresses, but who also obviously offered more general hospitality and comradeship. Instead of the atmospheric obbligato of guitars with which no Hollywood producer could have resisted backgrounding such a set, an enormous juke box blared deafening orchestrations out of its rococo edifice of plastic panels, behind which colored lights flowed and blended like delirious rainbows, a dazzling and stentorian witness to the irresistible march of North American culture.

Simon went to the counter and ordered a beer. The bartender, only a few hours more unshaven and a few hours dirtier than at their first meeting, looked at him curiously as he poured it.

'You are the *señor* who was looking for Consuelo.'

'Is she here now?'

'I will tell her,' the man said.

Simon took his glass over to the juke box and stood reading the list of its musical offerings, toying with the faint hope that he might find a title which suggested that in exchange for a coin some slightly less earsplitting melody might be evoked.

'You were asking for me?' a voice said at his shoulder.

The Saint turned.

He turned slowly, because the quality of the voice had jolted him momentarily off balance. It was an amazing thing for a mere voice to do at any time, and against the strident din through which he had to hear it it was almost incredible. Yet that was what it achieved, without effort. It was the loveliest speaking voice he had ever heard. It had the pure tones of cellos and crystal bells in it, and yet it held a true warmth and a caress and a passion that made the untrammeled sexiness of Jocelyn Ormond's voice sound like a crude rasp. Just those few words of it stippled goose-pimples up his spine. He wanted the space of a breath to re-establish his equanimity before he saw the owner.

Then he saw her; and the goose-pimples tightened and chilled as if at a touch of icy air, and the jolt he had felt turned to a leaden numbness.

She could have been under thirty, but she was aged in the cruel way that women of her racial mixture, in that climate, will age. You could see Spanish blood in her, and Indian, and undoubtedly some African. Her figure might once have been enticingly ripe, but now it was overblown and mushy. Her black hair was lank and greasy, her nose broad and flat, her painted mouth coarse and thick. Even under a heavy layer of powder that was several shades too light, her complexion showed dark and horribly ravaged with pock-marks. She smiled, showing several gold teeth.

'I am Consuelo,' she said in that magical voice.

Somehow the Saint managed to keep all reaction out of his face, or hoped he did.

'I am looking for an American, a Señor Yarn,' he said. 'He wrote a letter saying that one should come here and ask for you.'

Her eyes flickered over him oddly.

'*Si*,' she said. 'I remember. I will take you to him. *Un momentito*.'

She went to the bar and spoke briefly to the bartender, who scowled and shrugged. She came back.

'Come.'

Simon put down his glass and went out with her.

The sidewalk was so narrow that there was barely room for them both, and when they met any other walkers there was a subtle contest of bluff to decide which party should give way.

'It was a long time ago that he told me to expect someone,' she said. 'Why did you take so long?'

'His letter took a long time. And there were other delays.'

'You have the letter with you?'

'It was not written to me. I was sent by the person to whom he wrote.'

Some instinct of delicacy compelled him to evade a more exact naming of the person. He said, cautiously: 'You know what it was about?'

'I know nothing.'

Her high heels clicked a tattoo of fast short steps, hobbled by a skirt that was too tight from hip to knee.

'I have never met Señor Yarn,' he said. 'What kind of a man is he?'

She stopped looking up to search his face with a kind of vehement suddenness.

'He is a good man. The best I have ever known. I hope you are good for him!'

'I hope so, too,' said the Saint gently.

They walked on, zigzagging through alleys that grew steadily narrower and darker and more noisome; but the Saint, whose sense of direction could be switched on like a recording machine, never lost track of a turn. The people who shared the streets with them became fewer and vaguer shadows. Life went indoors, and barricaded itself against the night behind shutters through which only an occasional streak of yellow light leaked out. It revealed itself only as a muffled grumbling voice, a sharp ripple of shrill laughter, the wail of a baby, the faint tinny sound of a cheap radio or phonograph; and against that dim soundtrack the clatter of Consuelo's heels seemed to ring out like blows on an anvil. If the Saint had not stepped silently from incurable habit, he would have found himself doing it with a self-conscious impulse to minimize his intrusion. If he could conceivably have picked up Consuelo, or any of the other girls, in the Cantina de las Flores, without an introduction, and had found himself being led where he was for any other reason, he would have been tense with suspicion and wishing for the weight of a gun in his pocket. But he did not think he had anything to fear.

When she stopped, a faint tang of sea smells penetrating the hodgepodge of less natural aromas told his nostrils that they were near another part of the waterfront. The shack that loomed beside them was different only in details of outline from the others around it – a shanty of crumbling plaster and decaying timbers, with a rambling roof line which could consist of nothing but an accumulation of innumerable inadequate repairs.

'Here,' she said.

She opened the cracked plank door, and Simon followed her in.

The whole house was only one little room. There was a brass bedstead against one wall, with a faded chintz curtain across the corner beside it which might have concealed some sort of sanitary facilities. In another corner, there was an ancient oil cooking stove, and a bare counter board with a chipped enamel basin. On shelves above the counter, there were cheap dishes and utensils, and a few canned foods. Clothing hung on hooks in the walls, between an assortment of innocuous lithographs pinned up according to some unguessable system of selection.

'Ned,' Consuelo said very clearly, 'I have brought the *Americano* you sent for.'

The man sat in the one big chair in the room. It was an overstuffed chair of oldfashioned shape, with a heavily patched slipcover, but he looked comfortable in it, as if he had used it a lot. He had untidy blond hair and a powerful frame, but the flesh on his big bones was soft and shrunken and unhealthy, although his skin had a good tan; and his clean cotton shirt and trousers hung loosely on him. His face had the cragginess of a skull, an impression which was accentuated by the shadows of the dark glasses he wore even though the only light was an oil lamp turned down so low that it gave no more illumination than a candle. He turned only his head.

'I was afraid no one was ever coming,' he said.

'My name is Templar,' said the Saint. 'I was sent by – the party you wrote to.'

'My wife,' the man said. 'You don't have to be tactful. Consuelo knows about her.'

'Your ex-wife,' said the Saint.

Ned Yarn sat still, and the dark lenses over his eyes were a mask.

'I guess I'd sort of expected that. How did she get it? Desertion, I suppose.'

'Yes.'

'Is she . . . ?'

'She was married again, to a man named Ormond.'

'I don't know him.'

'They're divorced now.'

'I see.' Yarn's bony fingers moved nervously. 'And you?'

'Just an acquaintance. Nothing more. What with changing her name, and changing her address several times, apparently your letter took a long time to find her. And then she didn't want to come here alone, and couldn't decide who else to trust. Now I seem to be it.'

'Sit down,' Ned Yarn said.

Simon sat on a plain wooden chair by the oilcloth-covered table. Yarn looked around and said: 'Do we have anything to drink, Consuelo?'

'Some tequila.'

She brought a half-empty bottle and three small jelly-glasses, and poured a little for each of them. She put one of the glasses on the edge of the table nearest to Yarn. Yarn stretched out his hand, touched the edge of the table, and slid his fingers along it until they closed on the glass.

'You must excuse me seeming so helpless,' he said harshly. 'But you see, I'm blind.'

The Saint lighted a cigarette, and put his lighter away very quietly. He glanced at Consuelo for a moment as she sat down slowly on the other wooden chair at the table, and then he looked at Ned Yarn again.

'I'm sorry,' he said. 'How long ago did that happen?'

'Almost as soon as I got here.' The other gave a kind of short two-toned grunt that might have been meant for a laugh. 'How much did she tell you about all this?'

'As much as she knows, I think.'

'I can figure what else she thinks. And what everybody else thinks. But you know as much now as I knew when I came down here with Tiltman. That's the truth, so help me.'

'I hope you'll tell me the rest.'

Yarn sipped his drink, and put it down without a grimace, as if he was completely inured to the vile taste.

'We flew down here from Tijuana, and I thought it was all on the level. A chance to make some big money legitimately – that is, if we weren't bothered about bribing a few Mexicans not to watch us too closely. I'm just a sucker, I guess, but I fell for it like all the others. I was even carrying the money myself. We checked in at a hotel, the Perla.'

'And yet the American vice-consul and the police couldn't find any trace of you. That seems like an obvious place for them to have started asking.'

'Tiltman registered for us both – only he didn't use our names. If you want to check up on me, ask if they've got a record of Thompson and Young. He told me that later.'

'How long did he play it straight?'

'We had dinner. Tiltman was supposed to have arranged for a boat before we left Los Angeles. I was all excited and raring to go, of course. I didn't even want to wait till morning to look it over. I wanted to see it that night. He tried to stall me a bit, and then he gave in. We set out walking from the hotel. He led me through all kinds of back streets – I haven't the faintest idea where. Presently, in one of the darkest of them, we came to a bar, and he said let's stop in for a drink.'

'The Cantina de las Flores?'

'No. I don't even know the name of it. But anyway we went in. We had a drink. And then, as calmly as anything, he said: "Look, Ned, I'm going to stop beating about the bush. There isn't any boat. There isn't any diving equipment – all that stuff we ordered sent down here from Los Angeles, I canceled the order and got your money back." '

'And the great lost bed of pearl oysters?'

'He said: "That's just a rumor I heard when I was down here, sort of a local legend. But I don't know where it is, and nobody else does. It just gave me the idea for a good story to pick up a nice lot of money with. All that money you've got in your pocket," he said.'

'That must have called for another drink,' murmured the Saint.

'At first I thought he was kidding. But I soon knew he wasn't. He said: "I could've taken it from you tonight and left you holding the bag. But I like you, Ned, and I could use a partner. I've got tickets for both of us on a plane to Mazatlán. Let's split the money and go on and make a lot more like it." '

Simon barely touched his glass to his lips.

'And you said no?'

'I swear it. I told him he'd never get his hands on any of the money I had. I was taking it right back to Los Angeles, and I'd see what the police here could do about getting back the refund he'd gotten on the diving equipment. And I walked out.' Ned Yarn twisted his knuckles tensely together. 'I didn't get very far. He must have followed me and crept up behind me. Something hit me on the head, and I was out like a light. It's been lights out for me ever since.'

'The money was gone, of course.'

Yarn nodded. He said: 'You tell him, Consuelo.'

She said: 'I found him. It was just outside here. I was going to work. I thought he was drunk. Then I saw the blood. I could not leave him to die. I took him in my house. Then, when he did not get well quickly, I was afraid. I thought, if I call the police, they will say I did it to rob him. I sent for a doctor I know. Together we took care of him. He was sick for a long time. And then I could not turn him out, because he was blind.'

'And you've looked after him ever since,' said the Saint, and deliberately averted his eyes.

'I was glad to.' He heard only her voice. 'Because then I had fallen in love.'

And now the Saint understood at least a part of that strange story, with a fullness that left him for a little while without speech.

Ned Yarn had never seen Consuelo. He had met her only as a voice, a voice of indescribable sweetness, just as the Saint had first met her; but Ned Yarn had never been able to turn his eyes and have the mental vision that the voice created shattered by the sight of her coarse raddled face. And the woman who spoke with the voice had been kind to him in a way that fulfilled all the promise of its rich tenderness. Her figure would have been better then, and perhaps even her face less marred; and his fingers, when they clumsily explored her features, would not have been sensitive enough to trace them as they really were. They could easily have confirmed to him a picture that his imagination had already formed and was determined to believe. And in his perpetual darkness there could be no disillusion . . .

'Maybe you think I'm a bum,' Ned Yarn said. 'Maybe I am. But what could I do? I didn't have a penny, and I couldn't go more than a few steps by myself. Tiltman probably thought he'd killed me with that crack on the head. He might almost as well have. It was months before I really knew what was going on. And even then I still couldn't think straight, I guess.'

'You figured by that time everyone would have decided you'd run off with Tiltman and the money,' said the Saint.

'Even Joss. I couldn't blame her. I was just too ashamed to try to write and explain. I didn't think anyone would believe me. I guess I was wrong; but by the time I started to think it out properly, it was later still – that much more too late. And then . . .' The premature lines in his face softened amazingly. 'By then I was in love, too. I didn't really want to go back.'

Ash tumbled from the Saint's long-neglected cigarette as he put it to his mouth again.

'But you finally wrote to Jocelyn,' he said.

'I'm coming to that. After a while, I realized I couldn't go on forever doing nothing but being sorry for myself, letting Consuelo keep me on the money she made as a waitress.'

From the matter-of-fact way Yarn said it, Simon knew that the man could never have had any idea of the kind of place she worked in. He was aware of the woman's eyes on him, but he gave no sign of it.

'Her doctor thought there might be a chance of getting my sight back if I could go to a first-class specialist,' Ned Yarn said. 'But that would cost plenty of money. And I couldn't go back to the States for treatment when it'd probably mean being put in jail. I needed even more money, to pay everybody back what I'd helped them to lose through Tiltman. I wanted to do that anyway. When I finally got my guts back, I knew that was what I had to do somehow – pay everyone off, and get my eyes fixed, and make a fresh start.'

'You still believed in that overlooked oyster bed?'

'It was the only chance I could think of. Eventually I talked Consuelo into helping me. She has a friend who's a fisherman, and he'd let us borrow his boat sometimes. We went out as often as we could. We searched all over, everywhere.'

'You went diving, when you were blind?'

'No, Consuelo did that. With a face mask. She can swim like a fish, she tells me. I just sat in the boat. And then, when at last she found oysters, I'd haul up the baskets she filled, and help her to open them. And as I wrote to Joss, we finally did it. We found those pearls!'

'The jackpot?' Simon asked.

Ned Yarn shook his head.

'I don't know. Quite a few, so far. Consuelo sold a few small ones, to get money to make us just a little more comfortable. And six months ago we bought a boat of our own, so we could go out more often. Of course she got practically nothing for them, because of the way she had to sell them. And she couldn't show any of the big ones without attracting too much attention. That's why I had to get in touch with someone who'd know their real value, and perhaps be able to sell them properly up north.'

At Simon's side, the woman turned abruptly, her over-plucked eyebrows drawn together.

'Is he a buyer of pearls?' she asked. 'Is that why he is here? You did not tell me, Ned.'

'I know.' The man smiled awkwardly. 'I told you I was sending for someone who would help us to buy some real diving equipment, so we could really bring up those oysters after I taught you to use it. I was afraid of getting your hopes too high. But actually that's just what he might do.'

'If the pearls are not worth so much, you will use the money to buy diving equipment to look for more?'

'That's right.'

'But if they're worth enough,' said the Saint, 'you want to pay back $11,000 to various people, and see if something can be done about your eyes?'

'Yes.'

'And then come back to Consuelo,' said the Saint softly.

'Oh, no,' Ned Yarn said. 'I wouldn't leave here unless she came with me.'

Consuelo stood up with a sudden rough movement that shook the table. She stood beside Yarn with a hand on his shoulder, and his hand went up at once to cover hers.

'I do not like it,' she said. 'How do you know you can trust him?'

'I'll have to risk it,' Yarn said grimly. 'Show him the pearls, Consuelo.'

She stared at the Saint defensively, her eyes hot and hostile and shifting like the eyes of a cornered animal.

'I will not.'

'Consuelo!'

'I cannot,' she said. 'I have already sold them.'

'*What?*'

'*Si, si,*' she said quickly. 'I sold them. To a dealer I met at the Cantina. I was going to surprise you. He gave me $500 – '

'$500!'

'For a start. He will bring me the rest soon. I have it here.' She twisted away towards the bed and rummaged under the mattress. In a moment she was back, thrusting crumpled bills into his hands. 'There! Count them. It is all there. And there will be more!'

Ned Yarn did not count the bills. He did not even hold them. They spilled over his lap and fluttered down to the floor. He had caught one of Consuelo's wrists, and clung to it with both hands, and his blind face turned up towards her strickenly.

'What is this?' he said in a terrible hoarse voice. 'I never thought you lied to me. But you're lying now. Your voice tells me.'

'I do not lie!'

'Templar,' said Yarn, with a straining throat. 'Please help me. There's a pottery jar on the top shelf, in the corner over the stove. Look in it and tell me what you find.'

Simon got to his feet, a little uncertainly. Then he crossed to the corner in three quick strides. There was only one jar that fitted the description. With his height, he could just reach it.

Consuelo writhed and twisted in Yarn's grip like a lassoed wildcat, so that the chair he sat in rocked, and pounded on his head and shoulders with her free fist.

'No, no!' she screamed.

But the blind man's grip held her like an anchor, and she fell still at last as the Saint tilted the jar over one cupped hand, so that the ripple of things rolling from it could be heard over the heavy breathing which was the only other thing that broke the silence.

Simon Templar looked at the dozen or so cheap beads of various sizes brought together in the hollow of his palm, and looked up from them to the defiant streaming eyes of Ned Yarn's woman.

'I think these are the most beautiful pearls I ever saw,' he said.

The woman slid down to the floor beside Yarn and sat there with her face pressed against his thigh.

'Why did you lie, Consuelo?' Yarn asked puzzledly. 'What on earth upset you like that?'

'I think I can guess,' said the Saint. 'She was just trying to protect you. After all, neither of you knows me from Adam, and you are taking rather a lot on trust. Probably she wanted time to talk it over with you first.'

The woman sobbed.

Ned Yarn caressed her stringy hair, murmuring little soothing sounds as she clung to his legs.

'It's all right, *querida*.' His face was still troubled. 'But the money – the $500. Where did that come from?'

'I bet I can answer that too,' said the Saint. 'She'd held out two or three more small pearls and sold them, and she was saving the money for a surprise present of some kind. Is that right, Consuelo?'

She lifted her head and looked at the Saint.

'No,' she said. 'It is my own money. I earned it and saved it myself. I kept it from you, Ned. I did not want to spend quite all our money on the search for pearls. I thought, perhaps we will never find any pearls, but I would keep saving, and one day perhaps I could take you myself to see if you could be cured. That is the truth.'

Yarn lifted her up and kissed her.

'How blind can a man be?' he said huskily.

'Some people would give their eyes for what you've got,' Simon said.

'And I wish I had mine most so that I could see it. I know how beautiful she must be, but I would like to see her. She is beautiful, isn't she?'

'She is beautiful, Ned.'

'Please, you must both forgive me,' Consuelo said in a low voice. 'Let us have some tequila.'

Simon looked down at the little heap of beads in his hand.

'What do you want me to do with the pearls?' he asked.

The blind man's dark glasses held his gaze like hypnotic hungry eyes.

'Are they really valuable?'

'I'd say they were, but I'm not an expert,' Simon replied, improvising with infinite care. 'They'd have to be sold in the right place, of course. As you may know, individual pearls don't mean so much, unless they're really gigantic. Most pearls are made into necklaces and things like that, which means that they have to be matched, and they gain in value by being put together. And then it's a funny market these days, on account of all the cultured pearls that only an expert can tell from real ones. There are still people who'll spend a fortune on the genuine article, but you don't find them waiting on every jeweler's doorstep. It takes work, and preparation, and patience – and time.'

'But – eventually – they should be worth a lot?'

'Eventually,' said the Saint soberly, 'they may mean more to you than you'd believe right now.'

Ned Yarn's breath came and went in a long sigh.

'That's all I wanted to know,' he said. 'I can wait some more. I guess I'm used to waiting.'

'Do you want me to take the pearls back to the States and see what I can do with them?'

'Yes. And Consuelo and I will go on fishing for more. At least we'll know we aren't wasting our time. Where's that drink you were talking about, Consuelo?' She put the glass in his hand, and he raised it. 'Here's luck to all of us.'

'Especially to you two.' Simon looked at the woman over his glass and said: '*Salud!*'

He wrapped the beads carefully in a scrap of newspaper and tucked it into his pocket.

'Do you mind if Consuelo guides me back from here?' he asked. 'I don't want to get lost.'

'Of course, we don't want that. And thank you for coming.'

The night was the same, perhaps a little cooler, perhaps a little more muted in its secret sounds. The woman's heels tapped the same monotonous rhythm, perhaps a little slower. They walked quite a long way without speaking, as they had before; but now they kept silence as if to make sure that they were beyond the most fantastic range of a blind man's hearing before they spoke.

Simon Templar was glad that the silence lasted as long as it did. He had a lot to think about, to weigh and balance and to look ahead from.

Finally she said, almost timidly: 'I think you understand, *señor*.'

'I think so,' he said; but he waited to hear more from her.

'When he began to be discontented, we went out in the boat and began looking for pearls. For a long time that made him happy. But presently, when we found nothing he was unhappy again. At last we found some oysters. Then again he had hope. But there were no pearls. So presently, after some more time, he was sad again. It hurt too much to see him despair. So at last I let him find some pearls. At first they were real, I think. I took them from some earrings that my mother gave me. And after that, they were beads.'

'And when you said you sold them – '

'I did sell the real ones, for a few pesos. The rest was money I had saved for him, like the $500.'

'Did you mean what I heard you say – that if you could save enough, you meant to take him to a specialist somewhere who might be able to bring back his sight?'

There was a long pause before she answered.

'I would have done it when I had the courage,' she said. 'I will do it one day, when I am strong enough. But it will not be easy. Because I know that when he sees me with his eyes, he will not love me any more.'

He felt it all the way through him down to his toes, like the subsonic tremor of an earthquake, the tingling realization of what those few simple words meant.

She was not blind, and she used mirrors. If she had ever deluded herself, it had not been for long. She knew very well what they told her. Homely and aged and scarred as she was, no man such as she had dreamed of as a young girl would ever love her as a young girl dreams of love. Unless he was blind. Even before the aging had taken hold she had discovered that, and seen the infinite emptiness ahead.

But one night, some miracle had brought her a blind man . . .

She had taken him in and cared for him in his sickness, finding him clean and grateful, and lavished on him all the frustrated richness of her heart. And out of his helplessness, and for her kindness and the tender beauty of her voice, he had loved her in return. She had used what money she could earn in any way to humor his obsession, to bring him back from despair, to encourage hope and keep alive his dream. And one day she believed she might be able to make at least part of the hope come true, and have him made whole – and let him go.

Simon walked slowly through a night that no longer seemed dark and sordid.

'When he knows what you have done,' he said, 'he should think you the most beautiful woman in the world.'

'He will not love me,' she said without bitterness. 'I know men.'

'Now I can tell you something. He has been blind for nearly ten years. There will have been too many degenerative changes in his eyes by this time. There is hardly any chance at all that an operation could cure him now. And I never thought I could say any man was lucky to be blind, but I think Ned Yarn is that man.'

'Nevertheless, I shall have to try, one day.'

'It will be a long time still before you have enough money.'

She looked up at him.

'But the beads you took away. You told him they were worth much. What shall I tell him now?'

It was all clear to Simon now, the strangest crime that he had to put on his bizarre record.

'He will never hear another word from me. I shall just disappear. And presently it will be clear to him that I was a crook after all, as he believes you suspected from the start; and I stole them.'

'But the shock – what will it do to him?'

'He will get over it. He cannot blame you. He will think that your instinct was right all along, and he should have listened to you. You can help him to see that, without nagging him.'

'Then he will want to start looking for pearls again.'

'And you will find them. From time to time I will send you a few for you to put in the oysters. Real ones. You can make them last. You need not find them too often, to keep him hoping. And when you sell them, which you can do as a Mexican without getting in any trouble, you must do what your heart tells you with the money. I think you will be happy,' said the Saint.

* * *

Mrs Ormond, formerly Mrs Yarn, lay back in her chair and laughed, deeply and vibrantly in her exquisitely rounded throat, so that the ice cubes clinked in the tall glass she held.

'So the dope finally found his level,' she gurgled. 'Living in some smelly slum hovel with a frowzy native slut. While she's whoring in a crummy saloon and dredging up pearl beads to kid him he's something better than a pimp. I might have known it!'

She looked more unreally beautiful than ever in the dim light of the balcony, a sort of cross between a calendar picture and a lecherous trash-writer's imagining, in the diaphanous négligée that she had inevitably put on to await the Saint's return in. Her provocative breasts quivered visibly under the filmy nylon and crowded into its deep-slashed neckline as she laughed, and some of the beads rolled out of the unfolded paper in her lap and pattered on the bare floor.

Simon had told her only the skeletal facts, omitting the amplifications and additions which were his own, and waited for her reaction; and this was it.

'I hadn't realized it was quite so funny,' he said stonily.

'You couldn't,' she choked. 'My dear man, you don't know the half of it. Here I come dragging myself down to this ghastly dump, just in case Yarn has really got on to something I couldn't afford to miss; and all he's got is a mulatto concubine and a few beads. And all the time, right here in my jewel case, I've got a string of pearls that were good enough for Catherine of Russia!'

Simon stood very still.

'You have?' he said.

'Just one of those baubles that Ormond used to pass out when he was indulging his sultan complex. Like I told you. I think he only paid about fifteen grand for them at an auction. And me wasting all this time and effort, not to mention yours, on Ned Yarn's imaginary oyster bed!'

At last the Saint began to laugh too, very quietly.

'It is rather delirious,' he said. 'Let me fix you another drink, and let's go on with some unfinished business.'

THE SPECIALTY OF THE HOUSE

Stanley Ellin

'For those of you who have not yet had the pleasure of reading "The Specialty of the House", who approach it now for the very first time, a suggestion: read the story first, *and only* then *come back and read the introduction which follows.'*

Stanley Ellin writes:

"The Specialty of the House" was my first published story, and it won the prize as Best First Story in the Ellery Queen's Mystery Magazine *contest of 1948. Since then I have published a dozen novels and several dozen short stories, and have won four of the Edgar awards given by the Mystery Writers of America as well as, in 1975, the French* Grand Prix de Littérature Policière.

I still vividly remember how the idea for "The Specialty of the House" was born. My wife and I went out for a celebratory dinner when I returned from military service – a luxurious beefsteak dinner for which she had saved her precious meat-rationing coupons – and in the restaurant, after we gave our order, the waiter simply disappeared, apparently forever. After a long time went by, my wife remarked to me with a straight face, "Considering the shortage of beef nowadays, it's possible that the waiter himself is now in the oven, being roasted to a turn for us."

The black humor of this stuck in my mind afterward, and eventually led to the writing of the story – which, I have been told, has never been out of print somewhere in the world since the day of its first publication.

I am also happy to say that that same wife who saw me through all my trials in making a career for myself in writing is still at my side today, and has lost none of that mordant – and valuable – sense of humor.

'And this,' said Laffler, 'is Sbirro's.' Costain saw a square brown stone façade identical with the others that extended from either side into the clammy darkness of the deserted street. From the barred windows of the basement at his feet, a glimmer of light showed behind heavy curtains.

'Lord,' he observed, 'it's a dismal hole, isn't it?'

'I beg you to understand,' said Laffler stiffly, 'that Sbirro's is the restaurant without pretensions. Besieged by these ghastly, neurotic times, it has refused to compromise. It is perhaps the last important establishment in this city lit by gas jets. Here you will find the same honest furnishings, the same magnificent Sheffield service, and possibly, in a far corner, the very same spider webs that were remarked by the patrons of a half century ago!'

'A doubtful recommendation,' said Costain, 'and hardly sanitary.'

'When you enter,' Laffler continued, 'you leave the insanity of this year, this day and this hour, and you find yourself for a brief span restored in spirit, not by opulence, but by dignity, which is the lost quality of our time.'

Costain laughed uncomfortably. 'You make it sound more like a cathedral than a restaurant,' he said.

In the pale reflection of the street lamp overhead, Laffler peered at his companion's face. 'I wonder,' he said abruptly, 'whether I have not made a mistake in extending this invitation to you.'

Costain was hurt. Despite an impressive title and large salary, he was no more than clerk to this pompous little man, but he was impelled to make some display of his feelings. 'If you wish,' he said coldly, 'I can make other plans for my evening with no trouble.'

With his large, cowlike eyes turned up to Costain, the mist drifting into the ruddy, full moon of his face, Laffler seemed strangely ill at ease. Then, 'No, no,' he said at last, 'absolutely not. It's important that you dine at Sbirro's with me.' He grasped Costain's arm firmly and led the way to the wrought-iron gate of the basement. 'You see, you're the sole person in my office who seems to know anything at all about good food. And on my part, knowing about Sbirro's but not having some appreciative friend to share it is like having a unique piece of art locked in a room where no one else can enjoy it.'

Costain was considerably mollified by this. 'I understand there are a great many people who relish that situation.'

'I'm not one of that kind!' Laffler said sharply.

'And having the secret of Sbirro's locked in myself for years has finally become unendurable.' He fumbled at the side of the gate and from within could be heard the small, discordant jangle of an ancient pull bell. An interior door opened with a groan, and Costain found himself peering into a dark face whose only discernible feature was a row of gleaming teeth.

'Sair?' said the face.

'Mr Laffler and a guest.'

'Sair,' the face said again, this time in what was clearly an invitation. It moved aside and Costain stumbled down a single step behind his host. The door and gate creaked behind him, and he stood blinking in a small foyer. It took him a moment to realize that the figure he now stared at was his own reflection in a gigantic pier glass that extended from floor to ceiling. 'Atmosphere,' he said under his breath and chuckled as he followed his guide to a seat.

He faced Laffler across a small table for two and peered curiously around the dining room. It was no size at all, but the half-dozen guttering gas jets, which provided the only illumination, threw such a deceptive light that the walls flickered and faded into uncertain distance.

There were no more than eight or ten tables about, arranged to insure the maximum privacy. All were occupied, and the few waiters serving them moved with quiet efficiency. In the air was a soft clash and scrape of cutlery and a soothing murmur of talk. Costain nodded appreciatively.

Laffler breathed an audible sigh of gratification. 'I knew you would share my enthusiasm,' he said. 'Have you noticed, by the way, that there are no women present?'

Costain raised inquiring eyebrows.

'Sbirro,' said Laffler, 'does not encourage members of the fair sex to enter the premises. And, I can tell you, his method is decidedly effective. I had the experience of seeing a woman get a taste of it not long ago. She sat at a table for not less than an hour waiting for service which was never forthcoming.'

'Didn't she make a scene?'

'She did.' Laffler smiled at the recollection. 'She succeeded in annoying the customers, embarrassing her partner, and nothing more.'

'And what about Mr Sbirro?'

'He did not make an appearance. Whether he directed affairs from behind the scenes or was not even present during the episode, I don't know. Whichever it was, he won a complete victory. The woman never reappeared nor, for that matter, did the witless gentleman who by bringing her was really the cause of the entire contretemps.'

'A fair warning to all present,' laughed Costain.

A waiter now appeared at the table. The chocolate-dark skin, the thin, beautifully-molded nose and lips, the large liquid eyes, heavily lashed, and the silver-white hair so heavy and silken that it lay on the skull like a cap, all marked him definitely as an East Indian. The man arranged the stiff table linen, filled two tumblers from a huge, cut-glass pitcher, and set them in their proper places.

'Tell me,' Laffler said eagerly, 'is the special being served this evening?'

The waiter smiled regretfully and showed teeth as spectacular as those of the major-domo. 'I am sorry, sair. There is no special this evening.'

Laffler's face fell into lines of heavy disappointment. 'After waiting so long. It's been a month already, and I hoped to show my friend here – '

'You understand the difficulties, sair.'

'Of course, of course.' Laffler looked at Costain sadly and shrugged. 'You see, I had in mind to introduce you to the greatest treat that Sbirro's offers, but unfortunately it isn't on the menu this evening.'

The waiter said, 'Do you wish to be served now, sair?' and Laffler nodded. To Costain's surprise the waiter made his way off without waiting for any instructions.

'Have you ordered in advance?' he asked.

'Ah,' said Laffler, 'I really should have explained. Sbirro's offers no choice whatsoever. You will eat the same meal as everyone else in this room. Tomorrow evening you would eat an entirely different meal, but again without designating a single preference.'

'Very unusual,' said Costain, 'and certainly unsatisfactory at times. What if one doesn't have a taste for the particular dish set before him?'

'On that score,' said Laffler solemnly, 'you need have no fears. I give you my word that no matter how exacting your tastes, you will relish every mouthful you eat in Sbirro's.'

Costain looked doubtful, and Laffler smiled. 'And consider the subtle advantages of the system,' he said. 'When you pick up the menu of a popular restaurant, you find yourself confronted with innumerable choices. You are forced to weigh, to evaluate, to make uneasy decisions which you may instantly regret. The effect of all this is a tension which, however slight, must make for discomfort.

'And consider the mechanics of the process. Instead of a hurly-burly of sweating cooks rushing about a kitchen in a frenzy to prepare a hundred varying items, we have a chef who stands serenely alone, bringing all his talents to bear on one task, with all assurance of a complete triumph!'

'Then you have seen the kitchen?'

'Unfortunately, no,' said Laffler sadly. 'The picture I offer is hypothetical, made of conversational fragments I have pieced together over the years. I must admit, though, that my desire to see the functioning of the kitchen here comes very close to being my sole obsession nowadays.'

'But have you mentioned this to Sbirro?'

'A dozen times. He shrugs the suggestion away.'

'Isn't that a rather curious foible on his part?'

'No, no,' Laffler said hastily, 'a master artist is never under the compulsion of petty courtesies. Still,' he sighed, 'I have never given up hope.'

The waiter now reappeared bearing two soup bowls, which he set in place with mathematical exactitude, and a small tureen from which he slowly ladled a measure of clear, thin broth. Costain dipped his spoon into the broth and tasted it with some curiosity. It was delicately flavored, bland to the verge of tastelessness. Costain frowned, tentatively reached for the salt and pepper cellars, and discovered there were none on the table. He looked up, saw Laffler's eyes on him, and although unwilling to compromise with his own tastes, he hesitated to act as a damper on Laffler's enthusiasm. Therefore he smiled and indicated the broth.

'Excellent,' he said.

Laffler returned his smile. 'You do not find it excellent at all,' he said coolly. 'You find it flat and badly in need of condiments. I know this,' he continued as Costain's eyebrows shot upward, 'because it was my own reaction many years ago, and because like yourself I found myself reaching for salt and pepper after the first mouthful. I also learned with surprise that condiments are not available in Sbirro's.'

Costain was shocked. 'Not even salt!' he exclaimed.

'Not even salt. The very fact that you require it for your soup stands as evidence that your taste is unduly jaded. I am confident that you will now make the same discovery that I did: by the time you have nearly finished your soup, your desire for salt will be nonexistent.'

Laffler was right; before Costain had reached the bottom of his plate, he was relishing the nuances of the broth with steadily increasing delight. Laffler thrust aside his own empty bowl and rested his elbows on the table. 'Do you agree with me now?'

'To my surprise,' said Costain, 'I do.'

As the waiter busied himself clearing the table, Laffler lowered his voice significantly. 'You will find,' he said, 'that the absence of condiments is but one of several noteworthy characteristics which mark Sbirro's. I may as well prepare you for these. For example, no alcoholic beverages of any sort are served here, nor for that matter any beverage except clear, cold water, first and only drink necessary for a human being.'

'Outside of mother's milk,' suggested Costain dryly.

'I can answer that in like vein by pointing out that the average patron of Sbirro's has passed that primal stage of his development.'

Costain laughed. 'Granted,' he said.

'Very well. There is also a ban on the use of tobacco in any form.'

'But good heavens,' said Costain, 'doesn't that make Sbirro's more a teetotaler's retreat than a gourmet's sanctuary?'

'I fear,' said Laffler solemnly, 'that you confuse the words *gourmet* and *gourmand*. The gourmand, through glutting himself, requires a wider and wider latitude of experience to stir his surfeited senses, but the very nature of the gourmet is simplicity. The ancient Greek in his coarse chiton savoring the ripe olive; the Japanese in his bare room contemplating the curve of a single flower stem – these are the true gourmets.'

'But an occasional drop of brandy or pipeful of tobacco,' said Costain dubiously, 'are hardly over-indulgences.'

'By alternating stimulant and narcotic,' said Laffler, 'you seesaw the delicate balance of your taste so violently that it loses its most precious quality: the appreciation of fine food. During my years as a patron of Sbirro's, I have proved this to my satisfaction.'

'May I ask,' said Costain, 'why you regard the ban on these things as having such deep aesthetic motives? What about such mundane reasons as the high cost of a liquor license, or the possibility that patrons would object to the smell of tobacco in such confined quarters?'

Laffler shook his head violently. 'If and when you meet Sbirro,' he said, 'you will understand at once that he is not the man to make decisions on a mundane basis. As a matter of fact, it was Sbirro himself who first made me cognizant of what you call "aesthetic" motives.'

'An amazing man,' said Costain as the waiter prepared to serve the entrée.

Laffler's next words were not spoken until he had savored and swallowed a large portion of meat. 'I hesitate to use superlatives,' he said, 'but to my way of thinking, Sbirro represents man at the apex of his civilization!'

Costain cocked an eyebrow and applied himself to his roast, which rested in a pool of stiff gravy ungarnished by green or vegetable. The thin steam rising from it carried to his nostrils a subtle, tantalizing odor which made his mouth water. He chewed a piece as slowly and thoroughly as if he were analyzing the intricacies of a Mozart symphony. The range of taste he discovered was really extraordinary, from the pungent nip of the crisp outer edge to the peculiarly flat yet soul-satisfying ooze of blood which the pressure of his jaws forced from the half-raw interior.

Upon swallowing he found himself ferociously hungry for another piece, and then another, and it was only with an effort that he prevented himself from wolfing down all his share of the meat and gravy without waiting to get the full voluptuous satisfaction from each mouthful. When he had scraped his platter clean, he realized that both he and Laffler had completed the entire course without exchanging a single word. He commented on this, and Laffler said: 'Can you see any need for words in the presence of such food?'

Costain looked around at the shabby, dimly-lit room, the quiet diners, with a new perception. 'No,' he said humbly, 'I cannot. For any doubts I had I apologize unreservedly. In all your praise of Sbirro's there was not a single word of exaggeration.'

'Ah,' said Laffler delightedly. 'And that is only part of the story. You heard me mention the special which unfortunately was not on the menu tonight. What you have just eaten is nothing when compared to the absolute delights of that special!'

'Good Lord!' cried Costain. 'What is it? Nightingales' tongues? Filet of unicorn?'

'Neither,' said Laffler. 'It is lamb.'

'Lamb?'

Laffler remained lost in thought for a minute. 'If,' he said at last, 'I were to give you in my unstinted words my opinion of this dish, you would judge me completely insane. That is how deeply the mere thought of it affects me. It is neither the fatty chop, nor the too-solid leg; it is, instead, a select portion of the rarest sheep in existence and is named after the species – lamb Amirstan.'

Costain knit his brows. 'Amirstan?'

'A fragment of desolation almost lost on the border which separates Afghanistan and Russia. From chance remarks dropped by Sbirro, I gather it is no more than a plateau which grazes the pitiful remnants of a flock of superb sheep. Sbirro, through some means or other, obtained rights to the traffic in this flock and is, therefore, the sole restaurateur ever to have lamb Amirstan on his bill of fare. I can tell you that the appearance of this dish is a rare occurrence indeed, and luck is the only guide in determining for the clientele the exact date when it will be served.'

'But surely,' said Costain, 'Sbirro could provide some advance knowledge of this event.'

'The objection to that is simply stated,' said Laffler. 'There exists in this city a huge number of professional gluttons. Should advance information slip out, it is quite likely that they would, out of curiosity, become familiar with the dish and thenceforth supplant the regular patrons at these tables.'

'But you don't mean to say,' objected Costain, 'that these few people present are the only ones in the entire city, or for that matter, in the whole wide world, who know of the existence of Sbirro's!'

'Very nearly. There may be one or two regular patrons who, for some reason, are not present at the moment.'

'That's incredible.'

'It is done,' said Laffler, the slightest shade of menace in his voice, 'by every patron making it his solemn obligation to keep the secret. By accepting my invitation this evening, you automatically assume that obligation. I hope you can be trusted with it.'

Costain flushed. 'My position in your employ should vouch for me. I only question the wisdom of a policy which keeps such magnificent food away from so many who would enjoy it.'

'Do you know the inevitable result of the policy you favor?' asked Laffler bitterly. 'An influx of idiots who would nightly complain that they are never served roast duck with chocolate sauce. Is that picture tolerable to you?'

'No,' admitted Costain, 'I am forced to agree with you.'

Laffler leaned back in his chair wearily and passed his hand over his eyes in an uncertain gesture. 'I am a solitary man,' he said quietly, 'and not by choice alone. It may sound strange to you, it may border on eccentricity, but I feel to my depths that this restaurant, this warm heaven in a coldly insane world, is both family and friend to me.'

And Costain, who to this moment had never viewed his companion as other than tyrannical employer or officious host, now felt an overwhelming pity twist inside his comfortably expanded stomach.

By the end of two weeks the invitations to join Laffler at Sbirro's had become something of a ritual. Every day, at a few minutes after five, Costain would step out into the office corridor and lock his cubicle behind him; he would drape his overcoat neatly over his left arm, and peer into the glass of the door to make sure his Homburg was set at the proper angle. At one time he would have followed this by lighting a cigarette, but under Laffler's prodding he had decided to give abstinence a fair trial. Then he would start down the corridor, and Laffler would fall in step at his elbow, clearing his throat. 'Ah, Costain. No plans for this evening, I hope.'

'No,' Costain would say, 'I'm foot-loose and fancy-free,' or 'At your service,' or something equally inane. He wondered at times whether it would not be more tactful to vary the ritual with an occasional refusal, but the glow with which Laffler received his answer, and the rough friendliness of Laffler's grip on his arm, forestalled him.

Among the treacherous crags of the business world, reflected Costain, what better way to secure your footing than friendship with one's employer. Already, a secretary close to the workings of the inner office had commented publicly on Laffler's highly favorable opinion of Costain. That was all to the good.

And the food! The incomparable food at Sbirro's! For the first time in his life, Costain, ordinarily a lean and bony man, noted with gratification that he was certainly gaining weight; within two weeks his bones had disappeared under a layer of sleek, firm flesh, and here and there were even signs of incipient plumpness. It struck Costain one night, while surveying himself in his bath, that the rotund Laffler himself might have been a spare and bony man before discovering Sbirro's.

So there was obviously everything to be gained and nothing to be lost by accepting Laffler's invitations. Perhaps after testing the heralded wonders of lamb Amirstan and meeting Sbirro, who thus far had not made an appearance, a refusal or two might be in order. But certainly not until then.

That evening, two weeks to a day after his first visit to Sbirro's, Costain had both desires fulfilled: he dined on lamb Amirstan, and he met Sbirro. Both exceeded all his expectations.

When the waiter leaned over their table immediately after seating them and gravely announced: 'Tonight is special, sair,' Costain was shocked to find his heart pounding with expectation. On the table before him he saw Laffler's hands trembling violently. 'But it isn't natural,' he thought suddenly. 'Two grown men, presumably intelligent and in the full possession of their senses, as jumpy as a pair of cats waiting to have their meat flung to them!'

'This is it!' Laffler's voice startled him so that he almost leaped from his seat. 'The culinary triumph of all times! And faced by it you are embarrassed by the very emotions it distils.'

'How did you know that?' Costain asked faintly.

'How? Because a decade ago I underwent your embarrassment. Add to that your air of revulsion and it's easy to see how affronted you are by the knowledge that man has not yet forgotten how to slaver over his meat.'

'And these others,' whispered Costain, 'do they all feel the same thing?'

'Judge for yourself.'

Costain looked furtively around at the nearby tables. 'You are right,' he finally said. 'At any rate, there's comfort in numbers.'

Laffler inclined his head slightly to the side.

'One of the numbers,' he remarked, 'appears to be in for a disappointment.'

Costain followed the gesture. At the table indicated, a gray-haired man sat conspicuously alone, and Costain frowned at the empty chair opposite him.

'Why, yes,' he recalled, 'that very stout, bald man, isn't it? I believe it's the first dinner he's missed here in two weeks.'

'The entire decade more likely,' said Laffler sympathetically. 'Rain or shine, crisis or calamity, I don't think he's missed an evening at Sbirro's since the first time I dined here. Imagine his expression when he's told that, on his very first defection, lamb Amirstan was the *plat du jour*.'

Costain looked at the empty chair again with a dim discomfort. 'His very first?' he murmured.

'Mr Laffler! And friend! I am so pleased. So very, very pleased. No, do not stand; I will have a place made.' Miraculously a seat appeared under the figure standing there at the table. 'The lamb Amirstan will be an unqualified success, hurr? I myself have been stewing in the miserable kitchen all the day, prodding the foolish chef to do everything just so. The just so is the important part, hurr? But I see your friend does not know me. An introduction, perhaps?'

The words ran in a smooth, fluid eddy. They rippled, they purred, they hypnotized Costain so that he could do no more than stare. The mouth that uncoiled this sinuous monologue was alarmingly wide, with thin mobile lips that curled and twisted with every syllable. There was a flat nose with a straggling line of hair under it; wide-set eyes, almost oriental in appearance, that glittered in the unsteady flare of gaslight; and long, sleek hair that swept back from high on the unwrinkled forehead – hair so pale that it might have been bleached of all color. An amazing face, surely, and the sight of it tortured Costain with the conviction that it was somehow familiar. His brain twitched and prodded but could not stir up any solid recollection.

Laffler's voice jerked Costain out of his study. 'Mr Sbirro. Mr Costain, a good friend and associate.' Costain rose and shook the proffered hand. It was warm and dry, flint-hard against his palm.

'I am so very pleased, Mr Costain. So very, very pleased,' purred the voice. 'You like my little establishment, hurr? You have a great treat in store, I assure you.'

Laffler chuckled. 'Oh, Costain's been dining here regularly for two weeks,' he said. 'He's by way of becoming a great admirer of yours, Sbirro.'

The eyes were turned on Costain. 'A very great compliment. You compliment me with your presence and I return same with my food, hurr? But the lamb Amirstan is far superior to anything of your past experience, I assure you. All the trouble of obtaining it, all the difficulty of preparation, is truly merited.'

Costain strove to put aside the exasperating problem of that face. 'I have wondered,' he said, 'why with all these difficulties you mention, you even bother to present lamb Amirstan to the public. Surely your other dishes are excellent enough to uphold your reputation.'

Sbirro smiled so broadly that his face became perfectly round. 'Perhaps it is a matter of the psychology, hurr? Someone discovers a wonder and must share it with others. He must fill his cup to the brim, perhaps, by observing the so-evident pleasure of those who explore it with him. Or,' he shrugged, 'perhaps it is just a matter of good business.'

'Then in the light of all this,' Costain persisted, 'and considering all the conventions you have imposed on your customers, why do you open the restaurant to the public instead of operating it as a private club?'

The eyes abruptly glinted into Costain's, then turned away. 'So perspicacious, hurr? Then I will tell you. Because there is more privacy in a public eating place than in the most exclusive club in existence! Here no one inquires of your affairs; no one desires to know the intimacies of your life. Here the business is eating. We are not curious about names and addresses or the reasons for the coming and going of our guests. We welcome you when you are here; we have no regrets when you are here no longer. That is the answer, hurr?'

Costain was startled by this vehemence. 'I had no intention of prying,' he stammered.

Sbirro ran the tip of his tongue over his thin lips. 'No, no,' he reassured, 'you are not prying. Do not let me give you that impression. On the contrary, I invite your questions.'

'Oh, come, Costain,' said Laffler. 'Don't let Sbirro intimidate you. I've known him for years and I guarantee that his bark is worse than his bite. Before you know it, he'll be showing you all the privileges of the house – outside of inviting you to visit his precious kitchen, of course.'

'Ah,' smiled Sbirro, 'for that, Mr Costain may have to wait a little while. For everything else I am at his beck and call.'

Laffler slapped his hand jovially on the table. 'What did I tell you!' he said. 'Now let's have the truth, Sbirro. Has anyone, outside of your staff, ever stepped into the sanctum sanctorum?'

Sbirro looked up. 'You see on the wall above you,' he said earnestly, 'the portrait of one to whom I did the honor. A very dear friend and a patron of most long standing, he is evidence that my kitchen is not inviolate.'

Costain studied the picture and started with recognition. 'Why,' he said excitedly, 'that's the famous writer – you know the one, Laffler – he used to do such wonderful short stories and cynical bits and then suddenly took himself off and disappeared in Mexico!'

'Of course!' cried Laffler, 'and to think I've been sitting under his portrait for years without even realizing it!' He turned to Sbirro. 'A dear friend, you say? His disappearance must have been a blow to you.'

Sbirro's face lengthened. 'It was, it was, I assure you. But think of it this way, gentlemen: he was probably greater in his death than in his life, hurr? A most tragic man, he often told me that his only happy hours were spent here at this very table. Pathetic, is it not? And to think the only favor I could ever show him was to let him witness the mysteries of my kitchen, which is, when all is said and done, no more than a plain, ordinary kitchen.'

'You seem very certain of his death,' commented Costain. 'After all, no evidence has ever turned up to substantiate it.'

Sbirro contemplated the picture. 'None at all,' he said softly. 'Remarkable, hurr?'

With the arrival of the entrée Sbirro leaped to his feet and set about serving them himself. With his eyes alight he lifted the casserole from the tray and sniffed at the fragrance from within with sensual relish. Then, taking great care not to lose a single drop of gravy, he filled two platters with chunks of dripping meat. As if exhausted by this task, he sat back in his chair, breathing heavily. 'Gentlemen,' he said, 'to your good appetite.'

Costain chewed his first mouthful with great deliberation and swallowed it. Then he looked at the empty tines of his fork with glazed eyes.

'Good God!' he breathed.

'It is good, hurr? Better than you imagined?'

Costain shook his head dazedly. 'It is as impossible,' he said slowly, 'for the uninitiated to conceive the delights of lamb Amirstan as for mortal man to look into his own soul.'

'Perhaps,' Sbirro thrust his head so close that Costain could feel the warm, fetid breath tickle his nostrils, 'perhaps you have just had a glimpse into your soul, hurr?'

Costain tried to draw back slightly without giving offense. 'Perhaps,' he laughed, 'and a gratifying picture it made: all fang and claw. But without intending any disrespect, I should hardly like to build my church on lamb *en casserole*.'

Sbirro rose and laid a hand gently on his shoulder. 'So perspicacious,' he said. 'Sometime when you have nothing to do, nothing, perhaps, but sit for a very little while in a dark room and think of this world – what it is and what it is going to be – then you must turn your thoughts a little to the significance of the Lamb in religion. It will be so interesting. And now,' he bowed deeply to both men. 'I have held you long enough from your dinner. I was most happy' – he nodded to Costain – 'and I am sure we will meet again.' The teeth gleamed, the eyes glittered, and Sbirro was gone down the aisle of tables.

Costain twisted around to stare after the retreating figure. 'Have I offended him in some way?' he asked.

Laffler looked up from his plate. 'Offended him? He loves that kind of talk. Lamb Amirstan is a ritual with him; get him started and he'll be back at you a dozen times worse than a priest making a conversion.'

Costain turned to his meal with the face still hovering before him. 'Interesting man,' he reflected. 'Very.'

It took him a month to discover the tantalizing familiarity of that face, and when he did, he laughed aloud in his bed. Why, of course! Sbirro might have sat as the model for the Cheshire cat in *Alice!*

He passed this thought on to Laffler the very next evening as they pushed their way down the street to the restaurant against a chill, blustering wind. Laffler only looked blank.

'You may be right,' he said, 'but I'm not a fit judge. It's a far cry back to the days when I read the book. A far cry, indeed.'

As if taking up his words, a piercing howl came ringing down the street and stopped both men short in their tracks. 'Someone's in trouble there,' said Laffler. 'Look!'

Not far from the entrance to Sbirro's two figures could be seen struggling in the near darkness. They swayed back and forth and suddenly tumbled into a writhing heap on the sidewalk. The piteous howl went up again, and Laffler, despite his girth, ran toward it at a fair speed with Costain tagging cautiously behind.

Stretched out full length on the pavement was a slender figure with the dusky complexion and white hair of one of Sbirro's servitors. His fingers were futilely plucking at the huge hands which encircled his throat, and his knees pushed weakly up at the gigantic bulk of a man who brutally bore down with his full weight.

Laffler came up panting. 'Stop this!' he shouted. 'What's going on here?'

The pleading eyes almost bulging from their sockets turned toward Laffler. 'Help, sair. This man – drunk – '

'Drunk am I, ya dirty – ' Costain saw now that the man was a sailor in a badly-soiled uniform. The air round him reeked with the stench of liquor. 'Pick me pocket and then call me drunk, will ya!' He dug his fingers in harder, and his victim groaned.

Laffler seized the sailor's shoulder. 'Let go of him, do you hear! Let go of him at once!' he cried, and the next instant was sent careening into Costain, who staggered back under the force of the blow.

The attack on his own person sent Laffler into immediate and berserk action. Without a sound he leaped at the sailor, striking and kicking furiously at the unprotected face and flanks. Stunned at first, the man came to his feet with a rush and turned on Laffler. For a moment they stood locked together, and then as Costain joined the attack, all three went sprawling to the ground. Slowly Laffler and Costain got to their feet and looked down at the body before them.

'He's either out cold from liquor,' said Costain, 'or he struck his head going down. In any case, it's a job for the police.'

'No, no, sair!' The waiter crawled weakly to his feet, and stood swaying. 'No police, sair. Mr Sbirro do not want such. You understand, sair.' He caught hold of Costain with a pleading hand, and Costain looked at Laffler.

'Of course not,' said Laffler. 'We won't have to bother with the police. They'll pick him up soon enough, the murderous sot. But what in the world started all this?'

'That man, sair. He make most erratic way while walking, and with no meaning I push against him. Then he attack me, accusing me to rob him.'

'As I thought.' Laffler pushed the waiter gently along. 'Now go on in and get yourself attended to.'

The man seemed ready to burst into tears. 'To you, sair, I owe my life. If there is anything I can do – '

Laffler turned into the areaway that led to Sbirro's door. 'No, no, it was nothing. You go along, and if Sbirro has any questions send him to me. I'll straighten it out.'

'My life, sair,' were the last words they heard as the inner door closed behind them.

'There you are, Costain,' said Laffler, as a few minutes later he drew his chair under the table, 'civilized man in all his glory. Reeking with alcohol, strangling to death some miserable innocent who came too close.'

Costain made an effort to gloss over the nerve-shattering memory of the episode. 'It's the neurotic cat that takes to alcohol,' he said. 'Surely there's a reason for that sailor's condition.'

'Reason? Of course there is. Plain atavistic savagery!' Laffler swept his arm in an all-embracing gesture. 'Why do we all sit here at our meat? Not only to appease physical demands, but because our atavistic selves cry for release. Think back, Costain. Do you remember that I once described Sbirro as the epitome of civilization? Can you now see why? A brilliant man, he fully understands the nature of human beings. But, unlike lesser men, he bends all his efforts to the satisfaction of our innate natures without resultant harm to some innocent bystander.'

'When I think back on the wonders of lamb Amirstan,' said Costain, 'I quite understand what you're driving at. And, by the way, isn't it nearly due to appear on the bill of fare? It must have been over a month ago that it was last served.'

The waiter, filling the tumblers, hesitated. 'I am so sorry, sair. No special this evening.'

'There's your answer,' Laffler grunted, 'and probably just my luck to miss out on it altogether the next time.'

Costain stared at him. 'Oh, come, that's impossible.'

'No, blast it.' Laffler drank off half his water at a gulp and the waiter immediately refilled the glass. 'I'm off to South America for a surprise tour of inspection. One month, two months, Lord knows how long.'

'Are things that bad down there?'

'They could be better.' Laffler suddenly grinned. 'Mustn't forget it takes very mundane dollars and cents to pay the tariff at Sbirro's.'

'I haven't heard a word of this around the office.'

'Wouldn't be a surprise tour if you had. Nobody knows about this except myself – and now you. I want to walk in on them completely unsuspected. Find out what flimflammery they're up to down there. As far as the office is concerned, I'm off on a jaunt somewhere. Maybe recuperating in some sanatorium from my hard work. Anyhow, the business will be in good hands. Yours, among them.'

'Mine?' said Costain, surprised.

'When you go in tomorrow you'll find yourself in receipt of a promotion, even if I'm not there to hand it to you personally. Mind you, it has nothing to do with our friendship either; you've done fine work, and I'm immensely grateful for it.'

Costain reddened under the praise. 'You don't expect to be in tomorrow. Then you're leaving tonight?'

Laffler nodded. 'I've been trying to wangle some reservations. If they come through, well, this will be in the nature of a farewell celebration.'

'You know,' said Costain slowly, 'I devoutly hope that your reservations don't come through. I believe our dinners here have come to mean more to me than I ever dared imagine.'

The waiter's voice broke in. 'Do you wish to be served now, sair?' and they both started.

'Of course, of course,' said Laffler sharply. 'I didn't realize you were waiting.'

'What bothers me,' he told Costain as the waiter turned away, 'is the thought of the lamb Amirstan I'm bound to miss. To tell you the truth, I've already put off my departure a week, hoping to hit a lucky night, and now I simply can't delay any more. I do hope that when you're sitting over your share of lamb Amirstan, you'll think of me with suitable regrets.'

Costain laughed. 'I will indeed,' he said as he turned to his dinner.

Hardly had he cleared the plate when a waiter silently reached for it. It was not their usual waiter, he observed; it was none other than the victim of the assault.

'Well,' Costain said, 'how do you feel now? Still under the weather?'

The waiter paid no attention to him. Instead, with the air of a man under great strain, he turned to Laffler. 'Sair,' he whispered. 'My life. I owe it to you. I can repay you!'

Laffler looked up in amazement, then shook his head firmly. 'No,' he said; 'I want nothing from you, understand? You have repaid me sufficiently with your thanks. Now get on with your work and let's hear no more about it.'

The waiter did not stir an inch, but his voice rose slightly. 'By the body and blood of your God, sair, I will help you even if you do not want! *Do not go into the kitchen, sair*. I trade you my life for yours, sair, when I speak this. Tonight or any night of your life, do not go into the kitchen at Sbirro's!'

Laffler sat back completely dumbfounded. 'Not go into the kitchen? Why shouldn't I go into the kitchen if Mr Sbirro ever took it into his head to invite me there? What's all this about?'

A hard hand was laid on Costain's back, and another gripped the waiter's arm. The waiter remained frozen to the spot, his lips compressed, his eyes downcast.

'What is all *what* about, gentlemen?' purred the voice. 'So opportune an arrival. In time as ever, I see, to answer all the questions, hurr?'

Laffler breathed a sigh of relief. 'Ah, Sbirro, thank heaven you're here. This man is saying something about my not going into your kitchen. Do you know what he means?'

The teeth showed in a broad grin. 'But of course. This good man was giving you advice in all amiability. It so happens that my too-emotional chef heard some rumor that I might have a guest into his precious kitchen, and he flew into a fearful rage. Such a rage, gentlemen! He even threatened to give notice on the spot, and you can understand what that should mean to Sbirro's, hurr? Fortunately, I succeeded in showing him what a signal honor it is to have an esteemed patron and true connoisseur observe him at his work first-hand, and now he is quite amenable. Quite, hurr?'

He released the waiter's arm. 'You are at the wrong table,' he said softly. 'See that it does not happen again.'

The waiter slipped off without daring to raise his eyes and Sbirro drew a chair to the table. He seated himself and brushed his hand lightly over his hair. 'Now I am afraid that the cat is out of the bag, hurr? This invitation to you, Mr Laffler, was to be a surprise; but the surprise is gone, and all that is left is the invitation.'

Laffler mopped beads of perspiration from his forehead. 'Are you serious?' he said huskily. 'Do you mean that we are really to witness the preparation of your food tonight?'

Sbirro drew a sharp fingernail along the table-cloth, leaving a thin, straight line printed in the linen. 'Ah,' he said, 'I am faced with a dilemma of great proportions.' He studied the line soberly. 'You, Mr Laffler, have been my guest for ten long years. But our friend here – '

Costain raised his hand in protest. 'I understand perfectly. This invitation is solely to Mr Laffler, and naturally my presence is embarrassing. As it happens, I have an early engagement for this evening and must be on my way anyhow. So you see there's no dilemma at all, really.'

'No,' said Laffler, 'absolutely not. That wouldn't be fair at all. We've been sharing this until now, Costain, and I won't enjoy this experience half as much if you're not along. Surely Sbirro can make his conditions flexible, this one occasion.'

They both looked at Sbirro who shrugged his shoulders regretfully.

Costain rose abruptly. 'I'm not going to sit here, Laffler, and spoil your great adventure. And then, too,' he bantered, 'think of that ferocious chef waiting to get his cleaver on you. I prefer not to be at the scene. I'll just say good-by,' he went on, to cover Laffler's guilty silence, 'and leave you to Sbirro. I'm sure he'll take pains to give you a good show.' He held out his hand and Laffler squeezed it painfully hard.

'You're being very decent, Costain,' he said. 'I hope you'll continue to dine here until we meet again. It shouldn't be too long.'

Sbirro made way for Costain to pass. 'I will expect you,' he said. '*Au 'voir*.'

Costain stopped briefly in the dim foyer to adjust his scarf and fix his Homburg at the proper angle. When he turned away from the mirror, satisfied at last, he saw with a final glance that Laffler and Sbirro were already at the kitchen door; Sbirro holding the door invitingly wide with one hand, while the other rested, almost tenderly, on Laffler's meaty shoulders.

THE UNSTOPPABLE MAN

Michael Gilbert

'The Unstoppable Man' (or 'Amateur in Violence', as it came to be called later) had a curious publishing history. At the time that I wrote it, I was beginning to get my stories published in a magazine called John Bull, *which was started as a scandal sheet during the 1914–18 War but, by the time I am talking about, had developed into a most prestigious vehicle for short stories. Its story editor was Lionel Davidson, now himself a well-known writer, and it employed top-line artists and designers. I was delighted to appear in it.*

Then disaster struck. In the third story which I wrote for them, I inadvertently libelled a well-known solicitor. An injunction was sought, that particular number disappeared from the bookstalls, and a large sum of damages was demanded and was paid by the publishers.

I was not only horrified, but was also sad to think that no further stories of mine would appear in John Bull. *I made up my mind that I would do what I could to repair the damage: I would write the best short story of which I was capable, and would present it to them free of charge.*

As I cast round in my mind for a theme which would have universal appeal, it occurred to me that most crimes are somewhat distant to the average reader, who does not easily identify with bank robbery or forgery or murder. But there is one situation which every parent, at least, must have considered: what would he do if – perish the thought – one of his own children was to be kidnapped? Would he keep quiet and try to raise the money? Would he inform the police and co-operate with them? Or might he, conceivably, take the law into his own hands and endeavour to rescue his child? A fantasy, maybe, but one which must have crossed many minds. And that is how 'The Unstoppable Man' was born.

A footnote: John Bull *not only liked the story, but they insisted on paying me for it, after all.*

We were talking about violence. 'Some people,' I said, 'are afraid of people and some people are afraid of things.'

Chief Inspector Hazlerigg gave this remark more consideration than it seemed to merit and then said: 'Illustration, please.'

'Well, some people are afraid of employers and some of razors.'

'I don't think that sort of fear is a constant,' said Hazlerigg. 'It changes as you grow older, you know – or get more experienced. I haven't much occasion for bodily violence in my present job.' (He was one of the chief inspectors at Scotland Yard.) 'When I was a young constable the customers I chiefly disliked were drunken women. Nowadays – well, perhaps I should look at it the other way round. Perhaps I could describe the sort of man whom *I* should hate to have after *me*.'

In the pause that followed I tried hard to visualize what precise mixture of thug and entrepreneur would terrify the red-faced, gray-eyed, bulky, equitable man sitting beside me.

'He'd be English,' said Hazlerigg at last, 'Anglo-Saxon anyway, getting on for middle-age and a first-class businessman. He would have had some former experience of lethal weapons – as an infantry soldier, perhaps, in one of the world wars. But definitely an amateur – an amateur in violence. He would believe passionately in the justice of what he was doing – but without ever allowing the fanatic to rule the businessman. Now that's a type I should hate to have after me! He's unstoppable.'

'Is that a portrait from life?' I said.

'Yes,' said Hazlerigg slowly. 'Yes, it's a portrait from life. It all happened a good time ago – in the early thirties, when I was a junior inspector. Even now, you'll have to be very careful about names, you know, because if the real truth came out – however, judge for yourself.'

Inspector Hazlerigg first met Mr Collet (*the* Collets, the shipping people – this one was the third of the dynasty) in his managing director's mahogany-lined office. Hazlerigg was there by appointment. He had arrived at the building in a plain van and had been introduced via the goods entrance, but once inside he had been treated with every consideration.

Even during the few minutes which had elapsed before he could be brought face to face with Mr Collet, Hazlerigg had managed to collect a few impressions. Small things, from the way the commissionaire and the messenger spoke about him, and more still from the way his secretary spoke *to* him: that they liked him and liked working for him; that they knew something was wrong and were sorry.

They didn't, of course, know exactly what the trouble was. Hazlerigg did.

Kidnapping – the extorting of money by kidnapping – is a filthy thing. Fortunately, it does not seem to come very easily to the English criminal. But there was a little wave of it that year.

Mr Collet had an only child, a boy of nine. On the afternoon of the previous day he had been out with his aunt, Mr Collet's sister, in the park. A car had overtaken them on an empty stretch. A man had got out, pitched the boy into the back of the car, and driven off. As simple as that.

'So far as we know,' said Hazlerigg, 'there's just the one crowd. I'll be quite frank. We know very little about them. But there have been four cases already, and the features have been too much alike for coincidence.'

'Such as – ?' said Mr Collet. His voice and his hands, Hazlerigg noticed, were under control. He couldn't see the eyes. Mr Collet was wearing heavy sunglasses.

'Well – they don't ask for too much to start with, that's one thing. The first demand has always been quite modest. The idea being that a man will be more likely to go on paying once he has started.'

'Right so far,' said Mr Collet. 'They asked for only £5,000 – they could have had it this morning, if I'd thought it would do any good.'

'Then there's also their method of collecting. It's disarming. They employ known crooks. I don't know what they pay them – just enough to make it worth their while to take the risk. These crooks are strictly carriers only. We could arrest them at the moment they contact you without getting any nearer to the real organizers.'

'The Piccadilly side of Green Park, at 2 o'clock tomorrow,' said Mr Collet. 'I got the rendezvous quite openly over the telephone. Could they be followed?'

'That's where the organization really starts,' said Hazlerigg. 'Every move after that is worked out – and when you come to think about it, the cards are very heavily stacked in their favour. All they've got to do is to hand the money on. There are a hundred ways of doing it. They might pass it over in a crowd in an underground train or a bus in the rush hour, or they might be picked up by car and driven somewhere fast, or they might hand it over in a cinema. They might get rid of the money the same day, or they might wait a week.'

'Yes,' said Mr Collet, 'a little organization and that part shouldn't be too difficult. Any other peculiarities about this crowd?'

He said this as a businessman might inquire about a firm with whom he was going to trade.

Hazlerigg hesitated. What he was going to say had to be said some time. It might as well be said now.

'Yes, sir,' he said. 'There's this to consider. However much the victim pays – however often he pays – however promptly he pays – he doesn't get the child back. You've given us the best chance so far by coming to us immediately.' Mr Collet said nothing. 'You know Roger Barstow – he lost his little girl – Zilla was her name. He paid nine times. More than £100,000 – until he had no more left and said so. Next morning they found Zilla; in the swill bin at the back of his house.'

There was another silence. Hazlerigg saw the whites of the knuckle-bones start up for a moment on one of Mr Collet's thin brown hands. At last he got to his feet and said: 'Thank you, Inspector. I have your contact number. I'll get hold of you as soon as I – as soon as anything happens.'

As he walked to the door he took off his glasses for the first time and Hazlerigg saw in his eyes that he had got his ally. It had been a risk, but it had come off.

Mr Collet was going to fight.

When the door had closed behind the chief inspector Mr Collet thought for a few moments and then rang the bell and asked for Mr Stevens.

Mr Stevens, who was a month or two short of fifteen, was the head of the Collet messenger service, and a perfectly natural organizer. He spent a good deal of his time organizing the messenger boys of the firm into a sort of trade union, and he had already engineered two beautifully-timed strikes, the second of which had called for Mr Collet's personal intervention.

It says a good deal for both parties that when Mr Collet sent for him and asked for his help, young Stevens listened carefully to what he had to say and promised him the fullest assistance of himself and his organization.

'No film stuff,' said Mr Collet. 'These men are real crooks. They're dangerous. And they're wide awake. They expect to be followed. We're going to do this on business lines.'

That was Wednesday. At 4 o'clock on Thursday afternoon Inspector Hazlerigg again visited Archangel Street, taking the same precautions. Mr Collet was at his desk. 'You've got something for me . . .' It was more a statement than a question.

'Before I answer that,' said Mr Collet, 'I want something from you. I want your promise that you won't act on my information without my permission.'

Hazlerigg said: 'All right. I can't promise not to go on with such steps as I'm already taking. But I promise not to use your information until you say so. What do you know?'

'I know the names of most of the men concerned,' said Mr Collet. 'I know where my son is – I know where these people are hiding.'

When Hazlerigg had recovered his breath he said: 'Perhaps you'll explain.'

'I thought a good deal,' said Mr Collet, 'about what you told me – about the sort of people we were dealing with. Particularly about the men who would make contact with me and carry back the money. It was obvious that they weren't afraid of violence. They weren't even, basically, afraid of being arrested. That was part of the risk. They certainly weren't open to any sort of persuasion. If they observed the routine, which had no doubt been carefully laid down for them, they would take the money from me and get it back to their employers, without giving us any chance of following them. Their position seemed to be pretty well impregnable. In the circumstances it seemed – do you play bridge, Inspector?'

'Badly,' said Hazlerigg. 'But I'm very fond of it.'

'Then you understand the Vienna Coup.'

'In theory – though I could never work it. It's a sort of squeeze. You start by playing away one of your winning aces, isn't that it?'

'Exactly,' said Mr Collet. 'You give – or appear to give – your opponents an unexpected gift. And like all unexpected gifts it throws them off balance and upsets their defence. I decided to do the same. To be precise, I gave them £5,000 *more* than they asked for. I met these men – there were two of them as I told you – by appointment in Green Park. I simply opened my brief-case and put a brown paper packet into their hands. They opened it quickly, and as they were doing so I said: "Ten thousand pounds in one pound notes – that's right, isn't it?" I could almost see it hit them. To give them time to cover up I said: "When do I see my boy?" The elder of the two men said: "You'll be seeing him soon. We'll ring you tomorrow." Then they pushed off. I could see them starting to argue.'

Mr Collet paused. Inspector Hazlerigg, who was still trying to work out the angles, said nothing.

'The way I figured it out,' said Mr Collet, 'they'd have all their plans made for handing on £5,000 to their employers. So I gave them

£10,000. That meant £5,000 for themselves if they kept quiet about it, and played it right. But I'd put all the notes in one packet, you see. They had to be divided out. Then they had to split the extra £5,000 among themselves – they were both in on it. Above all, they had to get somewhere safe and somewhere quiet and talk it out. You see what that meant. Their original plan – the careful one laid down for them by the bosses – had to be scrapped.

'They had to make another plan, and make it rather quickly. It would be something simple. They'd either go to one of their own houses, or a safe friend's house – and it would probably be somewhere with a telephone – because they'd have to invent some sort of story for the bosses to explain why they'd abandoned the original plan. That last bit was only surmise, but it was a fair business risk.'

'Yes,' said Hazlerigg. 'I see. You still had to follow them, though.'

'Not me,' said Mr Collet. 'It was the boys who did that. The streets round the park were full of them. They're a sort of car-watching club – you see them anywhere in the streets of London if you look. They collect car numbers. Boy of mine called Stevens ran it. He's a born organizer. I went straight back to the office. Fifteen minutes later I got a call. Just an address, near King's Cross.

'I passed it on to a friend of mine – he's quite a senior official, so I won't give you his name. Inside five minutes he had the line from that house tapped. He was just in time to collect the outgoing call. That was that. It was to a house in Essex. Here's the address.' He pushed a slip of paper across. 'That's the name.'

'Just like that,' said Hazlerigg. 'Simple. Scotland Yard have been trying to do it for six months.'

'I had more at stake than you.'

'Yes,' said Hazlerigg. 'What happens now?'

'Now,' said Mr Collet, 'we sit back and wait.'

Continuing the story, Hazlerigg said to me: 'I think that was one of the bravest and coolest things I ever saw a man do. He was quite right, of course. The people we were dealing with moved by instinct – that sort of deadly instinct which those people get who sleep with one finger on the trigger.

'When their messengers reported the change of plan – I don't know what sort of story they put up – their bristles must have been on end. These people can smell when something's wrong. They're so used to double-crossing other people that they get a sort of second sight about it themselves. If we'd rushed them then, we should never have got the boy alive. So we waited. We had a man watch the house – it was a big, rather lonely house, between Pitsea and Rayleigh on the north of the Thames.'

And, meanwhile, Mr Collet sat in his mahogany-lined office and transacted the business of his firm. On the fourth morning he got a letter, in a painstaking schoolboy script.

> Dear Father,
>
> I am to write this to you. You are to pay £5,000 more. They will telephone you how to pay. I am quite well. It is quite a nice house. It is quite a nice room. The sun wakes me in the early morning.
>
> Love from David.
>
> P.S. Please be quick.

Mr Andrews, senior partner in the firm of Andrews and Mackay, house agents of Pitsea, summed up his visitor at one glance which took in the silk tie, the pigskin brief-case and the hood of the chauffeur-driven Daimler standing outside the office, and said in his most deferential voice: 'Certainly, Mr – er – Robinson. Anything we can do to help you. It's not everybody's idea of a house, but if you're looking for something quiet and secluded – '

'I understand that it's occupied at the moment,' said Mr Robinson.

'Temporarily,' agreed Mr Andrews. 'But you could have possession. The owner let it on short notice to a syndicate of men who are interested in a new color process. They needed the big grounds – the quiet, you understand, and the freedom from interruption. The only difficulty which occurs to me is that you will not be able to inspect the house today. By the terms of our arrangement we have to give at least forty-eight hours' notice.'

Mr Robinson thought for a moment and then said: 'Have you such a thing as a plan of the house?'

'Why, certainly,' said Mr Andrews. 'We had a very careful survey made when the house was put up for sale. Here you are – on two floors only, you see.'

'Only one bedroom,' said Mr Robinson, 'looks due east?'

'Why, yes.' Mr Andrews was hardened to the vagaries of clients.

'The sun wakes me in the early morning,' said Mr Robinson softly.

'I beg your pardon?'

'Nothing,' said Mr Robinson. 'Nothing. Thinking aloud. A bad habit. Would it be asking too much if I borrowed these plans for a day?'

'Why, of course,' said Mr Andrews. 'Keep them for as long as you like.'

Four o'clock of a perfect summer afternoon. It was so silent that the clack of a scythe blade on a stone sounded clear across the valley where the big gray house dozed in the sun.

As the double chime of the half hour sounded from Rayleigh Church, a figure appeared on the dusty road. It was a man, in postman's uniform, wheeling a bicycle.

The woman in the lodge answered the bell and unlocked one of the big gates, without comment. Then she returned to her back room, picked up the house telephone, and said: 'All right. It's only the postman.'

It was a mistake which might have cost her very dearly.

As Mr Collet wheeled his borrowed machine slowly up the long drive, he was thinking about the bulky sack which rested on the saddle and balanced there with difficulty. He knew that some very sharp eyes would be watching his approach. It couldn't be helped though. He had been able to see no better method of getting this particular apparatus up to the house.

He propped his bicycle against the pillar of the front door, lifted the sack down, keeping the mouth of it gathered in his left hand, and rang the bell. So far, so good.

The door was opened by a man in corduroys and a tweed jacket. He might have been a gardener or a gamekeeper. Mr Collet, looking at his eyes, knew better.

'Don't shout,' he said. The gun in his hand was an argument.

For a moment the man stared. Then he jumped to one side and started to open his mouth.

Even for an indifferent shot three yards is not a long range. The big bullet lifted the man back onto his heels like a punch under the heart and crumpled him onto the floor.

In the deep silence which followed the roar of the gun, Mr Collet raced for the stairs. The heavy sack was against him but he made good time.

At the top he turned left with the sureness of a man who knows his mind and made for the room at the end of the corridor.

He saw that it was padlocked.

He put the muzzle of his gun as near to the padlock as he dared and pulled the trigger.

The jump of the gun threw the bullet up into the door jamb, missing the padlock altogether. He took a lower aim and tried again. Once, twice, again. The padlock buckled.

Mr Collet kicked the door open and went in.

The boy was half-sitting, half-kneeling in one corner. Mr Collet grinned at him with a good deal more confidence than he felt and said: 'Stand out of the way, son. The curtain's going up for the last act.'

As he spoke he was piling together mattresses, bedclothes, a rug and a couple of small chairs into a barricade. When he had done this he opened the sack, pulled out the curious-looking instrument from inside it, laid it beside his home-made parapet, and started working on it.

'Get into that far corner, son,' said Mr Collet. 'And you might keep an eye on the window, just in case it occurs to the gentry to run a ladder up. Keep your head down, though. Here they come.'

Joe Keller had tortured children and had killed for pleasure as well as for profit, but he was not physically a coward.

As he watched his henchman twitching on the hall floor, with the indifference of a man who has seen many men die, he was already working out his plan of attack.

'Take a long ladder,' he said to one man, 'and run it up to the window. Not the bedroom window – be your age. Put it against the landing window, this end. You can see the bedroom door from there, can't you? If it's shut, wait. If it's open, start shooting into the room – aim high. We'll go in together along the floor.'

'He'll pick us off as we come.'

'Not if Hoppy keeps him pinned down,' said Keller. 'Besides, I reckon he doesn't know much about guns. It took him four shots to knock off that lock, didn't it? Any more arguments?'

Half a mile away, at points round the lip of the valley, four police cars had started up their engines at the sound of the first shot.

Hazlerigg was lying full length on the roof of one of them, a pair of long binoculars in his hands.

The Essex Superintendent looked up at him.

'I made that five shots,' he said. 'Do we start?'

'No, sir,' said Hazlerigg. 'You remember the signal we arranged.'

'Do you think he can do his stuff?' The Superintendent sounded worried.

'He hasn't done badly so far,' said Hazlerigg shortly, and silence settled down once more.

It was the driver of their car who saw it first, and gave a shout. From one of the first-floor windows of the house, unmistakable and ominous, a cloud of black and sooty smoke rolled upward.

The four cars started forward as one.

* * *

In that long upstairs passage, things had gone according to plan – at first. Covered by a fusillade from the window, Joe Keller and his two assistants had inched their way forward on elbows and knees, their guns ahead of them. At the end of the passage stood the door, open and inviting. The outer end of Mr Collet's barricade came into sight as they advanced, but it was offset from the doorway, and Mr Collet himself was still invisible.

Five yards to go.

Then, as the three men bunched for the final jump, it came out to meet them. A great red-and-yellow river of flame, overmantled with black smoke, burning and hissing and dripping with oil. As they turned to fly it caught them . . .

'There was nothing very much for us to do when we did get there,' said Inspector Hazlerigg. 'We had to get Mr Collet and the boy out of the window – the passage floor was red-hot. We caught one man in the garden. His nerve was gone – he seemed glad to give himself up.

'As for the other three – an infantry flame-thrower is not a discriminating sort of weapon, particularly at close quarters. There was just about enough left of them – well – say just about enough of the three of them to fill the swill bin where they found little Zilla Barstow.

'No, never tangle with a wholehearted amateur.'

GOODBYE, POPS

Joe Gores

I was born in Minnesota in 1931, received degrees in English Literature from Notre Dame and Stanford, and spent my two years as a draftee at the Pentagon, writing biographies of Army generals. Other jobs I held while learning the craft of fiction-writing included truck driver, construction worker, instructor in a gymnasium, lumberjack in Alaska, schoolteacher in Kenya and, for twelve years, private investigator in California.

My grandfather, whom I loved very much, died in 1952, while I was a student at Notre Dame. Upon my return to school from his funeral, I wrote an angry little memoir called 'Epitaph' on his death, because it had affected me so deeply. Fifteen years later, after I had become a professional writer, I ran across 'Epitaph' and realized it was the basis for a short story. I constructed the current plot line for it, and Fred Dannay, the editorial half of Ellery Queen, worked with me on honing and heightening emotion, then bought it, as 'Goodbye, Pops', for Ellery Queen's Mystery Magazine. *In 1970, 'Goodbye, Pops' won the Mystery Writers of America's Edgar as the best mystery short story of the previous year. (My first novel,* A Time of Predators, *was published in 1969, and awarded the MWA Edgar as best first novel the same year that 'Goodbye, Pops' won as best short story. I was also given an Edgar in 1976 for my* Kojak *teleplay,* 'No Immunity for Murder.'*)*

To date, I have published six novels, a massive non-fiction work on marine salvage, and some 100 short stories and articles; I have also written eight screenplays and 11 teleplays.

'Goodbye, Pops,' because it began with a true and honest emotion, deeply felt, has always been one of my favorite works, at any length and in whatever form. And I have always credited Mr Dannay's astute editorial advice for much of the success of the story.

I got off the Greyhound and stopped to draw icy Minnesota air into my lungs. A bus had brought me from Springfield, Illinois to Chicago the day before; a second bus had brought me here. I caught my passing reflection in the window of the old-fashioned depot – a tall, hard man with a white and savage face, wearing an ill-fitting overcoat. I caught another reflection, too, one that froze my guts: a cop in uniform. Could they already know it was someone else in that burned-out car?

Then the cop turned away, chafing his arms with gloved hands through his blue stormcoat, and I started breathing again. I went quickly over to the cab line. Only two hackies were waiting there; the front one rolled down his window as I came up.

'You know the Miller place north of town?' I asked.

He looked me over. 'I know it. Five bucks – now.'

I paid him from the money I'd rolled a drunk for in Chicago and eased back against the rear seat. As he nursed the cab out into ice-rimed Second Street, my fingers gradually relaxed from their rigid chopping position. I deserved to go back inside if I let a clown like this get to me.

'Old man Miller's pretty sick, I hear.' He half-turned to catch me with a corner of an eye. 'You got business with him?'

'Yeah. My own.'

That ended that conversation. It bothered me that Pops was sick enough for this clown to know about it; but maybe my brother Rod being vice-president at the bank would explain that. There was a lot of new construction and a freeway west of town with a tricky overpass to the old county road. A mile beyond a new sub-division were the 200 wooded hilly acres I knew so well.

After my break from the Federal pen at Terre Haute, Indiana two days before, I'd gotten outside their cordon through woods like these. I'd gone out in a prison truck, in a pail of swill meant for the prison farm pigs, had headed straight west, across the Illinois line. I'm good in open country, even when I'm in prison condition, so by dawn I was in a hayloft near Paris, Illinois, some 20 miles from the pen. You can do what you have to do.

The cabby stopped at the foot of the private road, looking dubious. 'Listen, buddy, I know that's been plowed, but it looks damned icy. If I try it and go into the ditch – '

'I'll walk from here.'

I waited beside the road until he'd driven away, then let the north wind chase me up the hill and into the leafless hardwoods. The cedars that Pops and I had put in as a windbreak were taller and fuller; rabbit paths were pounded hard into the snow under the barbed-wire tangles of wild raspberry bushes. Under the oaks at the top of the hill was the old-fashioned, two-story house, but I detoured to the kennels first. The snow was deep and undisturbed inside them. No more foxhounds. No cracked corn in the bird feeder outside the kitchen window, either. I rang the front doorbell.

My sister-in-law Edwina, Rod's wife, answered it. She was three years younger than my 35, and she'd started wearing a girdle.

'Good Lord! Chris!' Her mouth tightened. 'We didn't – '

'Ma wrote that the old man was sick.' She'd written, all right. *Your father is very ill. Not that you have ever cared if any of us lives or dies*. . . . And then Edwina decided that my tone of voice had given her something to get righteous about.

'I'm amazed you'd have the nerve to come here, even if they did let you out on parole or something.' So nobody had been around asking yet. 'If you plan to drag the family name through the mud again – '

I pushed by her into the hallway. 'What's wrong with the old man?' I called him Pops only inside myself, where no one could hear.

'He's dying, that's what's wrong with him.'

She said it with a sort of baleful pleasure. It hit me, but I just grunted and went by into the living room. Then the old girl called down from the head of the stairs.

'Eddy? What – who is it?'

'Just – a salesman, Ma. He can wait until Doctor's gone.'

Doctor. As if some damned croaker was generic physician all by himself. When he came downstairs Edwina tried to hustle him out before I could see him, but I caught his arm as he poked it into his overcoat sleeve.

'Like to see you a minute, Doc. About old man Miller.'

He was nearly six feet, a couple of inches shorter than me, but outweighing me by 40 pounds. He pulled his arm free.

'Now see here, fellow – '

I grabbed his lapels and shook him, just enough to pop a button off his coat and put his glasses awry on his nose. His face got red.

'Old family friend, Doc.' I jerked a thumb at the stairs. 'What's the story?'

It was dumb, dumb as hell, of course, asking him; at any second the cops would figure out that the farmer in the burned-out car wasn't me after all. I'd dumped enough gasoline before I struck the match so they couldn't lift prints off anything except the shoe I'd planted: but they'd make him through dental charts as soon as they found out he was missing. When they did they'd come here asking questions, and then the croaker would realize who I was. But I wanted to know whether

Pops was as bad off as Edwina said he was, and I've never been a patient man.

The croaker straightened his suitcoat, striving to regain lost dignity. 'He – Judge Miller is very weak, too weak to move. He probably won't last out the week.' His eyes searched my face for pain, but there's nothing like a Federal pen to give you control. Disappointed, he said, 'His lungs. I got to it much too late, of course. He's resting easily.'

I jerked the thumb again. 'You know your way out.'

Edwina was at the head of the stairs, her face righteous again. It seems to run in the family, even with those who married in. Only Pops and I were short of it.

'Your father is very ill. I forbid you – '

'Save it for Rod; it might work on him.'

In the room I could see the old man's arm hanging limply over the edge of the bed, with smoke from the cigarette between his fingers running up to the ceiling in a thin unwavering blue line. The upper arm, which once had measured an honest 18 and had swung his small tight fist against the side of my head a score of times, could not even hold a cigarette up in the air. It gave me the same wrench as finding a good foxhound that's gotten mixed up with a bobcat.

The old girl came out of her chair by the foot of the bed, her face blanched. I put my arms around her. 'Hi, Ma,' I said. She was rigid inside my embrace, but I knew she wouldn't pull away. Not there in Pops' room.

He had turned his head at my voice. The light glinted from his silky white hair. His eyes, translucent with imminent death, were the pure, pale blue of birch shadows on fresh snow.

'Chris,' he said in a weak voice. 'Son of a biscuit, boy . . . I'm glad to see you.'

'You ought to be, you lazy devil,' I said heartily. I pulled off my suit jacket and hung it over the back of the chair, and tugged off my tie. 'Getting so lazy that you let the foxhounds go!'

'That's enough, Chris.' She tried to put steel into it.

'I'll just sit here a little, Ma,' I said easily. Pops wouldn't have long, I knew, and any time I got with him would have to do me. She stood in the doorway, a dark indecisive shape; then she turned and went silently out, probably to phone Rod at the bank.

For the next couple of hours I did most of the talking; Pops just lay there with his eyes shut, like he was asleep. But then he started in, going way back, to the trapline he and I had run when I'd been a kid; to the big white-tail buck that followed him through the woods one rutting season until Pops whacked it on the nose with a tree branch. It was only after his law practice had ripened into a judgeship that we began to draw apart; I guess that in my twenties I was too wild, too much what he'd been himself 30 years before. Only I kept going in that direction.

About seven o'clock my brother Rod called from the doorway. I went out, shutting the door behind me. Rod was taller than me, broad and big-boned, with an athlete's frame – but with mush where his guts should have been. He had close-set pale eyes and not quite enough chin, and hadn't gone out for football in high school.

'My wife reported the vicious things you said to her.' It was his best give-the-teller-hell voice. 'We've talked this over with mother and we want you out of here tonight. We want – '

'*You* want? Until he kicks off it's still the old man's house, isn't it?'

He swung at me then – being Rod, it was a right-hand lead – and I blocked it with an open palm. Then I back-handed him, hard, twice across the face each way, jerking his head from side to side with the slaps and crowding him up against the wall. I could have fouled his groin to bend him over, then driven locked hands down on the back of his neck as I jerked a knee into his face; and I wanted to. The need to get away before they came after me was gnawing at my gut like a weasel in a trap gnawing off his own paw to get loose. But I merely stepped away from him.

'You – you murderous animal!' He had both hands up to his cheeks like a woman might have done. Then his eyes widened theatrically, as the realization struck him. I wondered why it had taken so long. 'You've *broken out*!' he gasped. '*Escaped*! A fugitive from – from justice!'

'Yeah. And I'm staying that way. I know you, kid, all of you. The last thing any of you want is for the cops to take me here.' I tried to put his tones into my voice. '*Oh!* The *scandal*!'

'But they'll be after you – '

'They think I'm dead,' I said flatly. 'I went off an icy road in a stolen car in down-state Illinois, and it rolled and burned with me inside.'

His voice was hushed, almost horror-stricken. 'You mean – that there *is* a body in the car?'

'Right.'

I knew what he was thinking, but I didn't bother to tell him the truth – that the old farmer who was driving me to Springfield, because he thought my doubled-up fist in the overcoat pocket was a gun, hit a patch of ice and took the car right off the lonely country road. He was impaled on the steering post, so I took his shoes and put one of mine on his foot. The other I left, with my fingerprints on it, lying near enough so they'd find it but not so near that it'd burn along with the car. Rod wouldn't have believed the truth anyway. If they caught me, who would?

I said, 'Bring me up a bottle of bourbon and a carton of cigarettes. And make sure Eddy and Ma keep their mouths shut if anyone asks about me.' I opened the door so Pops could hear. 'Well, thanks, Rod. It *is* nice to be home again.'

Solitary in the pen makes you able to stay awake easily or snatch sleep easily, whichever is necessary. I stayed awake for the last 37 hours that Pops had, leaving the chair by his bed only to go to the bathroom and to listen at the head of the stairs whenever I heard the phone or the doorbell ring. Each time I thought: *this is it*. But my luck held. If they'd just take long enough so I could stay until Pops went; the second that happened, I told myself, I'd be on my way.

Rod and Edwina and Ma were there at the end, with Doctor hovering in the background to make sure he got paid. Pops finally moved a pallid arm and Ma sat down quickly on the edge of the bed – a small, erect, rather indomitable woman with a face made for wearing a lorgnette. She wasn't crying yet; instead, she looked purely luminous in a way.

'Hold my hand, Eileen.' Pops paused for the terrible strength to speak again. 'Hold my hand. Then I won't be frightened.'

She took his hand and he almost smiled, and shut his eyes. We waited, listening to his breathing get slower and slower and then just stop, like a grandfather clock running down. Nobody moved, nobody spoke. I looked around at them, so soft, so unused to death, and I felt like a marten in a brooding house. Then Ma began to sob.

It was a blustery day with snow flurries. I parked the jeep in front of the funeral chapel and went up the slippery walk with wind plucking at my coat, telling myself for the hundredth time just how nuts I was to stay for the service. By now they *had* to know that the dead farmer wasn't me; by now some smart prison censor *had* to remember Ma's letter about Pops being sick. He was two days dead, and I should have been in Mexico by this time. But it didn't seem complete yet, somehow. Or maybe I was kidding myself, maybe it was just the old need to put down authority that always ruins guys like me.

From a distance it looked like Pops but up close you could see the cosmetics and that his collar was three sizes too big. I felt his hand: it was a statue's hand, unfamiliar except for the thick, slightly down-curved fingernails.

Rod came up behind me and said, in a voice meant only for me, 'After today I want you to leave us alone. I want you out of my house.'

'Shame on you, brother,' I grinned. 'Before the will is even read, too.'

We followed the hearse through snowy streets at the proper funeral pace, lights burning. Pallbearers wheeled the heavy casket out smoothly on oiled tracks, then set it on belts over the open grave. Snow whipped and swirled from a gray sky, melting on the metal and forming rivulets down the sides.

I left when the preacher started his scam, impelled by the need to get moving, get away, yet impelled by another urgency, too. I wanted something out of the house before all the mourners arrived to eat and guzzle. The guns and ammo already had been banished to the garage, since Rod never had fired a round in his life; but it was easy to dig out the beautiful little .22 target pistol with the long barrel. Pops and I had spent hundreds of hours with that gun, so the grip was worn smooth and the blueing was gone from the metal that had been out in every sort of weather.

Putting the jeep on four-wheel I ran down through the trees to a cut between the hills, then went along on foot through the darkening hardwoods. I moved slowly, evoking memories of Korea to neutralize the icy bite of the snow through my worn shoes. There was a flash of brown as a cotton-tail streaked from under a deadfall toward a rotting woodpile I'd stacked years before. My slug took him in the spine, paralyzing the back legs. He jerked and thrashed until I broke his neck with the edge of my hand.

I left him there and moved out again, down into the small marshy triangle between the hills. It was darkening fast as I kicked at the frozen tussocks. Finally a ringneck in full plumage burst out, long tail fluttering and stubby pheasant wings beating to raise his heavy body. He was quartering up and just a bit to my right, and I had all the time in the world. I squeezed off in mid-swing, knowing it was perfect even before he took that heart-stopping pinwheel tumble.

I carried them back to the jeep; there was a tiny ruby of blood on the pheasant's beak, and the rabbit was still hot under the front legs. I was using headlights when I parked on the curving cemetery drive. They hadn't put the casket down yet, so the snow had laid a soft blanket over it. I put the rabbit and pheasant on top and stood without moving for a minute or two. The wind must have been strong, because I found that tears were burning on my cheeks.

Goodbye, Pops. Goodbye to deer-shining out of season in the hardwood belt across the creek. Goodbye to jump-shooting mallards down in the river bottoms. Goodbye to woodsmoke and mellow bourbon by firelight and all the things that made a part of you mine. The part they could never get at.

I turned away, toward the jeep – and stopped dead. I hadn't even heard them come up. Four of them, waiting patiently as if to pay their respects to the dead. In one sense they were: to them that dead farmer in the burned-out car was Murder One. I tensed, my mind going to the .22 pistol that they didn't know about in my overcoat pocket. Yeah. Except that it had all the stopping power of a fox's bark. If only Pops had run to handguns of a little heavier caliber. But he hadn't.

Very slowly, as if my arms suddenly had grown very heavy, I raised my hands above my head.

THE TERRAPIN
Patricia Highsmith

'Patricia Highsmith is perhaps best known for her novels: Strangers on a Train *(brilliantly filmed by Alfred Hitchcock in 1951, with a screenplay by Raymond Chandler),* The Tremor of Forgery, A Suspension of Mercy, *four books about the talented – and dangerous – Tom Ripley, plus almost a dozen more.*

She has also published five volumes of short stories, and, in many of those stories, the main characters are animals, rather than people. Dogs, cats, hamsters, snails, pigs . . . Miss Highsmith has the unique ability to make such beasts come every bit as alive as the marvellously-drawn humans of her novels.

In the drama which follows, specially selected for this collection by its author as her finest short story, the dramatis personae *include a frustrated 11-year-old boy, his overbearing mother – and a turtle . . .'*

Victor heard the elevator door open, his mother's quick footsteps in the hall, and he flipped his book shut. He shoved it under the sofa pillow out of sight, and winced as he heard it slip between sofa and wall to the floor with a thud. Her key was in the lock.

'Hello, Vee-ector-r!' she cried, raising one arm in the air. Her other arm circled a brown paper bag, her hand held a cluster of little bags. 'I have been to my publisher and to the market and also to the fish market,' she told him. 'Why aren't you out playing? It's a lovely, lovely day!'

'I was out,' he said. 'For a little while. I got cold.'

'Ugh!' She was unloading the grocery bag in the tiny kitchen off the foyer. 'You are seeck, you know that? In the month of October, you are cold? I see all kinds of children playing on the sidewalk. Even, I think, that boy you like. What's his name?'

'I don't know,' Victor said. His mother wasn't really listening anyway. He pushed his hands into the pockets of his short, too-small shorts, making them tighter than ever, and walked aimlessly around the living room, looking down at his heavy, scuffed shoes. At least his mother had to buy him shoes that fit him, and he rather liked these shoes, because they had the thickest soles of any he had ever owned, and they had heavy toes that rose up a little, like mountain climbers' shoes. Victor paused at the window and looked straight out at a toast-coloured apartment building across Third Avenue. He and his mother lived on the 18th floor, next to the top floor where the penthouses were. The building across the street was even taller than this one. Victor had liked their Riverside Drive apartment better. He had liked the school he had gone to there better. Here they laughed at his clothes. In the other school, they had finally got tired of laughing at them.

'You don't want to go out?' asked his mother, coming into the living room, wiping her hands briskly on a paper bag. She sniffed her palms. 'Ugh! That stee-enk!'

'No, Mama,' Victor said patiently.

'Today is Saturday.'

'I know.'

'Can you say the days of the week?'

'Of course.'

'Say them.'

'I don't want to say them. I know them.' His eyes began to sting around the edges with tears. 'I've known them for years. Years and years. Kids five years old can say the days of the week.'

But his mother was not listening. She was bending over the drawing-table in the corner of the room. She had worked late on something last night. On his sofa bed in the opposite corner of the room, Victor had not been able to sleep until two in the morning, when his mother had gone to bed on the studio couch.

'Come here, Veector. Did you see this?'

Victor came on dragging feet, hands still in his pockets. No, he hadn't even glanced at her drawing-board this morning, hadn't wanted to.

'This is Pedro, the little donkey. I invented him last night. What do you think? And this is Miguel, the little Mexican boy who rides him. They ride and ride all over Mexico, and Miguel thinks they are lost, but Pedro knows the way home all the time, and . . .'

Victor did not listen. He deliberately shut his ears in a way he had learned to do from many years of practice, but boredom, frustration – he knew the word frustration, had read all about it – clamped his shoulders, weighted like a stone in his body, pressed hatred and tears up to his eyes, as if a volcano were churning in him. He had hoped his mother might take a hint from his saying that he was cold in his silly short-shorts. He had hoped his mother might remember what he had told her, that the fellow he had wanted to get acquainted with downstairs, a fellow who looked about his own age, eleven, had laughed at his short pants on Monday afternoon. *They make you wear your kid brother's pants or something?* Victor had drifted away, mortified. What if the fellow knew he didn't even own any longer pants, not even a pair of knickers, much less *long* pants, even blue jeans! His mother, for some cock-eyed reason, wanted him to look 'French,' and made him wear short-shorts and stockings that came to just below his knees, and dopey shirts with round collars. His mother wanted him to stay about six years old, for ever, all his life. She liked to test out her drawings on him. *Veector is my sounding board*, she sometimes said to her friends. *I show my drawings to Veector and I know if children will like them*. Often Victor said he liked stories that he did not like, or drawings that he was indifferent to, because he felt sorry for his mother and because it put her in a better mood if he said he liked them. He was quite tired now of children's book illustrations, if he had ever in his life liked them – he really couldn't remember – and now he had two favourites: Howard Pyle's illustrations in some of Robert Louis Stevenson's books and Cruikshank's in Dickens. It was too bad, Victor thought, that he was absolutely the last person of whom his mother should have asked an opinion, because he simply *hated* children's illustrations. And it was a wonder his mother didn't see this, because she hadn't sold any illustrations for books for years and years, not since *Wimple-Dimple*, a book whose jacket was all torn and turning yellow now from age, which sat in the centre of the bookshelf in a little cleared spot, propped up against the back of the bookcase so everyone could see it. Victor had been seven years old when that book was printed. His mother liked to tell people and remind him, too, that he had told her what he had wanted to see her draw, had watched her make every drawing, had shown his opinion by laughing or not, and that she had been absolutely guided by him. Victor doubted this very much, because first of all the story was somebody else's and had been written before his mother did the drawings, and her drawings had had to follow the story, naturally. Since then, his mother had done only a few illustrations now and then for magazines for children, how to make paper pumpkins and black paper cats for Hallowe'en and things like that, though she took her portfolio around to publishers all the time. Their income came from his father, who was a wealthy businessman in France, an exporter of perfumes. His mother said he was very wealthy and very handsome. But he married again, he never wrote, and Victor had no interest in him, didn't even care if he never saw a picture of him, and he never had. His father was French with some Polish, and his mother was Hungarian with some French. The word Hungarian made Victor think of gypsies, but when he had asked his mother once, she had said emphatically that she hadn't any gypsy blood, and she had been annoyed that Victor brought the question up.

And now she was sounding him out again, poking him in the ribs to make him wake up, as she repeated:

'Listen to me! Which do you like better, Veector? "In all Mexico there was no bur-r-ro as wise as Miguel's Pedro," or "Miguel's Pedro was the wisest bur-r-ro in all Mexico"?'

'I think – I like it the first way better.'

'Which way is that?' demanded his mother, thumping her palm down on the illustration.

Victor tried to remember the wording, but realized he was only staring at the pencil smudges, the thumbprints on the edge of his mother's illustration board. The coloured drawing in the centre did not interest him at all. He was not-thinking. This was a frequent, familiar sensation to him now, there was something exciting and important about not-thinking, Victor felt, and he thought one day he would find something about it – perhaps under another name – in the Public Library or in the psychology books around the house that he browsed in when his mother was out.

'Veec-tor! What are you doing?'

'Nothing, Mama!'

'That is exactly it! Nothing! Can you not even *think*?'

A warm shame spread through him. It was as if his mother read his thoughts about not-thinking. 'I *am* thinking,' he protested. 'I'm thinking about *not*-thinking.' His tone was defiant. What could she do about it, after all?

'About what?' Her black, curly head tilted, her mascaraed eyes narrowed at him.

'Not-thinking.'

His mother put her jewelled hands on her hips. 'Do you know, Veec-tor, you are a little bit strange in the head?' She nodded. 'You are seeck. Psychologically seeck. And retarded, do you know that? You have the behaviour of a leetle boy five years old,' she said slowly and weightily. 'It is just as well you spend your Saturdays indoors. Who knows if you would not walk in front of a car, eh? But that is why I love you, little Veector.' She put her arm around his shoulders, pulled him against her, and for an instant Victor's nose pressed into her large, soft bosom. She was wearing her flesh-coloured dress, the one you could see through a little where her breast stretched it out.

Victor jerked his head away in a confusion of emotions. He did not know if he wanted to laugh or cry.

His mother was laughing gaily, her head back. 'Seeck you are! Look at you! My lee-tle boy still, lee-tle short pants – Ha! Ha!'

Now the tears showed in his eyes, he supposed, and his mother acted as if she were enjoying it! Victor turned his head away so she would not see his eyes. Then suddenly he faced her. 'Do you think I like these pants? *You* like them, not me, so why do you have to make fun of them?'

'A lee-tle boy who's crying!' she went on, laughing.

Victor made a dash for the bathroom, then swerved away and dived onto the sofa, his face toward the pillows. He shut his eyes tight and opened his mouth, crying but not-crying in a way he had learned through practice also. With his mouth open, his throat tight, not breathing for nearly a minute, he could somehow get the satisfaction of crying, screaming even, without anybody knowing it. He pushed his nose, his open mouth, his teeth, against the tomato-red sofa pillow, and though his mother's voice went on in a lazily mocking tone, and her laughter went on, he imagined that it was getting fainter and more distant from him. He imagined, rigid in every muscle, that he was suffering the absolute worst that any human being could suffer. He imagined that he was dying. But he did not think of death as an escape, only as a concentrated and a painful incident. This was the climax of his not-crying. Then he breathed again, and his mother's voice intruded:

'Did you hear me? – *Did you hear me?* Mrs Badzerkian is coming for tea. I want you to wash your face and put on a clean shirt. I want you to recite something for her. Now what are you going to recite?'

' "In winter when I go to bed",' said Victor. She was making him memorize every poem in *A Child's Garden of Verses*. He had said the first one that came into his head, and now there was an argument, because he had recited that one the last time. 'I said it, because I couldn't think of any other one right off the bat!' Victor shouted.

'Don't yell at me!' his mother cried, storming across the room at him.

She slapped his face before he knew what was happening.

He was up on one elbow on the sofa, on his back, his long, knobby-kneed legs splayed out in front of him. All right, he thought, if that's the way it is, that's the way it is. He looked at her with loathing. He would not show the slap had hurt, that it still stung. No more tears for today, he swore, no more even not-crying. He would finish the day, go through the tea, like a stone, like a soldier, not wincing. His mother paced around the room, turning one of her rings round and round, glancing at him from time to time, looking quickly away from him. But his eyes were steady on her. He was not afraid. She could even slap him again and he wouldn't care.

At last she announced that she was going to wash her hair, and she went into the bathroom.

Victor got up from the sofa and wandered across the room. He wished he had a room of his own to go to. In the apartment on Riverside Drive, there had been three rooms, a living room and his and his mother's rooms. When she was in the living room, he had been able to go into his bedroom, and vice versa, but here . . . They were going to tear down the old building they had lived in on Riverside Drive. It was not a pleasant thing for Victor to think about. Suddenly remembering the book that had fallen, he pulled out the sofa and reached for it. It was Menninger's *The Human Mind*, full of fascinating case histories of people. Victor put it back on the bookshelf between an astrology book and *How to Draw*. His mother did not like him to read psychology books, but Victor loved them, especially ones with case histories in them. The people in the case histories did what they wanted to do. They were natural. Nobody bossed them. At the local branch library, he spent hours browsing through the psychology shelves. They were in the adults' section, but the librarian did not mind his sitting at the tables there, because he was quiet.

Victor went into the kitchen and got a glass of water. As he was standing there drinking it, he heard a scratching noise coming from one of the paper bags on the counter. A mouse, he thought, but when he moved a couple of the bags, he didn't see any mouse. The scratching was coming from inside one of the bags. Gingerly, he opened the bag with his fingers, and waited for something to jump out. Looking in, he saw a white paper carton. He pulled it out slowly. Its bottom was damp. It opened like a pastry box. Victor jumped in surprise. It was a turtle on its back, a live turtle. It was wriggling its legs in the air, trying to turn over. Victor moistened his lips and, frowning with concentration, took the turtle by its sides with both hands, turned him over and let him down gently into the box again. The turtle drew in its feet then, and its head stretched up a little and it looked straight at him. Victor smiled. Why hadn't his mother told him she'd brought him a present? A live turtle. Victor's eyes glazed with anticipation as he thought of taking the turtle down, maybe with a leash around its neck, to show the fellow who'd laughed at his short pants. He might change his mind about being friends with him, if he found he owned a turtle.

'Hey, Mama! Mama!' Victor yelled at the bathroom door. 'You brought me a tur-rtle?'

'A what?' The water shut off.

'A turtle! In the kitchen!' Victor had been jumping up and down in the hall. He stopped.

His mother had hesitated, too. The water came on again, and she said in a shrill tone, '*C'est une terrapène! Pour un ragoût!*'

Victor understood, and a small chill went over him because his mother had spoken in French. His mother addressed him in French when she was giving an order that had to be obeyed, or when she anticipated resistance from him. So the terrapin was for a stew. Victor nodded to himself with a stunned resignation, and went back to the kitchen. For a stew. Well, the terrapin was not long for this world, as they say. What did the terrapin like to eat? Lettuce? Raw bacon? Boiled potato? Victor peered into the refrigerator.

He held a piece of lettuce near the terrapin's horny mouth. The terrapin did not open its mouth, but it looked at him. Victor held the lettuce near the two little dots of its nostrils, but if the terrapin smelled it, it showed no interest. Victor looked under the sink and pulled out a large wash pan. He put two inches of water into it. Then he gently dumped the terrapin into the pan. The terrapin paddled for a few seconds, as if it had to swim, then finding that its stomach sat on the bottom of the pan, it stopped and drew its feet in. Victor got down on his knees and studied the terrapin's face. Its upper lip overhung the lower, giving it a rather stubborn and unfriendly expression, but its eyes – they were bright and shining. Victor smiled when he looked hard at them.

'Okay, *monsieur terrapène*,' he said, 'just tell me what you'd like to eat and we'll get it for you! – Maybe some tuna?'

They had had tuna fish salad yesterday for dinner, and there was a small bowl of it left over. Victor got a little chunk of it in his fingers and presented it to the terrapin. The terrapin was not interested. Victor looked around the kitchen, wondering, then seeing the sunlight on the floor of the living room, he picked up the pan and carried it to the living room and set it down so the sunlight would fall on the terrapin's back. All turtles liked sunlight, Victor thought. He lay down on the floor on his side, propped up on an elbow. The terrapin stared at him for a moment, then very slowly and with an air of forethought and caution, put out its legs and advanced, found the circular boundary of the pan, and moved to the right, half its body out of the shallow water. It wanted out, and Victor took it in one hand, by the sides, and said:

'You can come out and have a little walk.'

He smiled as the terrapin started to disappear under the sofa. He caught it easily, because it moved so slowly. When he put it down on the carpet, it was quite still, as if it had withdrawn a little to think what it should do next, where it should go. It was a brownish green. Looking at it, Victor thought of river bottoms, of river water flowing. Or maybe oceans. Where did terrapins come from? He jumped up and went to the dictionary on the bookshelf. The dictionary had a picture of a terrapin, but it was a dull, black-and-white drawing, not so pretty as the live one. He learned nothing except that the name was of Algonquian origin, that the terrapin lived in fresh or brackish water, and that it was edible. Edible. Well, that was bad luck, Victor thought. But he was not going to eat any *terrapène* tonight. It would be all for his mother, that *ragoût*, and even if she slapped him and made him learn an extra two or three poems, he would not eat any terrapin tonight.

His mother came out of the bathroom. 'What are you doing there? – Veector?'

Victor put the dictionary back on the shelf. His mother had seen the pan. 'I'm looking at the terrapin,' he said, then realized the terrapin had disappeared. He got down on hands and knees and looked under the sofa.

'Don't put him on the furniture. He makes spots,' said his mother. She was standing in the foyer, rubbing her hair vigorously with a towel.

Victor found the terrapin between the wastebasket and the wall. He put him back in the pan.

'Have you changed your shirt?' asked his mother.

Victor changed his shirt, and then at his mother's order sat down on the sofa with *A Child's Garden of Verses* and tackled another poem, a brand-new one for Mrs Badzerkian. He learned two lines at a time, reading it aloud in a soft voice to himself, then repeating it, then putting two, four and six lines together, until he had the whole thing. He recited it to the terrapin. Then Victor asked his mother if he could play with the terrapin in the bathtub.

'No! And get your shirt all splashed?'

'I can put on my other shirt.'

'No! It's nearly four o'clock now. Get that pan out of the living room!'

Victor carried the pan back to the kitchen. His mother took the terrapin quite fearlessly out of the pan, put it back into the white paper box, closed its lid, and stuck the box in the refrigerator. Victor jumped a little as the refrigerator door slammed. It would be awfully cold in there for the terrapin. But then, he supposed, fresh or brackish water was cold now and then, too.

'Veector, cut the lemon,' said his mother. She was preparing the big round tray with cups and saucers. The water was boiling in the kettle.

Mrs Badzerkian was prompt as usual, and his mother poured the tea as soon as she had deposited her coat and pocketbook on the foyer chair and sat down. Mrs Badzerkian smelled of cloves. She had a small, straight mouth and a thin moustache on her upper lip, which fascinated Victor, as he had never seen one on a woman before, not one at such short range, anyway. He never mentioned Mrs Badzerkian's moustache to his mother, knowing it was considered ugly, but in a strange way, her moustache was the thing he liked best about her. The rest of her was dull, uninteresting, and vaguely unfriendly. She always pretended to listen carefully to his poetry recitals, but he felt that she fidgeted, thought of other things while he spoke, and was glad when it was over. Today, Victor recited very well and without any hesitation, standing in the middle of the living room floor and facing the two women, who were then having their second cups of tea.

'*Très bien*,' said his mother. 'Now you may have a cookie.'

Victor chose from the plate a small round cookie with a drop of orange goo in its centre. He kept his knees close together when he sat down. He always felt Mrs Badzerkian looked at his knees with distaste. He often wished she would make some remark to his mother about his being old enough for long pants, but she never had, at least not within his hearing. Victor learned from his mother's conversation with Mrs Badzerkian that the Lorentzes were coming for dinner tomorrow evening. It was probably for them that the terrapin stew was going to be made. Victor was glad that he would have the terrapin one more day to play with. Tomorrow morning, he thought, he would ask his mother if he could take the terrapin down on the sidewalk for a while, either on a leash or in the paper box, if his mother insisted.

' – like a chi-ild!' his mother was saying, laughing, with a glance at him, and Mrs Badzerkian smiled shrewdly at him with her small, tight mouth.

Victor had been excused, and was sitting across the room with a book on the studio couch. His mother was telling Mrs Badzerkian how he had played with the terrapin. Victor frowned down at his book, pretending not to hear. His mother did not like him to open his mouth to her or her guests once he had been excused. But now she was calling him her 'lee-tle ba-aby Veec-tor . . .'

He stood up with his finger in the place in his book. 'I don't see why it's childish to look at a terrapin!' he said, flushing with sudden anger. 'They are very interesting animals, they – '

His mother interrupted him with a laugh, but at once the laugh disappeared and she said sternly, 'Veector, I thought I had excused you. Isn't that correct?'

He hesitated, seeing in a flash the scene that was going to take place when Mrs Badzerkian had left. 'Yes, Mama, I'm sorry,' he said. Then he sat down and bent over his book again. Twenty minutes later, Mrs Badzerkian left. His mother scolded him for being rude, but it was not a five- or ten-minute scolding of the kind he had expected. It lasted hardly two minutes. She had forgotten to buy heavy cream, and she wanted Victor to go downstairs and get some. Victor put on his grey woollen jacket and went out. He always felt embarrassed and conspicuous in the jacket, because it came just a little bit below his short pants and he looked as if he had nothing on underneath the coat.

Victor looked around for Frank on the sidewalk, but he didn't see him. He crossed Third Avenue and went to a delicatessen in the big building that he could see from the living room window. On his way back, he saw Frank walking along the sidewalk, bouncing a ball. Now Victor went right up to him.

'Hey,' Victor said. 'I've got a terrapin upstairs.'

'A what?' Frank caught the ball and stopped.

'A terrapin. You know, like a turtle. I'll bring him down tomorrow morning and show you, if you're around. He's pretty big.'

'Yeah? – why don't you bring him down now?'

'Because we're gonna eat now,' said Victor. 'See you.' He went into his building. He felt he had achieved something. Frank had looked really interested. Victor wished he could bring the terrapin down now, but his mother never liked him to go out after dark, and it was practically dark now.

When Victor got upstairs, his mother was still in the kitchen. Eggs were boiling and she had put a big pot of water on a back burner. 'You took him out again!' Victor said, seeing the terrapin's box on the counter.

'Yes, I prepare the stew tonight,' said his mother. 'That is why I need the cream.'

Victor looked at her. 'You're going to – You have to kill it tonight?'

'Yes, my little one. Tonight.' She jiggled the pot of eggs.

'Mama, can I take him downstairs to show Frank?' Victor asked quickly. 'Just for five minutes, Mama. Frank's down there now.'

'Who is Frank?'

'He's that fellow you asked me about today. The blond fellow we always see. Please, Mama.'

His mother's black eyebrows frowned. 'Take the *terrapène* downstairs? Certainly not. Don't be absurd, my baby! The *terrapène* is not a toy!'

Victor tried to think of some other lever of persuasion. He had not removed his coat. 'You wanted me to get acquainted with Frank – '

'Yes. What has that got to do with a terrapin?'

The water on the back burner began to boil.

'You see, I promised him I'd – ' Victor watched his mother lift the terrapin from the box, and as she dropped it into the boiling water, his mouth fell open. '*Mama!*'

'What is this? What is this noise?'

Victor, open-mouthed, stared at the terrapin, whose legs were now racing against the steep sides of the pot. The terrapin's mouth opened, its eyes looked directly at Victor for an instant, its head arched back in torture, the open mouth sank beneath the seething water – and that was the end. Victor blinked. It was dead. He came closer, saw the four legs and the tail stretched out in the water, its head. He looked at his mother.

She was drying her hands on a towel. She glanced at him, then said, 'Ugh!' She smelled her hands, then hung the towel back.

'Did you have to kill him like that?'

'How else? The same way you kill a lobster. Don't you know that? It doesn't hurt them.'

He stared at her. When she started to touch him, he stepped back. He thought of the terrapin's wide-open mouth, and his eyes suddenly flooded with tears. Maybe the terrapin had been screaming and it hadn't been heard over the bubbling of the water. The terrapin had looked at him, wanting him to pull him out, and he hadn't moved to help him. His mother had tricked him, done it so fast, he couldn't save him. He stepped back again. 'No, don't touch me!'

His mother slapped his face, hard and quickly.

Victor set his jaw. Then he about-faced and went to the closet and threw his jacket on to a hanger and hung it up. He went into the living room and fell down on the sofa. He was not crying now, but his mouth opened against the soft pillow. Then he remembered the terrapin's mouth and he closed his lips. The terrapin had suffered, otherwise it would not have moved its legs fast to get out. Then he wept, soundlessly as the terrapin, his mouth open. He put both hands over his face, so as not to wet the sofa. After a long while, he got up. In the kitchen, his mother was humming, and every few minutes he heard her quick, firm steps as she went about her work. Victor had set his teeth again. He walked slowly to the kitchen doorway.

The terrapin was out on the wooden chopping board, and his mother, after a glance at him, still humming, took a knife and bore down on its blade, cutting off the terrapin's little nails. Victor half closed his eyes, but he watched steadily. The nails, with bits of skin attached to them, his mother scooped off the board into her palm and dumped into the garbage bag. Then she turned the terrapin on to its back and, with the same sharp, pointed knife, she began to cut away the pale bottom shell. The terrapin's neck was bent sideways. Victor wanted to look away, but still he stared. Now the terrapin's insides were all exposed, red and white and greenish. Victor did not listen to what his mother was saying, about cooking terrapins in Europe, before he was born. Her voice was gentle and soothing, not at all like what she was doing.

'All right, don't look at me like that!' she suddenly threw at him, stomping her foot. 'What's the matter with you? Are you crazy? Yes, I think so! You are seeck, you know that?'

Victor could not touch any of his supper, and his mother could not force him to, even though she shook him by the shoulders and threatened to slap him. They had creamed chipped beef on toast. Victor did not say a word. He felt very remote from his mother, even when she screamed right into his face. He felt very odd, the way he did sometimes when he was sick at his stomach, but he was not sick at his stomach. When they went to bed, he felt afraid of the dark. He saw the terrapin's face very large, its mouth open, its eyes wide and full of pain. Victor wished he could walk out the window and float, go anywhere he wanted to, disappear, yet be everywhere. He imagined his mother's hands on his shoulders, jerking him back, if he tried to step out the window. He hated his mother.

He got up and went quietly into the kitchen. The kitchen was absolutely dark, as there was no window, but he put his hand accurately on the knife rack and felt gently for the knife he wanted. He thought of the terrapin, in little pieces now, all mixed up in the sauce of cream and egg yolks and sherry in the pot in the refrigerator.

His mother's cry was not silent; it seemed to tear his ears off. His second blow was in her body, and then he stabbed her throat again. Only tiredness made him stop, and by then people were trying to bump the door in. Victor at last walked to the door, pulled the chain bolt back, and opened it for them.

He was taken to a large, old building full of nurses and doctors. Victor was very quiet and did everything he was asked to do, and answered the questions they put to him, but only those questions, and since they didn't ask him anything about a terrapin, he did not bring it up.

THE LEOPOLD LOCKED ROOM

Edward D. Hoch

It's not easy to choose a best or favorite story from among the nearly 600 that I've published since 1955. During that period I've also found time to publish five novels, four story collections, nine anthologies and one juvenile book, but my first love has always been writing short detective stories for publications like Ellery Queen's Mystery Magazine, *where I've appeared in every issue since May, 1973.*

This year, serving as president of the Mystery Writers of America, I've had an opportunity to look back at my writing career and to consider some of its accomplishments. As an editor, I've been called on to judge the works of my contemporaries – and perhaps I've been harder on them than I've been on myself. Still, I know which of my own *stories I enjoy re-reading, and I believe that's an important test of quality, especially in the mystery field.*

My stories about series characters – detectives like Captain Leopold and thieves like Nick Velvet – have always been the most popular of my works, though some non-series tales have also been widely reprinted. After much thought, I've chosen a Captain Leopold story, 'The Leopold Locked Room', for inclusion in this volume. It's not the most profitable of my short stories, nor did it win me an Edgar award or nomination, as other Leopold stories have done. But its fame seems to have grown since its first publication, in the October, 1971 issue of EQMM.

The story was reprinted in a 1972 anthology edited by Ellery Queen, and from there it was purchased by Universal Pictures for transformation into a popular episode of the hit television series, McMillan & Wife, *where it was retitled 'Cop of the Year'. The story has also been published in Brazil, France, Japan and England, and has been dramatized on both BBC radio and South African radio.*

Anthology appearances have also been frequent. 'The Leopold Locked Room' was included in the 1976 Mystery Writers of America anthology, Tricks and Treats, *and in a 1982 collection called* Tantalizing Locked Room Mysteries. *It is one of four of my stories included in Ellery Queen's 20-volume* Masterpieces of Mystery *set, and one of three Hoch stories chosen by Jan Broberg for his six-volume* Mystery Masters *set, published in Sweden.*

But perhaps I'm most pleased with the story's inclusion in a 1979 college literature textbook, Story to Anti-Story, *along with work by Faulkner, Hemingway, Fitzgerald, Steinbeck – just about every important modern writer of mainstream fiction. There was one science-fiction story in the book (by Arthur C. Clarke), and mine was the only mystery. Since 'The Leopold Locked Room' was chosen to represent the modern mystery story in that prestigious collection, I'm quite content to let it stand here as my choice for the best of my works up to now.*

Captain Leopold had never spoken to anyone about his divorce, and it was a distinct surprise to Lieutenant Fletcher when he suddenly said, 'Did I ever tell you about my wife, Fletcher?'

They were just coming up from the police pistol range in the basement of headquarters after their monthly target practise, and it hardly seemed a likely time to be discussing past marital troubles. Fletcher glanced at him sideways and answered, 'No, I guess you never did, Captain.'

They had reached the top of the stairs and Leopold turned in to the little room where the coffee, sandwich, and soft-drink machines were kept. They called it the lunchroom, but only by the boldest stretch of the imagination could the little collection of tables and chairs qualify as such. Rather it was a place where off-duty cops could sit and chat, which was what Leopold and Fletcher were doing now.

Fletcher bought the coffee and put the steaming paper cups on the table between them. He had never seen Leopold quite this open and personal before, anxious to talk about a life that had existed far beyond the limits of Fletcher's friendship. 'She's coming back,' Leopold said simply, and it took Fletcher an instant to grasp the meaning of his words.

'Your wife is coming back?'

'My ex-wife.'

'Here? What for?'

Leopold sighed and played with the little bag of sugar that Fletcher had given him with his coffee. 'Her niece is getting married. Our niece.'

'I never knew you had one.'

'She's been away at college. Her name is Vicki Nelson, and she's marrying a young lawyer named Moore. And Monica is coming back east for the wedding.'

'I never even knew her name,' Fletcher observed, taking a sip of his coffee. 'Haven't you seen her since the divorce?'

Leopold shook his head. 'Not for fifteen years. It was a funny thing. She wanted to be a movie star, and I guess fifteen years ago lots of girls still thought about being movie stars. Monica was intelligent and very pretty – but probably no prettier than hundreds of other girls who used to turn up in Hollywood every year back in those days. I was just starting on the police force then, and the future looked pretty bright for me here. It would have been foolish of me to toss up everything just to chase her wild dream out to California. Well, pretty soon it got to be an obsession with her, really bad. She'd spend her afternoons in movie theaters and her evenings watching old films on television. Finally, when I still refused to go west with her, she left me.'

'Just walked out?'

Leopold nodded. 'It was a blessing, really, that we didn't have children. I heard she got a few minor jobs out there – as an extra, and some technical stuff behind the scenes. Then apparently she had a nervous breakdown. About a year later I received the official word that she'd divorced me. I heard that she recovered and was back working, and I think she had another marriage that didn't work out.'

'Why would she come back for the wedding?'

'Vicki is her niece and also her godchild. We were just married when Vicki was born, and I suppose Monica might consider her the child we never had. In any event, I know she still hates me and blames me for everything that's gone wrong with her life. She told a friend once a few years ago she wished I were dead.'

'Do you have to go to this wedding, too, Captain?'

'Of course. If I stayed away it would be only because of her. At least I have to drop by the reception for a few minutes.' Leopold smiled ruefully. 'I guess that's why I'm telling you all this, Fletcher. I want a favor from you.'

'Anything, Captain. You know that.'

'I know it seems like a childish thing to do, but I'd like you to come out there with me. I'll tell them I'm working and that I can only stay for a few minutes. You can wait outside in the car if you want. At least they'll see you there and believe my excuse.'

Fletcher could see the importance of it to Leopold, and the effort that had gone into the asking. 'Sure,' he said. 'Be glad to. When is it?'

'This Saturday. The reception's in the afternoon, at Sunset Farms.'

Leopold had been to Sunset Farms only once before, at the wedding of a patrolman whom he'd especially liked. It was a low rambling place at the end of a paved driveway, overlooking a wooded valley and a gently flowing creek. If it had ever been a farm, that day was long past; but for wedding receptions and retirement parties it was the ideal place. The interior of the main building was, in reality, one huge square room, divided by accordion doors to make up to four smaller square rooms.

For the wedding of Vicki Nelson and Ted Moore, three-quarters of the large room was in use, with only the last set of accordion doors pulled shut its entire width and locked. The wedding party occupied a head table along one wall, with smaller tables scattered around the room for the families and friends. When Leopold entered the place at five minutes of two on Saturday afternoon, the hired combo was just beginning to play music for dancing.

He watched for a moment while Vicki stood, radiant, and allowed her new husband to escort her to the center of the floor. Ted Moore was a bit older than Leopold had expected, but as the pair glided slowly across the floor, he could find no visible fault with the match. He helped himself to a glass of champagne punch and stood ready to intercept them as they left the dance floor.

'It's Captain Leopold, isn't it?' someone asked. A face from his past loomed up, a tired man with a gold tooth in the front of his smile. 'I'm Immy Fontaine, Monica's stepbrother.'

'Sure,' Leopold said, as if he'd remembered the man all along. Monica had rarely mentioned Immy, and Leopold recalled meeting him once or twice at family gatherings. But the sight of him now, gold tooth and all, reminded Leopold that Monica was somewhere nearby, that he might confront her at any moment.

'We're so glad you could come,' someone else said, and he turned to greet the bride and groom as they came off the dance floor. Up close, Vicki was a truly beautiful girl, clinging to her new husband's arm like a proper bride.

'I wouldn't have missed it for anything,' he said.

'This is Ted,' she said, making the introductions. Leopold shook his hand, silently approving the firm grip and friendly eyes.

'I understand you're a lawyer,' Leopold said, making conversation.

'That's right, sir. Mostly civil cases, though. I don't tangle much with criminals.'

They chatted for a few more seconds before the pressure of guests broke them apart. The luncheon was about to be served, and the more hungry ones were already lining up at the buffet tables. Vicki and Ted went over to start the line, and Leopold took another glass of champagne punch.

'I see the car waiting outside,' Immy Fontaine said, moving in again. 'You got to go on duty?'

Leopold nodded. 'Just this glass and I have to leave.'

'Monica's in from the West Coast.'

'So I heard.'

A slim man with a mustache jostled against him in the crush of the crowd and hastily apologized. Fontaine seized the man by the arm and introduced him to Leopold. 'This here's Dr Felix Thursby. He came east with Monica. Doc, I want you to meet Captain Leopold, her ex-husband.'

Leopold shook hands awkwardly, embarrassed for the man and for himself. 'A fine wedding,' he mumbled. 'Your first trip east?'

Thursby shook his head. 'I'm from New York. Long ago.'

'I was on the police force there once,' Leopold remarked.

They chatted for a few more minutes before Leopold managed to edge away through the crowd.

'Leaving so soon?' a harsh, unforgettable voice asked.

'Hello, Monica. It's been a long time.'

He stared down at the handsome, middle-aged woman who now blocked his path to the door. She had gained a little weight, especially in the bosom, and her hair was graying. Only the eyes startled him, and frightened him just a bit. They had the intense, wild look he'd seen before on the faces of deranged criminals.

'I didn't think you'd come. I thought you'd be afraid of me,' she said.

'That's foolish. Why should I be afraid of you?'

The music had started again, and the line from the buffet tables was beginning to snake lazily about the room. But for Leopold and Monica they might have been alone in the middle of a desert.

'Come in here,' she said, 'where we can talk.' She motioned toward the end of the room that had been cut off by the accordion doors. Leopold followed her, helpless to do anything else. She unlocked the doors and pulled them apart, just wide enough for them to enter the unused quarter of the large room. Then she closed and locked the doors behind them, and stood facing him. They were two people, alone in a bare unfurnished room.

They were in an area about thirty feet square, with the windows at the far end and the locked accordion doors at Leopold's back. He could see the afternoon sun cutting through the trees outside, and the gentle hum of the air-conditioner came through above the subdued murmur of the wedding guests.

'Remember the day we got married?' she asked.

'Yes. Of course.'

She walked to the middle window, running her fingers along the frame, perhaps looking for the latch to open it. But it stayed closed as she faced him again. 'Our marriage was as drab and barren as this room. Lifeless, unused!'

'Heaven knows I always wanted children, Monica.'

'You wanted nothing but your damned police work!' she shot back, eyes flashing as her anger built.

'Look, I have to go. I have a man waiting in the car.'

'Go! That's what you did before, wasn't it? *Go, go!* Go out to your damned job and leave me to struggle for myself. Leave me to – '

'You walked out on me, Monica. Remember?' he reminded her softly. She was so defenseless, without even a purse to swing at him.

'Sure I did! Because I had a career waiting for me! I had all the world waiting for me! And you know what happened because you wouldn't come along? You know what happened to me out there? They took my money and my self-respect and what virtue I had left. They made me into a tramp, and when they were done they locked me up in a mental hospital for three years. Three years!'

'I'm sorry.'

'Every day while I was there I thought about you. I thought about how it would be when I got out. Oh, I thought. And planned. And schemed. You're a big detective now. Sometimes your cases even get reported in the California papers.' She was pacing back and forth, caged, dangerous. 'Big detective. But I can still destroy you just as you destroyed me!'

He glanced over his shoulder at the locked accordion doors, seeking a way out. It was a thousand times worse than he'd imagined it would be. She was mad – mad and vengeful and terribly dangerous. 'You should see a doctor, Monica.'

Her eyes closed to mere slits. 'I've seen doctors.' Now she paused before the middle window, facing him. 'I came all the way east for this day, because I thought you'd be here. It's so much better than your apartment, or your office, or a city street. There are 150 witnesses on the other side of those doors.'

'What in hell are you talking about?'

Her mouth twisted in a horrible grin. 'You're going to know what I knew. Bars and cells and disgrace. You're going to know the despair I felt all those years.'

'Monica – '

At that instant perhaps twenty feet separated them. She lifted one arm, as if to shield herself, then screamed in terror. 'No! Oh, God, no!'

Leopold stood frozen, unable to move, as a sudden gunshot echoed through the room. He saw the bullet strike her in the chest, toppling her backward like the blow from a giant fist. Then somehow he had his own gun out of its belt holster and he swung around toward the doors.

They were still closed and locked. He was alone in the room with Monica.

He looked back to see her crumple on the floor, blood spreading in a widening circle around the torn black hole in her dress. His eyes went to the windows, but all three were still closed and unbroken. He shook his head, trying to focus his mind on what had happened.

There was noise from outside, and a pounding on the accordion doors. Someone opened the lock from the other side, and the gap between the doors widened as they were pulled open. 'What happened?' someone asked. A woman guest screamed as she saw the body. Another toppled in a faint.

Leopold stepped back, aware of the gun still in his hand, and saw Lieutenant Fletcher fighting his way through the mob of guests. 'Captain, what is it?'

'She – someone shot her.'

Fletcher reached out and took the gun from Leopold's hand – carefully, as one might take a broken toy from a child. He put it to his nose and sniffed, then opened the cylinder to inspect the bullets. 'It's been fired recently, Captain. One shot.' Then his eyes seemed to cloud over, almost to the point of tears. 'Why the hell did you do it?' he asked. 'Why?'

Leopold saw nothing of what happened then. He only had vague and splintered memories of someone examining her and saying she was still alive, of an ambulance and much confusion. Fletcher drove him down to headquarters, to the commissioner's office, and he sat there and waited, running his moist palms up and down his trousers. He was not surprised when they told him she had died on the way to Southside Hospital. Monica had never been one to do things by halves.

The men – the detectives who worked under him – came to and left the commissioner's office, speaking in low tones with their heads together, occasionally offering him some embarrassed gesture of condolence. There was an aura of sadness over the place, and Leopold knew it was for him.

'You have nothing more to tell us, Captain?' the commissioner asked. 'I'm making it as easy for you as I can.'

'I didn't kill her,' Leopold insisted again. 'It was someone else.'

'Who? How?'

He could only shake his head. 'I wish I knew. I think in some mad way she killed herself, to get revenge on me.'

'She shot herself with *your* gun, while it was in *your* holster, and while *you* were standing twenty feet away?'

Leopold ran a hand over his forehead. 'It couldn't have been my gun. Ballistics will prove that.'

'But your gun had been fired recently, and there was an empty cartridge in the chamber.'

'I can't explain that. I haven't fired it since the other day at target practice, and I reloaded it afterwards.'

'Could she have hated you that much, Captain?' Fletcher asked. 'To frame you for her murder?'

'She could have. I think she was a very sick woman. If I did that to her – if I was the one who made her sick – I suppose I deserve what's happening to me now.'

'The hell you do,' Fletcher growled. 'If you say you're innocent, Captain, I'm sticking by you.' He began pacing again and finally turned to the commissioner. 'How about giving him a paraffin test, to see if he's fired a gun recently?'

The commissioner shook his head. 'We haven't used that in years. You know how unreliable it is, Fletcher. Many people have nitrates or nitrites on their hands. They can pick them up from dirt, or fertilizers, or fireworks, or urine, or even from simply handling peas or beans. Anyone who smokes tobacco can have deposits on his hands. There are some newer tests for the presence of barium or lead, but we don't have the necessary chemicals for those.'

Leopold nodded. The commissioner had risen through the ranks. He wasn't simply a political appointee, and the men had always respected him. Leopold respected him. 'Wait for the ballistics report,' he said. 'That'll clear me.'

So they waited. It was another forty-five minutes before the phone rang and the commissioner spoke to the ballistics man. He listened, and grunted, and asked one or two questions. Then he hung up and faced Leopold across the desk.

'The bullet was fired from your gun,' he said simply. 'There's no possibility of error. I'm afraid we'll have to charge you with homicide.'

The routines he knew so well went on into Saturday evening, and when they were finished Leopold was escorted from the courtroom to find young Ted Moore waiting for him. 'You should be on your honeymoon,' Leopold told him.

'Vicki couldn't leave till I'd seen you and tried to help. I don't know much about criminal law, but perhaps I could arrange bail.'

'That's already been taken care of,' Leopold said. 'The grand jury will get the case next week.'

'I – I don't know what to say. Vicki and I are both terribly sorry.'

'So am I.' He started to walk away, then turned back. 'Enjoy your honeymoon.'

'We'll be in town overnight, at the Towers, if there's anything I can do.'

Leopold nodded and kept on walking. He could see the reflection of his guilt in young Moore's eyes. As he got to his car, one of the patrolmen he knew glanced his way and then quickly in the other direction. On a Saturday night, no one talked to wife murderers. Even Fletcher had disappeared.

Leopold decided he couldn't face the drab walls of his office, not with people avoiding him. Besides, the commissioner had been forced to suspend him from active duty pending grand-jury action and the possible trial. The office didn't even belong to him anymore. He cursed silently and drove home to his little apartment, weaving through the dark streets with one eye out for a patrol car. He wondered if they'd be watching him, to prevent his jumping bail. He wondered what he'd have done in the commissioner's shoes.

The eleven o'clock news on television had it as the lead item, illustrated with a black-and-white photo of him taken during a case last year. He shut off the television without listening to their comments and went back outside, walking down to the corner for an early edition of the Sunday paper. The front-page headline was as bad as he'd expected: DETECTIVE CAPTAIN HELD IN SLAYING OF EX-WIFE.

On the way back to his apartment, walking slowly, he tried to remember what she'd been like – not that afternoon, but before the divorce. He tried to remember her face on their wedding day, her soft laughter on their honeymoon. But all he could remember were those mad vengeful eyes. And the bullet ripping into her chest.

Perhaps he had killed her after all. Perhaps the gun had come into his hand so easily he never realized it was there.

'Hello, Captain.'

'I – Fletcher! What are you doing here?'

'Waiting for you. Can I come in?'

'Well . . .'

'I've got a six-pack of beer. I thought you might want to talk about it.'

Leopold unlocked his apartment door. 'What's there to talk about?'

'If you say you didn't kill her, Captain, I'm willing to listen to you.'

Fletcher followed him into the tiny kitchen and popped open two of the beer cans. Leopold accepted one of them and dropped into the nearest chair. He felt utterly exhausted, drained of even the strength to fight back.

'She framed me, Fletcher,' he said quietly. 'She framed me as neatly as anything I've ever seen. The thing's impossible, but she did it.'

'Let's go over it step by step, Captain. Look, the way I see it there are only three possibilities: Either you shot her, she shot herself, or someone else shot her. I think we can rule out the last one. The three windows were locked on the outside and unbroken, the room was bare of any hiding place, and the only entrance was through the accordion doors. These were closed and locked, and although they could have been opened from the other side, you certainly would have seen or heard it happen. Besides, there were 150 wedding guests on the other side of those doors. No one could have unlocked and opened them and then fired the shot, all without being seen.'

Leopold shook his head. 'But it's just as impossible that she could have shot herself. I was watching her every minute. I never looked away once. There was nothing in her hands, not even a purse. And the gun that shot her was in my holster, on my belt. I never drew it till *after* the shot was fired.'

Fletcher finished his beer and reached for another can. 'I didn't look at her close, Captain, but the size of the hole in her dress and the powder burns point to a contact wound. The medical examiner agrees, too. She was shot from no more than an inch or two away. There were grains of powder in the wound itself, though the bleeding had washed most of them away.'

'But she had nothing in her hand,' Leopold repeated. 'And there was nobody standing in front of her with a gun. Even I was twenty feet away.'

'The thing's impossible, Captain.'

Leopold grunted. 'Impossible – unless I killed her.'

Fletcher stared at his beer. 'How much time do we have?'

'If the grand jury indicts me for first-degree murder, I'll be in a cell by next week.'

Fletcher frowned at him. 'What's with you, Captain? You almost act resigned to it! Hell, I've seen more fight in you on a routine holdup!'

'I guess that's it, Fletcher. The fight is gone out of me. She's drained every drop out of me. She's had her revenge.'

Fletcher sighed and stood up. 'Then I guess there's really nothing I can do for you, Captain. Good night.'

Leopold didn't see him to the door. He simply sat there, hunched over the table. For the first time in his life he felt like an old man.

Leopold slept late Sunday morning and awakened with the odd sensation that it had all been a dream. He remembered feeling the same way when he'd broken his wrist chasing a burglar. In the morning, on just awakening, the memory of the heavy cast had always been a dream, until he moved his arm. Now, rolling over in his narrow bed, he saw the Sunday paper where he'd tossed it the night before. The headline was still the same. The dream was a reality.

He got up and showered and dressed, reaching for his holster out of habit before he remembered he no longer had a gun. Then he sat at the kitchen table staring at the empty beer cans, wondering what he would do with his day. With his life.

The doorbell rang and it was Fletcher. 'I didn't think I'd be seeing you again,' Leopold mumbled, letting him in.

Fletcher was excited, and the words tumbled out of him almost before he was through the door. 'I think I've got something, Captain! It's not much, but it's a start. I was down at headquarters first thing this morning, and I got hold of the dress Monica was wearing when she was shot.'

Leopold looked blank. 'The dress?'

Fletcher was busy unwrapping the package he'd brought. 'The commissioner would have my neck if he knew I brought this to you, but look at this hole!'

Leopold studied the jagged, blood-caked rent in the fabric. 'It's large,' he observed, 'but with a near-contact wound the powder burns would cause that.'

'Captain, I've seen plenty of entrance wounds made by a .38 slug. I've even caused a few of them. But I never saw one that looked like this. Hell, it's not even round!'

'What are you trying to tell me, Fletcher?' Suddenly something stirred inside him. The juices were beginning to flow again.

'The hole in her dress is much larger and more jagged than the corresponding wound in her chest, Captain. That's what I'm telling you. The bullet that killed her couldn't have made this hole. No way! And that means maybe she wasn't killed when we thought she was.'

Leopold grabbed the phone and dialed the familiar number of the Towers Hotel. 'I hope they slept late this morning.'

'Who?'

'The honeymooners.' He spoke sharply into the phone, giving the switchboard operator the name he wanted, and then waited. It was a full minute before he heard Ted Moore's sleepy voice answering on the other end. 'Ted, this is Leopold. Sorry to bother you.'

The voice came alert at once. 'That's all right, Captain. I told you to call if there was anything – '

'I think there is. You and Vicki between you must have a pretty good idea of who was invited to the wedding. Check with her and tell me how many doctors were on the invitation list.'

Ted Moore was gone for a few moments and then he returned. 'Vicki says you're the second person who asked her that.'

'Oh? Who was the first?'

'Monica. The night before the wedding, when she arrived in town with Dr Thursby. She casually asked if he'd get to meet any other doctors at the reception. But Vicki told her he was the only one. Of course we hadn't invited him, but as a courtesy to Monica we urged him to come.'

'Then after the shooting, it was Thursby who examined her? No one else?'

'He was the only doctor. He told us to call an ambulance and rode to the hospital with her.'

'Thank you, Ted. You've been a big help.'

'I hope so, Captain.'

Leopold hung up and faced Fletcher. 'That's it. She worked it with this guy Thursby. Can you put out an alarm for him?'

'Sure can,' Fletcher said. He took the telephone and dialled the unlisted squad-room number. 'Dr Felix Thursby? Is that his name?'

'That's it. The only doctor there, the only one who could help Monica with her crazy plan of revenge.'

Fletcher completed issuing orders and hung up the phone. 'They'll check his hotel and call me back.'

'Get the commissioner on the phone, too. Tell him what we've got.'

Fletcher started to dial and then stopped, his finger in mid-air. 'What *have* we got, Captain?'

The commissioner sat behind his desk, openly unhappy at being called to headquarters on a Sunday afternoon, and listened bleakly to what Leopold and Fletcher had to tell him. Finally he spread his fingers on the desk-top and said, 'The mere fact that this Dr Thursby seems to have left town is hardly proof of his guilt, Captain. What you're saying is that the woman wasn't killed until later – that Thursby killed her in the ambulance. But how could he have done that with a pistol that was already in Lieutenant Fletcher's possession, tagged as evidence? And how could he have fired the fatal shot without the ambulance attendants hearing it?'

'I don't know,' Leopold admitted.

'Heaven knows, Captain, I'm willing to give you every reasonable chance to prove your innocence. But you have to bring me more than a dress with a hole in it.'

'All right,' Leopold said. 'I'll bring you more.'

'The grand jury gets the case this week, Captain.'

'I know,' Leopold said. He turned and left the office, with Fletcher tailing behind.

'What now?' Fletcher asked.

'We go talk to Immy Fontaine, my ex-wife's stepbrother.'

Though he'd never been friendly with Fontaine, Leopold knew where to find him. The tired man with the gold tooth lived in a big old house overlooking the Sound, where on this summer Sunday they found him in the back yard, cooking hot dogs over a charcoal fire.

He squinted into the sun and said, 'I thought you'd be in jail, after what happened.'

'I didn't kill her,' Leopold said quietly.

'Sure you didn't.'

'For a stepbrother you seem to be taking her death right in stride,' Leopold observed, motioning toward the fire.

'I stopped worrying about Monica fifteen years ago.'

'What about this man she was with? Dr Thursby?'

Immy Fontaine chuckled. 'If he's a doctor, I'm a plumber! He has the fingers of a surgeon, I'll admit, but when I asked him about my son's radius that he broke skiing, Thursby thought it was a leg bone. What the hell, though, I was never one to judge Monica's love life. Remember, I didn't even object when she married you.'

'Nice of you. Where's Thursby staying while he's in town?'

'He was at the Towers with Monica.'

'He's not there anymore.'

'Then I don't know where he's at. Maybe he's not even staying for her funeral.'

'What if I told you Thursby killed Monica?'

He shrugged. 'I wouldn't believe you, but then I wouldn't particularly care. If you were smart you'd have killed her fifteen years ago, when she walked out on you. That's what I'd have done.'

Leopold drove slowly back downtown, with Fletcher grumbling beside him. 'Where are we, Captain? It seems we're just going in circles.'

'Perhaps we are, Fletcher, but right now there are still too many questions to be answered. If we can't find Thursby I'll have to tackle it from another direction. The bullet, for instance.'

'What about the bullet?'

'We're agreed it could not have been fired by my gun, either while it was in my holster or later, while Thursby was in the ambulance with Monica. Therefore, it must have been fired earlier. The last time I fired it was at target practice. Is there any possibility – any chance at all – that Thursby or Monica could have gotten one of the slugs I fired into that target?'

Fletcher put a damper on it. 'Captain, we were both firing at the same target. No one could sort out those bullets and say which came from your pistol and which from mine. Besides, how would either of them gain access to the basement target range at police headquarters?'

'I could have an enemy in the department,' Leopold said.

'Nuts! We've all got enemies, but the thing is still impossible. If you believe people in the department are plotting against you, you might as well believe that the entire ballistics evidence was faked.'

'It was, somehow. Do you have the comparison photos?'

'They're back at the office. But with the narrow depth of field you can probably tell more from looking through the microscope yourself.'

Fletcher drove him to the lab, where they persuaded the Sunday-duty officer to let them have a look at the bullets. While Fletcher and the officer stood by in the interests of propriety, Leopold squinted through the microscope at the twin chunks of lead.

'The death bullet is pretty battered,' he observed, but he had to admit that the rifling marks were the same. He glanced at the identification tag attached to the test bullet: *Test slug fired from Smith & Wesson .38 Revolver, serial number 2420547.*

Leopold turned away with a sigh, then turned back.

2420547.

He fished into his wallet and found his pistol permit. *Smith & Wesson 2421622.*

'I remembered those two's on the end,' he told Fletcher. 'That's not my gun.'

'It's the one I took from you, Captain. I'll swear to it!'

'And I believe you, Fletcher. But it's the one fact I needed. It tells me how Dr Thursby managed to kill Monica in a locked room before my very eyes, with a gun that was in my holster at the time. And it just might tell us where to find the elusive Dr Thursby.'

By Monday morning Leopold had made six long-distance calls to California, working from his desk telephone while Fletcher used the squad-room phone. Then, a little before noon, Leopold, Fletcher, the commissioner, and a man from the district attorney's office took a car and drove up to Boston.

'You're sure you've got it figured?' the commissioner asked Leopold for the third time. 'You know we shouldn't allow you to cross the state line while awaiting grand-jury action.'

'Look, either you trust me or you don't,' Leopold snapped. Behind the wheel Fletcher allowed himself a slight smile, but the man from the D.A.'s office was deadly serious.

'The whole thing is so damned complicated,' the commissioner grumbled.

'My ex-wife was a complicated woman. And remember, she had fifteen years to plan it.'

'Run over it for us again,' the D.A.'s man said.

Leopold sighed and started talking. 'The murder gun wasn't mine. The gun I pulled after the shot was fired, the one Fletcher took from me, had been planted on me sometime before.'

'How?'

'I'll get to that. Monica was the key to it all, of course. She hated me so much that her twisted brain planned her own murder in order to get revenge on me. She planned it in such a way that it would have been impossible for anyone but me to have killed her.'

'Only a crazy woman would do such a thing.'

'I'm afraid she *was* crazy – crazy for vengeance. She set up the entire plan for the afternoon of the wedding reception, but I'm sure they had an alternative in case I hadn't gone to it. She wanted some place where there'd be lots of witnesses.'

'Tell them how she worked the bullet hitting her,' Fletcher urged.

'Well, that was the toughest part for me. I actually saw her shot before my eyes. I saw the bullet hit her and I saw the blood. Yet I was alone in a locked room with her. There was no hiding place, no opening from which a person or even a mechanical device could have fired the bullet at her. To you people it seemed I must be guilty, especially when the bullet came from the gun I was carrying.

'But I looked at it from a different angle – once Fletcher forced me to look at it at all! I *knew* I hadn't shot her, and since no one else physically could have, I knew no one did! If Monica was killed by a .38 slug, it must have been fired *after* she was taken from that locked room. Since she was dead on arrival at the hospital, the most likely time for her murder – to me, at least – became the time of the ambulance ride, when Dr Thursby must have hunched over her with careful solicitousness.'

'But you *saw* her shot!'

'That's one of the two reasons Fletcher and I were on the phones to Hollywood this morning. My ex-wife worked in pictures, at times in the technical end of movie-making. On the screen there are a number of ways to simulate a person being shot. An early method was a sort of compressed-air gun fired at the actor from just off-camera. These days, especially in the bloodiest of the Western and war films, they use a tiny explosive charge fitted under the actor's clothes. Of course the body is protected from burns, and the force of it is directed outward. A pouch of fake blood is released by the explosion, adding to the realism of it.'

'And this is what Monica did?'

Leopold nodded. 'A call to her Hollywood studio confirmed the fact that she worked on a film using this device. I noticed when I met her that she'd gained weight around the bosom, but I never thought to attribute it to the padding and the explosive device. She triggered it when she raised her arm as she screamed at me.'

'Any proof?'

'The hole in her dress was just too big to be an entrance hole from a .38, even fired at close range – too big and too ragged. I can thank Fletcher for spotting that. This morning the lab technicians ran a test on the bloodstains. Some of it was her blood, the rest was chicken blood.'

'She was a good actress to fool all those people.'

'She knew Dr Thursby would be the first to examine her. All she had to do was fall over when the explosive charge ripped out the front of her dress.'

'What if there had been another doctor at the wedding?'

Leopold shrugged. 'Then they would have postponed it. They couldn't take that chance.'

'And the gun?'

'I remembered Thursby bumping against me when I first met him. He took my gun and substituted an identical weapon – identical, that is, except for the serial number. He'd fired it just a short time earlier, to complete the illusion. When I drew it I simply played into their hands. There I was, the only person in the room with an apparently dying woman, and a gun that had just been fired.'

'But what about the bullet that killed her?'

'Rifling marks on slugs are made by the lands in the rifled barrel of a gun causing grooves in the lead of a bullet. A bullet fired through a smooth tube has no rifling marks.'

'What in hell kind of gun has a smooth tube for a barrel?' the commissioner asked.

'A homemade one, like a zip gun. Highly inaccurate, but quite effective when the gun is almost touching the skin of the victim. Thursby fired a shot from the pistol he was to plant on me, probably into a pillow or some other place where he could retrieve the undamaged slug. Then he reused the rifled slug on another cartridge and fired it with his homemade zip gun, right into Monica's heart. The original rifling marks were still visible and no new ones were added.'

'The ambulance driver and attendant didn't hear the shot?'

'They would have stayed up front, since he was a doctor riding with a patient. It gave him a chance to get the padded explosive mechanism off her chest, too. Once that was away, I imagine he leaned over her, muffling the zip gun as best he could, and fired the single shot that killed her. Remember, an ambulance on its way to a hospital is a pretty noisy place – it has a siren going all the time.'

They were entering downtown Boston now, and Leopold directed Fletcher to a hotel near the Common. 'I still don't believe the part about switching the guns,' the D.A.'s man objected. 'You mean to tell me he undid the strap over your gun, got out the gun, and substituted another one – all without your knowing it?'

Leopold smiled. 'I mean to tell you only one type of person could have managed it – an expert, professional pickpocket. The type you see occasionally doing an act in nightclubs and on television. That's how I knew where to find him. We called all over southern California till we came up with someone who knew Monica and knew she'd dated a man named Thompson who had a pickpocket act. We called

Thompson's agent and discovered he's playing a split week at a Boston lounge, and is staying at this hotel.'

'What if he couldn't have managed it without your catching on? Or what if you hadn't been wearing your gun?'

'Most detectives wear their guns off-duty. If I hadn't been, or if he couldn't get it, they'd simply have changed their plan. He must have signaled her when he'd safely made the switch.'

'Here we are,' Fletcher said. 'Let's go up.'

The Boston police had two men waiting to meet them, and they went up in the elevator to the room registered in the name of Max Thompson. Fletcher knocked on the door, and when it opened, the familiar face of Felix Thursby appeared. He no longer wore the mustache, but he had the same slim surgeonlike fingers that Immy Fontaine had noticed. Not a doctor's fingers, but a pickpocket's.

'We're taking you in for questioning,' Fletcher said and the Boston detectives issued the standard warnings of his legal rights.

Thursby blinked his tired eyes at them and grinned a bit when he recognized Leopold. 'She said you were smart. She said you were a smart cop.'

'Did you have to kill her?' Leopold asked.

'I didn't. I just held the gun there and she pulled the trigger herself. She did it all herself, except for switching the guns. She hated you that much.'

'I know,' Leopold said quietly, staring at something far away. 'But I guess she must have hated herself just as much.'

SECOND TALENT

James Holding

As a writer, I am a two-career man. When I was 12 years old, I sold some light verse to a magazine and immediately decided that what I wanted was to be a professional author. Someday. I attended high school, graduated from Yale University, then spent a year bicycling about Europe. On my return to America, I settled down to my first writing career: as a copywriter for the advertising agency Batten, Barton, Durstine and Osborn. I remained there for twenty-eight years, rising to Copy Chief and Vice President before retiring, at the age of 50, to try my hand at free-lance writing.

Since then I have published about 250 short mystery stories and travel articles, plus twenty children's books, while traveling extensively all over the world. Many of my stories have foreign backgrounds, are laid in far-off places which I have personally visited and observed.

As for my choice of 'Second Talent' for this book: Rio de Janeiro is one of my favorite cities, I have long enjoyed an intense interest in the pre-Columbian civilizations of South America (especially Peru), and I had, of course, a professional interest in photography from my advertising days. I thought it would be amusing to see if I could write a story that would involve all three of these rather diverse elements: 'Second Talent' is the result, and I confess to a special fondness for it.

Manuel Andradas walked to the back of the mansion through the formal gardens that encircled it. Senhor Martinho was sitting at ease on the patio overlooking his lily pond. He was sipping an iced drink and reading a pamphlet.

He glanced up in surprise as Manuel appeared. To his knowledge, he had never seen this small unremarkable fellow with the muddy brown eyes before. 'Who are you?' he asked sharply. 'I didn't hear you ring.' He put his drink down on the glass-topped table beside him.

The intruder had a camera case slung by a strap across his shoulder, and he presented his card with a half bow.

'Manuel Andradas, photographer,' Martinho read aloud. 'Oh, yes.' He looked up at Manuel. 'I know your work, Senhor. I've admired it often in *Rio Illustrated*.' With the casual politeness of the very rich, he invited Manuel to sit down.

Manuel thanked him and took a straight chair directly facing his host's chaise. He was very pleased that Martinho knew his work and recognized his name. He said obliquely, 'Since your servants are evidently out, I took the liberty of coming straight back, Senhor Martinho.' Behind him, sunlight glinted brightly on the surface of the lily pond where a pair of swans floated in stately silence.

'Ah, yes, the servants' picnic, a little treat I arrange for them annually. I had forgotten I am here alone today.' Martinho leaned back. 'Well, what do you wish of me, then, Senhor Andradas? Permission to photograph my collection?' His collection of pre-Columbian artifacts was world famous.

Manuel shook his head, then took a gun out of his jacket pocket. 'No, Senhor,' he said quietly. 'I am here to kill you.'

Aside from a startled flicker of the eyes, Martinho's lined face remained surprisingly calm. 'Indeed,' he said. 'How extraordinary. I thought you were a photographer.'

'I am,' said Andradas. 'A good one, I hope. Yet I have a second talent which pays better than photography.'

'Killing for money, you mean?'

'I prefer to call it nullification,' Manuel said with dignity. 'There is no malice in it, you understand. With me, it is purely a matter of business. I make a living, you might say, out of your dying.'

Martinho thought this might be intended as a joke. The photographer's thin lips, however, were not smiling, nor were his eyes. 'I see,' said Luis Martinho. 'You are a professional, then?'

'Exactly.'

'A professional would not sit here talking for two minutes before administering the *coup de grâce*. Therefore I think you bluff, Senhor. You attempt to put the fear of death in me so that you may thereby gain other ends. Am I not right?'

'Not even remotely right. I am here to kill you, and I shall do so. Never doubt it.'

'Then why not get it over?' Martinho reached out an arm and placed his pamphlet on the table beside his drink.

That question had been troubling Manuel, too. This was a job like any other, so why dawdle over it? Could the explanation lie in the empathy of one artist for another? Was he obscurely reluctant to nullify Martinho because the collector was a man of artistic judgment who admired his, Manuel's, work? He said to Martinho, 'I am in no hurry if you are not.'

Martinho licked his lips. 'Do you do this sort of thing frequently? Kill people, I mean?'

'Only occasionally, Senhor.'

'Who hired you to kill me?'

'I don't know. I know only the middleman, as it were. The broker.' Manuel paused. It was against his rule to mention his employers. Yet what harm could it do when Martinho was virtually a dead man? 'Have you ever heard of the Corporation? The Big Ones?'

'Isn't it some sort of criminal organization?'

Manuel nodded. 'It was the Corporation that arranged for me to nullify you . . . on behalf of some client unknown to me who will pay them generously for the service.'

'Oh.' Martinho sat quietly for a moment, then reached into his shirt pocket and drew out a packet of cigarettes. He offered one to Manuel. When the photographer refused with a shake of the head, the collector lit one for himself and returned the packet to his pocket. 'A broker, indeed. Well, there is no doubt in my mind,' Martinho said thoughtfully, 'who is paying this Corporation of yours for my removal.' He was very thoughtful.

'We all have enemies,' Manuel said sententiously.

Martinho ignored him. 'My nephew!' he said. 'Who else would wish me dead?' A certain frenetic excitement came into his voice. 'Of course. He is the poor relation. I am rich. He covets my collection for the second-rate museum of which he is curator. He knows he is my sole heir, but I am still quite robust, although old, as you see. So perhaps he has grown tired of waiting for me to die in the usual fashion, eh, in the natural way? And he is attempting to expedite matters with your help? Then he inherits my money and my collection now, not sometime in the uncertain future, but immediately. What do you think of that hypothesis? Can you find a flaw in it?'

Manuel sat like a stone. 'There are many reasons why men seek the Corporation's help.'

'The ingrate!' Martinho was at last in the grip of violent emotion. 'I refuse to die for him!'

'I'm afraid you have no choice, Senhor.' Manuel's gun pointed unwaveringly at his middle.

The collector jerked upright in his lounge chair. 'Wait! You said your killings pay better than your photography. Didn't you?'

The photographer nodded.

'Then you like money, quite obviously. Lots of it.'

'I like it.' An understatement.

'Look,' said Martinho, pointing. 'Those two Mochica vases beside the door over there are Peruvian antiquities. They are worth 5000 *novo* cruzeiros each.'

Manuel's eyes went to the vases for a moment, then switched back to Martinho. The gun didn't budge. He said nothing.

'And over on that table near you,' Martinho said, 'that's a piece of molded black-ware pottery of the Chimu Empire. It's worth 3000.'

Shocked into speech, Manuel said, 'If they are so valuable, you display them very carelessly, Senhor.'

'Oh, they are locked safely away behind my numerous burglar alarms at night, with the rest of my collection. I bring a few treasures to the patio here each day for my own pleasure, you understand. I love to look at them.'

'They don't look like much,' Manuel said.

'No they don't, do they? You'd rather have the money they'd bring?'

Manuel's expression did not change. 'You are trying to buy your life with them.'

'Well . . .'

'You can't. I told you, I am a professional. When I make a contract, I do the work.'

'That's a pity.' Martinho reached out for his drink, brought the glass to his lips and took a sip. He was perspiring. 'This thing I am using for an ashtray, do you know what it is?' he asked as he ground out his cigarette in it. 'It is a polychrome eating plate of the Incas, 500 years old, and worth 10,000 cruzeiros.'

The photographer allowed his eyes to flash to the plate on the table. Impossible, such a shabby thing! Ten thousand! Martinho choked on his drink and went into a paroxysm of coughing. Manuel looked back at him quickly. The old man was red in the face. His left hand was pressed against his chest. Finally he stopped coughing.

Manuel said, 'I am grateful to you for pointing out these valuable objects. I plan to take several of them with me when I leave.'

'To make my shooting seem the work of burglars? Art thieves?'

Andradas shrugged. 'Why not?'

Martinho's thin face took on an expression of resignation. He rubbed a hand over his white hair. 'In that case,' he said wryly, 'you'd better steal something that will make your stratagem credible.' His lips curved in a half-smile. 'I misled you about these objects on the patio. They're worthless.'

'I suspected as much.'

'Yes, trash. If you really want the authorities to believe I've been murdered by art thieves, you should steal my ear of corn.'

'Ear of corn?' Manuel tried to conceal his bewilderment.

'The treasure of my collection. A solid gold, hand-carved ear of corn, the only extant fragment of the famous golden cornfield planted by Inca goldsmiths in Cuzco's *Curi-canchi*, the Golden Enclosure, in the fifteenth century. . . .' Martinho looked into the photographer's dull eyes, saw none of his own enthusiasm for Inca culture reflected there. 'But never mind. The main thing is, my golden corn is literally priceless. Any collector, museum or dealer would give his soul to possess it.'

Manuel said, 'I don't doubt you, Senhor. Yet an ear of corn. . . .'

Martinho stood up. 'I'll show it to you,' he said.

Manuel moved the gun muzzle a fraction of an inch. 'Where is it?'

'In my study, through the doors there. I have never shown it to a stranger. But since I am to die, I would like to see it once more myself?' His voice rose at the end.

Manuel Andradas came to his feet like a cat. 'I will be right behind you.' What harm to indulge Martinho's whim? Besides, he was faintly curious about the ear of corn.

He followed Martinho across the patio and through the French doors into the collector's study, a large room lined with glass-fronted cases. On velvet-clad shelves inside the cases reposed the age-darkened objects that comprised Martinho's collection. Manuel gave them only a glance.

Martinho went directly to a waist-high steel safe of massive construction at one end of the room. Kneeling before it, he raised his eyes to the ceiling in momentary thought, then made mysterious movements with his hands before the safe door, above it, and on each side. 'I keep the corn here,' he said over his shoulder. 'This is a truly burglar-proof safe. It operates on a complex system of electrical impulses, activated and interrupted at specific points and intervals. No one can open it except me and my confidential secretary, you know.'

The safe door whispered open. Martinho removed from it a cylindrical-shaped object encased in padded velvet. He squatted on his heels and held the velvet bundle up toward Manuel. 'Here it is, Senhor Andradas. The ear of corn.'

Manuel stepped back a pace. His gun was steady. 'Unwrap it yourself,' he said.

Martinho did so. He put the velvet case on the floor before the open safe, and laid the golden ear of corn upon it. 'There,' he said, in a voice so low Manuel could scarcely hear him, 'is a finer piece than Pizarro ever plundered!' His eyes rested reverently upon the corn. 'Isn't it a marvel?' he asked. He took his packet of cigarettes from his shirt pocket and lit one, inhaling luxuriously, waiting for the photographer's comment.

Manuel said, 'Yes, it is handsome. To photograph it and get that exact sheen of ancient gold, the detail of each kernel of corn, would be . . .' He stopped. 'Close the safe. Pick up the corn and bring it to the patio.'

Martinho nodded. He pushed the door of the safe firmly shut, then picked up the ear of corn and preceded Manuel to the patio where he once more sank into his chaise. He set the golden relic on the table beside the pamphlet he had been reading.

Manuel resumed his chair. He said, 'It is well-known that you own this unique ear of corn?'

'Certainly. It is the finest item I possess.'

'Very well. I shall take it with me, as you suggest.'

'For verisimilitude only, I warn you. You cannot sell it without giving yourself away as my murderer. It is too well known.'

'I'll drop it off Sugar Loaf into the sea,' Manuel said. 'No one else shall own it. I promise you that.' The gun came up. 'Are you ready?'

'May I have a last cigarette? And a last look at my ear of corn?'

Out of respect for the old man's courage, Manuel said, 'Go ahead.'

'Can you give me a cigarette?'

'I don't smoke,' Manuel answered. 'I confine myself to cashew juice.' Then, 'But where are your own cigarettes? You had some in your shirt pocket.'

Martinho said, 'I locked those up in my safe just now.'

'Why?'

'The packet of cigarettes contained my new Japanese camera,' Martinho said. 'The Banzai Miniature. It is advertised as no bigger than a cigarette. You know it?' His tone was bland.

'I know it. I prefer the Minox, however.' Manuel paused. 'It was in your packet of cigarettes?'

'It was in my left hand until I snapped your picture with it,' said Martinho. 'I choked on my drink to cover the sound of the shutter-click. Remember? Then I slipped the camera into my packet of cigarettes.'

'You took a photograph of me?'

'Exactly. A medium close-up, I think you call it. It should show your features and your gun very clearly.'

Patiently Manuel said, 'Let us not joke, Senhor. You are telling me you had a miniature camera in your hand when I arrived here? That you took my photograph with it? That you then locked the camera in your burglar-proof safe?'

'A very precise summary.'

'Of an excellent bluff only. Oh, I take your intention: to make me suppose that when your secretary opens your safe in the course of the police investigation of your murder, they find a camera in the safe instead of this precious ear of corn. They will develop the film in the camera and will thus be presented with a picture of your murderer . . . who can be readily identified by hundreds of people as Manuel Andradas, the photographer. Is that it?'

'Precisely. Your analysis is masterly.'

'And your idea ingenious,' Manuel said, 'to lay a photographic trap for a photographer. I do not, however, believe you.'

'Why not?' Martinho was relaxed, smiling a little.

'I have watched you every moment since I arrived. You couldn't have taken my picture.'

'You looked at my Mochica vases, my Chimu black-ware and my Inca dinner plate, did you not?'

Manuel, suddenly finding it difficult to breathe, said, 'Perhaps, as you say. But that you had a miniature camera in your hand when I came upon you, that is stretching coincidence too far.'

Martinho shrugged. 'I do not usually lie, yet I might, to save my life. Perhaps this will convince you?' He handed Manuel the pamphlet he had been reading when the photographer arrived upon his patio.

A single glance revealed it was an instruction manual on how to use the new Banzai Miniature camera.

With the air of a man who has just lost a wager larger than he can afford to lose, Manuel put away his gun. 'The police, I suppose?' he asked after a painful pause.

'Not necessarily. Another idea occurs to me.' The creases in Martinho's face leading from nose to mouth corners momentarily deepened. 'My nephew's perfidy in this affair concerns me far more than your own purely mechanical involvement, Senhor Andradas.' Then he asked, 'How do you get your assignments from the Corporation?'

'A jackal named Rodolfo – '

'No, no. Do they point out your victims to you in the flesh, I mean?'

'I get only a name and address from my contact. Correct identification is entirely up to me.'

'In that case, the matter simplifies itself, I think.' Senhor Martinho nodded. 'The name and address only, eh?'

'That's all.'

'Then I suggest that what has happened, Sehnor Andradas, is that you have made an unfortunate mistake in identification today. The right name, the right address, yes, but the wrong man. Do you see?'

Manuel shook his head. 'I do not.'

Martinho's faded blue eyes narrowed. 'My nephew,' he said softly, 'happens to be my brother's son. His name is therefore Martinho, like mine. Luis Martinho, indeed, since he is my namesake.'

'Ah.' Manuel saw where the trail led now. 'But the address, Senhor?'

Martinho waved a hand at a building beyond the lily pond. 'That is my carriage house over there. I permit my nephew to live in it, rent-free. The same address, therefore, as mine.'

Manuel remained silent.

Martinho said, 'One does not arrange the sudden death of rich uncles with impunity, even in these corrupt days. My nephew must be taught a lesson.'

After a moment Manuel said without inflection, 'A permanent lesson, Senhor?'

'A permanent lesson, by all means. Will you see to it, then?'

'When?'

'Tonight? He will be at home, I know. The servants will not return from their picnic before eleven.'

'Where will you be?'

Martinho smiled. 'Across the city, dining with friends, from eight until midnight.'

'Very well,' said Manuel. '*Va bem.*'

'Then that is settled.'

'Except,' said Manuel, 'that the Corporation will withhold my money if I nullify the wrong man, especially their own client, and my reputation with them will no doubt suffer damage.'

Martinho shrugged. 'We must all pay for our mistakes – my nephew, you, I, everyone.'

Manuel sighed. 'I can think of no mistake that you have made, Senhor. For me, on the other hand, the day has been a disaster. I lose the money I was to earn for your removal. I am forced to nullify your nephew without recompense. I lose my anonymity as a Corporation employee. I, a professional photographer, am photographically tricked by an amateur. I also lose, I presume, this ear of golden corn.'

'You do, indeed.' Martinho picked up the corn and fondled it. 'However, once you have taught my nephew his lesson, I will give you the incriminating film.'

Manuel stared. 'Even though retaining it might prevent me from making another attempt on your life?'

'Even so. I'll guarantee to send the film, undeveloped, to your studio tomorrow – if you are successful tonight.'

It was evident from the blankness of the photographer's eyes that he failed to comprehend this quixotic gesture. Martinho laughed. 'You must understand that I bear you no ill will over this business. Instead, I'm grateful to you for opening my eyes to my own nephew's character. So I shall send you the film.'

'*Obrigado*,' murmured Manuel. 'Thanks.'

Martinho waved a hand at his vases, his black-ware, his ashtray. 'When you leave, you may wish to take one of these antiquities with you,' he said, 'as a slight token of my appreciation.' He rose, cradling his golden ear of corn in his hands as tenderly as one might hold a baby bird with a broken wing. 'I must say good-day to you now, Senhor Andradas. I tire rather easily these days. Thank you for relieving my tedium, however.' He shook his head. 'It is ironic that my nephew was so impatient. A few short weeks would have made all the difference to him.'

'How so?' asked Manuel.

Martinho flashed him a brilliant smile. 'My doctors assured me yesterday that I am incurably ill,' he said. 'They give me, at the most, two months to live.'

The old man walked into the house. Manuel watched him, hitching the strap of his camera case to ease its weight on his shoulder. When Martinho was gone, he thoughtfully dumped into a handy flowerpot the cigarette stubs and powdered ashes from Martinho's polychrome ashtray. Then he slipped it into his pocket.

With a trickster like Senhor Martinho, one never knew what to believe. The ashtray just might be worth something.

GUP

H.R.F. Keating

I wrote 'Gup' (the word is perhaps not so much used now as when I was a boy: it comes from the Hindi and means, according to my stern Hindustani dictionary published in Allahabad in 1916, 'idle or frivolous talk') for a particular purpose.

A few years ago the Detection Club (of Great Britain), that venerable but also rather idle and frivolous institution, began to be in financial difficulties. There was no doubt about the cause: the subscription had remained at an exceedingly modest level ever since, I think, the club's foundation under the presidency of G.K. Chesterton almost half a century earlier, while the cost of the dinners which members subsidized for themselves had risen with the rocket-like ascendant of inflation.

So it was suggested that the club might, as a fund-replenishing venture, publish a collection of stories, and that, as an added attraction, these might be linked by some sort of theme. Eventually we hit on the notion of a verdict. Each story was to be concerned with a jury and its conclusion. And, Detection Club members being the kind of person they are, it became somewhat of a point of honour deviously to make one's verdict as unverdict-like as possible while still coming within the terms of the bargain.

Hence my 'jury': the disregarded Indians of a hill-station at the height of the British Raj in the mid-1930s, with as a second, sort of sympathetic string, the committee of the local club. I might not have set my contribution in India at all, except that while lunching with the book's British publisher, Charles Monteith of Faber and Faber, to discuss the project, which eventually was given the title Verdict of 13, *he said, almost as a parting remark, 'I hope you're going to set your story in India, Harry.' Another challenge, and one I felt equally bound to accept.*

At ease in the shade on a warped wooden bench outside a tea stall in the bazaar, Sudhir Naik, the telegraph operator, blew skilfully across the milky liquid in his saucer.

'Yes,' he said, 'I sent the cable. To U.K. To the beautiful Webster Gardens, London W.5.'

For the benefit of those of his listeners who did not speak the language of the Angrezi-log he translated the word 'Gardens'. 'With many, many flowers,' he added. 'And the scent also of much frangipane. Beautiful.'

His hearers wagged their heads in appreciation. No one asked what had been said in the cable. They knew that in his own good time Sudhir Naik would tell them.

He did better. From the pocket of his uniform he drew out the crumpled sheet which he had had before him when he had operated his Morse key. There was a craning-forward of faces shining with delighted interest.

'Ah, yes,' said old Laloo, who was a servant at a bungalow on the outskirts of the hill-station and was sometimes concerned that he did not get to hear the news as quickly as others did. 'Yes, I knew Cadogan Sahib must be dead. I knew it at once when my Memsahib was saying to my Sahib, "But it's only a rumour, Peter, just bazaar gup".'

He had imitated to a nicety the strident voice of his mistress and received an appreciative chuckle from those members of the circle who came into direct contact with the English.

From the opposite pocket of his uniform Sudhir Naik then drew out his spectacles, polished them on the loose corner of the jacket, taking delicate care with the lens that was cracked, and placed them with ceremony upon his nose. He picked up the telegraph form, cleared his throat, looked round at them all and at last read out the English words.

'Mahadharwar, 13 September 1935. Miss Elizabeth Cadogan, 18 Webster Gardens, London W.5. Have to inform you with greatest regret your nephew Rupert passed away effects malaria. Letter follows. All condolences. Anketell-Brown Chairman Mahadharwar Club.'

He left a pause after the reading so that those of them with good enough English could fully savour what they had heard. Then he explained to the others that 'passed away' was what the Angrezi-log said when they meant 'died', and that Anketell-Brown Sahib was the burra sahib at the Club, and that 'effects malaria' was a lie.

Moti was only a boy. But there was always one of the long-established Club servants to explain things to him in the long sun-slowed hours while the sahibs slept in their homes under the burring drone of their new electric fans. Sometimes even the butler, Ram Lal, heavy brass-badged sash and stiff white turban laid aside, would enlighten his ignorance.

'Now Cadogan Sahib is Assistant Secretary Sahib. But Major Johnson Sahib, also known by the name of Horrible Horace, is Secretary Sahib. Understand that, little fool.'

'Oh, yes, khitmagar sahib. But if Cadogan Sahib is a burra sahib also, why is Major Johnson Sahib always angry against him?'

Ram Lal looked grave.

'That is because of Cadogan Sahib's *cigarette-case*,' he said, laying down the words, vernacular and English, one by one so that at last they formed an edifice that would stand up against even a hurricane.

Puzzled, Moti looked down for comfort to the lump of dirty rag with which he cleaned the floors of the Club's corridors, his particular charge.

'But, khitmagar sahib, why is this *cigarette-case* making Secretary Sahib always angry? Is it because Cadogan Sahib has stolen?'

The butler laughed.

'Oh, little one, you have plenty to learn. Cadogan Sahib is a true Angrezi sahib. Such a one does not steal. No, no. It is because on the *cigarette-case* there is *crest*. A *crest*, you know, is a very strong magical sign that is saying that Cadogan Sahib comes from a very, very great family across the black water.'

'But then,' asked the boy, who knew so little, 'why is not Cadogan Sahib the Secretary and Major Johnson Sahib Assistant Secretary only?'

'Ah, that is because, although Major Johnson Sahib is not at all from a great family and was Ranker Officer only before he was retiring and becoming Secretary of Mahadharwar Club, Cadogan Sahib's family is losing all, all their money. So Cadogan Sahib is having to come to India to take job. Because in U.K. now there are no jobs for foolish young men, even though they are from great families, like Cadogan Sahib.'

The boy Moti sighed, as did the other servants who were sitting or lying in this coolest spot in the Club's servant quarter.

'Yes,' said the butler, 'so that is why Major Johnson Sahib, whom the burra sahibs are calling Horrible Horace when it is behind his back, is always angry with Cadogan Sahib.'

'And it is for that reason,' added Gopal, Major Johnson's bearer, who had come across from the Johnsons' bungalow on the other side of the Club compound to join in talking the afternoon away, 'that soon after Cadogan Sahib had come Major Johnson Sahib was telling him that the servant he had got was a great badmash, when everybody is knowing he is altogether honest and good at his work also, and making him instead take that fellow Mangu who would steal from his own mother.'

'Yes, yes,' agreed Ram Lal. 'That is what Major Johnson Sahib is always doing. Moti, my boy, keep out of the way of Major Johnson Sahib. He is *not-quite-a-gentleman*.'

Moti gratefully inclined his head at the advice.

The evening before, Mangu, the thief, had been present at a small gathering of servants from here and there around the station who would meet, when they could, in the potting-shed in the corner of the garden at Ethel Cottage. Kanni, the mali whose responsibility the garden was, lived in the shed and liked to extend its hospitality to cronies whose special delight lay in discussing the sexual peccadilloes of the Angrezi-log.

'Maisie, the Man-eater,' Mangu had just proclaimed to them in English.

The others sitting round, comfortably cross-legged, all knew well that this was the name the European community had bestowed on the wife of Major Johnson, Secretary of the Mahadharwar Club. But they appreciated Mangu's reference with as much chuckling and elbow-digging as if this was the first time they had heard it.

'Maisie, the Man-eater,' Kanni repeated when the original impulse had at last died away.

He wagged his head marvellingly.

'And now,' added Mangu, 'she is beginning to gobble up Cadogan Sahib. In his sleep I have heard him mutter her name even. "Maisie, Maisie".'

His imitation was considered extraordinarily droll and he was pressed several times to repeat it.

'And,' asked Kanni at last, with a fearful leer, 'have the jaws snapped yet? Eh? Eh? Eh?'

'Ah,' Mangu answered, 'that is tonight. Tonight. Snap.'

And he brought his own stumpy and red betel-stained teeth together with a chomp that reverberated from side to side of the close, earth-smelling shed.

'Yes,' he went on after laughter, 'I heard her say to him yesterday, "Darling, Horace always plays in the Diwali Night Bridge Tournament. So tomorrow we can be together, at last." And afterwards she is telling him that always Major Johnson Sahib puts his own name on top of the pile when Anketell-Brown Sahib is making draw. And next he puts Hitchman Sahib's just underneath, so that in that way he makes sure of becoming partner with the best player in whole Mahadharwar Club. "Darling, we will have hours together, hours," she is saying. And Cadogan Sahib is saying, "Oh, Maisie".'

The laughter at Mangu's imitation of lonely, love-lorn Rupert Cadogan's voice was tremendous. It quite drowned the pops and bangs from the many crackers and rockets with which are celebrated Diwali when with lights and fireworks of every sort the Goddess Lakshmi is begged to bring modest prosperity to all in the year ahead.

That same firework-popping night Ram Lal, the butler, and Chandra, the Club billiards marker, chanced to pass each other in a dark passage as they went about their duties. They exchanged a few brief words.

'Oh, oh, great trouble, khitmagar sahib.'

'What trouble, Chandra bhai?'

'Anketell-Brown Sahib has done a terrible thing.'

'What thing, Chandra bhai?'

'When he was offered mighty bridge cup by Major Johnson Sahib to make draw for Diwali Night tournament he was not taking top piece of paper in customary manner.'

'Haiee,' said the butler, at once grasping the implications. 'So Major Johnson Sahib has not drawn Hitchman Sahib for partner?'

'Oh, khitmagar sahib, it is worse than that.'

'Worse than that, Chandra bhai?'

'Khitmagar sahib, he has drawn Murdoch Sahib.'

The butler patted his cheeks in dismay.

'Murdoch Sahib whom all are calling "rabbit",' he exclaimed.

'Already, khitmagar sahib, Major Johnson Sahib is saying, "Sorry you chaps, beastly headache, must take a stroll." But he is going, of course, back to his bungalow.'

The butler darted a glance along the passage. Beyond the open doors of the dining-room he could see that all his waiters seemed to be properly busy laying their tables. Perhaps he could afford to linger one moment more.

'And Johnson Memsahib?' he asked the billiards marker. 'Is Maisie the Man-eater playing mah-jongg tonight at Hitchman Memsahib's bungalow, as she told Major Johnson Sahib, or not?'

He hurried off then to the Dining-room. His question was not one that needed an answer.

Busy going to and fro with his arrangements for the late Diwali Night dinner – there were to be special flowers on each table as well as paper streamers criss-crossing the big dining-room this way and that – the butler did not at first believe little Moti when out in the smoky kitchen he told him that Major Johnson Sahib had returned to the Club.

'Nonsense, boy, nonsense. Secretary Sahib is having headache tonight. Secretary Sahib drew rabbit partner in Diwali Night bridge tournament. Keep a thousand times out of Secretary Sahib's way tomorrow, I warn you.'

But the boy persisted.

'Khitmagar sahib, I have seen. He was coming back. He was going again into card room. Chandra, who is on duty there tonight because nobody is playing billiards, told that Major Johnson Sahib is coming in there and he is saying, "Ha, need new score cards, I see, half a mo' and I'll fetch some".'

The butler was impressed by this wealth of detail.

'Very good, Moti,' he said. 'But all the same, keep clear of Secretary Sahib tonight and tomorrow. I have told you.'

'Yes, khitmagar sahib. And Chandra is saying that score cards were there all the time. Cadogan Sahib himself put many there before he was going.'

'Ah, Cadogan Sahib,' the butler said with a sigh.

The story of what happened when, within two minutes of leaving the Card Room to go and fetch fresh score cards from the store cupboard in his own bungalow, Major Johnson suddenly and unexpectedly returned was all over the bazaar at an early hour next day.

A huddle of boys sitting on the ground behind a flower stall busy threading garlands passed the news to and fro among themselves.

'Major Johnson Sahib came running into Club. "My wife, my wife," he was shouting.'

'Yes, "My wife, my wife, she has been shot".'

'Yes, yes. "She has been shot dead." Bang, bang. And the safe . . .'

'Yes. The burra safe of the Club in Major Johnson Sahib's bungalow, it was open. All the great cups were gone. All the money.'

'Yes, yes. Ten lakhs of rupees stolen.'

'No. Twenty. Twenty lakhs, and the Memsahib shot. Oh, that was done by terrible terrible goondas.'

'No, no. You are a fool only, Budhoo. That is what Anketell-Brown Sahib is saying. "Might be the work of some damned native," he is saying. But then Major Johnson Sahib is saying, " 'Fraid not, Anketell-Brown, I mean, damn it, you saw that cigarette-case there." '

'Yes, yes. It is the *cigarette-case* of Cadogan Sahib. The *cigarette-case* with the magic magic sign upon it to say what a great man is Cadogan Sahib. It was there by the safe.'

In the little group of women standing watching with mild envy as the bangle-seller works with his strong fingers on the hand of the young bride squatting in front of him, flexing the green glass bangle over the pliant bones, Sundari, wife of Gopal, Major Johnson's bearer, relays from time to time choice items from the unprecedentedly rich store that her husband has just acquired in the course of his duties.

'Anketell-Brown Sahib thought it might be a thing done by a damn-native.'

Her hearers sigh gustily at this. But, with a proud lift of her bosom, sending the red sari slipping a little, Sundari immediately trumps her own ace.

'But, no, they are saying, "It cannot be the work of some goonda because, look, here is the *cigarette-case* that the thief has left and it is the *cigarette-case* of Cadogan Sahib." '

Such indrawn breaths, such tongue-cluckings at this. Such glances from one to the other. The traditional moment of triumph when the banglewallah at last gets the thin ring of green glass over the mounded knuckles and on along in a rush to join its fellows at the slim wrist goes quite unmarked.

And Sundari has yet more to dole out.

She waits till the young bride has risen to her feet, modestly drawn her sari over her head and slipped to the outer edge of the circle, looking downwards always at her new acquisition. And she waits yet longer, until the bangle-seller's first burst of noisy salesmanship has petered away. And only then does she release the next morsel.

'My husband says it was Major Johnson Sahib himself who suggested what they should do.'

'Aiee, and what was that, Sundaribehn?'

Sundari looked round to make sure that every person in her audience was hanging on her lips, not excluding the bangle-seller from whom she hoped before all was told to get the offer of a bangle at even as little as half the regular price, and at last when she saw the moment was right she told them.

'Major Johnson Sahib is saying to Anketell-Brown Sahib, "My dear chap, do you think that is wise?".'

The old woman nearby who sold plantains, her little stock carefully laid out on a piece of gunny in front of her, each separate banana of the ten given its exact best place in the pattern, actually broke in on the circle at this point, her curiosity was so whetted and her understanding so bemused.

'What was wise? What was not wise? Oh, kind one, clear a poor old person's head.'

Sundari felt then that this was indeed a day of days. She pretended to ignore the old woman, turning elaborately to her neighbours on the other side.

'Yes,' she said, 'Major Johnson Sahib himself was saying that. Him it was and not another, as that Mangu fellow is trying to make out.'

'Oh, aiee, that one is a thief, a goonda of goondas.'

Such loyalty earned from Sundari a prompt reward.

'Yes,' she said. 'Very quietly Major Johnson Sahib is saying, "Do you think it is wise? To make it a police matter?" And then Anketell-Brown Sahib answered, "But we have to tell them." And Major Johnson Sahib said then, "But if he gets into the hands of the police, there'll have to be a trial. And think who the judge might be: a damned Indian. And what a field day it's going to make for the Indian papers, whoever's on the bench." '

Sundari, playing from strength, gave a little sigh.

'I am not knowing what "field day" means,' she said. 'And neither is my husband. But it is bad. Very bad.'

Devi, the wife of the sweetmeats merchant, who was making a concession by stopping to listen to such people as Sundari and her friends – but with such a story to be heard, the story of a lifetime even, some dignity had to be sacrificed – weighed in with a comment here, the comment of a woman of experience.

'Oh, the Angrezi-log, they are not at all liking that they should be written about in the Indian papers. It gives them what they call *a bad name*. It is as if there had been painted many times on a wall, "Down With British Sarkar". But papers cannot so easily be tarred over.'

There was a great deal of wise nodding and murmuring over that. Rather more than was necessary, only it was seldom one got a chance of agreeing with the wife of the sweetmeats merchant.

Sundari, feeling that attention was beginning to slip away from her, offered another juicy morsel to be gulped.

'Yes,' she said, 'so then Anketell-Brown Sahib and Hitchman Sahib and all the great ones of the Club are agreeing. "We'll flush the blighter out ourselves and settle the matter between gentlemen".'

'So they are hunting, hunting Cadogan Sahib?' asked one of the less well-informed wives.

Sundari waited to give her answer, that yet more appetizing gobbet than any before. She waited to feel the whole weight of everyone's curiosity tugging at her. Waited too long.

'Oh, no,' said the sweetmeats merchant's wife, 'everybody well knows how hunting and hunting was not necessary. Not at all necessary.'

And she laughed her jolly, well-fed, sugar-sweetened laugh, rolling up from deep in her rounded belly and lasting long and long.

The manager of Rivoli Talkies, the station's single cinema, came out to the sweetmeats shop himself instead of sending a boy to buy his customary midday badam halwa. He discussed the price of sugar with the sweetmeats merchant and the merits of replacing the cinema's great flapping punkahs with the new electric fans. He had hoped that Bhabi Rani might himself refer first to the subject of real interest. But before long he had to admit that that would have been too much to expect.

He took a breath.

'And what is all this about Cadogan Sahib?' he asked. 'They are saying that the hunt for him never found.'

The sweetmeats merchant wagged his many chins in agreement.

'Yes, yes, that is perfectly true, Manager Sahib. They did not find. They did not need to find. Because, although Cadogan Sahib did not return to his bungalow all night, in the morning he came into the Club daftar just as if it was an ordinary day. "Good morning, Chatterjee," he said to that Bengali clerk they have there. Just as he always does. He is not long from England, you know.'

'Yes, yes. To me also when I am showing him into best armchair seats he is saying always, "Thank you, Manager Sahib." But what after he came into the office, Mr Rani? What did they do to him then?'

It was galling to have to ask right out, but he had been away arranging the new films – there was the newsreel of the King-Emperor's Silver Jubilee, something that was bound to bring in customers, both European and Indian – and he had missed too much of the talk.

Bhabi Rani was generous.

'Manager Sahib,' he said as a preliminary, 'please try some of this new sweet my cook has made only this morning. I think you would find it very good.'

The cinema manager accepted graciously.

'Yes,' Bhabi Rani said, watching the fat pink tongue explore the crisp golden strands. 'Yes, all their hunting and punting had gone for nothing. In came Cadogan Sahib. At first they did not know at all what to do. So Cadogan Sahib went, with no one saying a word, into his own chota daftar where he works every day and he began as usual to do his accounts. Outside, they were having a long, long discussion with Anketell-Brown Sahib till in the end they were deciding just to lock him in where he was, and he was all the time protesting and exclaiming and saying, "Why is this?".'

'Yes, yes. Well, well. But he could do nothing but protest, a proved thief. Yes, he should be kept under lock and key. And a murderer also.'

'Yes, yes. That is what they are saying one to another. "The chap is a murderer after all, damn it." And so then they were sending messages to all members of the Club Committee. One I have read myself. The boy they sent much enjoyed that new sweet you are enjoying also, Manager Sahib.'

'Yes, yes?' inquired the manager, between hasty licks.

'Ah, yes. This is what the message said: "I hereby summon you to a Special Extraordinary Meeting of the Committee of the Mahadharwar Club to be held this day at 2 p.m. Agenda: private".'

'Yes,' said the manager, the last of the new sweet disposed of, 'that was very good, Mr Rani. Very good. Excellent.'

He sucked at his teeth.

'And we are well knowing what is that "private",' he added.

'Yes, yes,' said the sweetmeats merchant. 'It is the trial and execution of Cadogan Sahib, no less.'

Old Laloo, out in the bungalow – well called Heathview – on the outskirts of the station where, he was always afraid, the news penetrated much too slowly, took what compensatory pleasure he could for his isolation in instructing the ayah whom the sahibs had brought with them from the Punjab. But, since they shared only a few words in various languages, communication was not easy.

However, he did his best.

'Now, Bhagwati, listen. This is what I heard with my own ears. I heard it from Sudhir Naik, who is a big big telegraph operator.'

Here a little work on an imaginary Morse key and an assumed air of tremendous dignity conveyed much.

'So, listen, Bhagwati, and hear. This is the cable Anketell-Brown Sahib himself was sending across the black water to the beautiful Webster Gardens.'

The pretty Punjabi ayah's eyes were wide and expectant as dark parched pools in a dried-up river bed.

'*Nephew Rupert* – that is Cadogan Sahib, you are understanding – *Nephew Rupert is passing out from very bad malaria. Many bitter tears. Anketell-Brown Sahib, Chairman of Mahadharwar Club.*'

The girl repeated with carefully moving silent lips the awkward English words. When old Laloo thought they had thoroughly sunk in he explained laboriously that 'very bad malaria' was not the cause of Cadogan Sahib's death.

Bhatu, the sweeper at Major Johnson's bungalow, was the hero that day of the whole sweepers' colony tucked away in a narrow cleft at the edge of the station well downwind of the other inhabitants.

'Now I am telling you,' he said to the squatting group outside his dark little tumbledown hut. 'It was this way. There in the dark in the garden Cadogan Sahib was kneeling on the ground behind a big bed of tall canna plants. He had come running running out when they had heard the heavy steps of a sahib in shoes coming near. "Please go. Go," Maisie the Man-eater had cried. And then came the noise of a gun shooting.'

'Yes, yes,' agreed Bhatu's friend Jai, the sweeper at Cadogan Sahib's bungalow. 'A shot from a gun. Only a fool would think that was a Diwali cracker or a rocket. Like my sahib, Cadogan Sahib.'

'Yes, yes, yes,' Bhatu said. 'I was there, seeing all, and I knew that it was a gun. It was the gun Major Johnson Sahib had in the drawer of his bedside teapoy, the one that no damn-native is supposed to know about. But Cadogan Sahib, on the ground making his white white trousers all dirty, he thought it was another rocket only and that Maisie the Man-eater would lie and lie for him and all would be well.'

'But what was it that you did, Bhatu bhai, when you heard the gun?' asked Jai.

He knew, of course. But he was aware too of his duty as storyteller's best friend.

'Oh, bhai, then at once I was going quietly quietly to see what had happened in bungalow.'

'Good, good. And what was it that you saw?'

Bhatu's eyes shone. This was the best bit of all. His utter triumph.

'Oh, Jai bhai, what did I see? I saw Maisie the Man-eater shot dead, with what she is calling "my kimono" only just dragged on to her naked body. And then . . . And then . . .'

'Yes? Then?'

'Then I saw Major Johnson Sahib pull off that kimono and instead pull on first those clothes the memsahibs wear under their clothes and then the dress of the memsahib.'

'Yes, yes,' Jai explained to the others. 'It was necessary for Major Johnson Sahib to do that so that it was looking as if Maisie Memsahib had just come back from playing the game of mah-jongg with Hitchman Memsahib and she had found Cadogan Sahib stealing from safe.'

'That is so,' Bhatu agreed gravely. 'He had to do that, and he had also to move *cigarette-case* with magical crest, which in the end is not very strong magic, from bedside teapoy where Cadogan Sahib had left it to a place next to the safe, which he had also opened wide, so that there Anketell-Brown Sahib would see. Oh, yes, Major Johnson Sahib is very clever sahib, very clever sahib indeed'

It had taken a long time for little Moti, to whom almost everything that went on among the sahibs in the Club where his whole duty lay was so much arcane mystery, to learn the news. And even longer for him to acquire any glimmerings of an idea of its meaning. But at last now he had his questions to ask.

'Oh, Chandra, tell me please.'

The billiards marker, still buzzingly happy from all the things he knew, condescended to take notice.

'Tell what, little one? There is much, much, much to tell.'

'Oh, Chandra, say is it true that they have locked up Cadogan Sahib in his own daftar?'

Chandra smiled, a grim smile.

'Yes, in the chota daftar he is under lock and key.'

'But, Chandra, is it not that he is saying, and shouting even, "What is this? Why are you doing this?" '

'Oh, yes, little boy. Saying and protesting and repeating, that is what Cadogan Sahib was doing.'

Out in the bungalow called Heathview, that most distant of bungalows from the hub of activity, Bhagwati, the pretty little ayah, was reduced from lack of hearers capable of understanding her Punjabi to telling the little kicking white baby she looked after all about everything.

'And they are sending cable, babyji. Yes, cable, they are sending to the beautiful, beautiful Webster Gardens where there is a marble baradari in the middle of a big, big tank. And in the cable they are saying "Very bad malaria," and what is that meaning, babyji?'

She cooed at the little kicking pink-skinned creature.

'It is meaning they have made him shoot with his own gun, babyji. Bang, bang, bang, bang.'

But it was actually little Moti who turned out to have after all perhaps the best tale of them all to tell. Because it was he, too insignificant to be noticed squatting in the passage swirling his lump of grey rag round on the floor, hopping at intervals from one side to the other, who had seen, in the middle of the luncheon hour when none of the white sahibs was anywhere about, Major Johnson come quickly along, hastily pull from his pocket the key of the chota daftar where Rupert Cadogan was a prisoner awaiting trial, slip it into the lock, open the door a crack and slide rapidly in.

And it was Moti who, crouching up against the door, heard what that low intense voice on the far side had said.

'Oh, khitmagar sahib, this is how Major Johnson Sahib talked. This and this only, I am telling you.'

'Yes, yes. Repeat to me just what you heard, boy. And tell the truth. Tell the truth, you are not in court.'

'Yes, khitmagar sahib. This is, in truth, what Major Johnson Sahib said. "Now listen to me, Cadogan, because I shan't give you another chance".'

The boy's sharp ear had caught every nuance of the hardly understood English and he repeated the words now faithfully as a gramophone.

'And "Yes?" Cadogan Sahib said. Then Major Johnson Sahib said: "You know Maisie shot herself? Yes, shot herself from the sheer shame of it." And Cadogan Sahib is saying, "Oh, my God. I seduced her, Johnson. I seduced her".'

'Maisie the Man-eater,' the butler murmured, but only to himself.

'Then Major Johnson Sahib is saying this,' the boy went on. 'He is saying: "Do you want what you did, and what she did, to become so much common knowledge? Do you want everybody to know, even the servants perhaps?" And Cadogan Sahib is saying, "No, no. Not that. My God, not that".'

'And then?' the butler asked, all dignity forgotten.

'Then, khitmagar sahib, Major Johnson Sahib is saying: "Then you must do the decent thing, Cadogan. Plead guilty when the Committee sit, and take the gentleman's way out when they offer it." And then he gave a little laugh like this, khitmagar sahib.'

In the quiet of the compound where the two of them were standing in the shade of a darkly green neem tree there came into the hot, still air, extraordinarily lifelike, the sound of Major Johnson's curtly brutal laugh.

The boy looked up to the imposing figure of the butler.

'Then Major Johnson Sahib said: "In any case, man, you won't be believed if you do tell the truth. And if you don't take the chance that's offered you, I can tell you twenty years in an Indian gaol's a whole lot worse than a clean death".'

In the bazaar afterwards a score of versions of the trial by Committee were retailed. The embroidery differed. But the essentials were always there. Not one version, for instance, omitted the moment when Anketell-Brown Sahib had said, 'A thief. That's what I can't get over. No more than a common thief.' And there had followed a general murmur of sad assent.

And, like every other one, the version told by the barber, a sharp much-travelled man who had picked up a good deal of English, though much of it appallingly mispronounced, had of course included what was really the climactic moment of the whole trial.

Squatting on his heels, working his thin-as-a-wafer cut-throat razor round the lean square jawbone of the astrologer whose place of business was in the porch of St Thomas's Church, the fellow had paused the proper length of time and then had quoted with exact solemnity Anketell-Brown's most solemnly uttered words.

' "And that is werdict of you all?" '

THE LOCKED ROOM

Peter Lovesey

'I read nothing except the criminal news and the agony column,' said Sherlock Holmes in 'The Adventure of the Noble Bachelor'. 'The latter is always instructive.' Good old Sherlock! Good old Conan Doyle! I devoured those wonderful short stories as a boy. They were the first crime fiction I read.

But I owe a bigger debt to Holmes. I emulated him by studying the small ads in the newspapers, and there, one morning in The Times, *I found the announcement of a competition for a first crime novel. I wrote a book called* Wobble to Death, *set in London in 1879, and, happily, it won.*

Other novels followed, all set in the Victorian period. To get the details right, I researched the period carefully. A great discovery was a newspaper library, where I spent weeks studying the papers of the period: it was the nearest thing to a time machine that I have ever experienced. I turned the pages of those century-old papers, and the impact was amazing. The past was recaptured, with an immediacy that no history book could equal. I followed the daily progress of the hunt for Jack the Ripper, the building of the underground railway, the scandals of the Prince of Wales.

But back to Sherlock Holmes. In the newspaper library, I could study for myself the personal columns which Holmes found so instructive. I found them more fascinating than descriptions of historical events. Often, the personalities of those involved came vividly to life in the few words of the advertisements.

'The Locked Room' is my attempt to show how tantalizing such glimpses of the past can be. I found the advertisement mentioned in the story, and I knew that I had to use it, exactly as it was.

I won't say more: you must read it for yourself.

Sometimes, when the shop was quiet, Braid would look up at the ceiling and give a thought to the locked room overhead. He was mildly curious, no more. If the police had not taken an interest he would never have done anything about it.

The inspector appeared one Wednesday soon after eleven, stepping in from Leadenhall Street with enough confidence about him to show he was no tourist. Neither was he in business; it is one of the City's most solemn conventions that, between ten and four, nobody is seen on the streets in a coat. This was a brown imitation leather coat, categorically not City at any hour. Gaunt and pale, a band of black hair trained across his head to combat baldness, he stood back from the counter, not interested in buying cigarettes, waiting rather, one hand in a pocket of the coat, the other fingering his woollen tie, while the last genuine customer named his brand and took his change.

When the door was shut he came a step closer and told Braid, 'I won't take up much of your time. Detective Inspector Gent, C.I.D.' The hand that had been in the pocket now exhibited a card. 'Routine inquiry. You are Frank Russell Braid, the proprietor of this shop?'

Braid nodded, and moistened his lips. He was perturbed at hearing his name articulated in full like that, as if he were in court. He had never been in trouble with the police. Never done a thing he was ashamed of. Twenty-seven years he had served the public loyally over this counter. He had not received a single complaint he could recollect, nor made one. From the small turnover he achieved he had always paid whatever taxes the government imposed. Some of his customers – bankers, brokers and accountants – made fortunes and talked openly of tax dodges. That was not Frank Braid's way. He believed in fate. If it was decreed that he should one day be rich, it would happen. Meanwhile he would continue to retail cigarettes and tobacco honestly and without regret.

'I believe you also own the rooms upstairs, sir?'

'Yes.'

'There is a tenant, I understand.'

So Messiter had been up to something. Braid clicked his tongue, thankful that the suspicion was not directed his way, yet irritated at being taken in. From the beginning Messiter had made a good impression. The year of his tenancy had seemed to confirm it. An educated man, decently dressed, interesting to talk to and completely reliable with the rent. This was a kick in the teeth.

'His name, sir?'

'Messiter.' With deliberation Braid added, 'Norman Henry Messiter.'

'How long has Mr Messiter been a lodger here?'

'*Lodger* isn't the word. He uses the rooms as a business address. He lives in Putney. He started paying rent in September last year. That would be thirteen months, wouldn't it?'

It was obvious from the inspector's face that this was familiar information. 'Is he upstairs this morning, sir?'

'No. I don't see a lot of Mr Messiter. He calls on Tuesdays and Fridays to collect the mail.'

'Business correspondence?'

'I expect so. I don't examine it.'

'But you know what line Mr Messiter is in?'

It might have been drugs from the way the inspector put the question.

'He deals in postage stamps.'

'It's a stamp shop upstairs?'

'No. It's all done by correspondence. This is simply the address he uses when he writes to other dealers.'

'Odd,' the inspector commented. 'I mean, going to the expense of renting rooms when he could just as easily carry on the business from home.'

Braid would not be drawn. He would answer legitimate questions, but he was not going to volunteer opinions. He busied himself tearing open a carton of cigarettes.

'So it's purely for business?' the inspector resumed. 'Nothing happens up there?'

That started Braid's mind racing. Nothing *happens* . . . ? What did they suspect? Orgies? Blue films?

'It's an unfurnished flat,' he said. 'Kitchen, bathroom and living room. It isn't used.'

At that the inspector rubbed his hands. 'Good. In that case you can show me over the place without intruding on anyone's privacy.'

It meant closing for a while, but most of his morning regulars had been in by then.

'Thirteen months ago you first met Mr Messiter,' the inspector remarked on the stairs.

Strictly it was untrue. As it was not put as a question, Braid made no response.

'Handsome set of banisters, these, Mr Braid. Individually carved, are they?'

'The building is at least 200 years old,' Braid told him, grateful for the distraction. 'You wouldn't think so to look at it from Leadenhall Street. You see, the front has been modernized. I wouldn't mind an old-fashioned front if I were selling silk hats or umbrellas, but cigarettes – '

'Need a more contemporary display,' the inspector cut in as if he had heard enough. '*Was* it thirteen months ago you first met Mr Messiter?'

Clearly this had some bearing on the police enquiry. It was no use prevaricating. 'In point of fact, no. More like two years.' As the inspector's eyebrows peaked in interest, Braid launched into a rapid explanation. 'It was purely in connection with the flat. He came in here one day and asked if it was available. Just like that, without even seeing over the place. At the time, I had a young French couple as tenants. I liked them and I had no intention of asking them to leave. Besides, I know the law. You can't do that sort of thing. I told Mr Messiter. He said he liked the situation so much that he would wait till they moved out, and to show good faith he was ready to pay the first month's rent as a deposit.'

'Without even seeing inside?'

'It must seem difficult to credit, but that was how it was,' said Braid. 'I didn't take the deposit, of course. Candidly, I didn't expect to see him again. In my line of business you sometimes get people coming in off the street simply to make mischief. Well, the upshot was that he *did* come back – repeatedly. I must have seen the fellow once a fortnight for the next eleven months. I won't say I understood him any better, but at least I knew he was serious. So when the French people eventually went back to Marseilles, Mr Messiter took over the flat.' By now they were standing on the bare boards of the landing. 'The accommodation is unfurnished,' he said in explanation. 'I don't know what you hope to find.'

If Inspector Gent knew, he was not saying. He glanced through the open door of the bathroom. The place had the smell of disuse.

He reverted to his theme. 'Strange behaviour, waiting all that time for a flat he doesn't use.' He stepped into the kitchen and tried a tap. Water the colour of weak tea spattered out. 'No furniture about,' he went on. 'You must have thought it was odd, not bringing furniture.'

Braid passed no comment. He was waiting by the door of the locked room. This, he knew, was where the interrogation would begin in earnest.

'What's this – the living room?' the inspector asked. He came to Braid's side and tried the door. 'Locked. May I have the key, Mr Braid?'

'That isn't possible, I'm afraid. Mr Messiter changed the lock. We – er – came to an agreement.'

The inspector seemed unsurprised. 'Paid some more on the rent, did he? I wonder why.' He knelt by the door. 'Strong lock. Chubb mortice.

No good trying to open that with a piece of wire. How did he justify it, Mr Braid?'

'He said it was for security.'

'It's secure, all right.' Casually, the inspector asked, 'When did you last see Mr Messiter?'

'Tuesday.' Braid's stomach lurched. 'You don't suspect he is – '

'Dead in there? No, sir. Messiter is alive, no doubt of that. Active, I would say.' He grinned in a way Braid found disturbing. 'But I wouldn't care to force this without a warrant. I'll be arranging that. I'll be back.' He started downstairs.

'Wait,' said Braid, going after him. 'As the landlord, I think I have the right to know what you suspect is locked in that room.'

'Nothing dangerous or detrimental to health, sir,' the inspector told him without turning his head. 'That's all you need to know. You trusted Messiter enough to let him fit his own lock, so with respect you're in no position to complain about rights.'

After the inspector had left, Braid was glad he had not been stung into a response he regretted, but he was angry, and his anger refused to be subdued through the rest of the morning and afternoon. It veered between the inspector, Messiter and himself. He recognized now his mistake in agreeing to the fitting of the lock, but to be rebuked like a gullible idiot was unjust. Messiter's request had seemed innocent enough at the time. Well, it had crossed Braid's mind that what was planned could be the occasional afternoon up there with a girl, but he had no objection to that if it was discreet. He was not narrow-minded. In its two centuries of existence the room must have seen some passion. Crime was quite another thing, not to be countenanced.

He had trusted Messiter, been impressed by his sincerity. The man had seemed genuinely enthusiastic about the flat, its old-world charm, the high, corniced ceilings and the solid doors. To wait, as he had, over a year for the French people to leave had seemed a commitment, an assurance of good faith.

It was mean and despicable. Whatever was locked in that room had attracted the interest of the police. Messiter must have known this was a possibility when he took the rooms. He had cynically and deliberately put at risk the reputation of the shop. Customers were quick to pick up the taint of scandal. When this got into the paper years of goodwill and painstaking service would go for nothing.

That afternoon, when Braid's eyes turned to the ceiling, he was not merely curious about the locked room. He was asking questions. Angry, urgent questions.

By six, when he closed, the thing had taken a grip on his mind. He had persuaded himself he had a right to know the extent of Messiter's deceit. Dammit, the room belonged to him. He would not sleep without knowing what was behind that locked door.

And he had thought of a way of doing it.

In the back was a wooden ladder some nine feet long. Years before, when the shop was a glover's, it had been used to reach the high shelves behind the counter. Modern shop design kept everything in easy reach. Where gloves had once been stacked in white boxes were displays of Marlboro country and the pure gold of Benson and Hedges. One morning in the summer he had taken the ladder outside the shop to investigate the working of the sun-blind, which was jammed. Standing several rungs from the top, he had been able to touch the ledge below the window of the locked room.

The evening exodus was over, consigning Leadenhall Street to surrealistic silence, when Braid propped the ladder against the shop-front. The black marble and dark-tinted glass of banks and insurance blocks glinted funereally in the street-lights, only the brighter windows of the Bull's Head at the Aldgate end indicating that life was there, as he began to climb. If anyone chanced to pass that way and challenge him, he told himself, he would inform them with justification that the premises were his own and he was simply having trouble with a lock.

He stepped on to the ledge and drew himself level with the window, which was of the sash-type. By using a screwdriver from his pocket he succeeded in slipping aside the iron catch. The lower section was difficult to move, but once he had got it started it slid easily upwards. He climbed inside and took out a torch.

The room was empty.

Literally empty. No furniture, curtains, carpet. Bare floorboards, ceiling and walls, with paper peeled away in several places.

Uncomprehending, he shone the torch over the floorboards. They had not been disturbed in months. He examined the skirting-board, the plaster cornice and the window sill. He could not see how anything could be secreted here. The police were probably mistaken about Messiter. And so was he. With a sense of shame he climbed out of the window and drew it down.

On Friday Messiter came in about eleven as usual, relaxed, indistinguishable in dress from the stockbrokers and bankers: dark suit, old boys' tie, shoes gleaming. With a smile he peeled a note from his wallet and bought his box of five Imperial Panatellas, a ritual that from the beginning had signalled goodwill towards his landlord. Braid sometimes wondered if he actually smoked them. He did not carry conviction as a smoker of cigars. He was a quiet man, functioning best in private conversations. Forty-seven by his own admission, he looked ten years younger, dark-haired with brown eyes that moistened when he spoke of things that moved him.

'Any letters for me, Mr Braid?'

'Five or six.' Braid took them from the shelf behind him. 'How is business?'

'No reason to complain,' Messiter said, smiling. 'My work is my hobby, and there aren't many lucky enough to say that. And how is the world of tobacco? Don't tell me. You'll always do a good trade here, Mr Braid. All the pressures – you can see it in their faces. They need the weed and always will.' Mildly he enquired, 'Nobody called this week asking for me, I suppose?'

Braid had not intended saying anything, but Messiter's manner disarmed him. That and the shame he felt at the suspicions he had harboured impelled him to say, 'Actually, there *was* a caller. I had a detective in here – when was it? – Wednesday – asking about you. It was obviously a ridiculous mistake.' He described Inspector Gent's visit without mentioning his own investigation afterwards with the ladder. 'Makes you wonder what the police are up to these days,' he concluded. 'I believe we're all on the computer at Scotland Yard now. This sort of thing is bound to happen.'

'You trust me, Mr Braid. I appreciate that,' Messiter said, his eyes starting to glisten. 'You took me on trust from the beginning.'

'I'm sure you aren't stacking stolen goods upstairs, if that's what you mean,' Braid told him in sincerity.

'But the inspector was not so sure?'

'He said something about a search warrant. Probably by now he has realized his mistake. I don't expect to see him again.'

'I wonder what brought him here,' Messiter said, almost to himself.

'I wouldn't bother about it. It's a computer error.'

'I don't believe so. What did he say about the lock I fitted on the door, Mr Braid?'

'Oh, at the time he seemed to think it was quite sinister.' He grinned. 'Don't worry – it doesn't bother me at all. You consulted me about the damned thing and you pay a pound extra a week for it, so who am I to complain? What you keep in there – if anything – is your business.' He chuckled in a way intended to reassure. 'That detective carried on as if you had a fortune hidden away in there.'

'Oh, but I have.'

Braid felt a pulse throb in his temple.

'It's high time I told you,' said Messiter serenely. 'I suppose I should apologize for not saying anything before. Not that there's anything criminal, believe me. Actually it's a rather remarkable story. I'm a philatelist, as you know. People smile at that and I don't blame them. Whatever name you give it, stamp collecting is a hobby for kids. In the business, we're a little sensitive on the matter. We dignify it with its own technology – dies and watermarks and so forth – but I've always suspected this is partly to convince ourselves that the whole thing is serious and important. Well, it occurred to me four or five years ago that there was a marvellous way of justifying stamp collecting to myself and that was by writing a book about stamps. You must have heard of Rowland Hill, the fellow who started the whole thing off?'

'The Penny Post?'

Messiter nodded. '1840 – the world's first postage stamps, the Penny Black and the Twopence Blue. My idea was not to write a biography of Hill – that's been done several times over by cleverer writers than I – but to analyse the way his idea caught on. The response of the Victorian public was absolutely phenomenal, you know. It's all in the newspapers of the period. I went to the Newspaper Library at Colindale to do my research. I spent weeks over it.' His voice conveyed not fatigue at the memory, but excitement. 'There was so much to read. Reports of Parliament. Letters to the Editor. Special articles describing the collection and delivery of the mail.' He paused, pointing a finger at Braid. 'You're wondering what this has to do with the room upstairs. I'll tell you. Whether it was providence or pure good luck I wouldn't care to say, but one afternoon in that Newspaper Library I turned up *The Times* for a day in May, 1841, and my eye was caught – riveted, I should say – by an announcement in the Personal Column on the front page.' Messiter's hand went to his pocket and withdrew his wallet. From it he took a folded piece of paper. 'This is what I saw.'

Braid took it from him, a photocopy of what was unquestionably a column of old newspaper type. The significant words had been scored round in ballpoint.

A Young Lady, being desirous of covering her dressing-room with cancelled postage stamps, has been so far encouraged in her wish by private friends as to have succeeded in collecting 16,000. These, however, being insufficient, she will be greatly obliged if any good-natured person who may have these otherwise worthless little articles at their disposal would assist her in her whimsical project. Address to Miss E.D., Mr Butt's, Glover, Leadenhall Street.

Braid made the connection instantly. His throat went dry. He read it again. And again.

'You understand?' said Messiter. 'It's a stamp man's dream – a room literally papered with Penny Blacks!'

'But this was – '

'1841. Right. More than a century ago. Have you ever looked through a really old newspaper? It's quite astonishing how easy it is to get caught up in the immediacy of the events. When I read that announcement, I could see that dressing-room vividly in my imagination: chintz curtains, gas-brackets, brass bedstead, washstand and mirror. I could see Miss E.D. with her paste-pot and brush assiduously covering the wall with stamps. It was such an exciting idea that it came as a jolt to realize that it all had happened so long ago that Miss E.D. must have died about the turn of the century. And what of her dressing-room? That, surely, must have gone, if not in the Blitz, then in the wholesale rebuilding of the City. My impression of Leadenhall Street was that the banks and insurance companies had lined it from end to end with gleaming office buildings five storeys high. Even if by some miracle the shop that had been Butt's the Glover's *had* survived, and Miss E.D.'s room *had* been over the shop, common sense told me that those stamps must long since have been stripped from the walls.' He paused, smiled and lighted a cigar.

Braid waited, his heart pounding.

'Yet there was a possibility, remote, but tantalizing and irresistible, that someone years ago redecorated the room by papering over the stamps. Any decorator will tell you they sometimes find layer upon layer of wallpaper. Imagine peeling back the layers to find thousands of Penny Blacks and Twopence Blues unknown to the world of philately! These days the commonest are catalogued at £10 or so, but find some rarities – inverted watermarks, special cancellations – and you could be up to £500 a stamp. Maybe a thousand. Mr Braid, I don't exaggerate when I tell you the value of such a room could run to half a million pounds. Half a million for what that young lady in her innocence called worthless little articles!'

Braid had a momentary picture of her upstairs in her crinoline arranging the stamps on the wall. His wall!

As if he read the thought, Messiter said, 'It was my discovery. I went to a lot of trouble. Eventually I found the *Post Office Directory* for 1845 in the British Library. The list of residents in Leadenhall Street included a glover by the name of Butt.'

'So you got the number of this shop?'

Messiter nodded.

'And when you came to Leadenhall Street, here it was, practically the last-pre-Victorian building this side of Lloyd's?'

Messiter drew on his cigar, scrutinizing Braid.

'All those stamps,' Braid whispered. 'Twenty-seven years I've owned this shop and the flat without knowing that in the room upstairs was a fortune. It took you to tell me that.'

'Don't get the idea it was easy for me,' Messiter pointed out. 'Remember, I waited practically a year for those French people to move out. That was a test of character, believe me, not knowing what I would find when I took possession.'

Strangely, Braid felt less resentment towards Messiter than the young Victorian woman who had lived in this building, *his* building, and devised a pastime so sensational in its consequence that his own walls mocked him.

Messiter leaned companionably across the counter. 'Don't look so shattered, chum. I'm not the rat you take me for. Why do you think I'm telling you this?'

Braid shrugged. 'I really couldn't say.'

'Think about it. As your tenant, I did nothing underhand. When I took the flat, didn't I raise the matter of redecoration? You said I was free to go ahead whenever I wished. I admit you didn't know then that the walls were covered in Penny Blacks, but I wasn't certain myself till I peeled back the old layers of paper. What a moment that was!' He paused, savouring the recollection. 'I've had a great year thanks to those stamps. In fact, I've set myself up for some time to come. Best of all, I had the unique experience of finding that room.' He flicked ash from the cigar. 'I estimate there are still upwards of 20,000 stamps up there, Mr Braid. In all justice, they belong to you.'

Braid stared in amazement.

'I'm serious,' Messiter went on. 'I've made enough to buy a place in the country and write my book. The research is finished. That's been my plan for years, to earn some time, and I've done it. I want no more.'

Frowning, Braid said, 'I don't understand why you're doing this. Is it because of the police? You said there was nothing dishonest.'

'And I meant it, but you are right, Mr Braid. I am a little shaken to hear of your visit from the inspector.'

'What do you mean?'

Messiter asked obliquely, 'When you read your newspaper, do you ever bother with the financial pages?'

Braid gave him a long look. Messiter held his stare.

'If it really has any bearing on this, the answer is no. I don't have much interest in the stock market. Nor any capital to invest,' he added.

'Just as well in these uncertain times,' Messiter commented. 'Blue chip investments have been hard to find these last few years. That's why people have been putting their money into other things. Art, for instance. A fine work of art holds its value in real terms even in a fluctuating economy. So do jewellery and antiques. And stamps, Mr Braid. Lately a lot of money has been invested in stamps.'

'That I can understand.'

'Then you must also understand that information such as this' – he put his hand on the photostat between them – 'is capable of causing flutters of alarm. Over the last year or so I have sold to dealers a number of early English stamps unknown to the market. These people are not fools. Before they buy a valuable stamp, they like to know the history of its ownership. I have had to tell them my story and show them the announcement in *The Times*. That's all right. Generally they need no more convincing. But do you understand the difficulty? It's the prospect of 20,000 Penny Blacks and Twopence Blues unknown to the stamp world shortly coming onto the market. Can you imagine the effect?'

'I suppose it will reduce the value of stamps people already own.'

'Precisely. The rarities may not be so rare. Rumours begin, and it isn't long before there is a panic and prices tumble.'

'Which is when the sharks move in,' said Braid. 'I see it now. The police probably suspect the whole thing is a fraud.'

Messiter gave a nod.

'But you and I know it isn't a fraud,' Braid went on. 'We can show them the room. I still don't understand why you are giving it up.'

'I told you the reason. I always planned to write my book. And there is something else. It's right to warn you that there is sure to be publicity over this. Newspapers, television – this is the kind of story they relish, the unknown Victorian girl, the stamps undiscovered for over a century. Mr Braid, I value my privacy. I don't care for my name being printed in the newspapers. It will happen, I'm sure, but I don't intend to be around when it does. That's why I am telling nobody where I am going. After the whole thing has blown over, I'll send you a forwarding address, if you would be so kind . . .'

'Of course, but – '

A customer came in, one of the regulars. Braid gave him a nod and wished he had gone to the kiosk up the street.

Messiter picked up the conversation. 'Was it a month's notice we agreed? I'll see that my bank settles the rent.' He took the keys of the flat from his pocket and put them on the counter with the photostat. 'For you. I shan't need these again.' Putting a hand on Braid's arm, he added, 'some time we must meet and have a drink to Miss E.D.'s memory.'

He turned and left the shop and the customer asked for twenty Rothmans. Braid lifted his hand in a belated salute through the shop window and returned to his business. More customers came in. Fridays were always busy, with people collecting their cigarettes for the weekend. He was thankful for the activity. It compelled him to adjust by degrees and accept that he was a rich man now. Unlike Messiter, he would not object to the story getting into the press. Some of these customers who had used the shop for years and scarcely acknowledged him as a human being would choke on their toast and marmalade when they saw his name one morning in *The Times*.

It satisfied him most to recover what he owned. When Messiter had disclosed the secret of the building, it was as if the twenty-seven years of Braid's tenure were obliterated. The place was full of Miss E.D. That young lady – she would always be young – had in effect asserted her prior claim. He had doubted if he would ever again believe it was truly his own. But now that her 'whimsical project' had been ceded to him, he was going to take pleasure in dismantling the design, stamp by stamp, steadily accumulating a fortune Miss E.D. had never supposed would accrue. Vengeful it might be, but it would exorcise her from the building that belonged to him.

Ten minutes before closing time Inspector Gent entered the shop. As before, he waited for the last customer to leave.

'Sorry to disturb you again, sir. I have that warrant now.'

'You won't need it,' Braid cheerfully told him. 'I have the key. Mr Messiter was here this morning.' He started to recount the conversation.

'Then I suppose he took out his cutting from *The Times*?' put in the inspector.

'You *know* about that?'

'Do I?' he said caustically. 'The man has been round just about every stamp shop north of Birmingham telling the tale of that young woman and the Penny Blacks on her dressing-room wall.'

Braid frowned. 'There's nothing dishonest in that. The announcement really did appear in *The Times*, didn't it?'

'It did, sir. We checked. And this *is* the address mentioned.' The inspector eyed him expressionlessly. 'The trouble is that the Penny

Blacks our friend Messiter has been selling in the north aren't off any dressing-room wall. He buys them from a dealer in London, common specimens, about £10 each one. Then he works on them.'

'Works on them? What do you mean?'

'Penny Blacks are valued according to the plates they were printed from, sir. There are distinctive markings on each of the plates, most particularly in the shape of the guide letters that appear in the corners. The stamps Messiter has been selling are doctored to make them appear rare. He buys a common Plate 6 stamp in London, touches up the guide letters and sells it to a Manchester dealer as a Plate 11 stamp for a hundred pounds. As it's catalogued at twice that, the dealer thinks he has a bargain. Messiter picks his victims carefully: generally they aren't specialists in early English stamps, but almost any dealer is ready to look at a Penny Black in case it's a rare one.'

Braid shook his head. 'I don't understand this at all. Why should Messiter have needed to resort to forgery? There are 20,000 stamps upstairs.'

'Have you seen them?'

'No, but the newspaper announcement – '

'That fools everyone, sir.'

'You said it was genuine.'

'It is. And the idea of a roomful of Penny Blacks excites people's imagination. They *want* to believe it. That's the secret of all the best confidence tricks. Now why do you suppose Messiter had a mortice lock fitted on that room? You thought it was because the contents were worth a fortune? Has it occurred to you as a possibility that he didn't want anyone to know there was nothing there?'

Braid's dream disintegrated.

'It stands to reason, doesn't it,' the inspector went on, 'that the stamps were stripped off the wall generations ago? When Messiter found empty walls, he couldn't abandon the idea. It had taken a grip on him. That young woman who thought of papering her wall with stamps could never have supposed she would be responsible over a century later for turning a man to crime.' He held out his hand. 'If I could have that key, sir, I'd like to see the room for myself.'

Braid followed the inspector upstairs and watched him unlock the door. They entered the room.

'I don't mind admitting I have a sneaking respect for Messiter,' the inspector said. 'Imagine the poor beggar coming in here at last after going to all the trouble he did to find the place. Look, you can see where he peeled back the wallpaper layer by layer' – gripping a furl of paper, he drew it casually aside – 'to find absolutely – ' He stopped. 'My God!'

The stamps were there, neatly pasted in rows.

Braid said nothing, but the blood slowly drained from his face.

Miss E.D.'s scheme of interior decoration had been more ambitious than anyone expected. She had diligently blocked out each stamp in ink – red, blue or green – to form an intricate mosaic. Penny Blacks or Twopence Blues, Plate 6 or Plate 11, they were as she had described them in *The Times*, worthless little articles.

WOMAN TROUBLE

Florence V. Mayberry

I'm an American, born in Missouri. My husband David and I lived in Reno, Nevada for a long time, and joined the Bahá'i faith there. I became very widely traveled as a volunteer speaker for Bahá'i – I've been twice around the world, and even went to China in 1980. Thus my stories not only have a Nevada background; they may be set in Mexico, Hong Kong, Haifa, London, Rome, California, or elsewhere. Since 1973, David and I have lived in Israel, where I am a Counsellor member of the Bahá'i International Teaching Center in Haifa.

I've been writing since childhood: my first story was a mystery involving secret passages, strange sounds in the night and dastardly characters. The story was accepted – by my sixth-grade teacher. In addition to frequent appearances in Ellery Queen's Mystery Magazine, *my work has been published in Holland, Japan, France, Italy, England and Australia; a number of my stories have appeared in anthologies, and some have been scripted for radio production in South Africa. I've also published poetry, and one children's book,* The Dachshunds of Mama Island.

I have four or five stories which are favorites, but the edge goes to 'Woman Trouble', which is also the favorite of Eleanor Sullivan, editor of EQMM. *It was included in the 1974 edition of* Best Detective Stories of the Year *– rather surprisingly, I think, as no detective or police procedure exists in the story.*

I never did like living in Reno. I'm a desert woman, born and raised just outside Winnemucca, Nevada. Trees and buildings, and all those crowds milling around day and night on the streets get in my way. I like to see clear and far off. Horizons, mountains. Even people stand out better in the open desert. You can see them coming, all alone and separate instead of muffled up in all that town stuff.

Have you ever smelled, real good, the sage coming in off the desert after a rain? Clean, heady, sweet. Seems to scour out the lungs and makes your brain fresh. You can remember you've got a heart, even a soul. Well, that's what I wanted for Paddy.

Paddy belongs to the desert. Wyoming country, he was born there. Up where buttes are swept by winds and you have to struggle a little to fill your lungs with oxygen, it's so high in the sky, you know. Couple of years after we were married Paddy took me back to his old home ranch. Well, it wasn't his any longer – he'd lost it fooling around in Nevada's gambling clubs. But the people who bought it from the bank are nice folks, old friends of the family, and they pretended the ranch was still Paddy's.

Paddy and I rode alongside the buttes, sometimes stopping the horses and edging them together so we could kiss. 'Paddy,' I told him, 'let's save up and buy back your ranch. Town's no good for us, we're open-country people.' Especially town's no good for Paddy, I was thinking, and he knew it.

He grinned and said, 'You're right, girl. No dice tables out here on the open range.' He patted my arm and added, 'First big killing I make, and I sure ought to be due for one soon, we'll buy us a spread. Build us a brand-new house on it with all the fixings, good as back in Reno.'

Good as! My God. A two-room-with-kitchenette apartment. A stove with an oven which baked lopsided. A dwarf-sized refrigerator. And all the gambling tables in the world, it seemed, just down the street.

'Paddy, I don't need fine things, I'm not used to them. It would be fun to camp out in a cabin, cook on a wood-stove – nothing bakes good like a wood range. It would be like when I was a kid. Home-baked bread – my mother always did her own baking and she taught me. And we could have a little garden, Paddy. You'd be outdoors a lot – indoors don't suit you, Paddy, staying in that warehouse all the time, lifting those heavy loads.'

'Lifting loads, woman?' His face took on that remote expression he always got when he decided I had gone too far interfering in men's ways. 'You mean pushing so hard on those little levers that do all the lifting? With a 180-pounds, six-one of a man to do the pushing? Well, Angie, I sure got a hard life.'

I wanted to say it was lifting the dice, shaking them, tossing them out that was too much for a 180-pounds, six-one of a man. But when he got that look Paddy scared me. No, no, I don't mean he ever hit me or roughed me up. He never did. Why, Paddy would just spit on the ground when he heard about men who hit women. Said only feisty little men did that, who were too scared to tackle a man. But once, after that look, Paddy had walked out of our apartment and didn't come back. It took me a week to find him. Down in Vegas. And another week to beg him back.

That time I wished he had hit me instead. All the money we had in our joint savings account, $715, went that time. To the last penny. It takes a lot of standing on your feet and waiting on customers in a department store to get that much put away above what it costs to live these days.

Paddy didn't believe in savings accounts, even though I had his name on the bank book. Said it was for men who didn't have the guts to take a chance, or for women. That's why it didn't bother him when he drew it out. Grinned, patted me on the back, and said he'd pay it back one of these days with interest.

Me, I didn't care if he ever paid it back. All I wanted back was Paddy.

Like that evening later on when I was snuggling my face against his, whispering I wouldn't trade him for the whole world tied in ribbons.

He kissed me and whispered back, 'You're a good kid.' Then he scooted me off his lap, stood up, gave me a little smack on the bottom, and said, 'Think I'll hit the clubs a while. Think I'll begin my first million tonight. So I can get you that little ranch you're always talking about. Only it'll be a big one. Maybe I'll try for two million, so's I can fence it in with those ribbons you're always talking about.'

'Oh, Paddy, please! Don't go, Paddy. I don't want to be rich. I don't even need the ranch. Paddy, you know it's just you I need. And you've been away so much lately. Every night, Paddy, the last few weeks.'

'Maybe there'll be a few more nights, too,' he said easily. 'Stick with it, one of these nights I'll strike it rich.'

'I'll go with you, Paddy.'

His face set. 'No. You bug me at the tables.'

No use arguing with Paddy. Unless I wanted to set out on another search all over Nevada.

I remember it rained that night in Reno. A good steady rain. Once I thought, I'll just go along Virginia Street, down the alley by the clubs, find out which one Paddy's in, say it was raining hard and that I'd brought him an umbrella. But it scared me to think of the way his face would look – *I'm a man, Angie, don't wet-nurse me. You bug me at the tables, Angie.* Or maybe he wouldn't say anything. Just never come home.

I'd rather he hit me every day, honest I would.

I woke up in the morning and felt for him next to me. The sheet was cool, untouched. All around me, all through the apartment, was the sweet sage smell that rises off the desert after a rain. But it wouldn't make the ache in my head go away. I perked some coffee, waited a while to eat, and hoped he would show up before he had to go to work. And I said to myself, *Damn the gambling and the gamblers, damn Reno to hell.*

Reno could have been a nice place, you know. A sweet hometown with the Truckee River running through, willows all along it. Over to the west, Mount Rose with snow still on it in summer. Old brown fat Peavine Mountain squatting toward the north. And the clean lovely desert spread to the east. My God, it could have been nice to live in with the man you love. Only it wasn't.

I left a place set at the table in case he showed up. Then I went down on Virginia Street, making like I was window shopping. At 6:30 in the morning, yet! Hoping I'd see him, but that he wouldn't see me: *Angie, you trying to make a woman out of me? I thought you married me because I was a man*. At 6:30 he could be grabbing a bite to eat at one of the club lunch counters, because he had to be at work by seven.

Then I saw him. Coming out of a club with a tall red-blonde holding onto his arm, almost head-high with him. Laughing, throwing her head back, tossing her long shiny hair. She had on a long black dress and it fit her like she was the model on which all women ought to be patterned. I noticed that especially because I'm short and stocky-built. Not fat or anything, just short and stocky-built, the strong kind. I used to help my Dad chop wood – Mother and Dad never had any boys.

I wanted to walk over and sock the girl in the nose. But I always have a sense to be fair about things. It was Paddy who needed the sock in the nose. How would the girl know Paddy belonged to me if he didn't tell her?

I speeded up and came even with them just as she leaned toward him and kissed his cheek. Paddy had his arm up hailing a taxi. I said, 'Hi, Paddy, won't you be late for work?'

Paddy was a gambler. His face stayed cool and easy, and it was like hoods dropped over his eyes so I couldn't see into them. 'Hi, Angie,' he said with his mouth. But I could feel the inside of him saying, *Get the hell out of here*. That wasn't fair. He was the one on the spot, not me. Besides, this was woman trouble. I'd never had woman trouble with Paddy before. Far as I knew. A wife can't buckle under when it's woman trouble.

'I laid out your breakfast on the table – you shouldn't go to work on an empty stomach. Paddy, I don't think I've met your friend.'

I was talking to Paddy, but I was looking square at this woman.

Woman she was, somewhere between 25 and 30, not much younger than me. She had the skin and the looks of an 18-year-old, only young kids don't get that confident look on them. This woman looked strong and sure of herself, like maybe she'd fought her way up.

She was beautiful, I'll say that. Her eyes were so blue their color almost hurt you to look at. Big, too. Only thing, they stared at me bold as brass, shrewd too. Had me figured first look, and it was striking her funny. She took on a little half-smile like she was holding back a laugh.

She knew how to put on makeup, just enough to turn her skin to honey and rose. Or maybe the Lord shot the works on her, maybe she was born that way. Makeup on her eyes, though, and lashes that almost brushed her cheeks. And like a halo, all that red-blonde hair.

'Is this your wife?' she asked Paddy.

He nodded and said, easy, 'Sure is. Angie, meet Molly.'

She looked him level in the eye, laughed, and said, 'You're a cool one, I'll say that for you.' She turned to me. 'Chin up, lady, so he can take a poke at it for good measure.' She laughed again, climbed in the taxi and drove off.

What she said shook Paddy. He whipped his face away from the taxi like he'd been slapped, and he didn't give me that goodbye look like he had just before he'd hopped off for Vegas. He said, 'I'm sorry, Angie. But you shouldn't have come looking for me. And I'm not going to lie to you, tell you I was just coming out to put her in the taxi. I was going with her.'

Well, I couldn't hardly jump on him after that. I mean, he'd come square with me. So I said, 'I'm sorry too, Paddy. See you tonight. I've fixed up a good roast for dinner.' *Last night while you made up to this Molly with her bold, laughing, beautiful face, I was home cooking for you. I'm not ugly, Paddy. I got big brown eyes, nice features – you told me it's brown eyes you like, not blue like yours. You said brown eyes always got you.*

He let a deep breath sigh out and said, 'Okay. See you tonight.'

'You've never hit me, Paddy. Not once. She shouldn't have said that.'

Kind of like it hurt as the words came out he said, 'She's seen 'em hit.' Then he turned and walked off.

What do you do when you love a man and as far as you know he's never two-timed you before, and then you find out he did – or was going to? And you begin thinking maybe all those gambling nights and the money gone, that $715 out of the savings account – maybe it wasn't all for gambling?

You brood on it, if you're like me.

All day long while I was selling girdles, pantyhose and things, I couldn't stop thinking about that tall bold Molly. The way she laughed and told off Paddy, and him standing there looking like he could eat her. And the contempt she'd had for his little dumb wife.

Paddy was there when I got home. He didn't say anything, just pulled me down on his lap and kissed my forehead and my eyes. 'You got nice eyes, Angie,' he said. 'They never did see nothing bad about me. You got nice lovin' eyes.'

That's all. What I wanted to say was such a big lump in me that I was afraid to let it out. So I just kissed him.

But after dinner I said, 'Paddy, let's pull out and go on up to Wyoming. We could save for our own place up there as well – maybe better – as here in Reno. I could find a job and maybe you could get us a little house on a ranch where you'd work. There's an old cabin on your home place, maybe they'd rent it to us and we could fix it up. Get our roots in.'

'One of these days,' he said. 'Maybe.'

He helped me with the dishes that night – usually he didn't do that, said he felt silly lifting teacups with a rag in his hand. But that night he helped me. And he kissed me sweet. Tender, it was. Never once mentioned going to the clubs. It was wonderful.

But sometime in the night – well, it was two o'clock when I turned on the light – I found myself alone in the bed. Paddy was nowhere in the apartment.

Molly, her name was. *Angie, meet Molly*. That's all, no last name. How do you find a Molly in a place as big as Reno?

You get up and dress and go down to the gambling clubs and start looking for Paddy. Or Molly.

But I didn't go. Paddy needed some kind of honor, even if it was the kind I made up myself.

Around four o'clock I laid out some potatoes, ready to fry the way Paddy likes them. Set the table pretty. Listened for the creak of the elevator which meant somebody was coming up. Went to the bathroom to do what I could about my face. Bluish circles under my eyes smudged the upper part of my face. Face puffy from worry and lack of sleep – or like a puff adder getting mad, ready to strike. I was only in my early thirties, but this morning I looked 40 or more. Little dumpy woman. Why wouldn't Paddy, eyes blue as heaven, six-one of muscle, a sidewise grin, why wouldn't –

'Stop it!' I told myself in the mirror. 'Stop it!'

Paddy loved me. He told me so lots of times. And Paddy never lied, no matter what else he did.

I put the potatoes away in the refrigerator, drank a cup of coffee and walked to work. It wasn't far, and besides we didn't have a car any more. Used to, but Paddy hit a winning streak a year or so back and wanted to raise his bets. So I signed the car over – it was in my name – and Paddy sold it. Oh, well, it costs money for gas.

It's tough to stand on your feet all day, straightening up counters that customers are always messing up the minute you've folded things. It's tough smiling, when you ache all over from wondering where Paddy's gone to. I thought once I'd call him at work. But if he was there he'd be mad. And if he wasn't there his boss would be mad knowing Paddy's wife was hunting for him again.

I tried to eat a sandwich at lunch, but it just wouldn't go down. So I asked my boss could I go home, I didn't feel good. He was real nice, told me not to come back till I felt completely okay. They like me at work. Steady, always on time. Just a dumb, steady, day-after-day salesclerk that redheaded Molly wouldn't be caught dead being.

I went home and took a couple of aspirins. Tried to lie down and relax. Got up and mopped the kitchen and bathroom. Took a shower. Put on my new coral pants suit. Took it off. Broad as a barn door from the rear. Put on a long straight jersey dress. Looked like a Japanese wrestler in a nightgown. Finally put back on the dark dress I had worn to work. And it was past five o'clock and no Paddy.

Well, Reno's free and open – anybody can go in the clubs and play a few nickels and dimes in the slot machines. That's what I'd tell Paddy if I saw him. But maybe he wouldn't see me. I could hide behind the machines, leave once I knew where – no. Not if he was with Molly.

I walked my legs off that night. Tried to eat a hamburger. Couldn't make it. Got to bed around three in the morning. Alone.

Next morning I called at work and said I was still sick. It was no lie. I was sick. The boss was nice, said to take care of myself. So I was ashamed to walk the streets, running in and out of clubs. I stayed in the apartment. Which was good because Paddy's boss telephoned and asked what happened to him the last two days. 'We're sick,' I said. What kind of sick? 'We must have eaten something funny. Sick to our stomachs.'

'Yeah,' his boss said. 'Not down in Vegas again, is he, Angie, and you packing to go find him?'

'Listen, Pete, you got no right to say that – my God, can't a man have a stomachache without – '

'Okay, okay, Angie, cool it. Take care of yourselves. Tell Paddy to forget about tomorrow, it's Saturday, he might as well get a good start on Monday.'

'Thanks, Pete, I'll tell him.'

If Paddy was in the clubs he was like a ghost slipping in and out, because I hit them all. And that wasn't Paddy's style. Even losing, he'd stick at one table, waiting for the odds to break his way. And Paddy hadn't left for Vegas, he was still in Reno. My insides told me so.

They kept telling me something else. Paddy was with Molly.

So I concentrated on how I could find Molly.

You ever looked over the list of attorneys in the phone-book yellow pages? In Reno? You wonder how they all eat, except Reno's built on divorce as well as gambling – some fine recommendation for your hometown, huh? I started calling attorneys' offices and ran smack into, 'Molly? The last name, please? You say you saw this lady drop her purse in one of the clubs and there's no identification in it, so how do you know the name is Molly? Oh. One of the dealers. Well, my suggestion would be to ask that dealer about her, or turn over the purse to the cashier or the police.' A long pause. 'May I ask why you didn't just give it to the lady?' Or, 'I'm sorry but we never give out clients' names. Why don't you try the police?'

Well, it was a dumb try anyway.

I thought, why not go down to that club where I first saw Paddy with her and ask around?

Down to the clubs. Jangling, brassy sound of slot machines, busy, busy. Everybody pulling handles like it was a job doing some good, like cleaning up the world or something every time a coin dropped in. Most of the time nothing was coming out, no loaf of bread or can of beans, nothing. Once in a while a little money to be stuffed back into the machine.

'Say, do you know a pretty redhead named Molly? Tall girl, dressed good. She was here the other night. I – I've got something I think may belong to her. I got to find her.'

The dealer at the blackjack table grinned sidewise and said, 'Honey, I hope it's something nice you got for her. If it is, you might try the office. Something different, you better take it home. No, I don't know any tall redhead named Molly.'

I tried a couple of other dealers. Then the lunch counter. A waitress there said, 'Say, aren't you Paddy Finley's wife?'

I nodded and she said, 'I thought so. See, I used to live in your same apartment house, couple of floors below, but I used to see you come in together.'

'I've got something may be this Molly's,' I said again. 'The other day down here I saw her with – something like it. But I don't know where to find her. I just thought someone here might know her.'

She gave me a quirky smile. 'I don't know her, honey, but I do know Paddy, he's here a lot. Hard to miss Paddy, looks like kids used to think cowboy heroes ought to look. Eastern divorcees still think that. You know what I'd do, Mrs Finley – I'd go home, take two-three aspirins, and have yourself a nice rest. Then when Paddy came home you'd be in shape to flatten him. Wanta cup of coffee, I'll throw in the aspirin?'

It's peculiar, how when your mind's upset it's the middle of your stomach that hurts. Like a knot tied in it. But all the time the real hurt is in your mind where you can't touch it.

Out on the street, up a way, I got this queer feeling. Like I wanted to shake all over but was too frozen to do it. I felt something either pulling on me or breathing on me. I mean, it was screwy, like I was a Geiger counter and had run into what I was looking for. I turned.

Across Second Street, headed towards the alley that leads into the clubs, was Molly. Wearing a long bright-green skirt and a white turtleneck sweater. With all that pretty reddish hair in a big topknot, like she was deliberately making herself taller than she already was. Conspicuous, you know?

Paddy wasn't with her.

I was so relieved I felt like I ought to walk over and apologize to her. Instead I went close to the store windows, turned, and watched her swing along the street. Like she'd owned Reno so long she'd even forgotten it belonged to her.

Then I saw him, Paddy, Walking fast behind her, his long legs giving at the knee in that little bend that cowpunchers never quite lose. He came up to her, grabbed her arm, flung her face to face with him. She wasn't surprised. Just took on a strong bold look. Said something. Laughed. He grabbed her throat and shook her back and forth. Her long legs kicked at him, her fingers raked his cheeks. Her knee came up hard. Paddy staggered back, bent over. Even from across the street I could see he was pale, sick.

Molly turned away, cool as you please, not even touching her throat though it was bound to be hurting. Bold as brass. Still owning the town, she was.

I cut across the traffic to Paddy. He was leaning against a building, while people clustered around staring, eyes thrilled like they were watching a movie being shot.

'Paddy, let's go home.'

Somebody snickered.

Flames shot through me. Like a chimney long unused and then too much paper is put in the firepot and the soot blazes and sets the house on fire. I plunged into the ring of gawkers, punching, slapping, screaming for them to mind their own business, to leave my Paddy alone.

I felt hands on my shoulders. Paddy's hands. 'Angie, that's enough. Let's get out of here.'

The crowd parted and we walked through it, turned towards the river. Paddy hailed a taxi and we got in it. Paddy wasn't walking too good.

'That Molly – that Molly, why did you – ' I began after we shut the door of our apartment.

'I don't want to talk about it,' Paddy said, his face white and drawn. He went in the bathroom and closed the door.

I made some coffee, then stood by the stove wondering whether he'd rather have steak or soup. Or if either of us ever wanted to eat again.

It's hard for a wife of twelve years not to ask her man why he chokes a girl he's just met. If he just met her. Especially with Paddy always spitting on the ground at the mention of men who hit women. Said they ought to take out their mad on wrangling horses or find a man their size or bigger. Now he was choking Molly. Like she had set him crazy.

And then she bested him, right in the middle of Reno with his wife and a crowd watching. *Damn you, Paddy, how'd that look in the papers if a cop had been around and taken you both to the station and me, too? The papers saying your girl friend beat you up and your wife beat up the crowd for snickering. Like you were some ragdoll for women to toss around. Damn you, Paddy, how'd you like that?*

Paddy was a long time in the bathroom. I heard the bath water running. When he came out he was shaved and had on clean underthings I kept in a bureau for him in the bathroom. 'I got soup hot and steak ready to broil,' I said as he went through the living room to the bedroom, that's the screwy way our apartment was.

'I don't want anything.'

I heard him moving around the bedroom. Pretty soon he came out, dressed up, and his suitcase in his hand. 'So long, Angie,' he said.

'You can't go like this, Paddy. It's not right, it's not fair to me. We got to talk. Listen, Paddy, I can overlook what happened. Just tell me why, then we won't talk about it any more.'

'This time don't come looking for me,' he said, staring straight ahead at the outside door.

'Paddy, you don't want her after what she done – she don't want you, you don't want a woman don't want you. But I want you.'

'So long, Angie.'

'Paddy, let's pack up and head for Wyoming, get out of this damn state with its no-good life, gambling, and loose women like – '

He wheeled on me, his eyes blue fire. 'Don't say her name!'

He opened the door and went out. I just followed him, like a puppy dog that's been kicked but won't stay home. Down the hall after him. He took the stairs instead of the elevator, his long legs going fast. I kept up. Outside on the side-walk, down to the corner, me with no purse or anything.

He turned and said, 'Angie, I don't want you no more.' He started walking again, with me right behind.

He began running. I'm stubby-built, but I've got lasting power. I ran behind him, down almost to Virginia Street. Paddy stopped and I stood beside him.

'You want to go along and hear me tell her I love her before I kill her?'

'You're not going to kill anybody.'

'Okay, just keep hanging onto my tail.' He started walking, and I did too. We crossed the Truckee Bridge, over by the old Post Office, past the Holiday Hotel. Turned back again, the opposite direction, with him trying to lose me, up the hill above the river, then we turned again.

'You got no pride, Angie,' he said over his shoulder.

What's pride? It don't fill emptiness. I kept walking.

Finally he stopped in front of a fine old house above the river, not far from downtown, that was split into apartments. 'She lives here,' Paddy said. 'I'm going in. And if she's not there I'll wait for her. Because she's mine, she's not going to change her mind just because she's got her divorce and is tired of playing around. Angie, you go get you a divorce. I'm taking Molly. One way or another.'

He went up the porch steps, through the entrance, up the stairs. Me back of him. At the top of the stairs he turned and said, 'You're asking for it, Angie,' and hauled back his arm. I stood, waiting for it. If he hit me, maybe he'd think of me the way he did Molly. But his hand dropped.

He knocked on a door, with a number 3 on it. Inside were footsteps and a woman asked, 'Who is it?' Molly.

'You know who,' Paddy said.

She laughed. 'You want to get messed up again?' She slid a bolt on the other side and walked away.

Paddy stepped back and kicked the door. Ordinarily a kick that hard would have gone on through. But this was an old-fashioned house with heavy oak doors. Nothing happened except a big deep scar on the finish.

Paddy kicked again. Then he went crazy. Kept kicking that door like a bronco with a cactus under its saddle, his face a sick-gray and his eyes blazing. I pulled at him. He shook me off and kept kicking. Nobody came out of the apartment across the hall – the folks must have been gone. Downstairs a woman was yelling. The landlady, it turned out, who went back inside and called the police.

Suddenly the cops were there, no sirens or anything, and they were manhandling Paddy. It took the two of them to handcuff him and drag him downstairs. I stood there, frozen. One cop came back, knocked on Molly's door, asked her to open up and tell him what the trouble was. 'No trouble of mine,' she said through the door. 'I didn't call you. Nobody came in my apartment. Just some stupid idiot kicking my door. Go talk to the one who called you.'

'It's the police. We need information.'

She didn't answer. He turned to me, 'You in on this, lady? You trying to get inside, too?'

I shook my head. 'I'm his wife. I never touched the door. He just wanted to talk to her. She wouldn't talk to him and he got mad. There wasn't any more to it than that, he just lost his temper.'

'Some temper the way the door's beat up. You better come down to the station and tell the Chief about it.'

'I'm his wife. I've got no complaint. And if I did, you can't make me say anything against Paddy. I'm his wife. I've got no complaint.'

'Well, I have!' the landlady yelled behind us. 'Breaking up my door, disturbing my tenants, you bet I'll complain, I'll follow you down to the station in my car.'

'I'll pay for all the damage,' I said. 'You tell the Chief that.'

The policeman and the landlady left and I sat down on the top stairstep, shaking like a Washoe Zephyr had struck me. After a bit the bolt slid on Molly's door and the door slowly opened.

She saw me. 'Oh,' she said.

I didn't say anything.

'You're his wife, aren't you?' I nodded.

'Listen, I'll be straight with you. When I first hit this town I bumped into Paddy. In one of the clubs. I was just getting my bearings, had noplace to go or anyone to see. And Paddy – well, he has a way with him. Anyway, I didn't know he was married, so we played around. Then you showed up, talking about breakfast. So I split. But he looked me up after that and said he'd left you. Kept hanging around. But frankly, lady, I run on a different track than Paddy. With bosses, not hired help. So I said bye-bye and he wouldn't listen. So he tried muscling me around.' She laughed, high and hard. 'Shows how stupid a good-looking guy can be. I was trained by pros, and he's an amateur.'

'Paddy never once raised his hand to me.'

She looked at me wise, and a little sad. 'Maybe it would have worked out better if he had. Honest to God. Women!' She went back inside and closed the door.

I'd been trying to hate her. But I couldn't. I couldn't even hate Paddy. I felt nothing but sick, sitting there in a strange place like a cast-off ragdoll with its stuffing out.

I got up and went outdoors.

Like I said, it was an old-fashioned house turned into apartments. Whoever had changed it had made kind of a thing out of it being old-fashioned. They'd kept the old veranda, shaped like an L, and put up an old-time hanging porch swing around the corner from the house front. I felt so done in that I went and rested in the swing.

After a while a car drove up. It was the landlady looking like she'd bit into a chunk of iron. She stomped inside, never saw me. It got dark, but I just kept sitting there.

Maybe I had a hunch what would happen.

Molly came out of the house. She went down the steps to the sidewalk, her hair shimmering under the porch light and her long black dress swirled with embroidery that matched the color of her hair. When she reached the sidewalk, she turned towards town.

I heard footsteps, running from a clump of trees across the street. I stood up, my heart feeling like it filled my whole chest. Molly stopped, tall and defiant, turning towards the man who rushed at her. Paddy. I knew it would be Paddy. She laughed, never a flinch out of her. 'Did that poor fool woman bail you out?'

'They didn't hold me. I paid for the door.'

'Well, scram! You can't pay for me. The price is too high.'

He called her a name. Then pleading like, his hands reaching out almost as if he was trying to climb up some slick and muddy riverbank, 'Please, Molly. Please! I'm begging, Molly. I never felt this way before about anybody. I've got to have you, Molly!'

'Go to hell,' she said. 'I'm no horse you can break. So lay off the big he-man Wild West stuff with me.'

Paddy swung. She dodged but the blow glanced her head. She staggered back. He came at her again, both his hands grabbing.

She must have reached in her purse. I couldn't see. I only heard a sharp crack, the sound reverberating in my ears until it made me dizzy. Paddy was on the ground, crawling around like he was trying to find something.

I floated down the steps, no feet, out to the sidewalk. Then Molly was on the pavement and I was pounding her head onto the concrete.

See Paddy out there? Gentlest man in the world. Sweet and quiet, just rocking on the porch. Hums to himself and rocks. Oh, now and again he walks out to the little corral I built and pets the mare I bought after I moved us up here to Wyoming. But Paddy just stays gentle and quiet, that's his real nature. That Molly had no right to stir him up, make fun of him. Then try to kill him. She turned him crazy, her face and her bigtime ways.

Right after the trial I brought Paddy back to Wyoming.

Yes, the trial scared me. Not so much for myself as for Paddy. Because if I got sent to the penitentiary, who'd look after him? That shot of Molly's addled him. Struck his head. Made him like a child. Sometimes he cries at night, gets on the floor and crawls around. Just like he did that night. Like he's looking for something he'll never find.

Molly didn't die right away. Not for almost two weeks after that night. But that didn't get me off. Manslaughter it was. In the heat of passion. And my lawyer brought out that I was protecting my husband. So they gave me a suspended sentence. On probation for three years. I have to check in every month.

So I rent this little house on Paddy's old home place from the folks who own it now. Family friends. They keep an eye on Paddy while I'm at work. Except for some nights Paddy's happy. Thinks the mare is a whole string of horses, calls her a lot of different names.

Me?

Well, I'm kind of happy, too. Kind of. No more worry about Paddy running off to the clubs. And by now I'm used to it.

Used to what?

Oh, like with the mare, Paddy calls me by a different name. Just one. Molly. So it hurts a little, but I just figure it's me who answers. Me, Angie.

FIRST OFFENSE
Ed McBain

This story was first published under my own name, Evan Hunter. But because of its genesis, I've chosen now to have it reprinted under the Ed McBain pseudonym. Fair is fair, and justice should, in the long run, triumph. Here's how the story came into being.

When I began doing research for the first of the 87th Precinct novels, I spent a great deal of time with the police in New York, hanging around squadrooms, riding in radio motor patrol cars, accompanying officers to court, visiting the lab – and attending lineups, which at the time were very different from today's lineups, or 'showups' as they are sometimes called. Back then, felony offenders were taken on the morning after their arrest to be viewed by detectives from precincts all over the city. The purpose of these lineups, presided over by the Chief of Detectives, was to acquaint working detectives with the people committing crimes, on the assumption that a man who commits a crime once is likely to commit the same crime again, and it would be valuable for detectives to recognize *such an offender if ever they saw him on their turf.*

Nowadays this practice has been abandoned: scheduling two detectives from each precinct for lineup duty every Monday through Thursday seems a wasteful procedure when those men could better spend their time actually preventing or investigating crimes. Lineups today are usually conducted in the station house itself, for the sole purpose of positive identification of a suspect by the victim of a crime.

I used a lineup for plot purposes in the first of the 87th Precinct novels – Cop Hater, *published in 1956. But before that, I wrote 'First Offense'. I wrote it because I hoped to reach a great many young people who didn't understand the old police adage: 'If you can't do the time, don't do the crime.' I wanted to acquaint them with the cold, hard facts of arrest and possible conviction. I wanted to tell them, in terms they could easily understand, what it might mean for them if their thoughtless burglary or assault or armed robbery did not go exactly as planned. I wanted to alert them to the dangers and consequences of crime. I wanted to offer them a choice.*

It's rare, I feel, that a writer has an opportunity to present a persuasive argument in terms of a short, self-contained and (I hope) dramatic story. I felt I had something very important to say in 'First Offense', and I said it as honestly as I knew how. My hope then was that the story might cause someone out there to think *at least a little before taking the single step that could change his life forever.*

That is still my hope now.

He sat in the police van with the collar of his leather jacket turned up, the bright silver studs sharp against the otherwise unrelieved black. He was seventeen years old, and he wore his hair in a high black crown. He carried his head high and erect because he knew he had a good profile, and he carried his mouth like a switch knife, ready to spring open at the slightest provocation. His hands were thrust deep into his jacket pockets, and his gray eyes reflected the walls of the van. There was excitement in his eyes, too, an almost holiday excitement. He tried to tell himself he was in trouble, but he couldn't quite believe it. His gradual descent to disbelief had been a spiral that had spun dizzily through the range of his emotions. Terror when the cop's flash had picked him out; blind panic when he'd started to run; rebellion when the cop's firm hand had closed around the leather sleeve of his jacket; sullen resignation when the cop had thrown him into the RMP car; and then cocky stubbornness when they'd booked him at the local precinct.

The desk sergeant had looked him over curiously, with a strange aloofness in his Irish eyes.

'What's the matter, Fatty?' he'd asked.

The sergeant stared at him implacably. 'Put him away for the night,' the sergeant said.

He'd slept overnight in the precinct cell block, and he'd awakened with this strange excitement pulsing through his narrow body, and it was the excitement that had caused his disbelief. Trouble, hell! He'd been in trouble before, but it had never felt like this. This was different. This was a ball, man. This was like being initiated into a secret society some place. His contempt for the police had grown when they refused him the opportunity to shave after breakfast. He was only seventeen, but he had a fairly decent beard, and a man should be allowed to shave in the morning, what the hell! But even the beard had somehow lent to the unreality of the situation, made him appear – in his own eyes –

somehow more desperate, more sinister-looking. He knew he was in trouble, but the trouble was glamorous, and he surrounded it with the gossamer lie of make-believe. He was living the story-book legend. He was big time now. They'd caught him and booked him, and he should have been scared but he was excited instead.

There was one other person in the van with him, a guy who'd spent the night in the cell block, too. The guy was an obvious bum, and his breath stank of cheap wine, but he was better than nobody to talk to.

'Hey!' he said.

The bum looked up. 'You talking to me?'

'Yeah. Where we going?'

'The lineup, kid,' the bum said. 'This your first offense?'

'This's the first time I got caught,' he answered cockily.

'All felonies go to the lineup,' the bum told him. 'And also some special types of misdemeanors. You commit a felony?'

'Yeah,' he said, hoping he sounded nonchalant. What'd they have this bum in for anyway? Sleeping on a park bench?

'Well, that's why you're goin' to the lineup. They have guys from every detective squad in the city there, to look you over. So they'll remember you next time. They put you on a stage, and they read off the offense, and the Chief of Detectives starts firing questions at you. What's your name, kid?'

'What's it to you?'

'Don't get smart, punk, or I'll break your arm,' the bum said.

He looked at the bum curiously. He was a pretty big guy, with a heavy growth of beard, and powerful shoulders. 'My name's Stevie,' he said.

'I'm Jim Skinner,' the bum said. 'When somebody's trying to give you advice, don't go hip on him.'

'Yeah. Well, what's your advice?' he asked, not wanting to back down completely.

'When they get you up there, you don't have to answer anything. They'll throw questions, but you don't have to answer. Did you make a statement at the scene?'

'No,' he answered.

'Good. Then don't make no statement now, either. They can't force you to. Just keep your mouth shut, and don't tell them nothing.'

'I ain't afraid. They know all about it anyway,' Stevie said.

The bum shrugged and gathered around him the sullen pearls of his scattered wisdom. Stevie sat in the van whistling, listening to the accompanying hum of the tires, hearing the secret hum of his blood beneath the other, louder sound. He sat at the core of a self-imposed importance, basking in its warm glow, whistling contentedly, secretly happy. Beside him, Skinner leaned back against the wall of the van.

When they arrived at the Center Street Headquarters, they put them in detention cells, awaiting the lineup which began at nine. At ten minutes to nine they led him out of his cell, and the cop who'd arrested him originally took him into the special prisoners' elevator.

'How's it feel being an elevator boy?' he asked the cop.

The cop didn't answer him. They went upstairs to the big room where the lineup was being held. A detective in front of them was pinning on his shield so he could get past the cop at the desk. They crossed the large gymnasium-like compartment, walking past the men sitting in folded chairs before the stage.

'Get a nice turnout, don't you?' Stevie said.

'You ever tried vaudeville?' the cop answered.

The blinds in the room had not been drawn yet, and Stevie could see everything clearly. The stage itself with the permanently fixed microphone hanging from a narrow metal tube above; the height markers – four feet, five feet, six feet – behind the mike on the wide white wall. The men in the seats, he knew, were all detectives and his sense of importance suddenly flared again when he realized these bulls had come from all over the city just to look at him. Behind the bulls was a raised platform with a sort of lecturer's stand on it. A microphone rested on the stand, and a chair was behind it, and he assumed this was where the chief bull would sit. There were uniformed cops stationed here and there around the room, and there was one man in civilian clothing who sat at a desk in front of the stage.

'Who's that?' Stevie asked the cop.

'Police stenographer,' the cop answered. 'He's going to take down your words for posterity.'

They walked behind the stage, and Stevie watched as other felony offenders from all over the city joined them. There was one woman, but all the rest were men, and he studied their faces carefully, hoping to pick up some tricks from them, hoping to learn the subtlety of their expressions. They didn't look like much. He was better-looking than all of them, and the knowledge pleased him. He'd be the star of this little shindig. The cop who'd been with him moved over to talk to a big broad who was obviously a policewoman. Stevie looked around, spotted Skinner and walked over to him.

'What happens now?' he asked.

'They're gonna pull the shades in a few minutes,' Skinner said. 'Then they'll turn on the spots and start the lineup. The spots won't blind you, but you won't be able to see the faces of any of the bulls out there.'

'Who wants to see them mugs?' Stevie asked.

Skinner shrugged. 'When your case is called, your arresting officer goes back and stands near the Chief of Detectives, just in case the Chief needs more dope from him. The Chief'll read off your name and the borough where you was pinched. A number'll follow the borough. Like he'll say "Manhattan one" or "Manhattan two". That's just the number of the case from that borough. You're first, you get number one, you follow?'

'Yeah,' Stevie said.

'He'll tell the bulls what they got you on, and then he'll say either "Statement" or "No statement". If you made a statement, chances are he won't ask many questions 'cause he won't want you to contradict anything damaging you already said. If there's no statement, he'll fire questions like a machine-gun. But you don't have to answer nothing.'

'Then what?'

'When he's through, you go downstairs to get mugged and printed. Then they take you over to the Criminal Courts Building for arraignment.'

'They're gonna take my picture, huh?' Stevie asked.

'Yeah.'

'You think there'll be reporters here?'

'Huh?'

'Reporters.'

'Oh. Maybe. All the wire services hang out in a room across the street from where the vans pulled up. They got their own police radio in there, and they get the straight dope as soon as it's happening, in case they want to roll with it. There may be some reporters.' Skinner paused. 'Why? What'd do you?'

'It ain't so much what I done,' Stevie said. 'I was just wonderin' if we'd make the papers.'

Skinner stared at him curiously. 'You're all charged up, ain't you, Stevie?'

'Hell, no. Don't you think I know I'm in trouble?'

'Maybe you don't know just how much trouble,' Skinner said.

'What the hell are you talking about?'

'This ain't as exciting as you think, kid. Take my word for it.'

'Sure, you know all about it.'

'I been around a little,' Skinner said drily.

'Sure, on park benches all over the country. I know I'm in trouble, don't worry.'

'You kill anybody?'

'No,' Stevie said.

'Assault?'

Stevie didn't answer.

'Whatever you done,' Skinner advised, 'and no matter how long you been doin' it before they caught you, make like it's your first time. Tell them you done it, and then say you don't know why you done it, but you'll never do it again. It might help you, kid. You might get off with a suspended sentence.'

'Yeah?'

'Sure. And then keep your nose clean afterwards, and you'll be okay.'

'Keep my nose clean! Don't make me laugh, pal.'

Skinner clutched Stevie's arm in a tight grip. 'Kid, don't be a damn fool. If you can get out, get out now! I coulda got out a hundred times, and I'm still with it, and it's no picnic. Get out before you get started.'

Stevie shook off Skinner's hand. 'Come on, willya?' he said, annoyed.

'Knock it off there,' the cop said. 'We're ready to start.'

'Take a look at your neighbors, kid,' Skinner whispered. 'Take a hard look. And then get out of it while you still can.'

Stevie grimaced and turned away from Skinner. Skinner whirled him around to face him again, and there was a pleading desperation on the unshaven face, a mute reaching in the red-rimmed eyes before he spoke again. 'Kid,' he said, 'listen to me. Take my advice. I've been . . .'

'Knock it off!' the cop warned again.

He was suddenly aware of the fact that the shades had been drawn and the room was dim. It was very quiet out there, and he hoped they would take him first. The excitement had risen to an almost fever pitch inside him, and he couldn't wait to get on that stage. What the hell was Skinner talking about anyway? 'Take a look at your neighbors, kid.' The poor jerk probably had a wet brain. What the hell did the police bother with old drunks for, anyway?

A uniformed cop led one of the men from behind the stage, and Stevie moved a little to his left, so that he could see the stage, hoping none of the cops would shove him back where he wouldn't have a good view. His cop and the policewoman were still talking, paying no attention to him. He smiled, unaware that the smile developed as a smirk, and watched the first man mounting the steps to the stage.

The man's eyes were very small, and he kept blinking them, blinking them. He was bald at the back of his head, and he was wearing a Navy peacoat and dark tweed trousers, and his eyes were red-rimmed and sleepy-looking. He reached to the five-foot-six-inches marker on the wall behind him, and he stared out at the bulls, blinking.

'Assisi,' the Chief of Detectives said, 'Augustus, Manhattan one. Thirty-three years old. Picked up in a bar on 43rd and Broadway, carrying a .45 Colt automatic. No statement. How about it, Gus?'

'How about what?' Assisi asked.

'Were you carrying a gun?'

'Yes, I was carrying a gun.' Assisi seemed to realize his shoulders were slumped. He pulled them back suddenly, standing erect.

'Where, Gus?'

'In my pocket.'

'What were you doing with the gun, Gus?'

'I was just carrying it.'

'Why?'

'Listen, I'm not going to answer any questions,' Assisi said. 'You're gonna put me through a third-degree. I ain't answering nothing. I want a lawyer.'

'You'll get plenty opportunity to have a lawyer,' the Chief of Detectives said. 'And nobody's giving you a third-degree. We just want to know what you were doing with a gun. You know that's against the law, don't you?'

'I've got a permit for the gun,' Assisi said.

'We checked with Pistol Permits, and they say no. This is a Navy gun, isn't it?'

'Yeah.'

'What?'

'I said yeah, it's a Navy gun.'

'What were you doing with it? Why were you carrying it around?'

'I like guns.'

'Why?'

'Why what? Why do I like guns? Because . . .'

'Why were you carrying it around?'

'I don't know.'

'Well, you must have a reason for carrying a loaded .45. The gun *was* loaded, wasn't it?'

'Yeah, it was loaded.'

'You have any other guns?'

'No.'

'We found a .38 in your room. How about that one?'

'It's no good.'

'What?'

'The .38.'

'What do you mean, no good?'

'The firin' mechanism is busted.'

'You want a gun that works, is that it?'

'I didn't say that.'

'You said the .38's no good because it won't fire, didn't you?'

'Well, what good's a gun that won't fire?'

'Why do you need a gun that fires?'

'I was just carrying it. I didn't shoot anybody, did I?'

'No, you didn't. Were you planning on shooting somebody?'

'Sure,' Assisi said. 'That's just what I was planning.'

'Who?'

'I don't know,' Assisi said sarcastically. 'Anybody. The first guy I saw, all right? Everybody, all right? I was planning on wholesale murder.'

'Not murder, maybe, but a little larceny, huh?'

'Murder,' Assisi insisted, in his stride now. 'I was just going to shoot up the whole town. Okay? You happy now?'

'Where'd you get the gun?'

'In the Navy.'

'Where?'

'From my ship.'

'It's a stolen gun?'

'No, I found it.'

'You stole government property, is that it?'

'I found it.'

'When'd you get out of the Navy?'

'Three months ago.'

'You worked since?'

'No.'

'Where were you discharged?'

'Pensacola.'

'Is that where you stole the gun?'

'I didn't steal it.'

'Why'd you leave the Navy?'

Assisi hesitated for a long time.

'Why'd you leave the Navy?' the Chief of Detectives asked again.

'They kicked me out!' Assisi snapped.

'Why?'

'I was undesirable!' he shouted.

'Why?'

Assisi did not answer.

'Why?'

There was silence in the darkened room. Stevie watched Assisi's face, the twitching mouth, the blinking eyelids.

'Next case,' the Chief of Detectives said.

Stevie watched as Assisi walked across the stage and down the steps on the other side, where the uniformed cop met him. He'd handled himself well, Assisi had. They'd rattled him a little at the end there, but on the whole he'd done a good job. So the guy was lugging a gun around. So what? He was right, wasn't he? He didn't shoot nobody, so what was all the fuss about? Cops! They had nothing else to do, they went around hauling in guys who were carrying guns. Poor bastard was a veteran, too; that was really rubbing it in. But he did a good job up there, even though he was nervous, you could see he was very nervous.

A man and a woman walked past him and on to the stage. The man was very tall, topping the six-foot marker. The woman was shorter, a bleached blonde turning to fat.

'They picked them up together,' Skinner whispered. 'So they show them together. They figure a pair'll always work as a pair, usually.'

'How'd you like that Assisi?' Stevie whispered back. 'He really had them bulls on the run, didn't he?'

Skinner didn't answer. The Chief of Detectives cleared his throat.

'MacGregor, Peter, aged forty-five, and Anderson, Marcia, aged forty-two, Bronx one. Got them in a parked car on the Grand Concourse. Back seat of the car was loaded with goods, including luggage, a typewriter, a portable sewing machine and a fur coat. No statements. What about all that stuff, Pete?'

'It's mine.'

'The fur coat, too?'

'No, that's Marcia's.'

'You're not married, are you?'

'No.'

'Living together?'

'Well, you know,' Pete said.

'What about the stuff?' the Chief of Detectives said again.

'I told you,' Peter said. 'It's ours.'

'What was it doing in the car?'

'Oh. Well, we were – uh . . .' The man paused for a long time. 'We were going on a trip.'

'Where to?'

'Where? Oh. To – uh . . .' Again he paused, frowning, and Stevie smiled, thinking what a clown this guy was. This guy was better than a sideshow at Coney. This guy couldn't tell a lie without having to think about it for an hour. And the dumpy broad with him was a hot sketch, too. This act alone was worth the price of admission.

'Uh . . .' Pete said, still fumbling for words. 'Uh . . . we were going to – uh . . . Denver.'

'What for?'

'Oh, just a little pleasure trip, you know,' he said, attempting a smile.

'How much money were you carrying when we picked you up?'

'Forty dollars.'

'You were going to Denver on forty dollars?'

'Well, it was fifty dollars. Yeah, it was more like fifty dollars.'

'Come on, Pete, what were you doing with all that stuff in the car?'

'I told you. We were taking a trip.'

'With a sewing-machine, huh? You do a lot of sewing, Pete?'

'Marcia does.'

'That right, Marcia?'

The blonde spoke in a high, reedy voice. 'Yeah, I do a lot of sewing.'

'That fur coat, Marcia. Is it yours?'

'Sure.'

'It has the initials G.D. on the lining. Those aren't your initials, are they, Marcia?'

'No.'

'Whose are they?'

'Search me. We bought that coat in a hock shop.'

'Where?'

'Myrtle Avenue, Brooklyn. You know where that is?'

'Yes, I know where it is. What about that luggage? It had initials on it, too. And they weren't yours or Pete's. How about it?'

'We got that in a hock shop, too.'

'And the typewriter?'

'That's Pete's.'

'Are you a typist, Pete?'

'Well, I fool around a little, you know.'

'We're going to check all this stuff against our Stolen Goods list; you know that, don't you?'

'We got all that stuff in hock shops,' Pete said. 'If it's stolen, we don't know nothing about it.'

'Were you going to Denver with him, Marcia?'

'Oh, sure.'

'When did you both decide to go? A few minutes ago?'

'We decided last week sometime.'

'Were you going to Denver by way of the Grand Concourse?'

'Huh?' Pete said.

'Your car was parked on the Grand Concourse. What were you doing there with a carload of stolen goods?'

'It wasn't stolen,' Pete said.

'We were on our way to Yonkers,' the woman said.

'I thought you were going to Denver.'

'Yeah, but we had to get the car fixed first. There was something wrong with the . . .' She paused, turning to Pete. 'What was it, Pete? That thing that was wrong?'

Pete waited a long time before answering. 'Uh – the – uh . . . the flywheel, yeah. There's a garage up in Yonkers fixes them good, we heard. Flywheels, I mean.'

'If you were going to Yonkers, why were you parked on the Concourse?'

'Well, we were having an argument.'

'What kind of an argument?'

'Not an argument, really. Just a discussion, sort of.'

'About what?'

'About what to eat.'

'What!'

'About what to eat. I wanted to eat Chink's, but Marcia wanted a glass of milk and a piece of pie. So we were trying to decide whether we should go to the Chink's or the cafeteria. That's why we were parked on the Concourse.'

'We found a wallet in your coat, Pete. It wasn't yours, was it?'

'No.'

'Whose was it?'

'I don't know.' He paused, then added hastily, 'There wasn't no money in it.'

'No, but there was identification. A Mr Simon Granger. Where'd you get it, Pete?'

'I found it in the subway. There wasn't no money in it.'

'Did you find all that other stuff in the subway, too?'

'No, sir, I bought that.' He paused. 'I was going to return the wallet, but I forgot to stick it in the mail.'

'Too busy planning for the Denver trip, huh?'

'Yeah, I guess so.'

'When's the last time you earned an honest dollar, Pete?'

Pete grinned. 'Oh, about two, three years ago, I guess.'

'Here're their records,' the Chief of Detectives said. 'Marcia, 1938, Sullivan Law; 1939, Concealing Birth of Issue; 1940, Possession of Narcotics – you still on the stuff, Marcia?'

'No.'

'1942, dis cond; 1943, Narcotics again; 1947 – you had enough, Marcia?'

Marcia didn't answer.

'Pete,' the Chief of Detectives said, '1940, Attempted Rape; 1941, Selective Service Act; 1942, dis cond; 1943, Attempted Burglary; 1945, Living on Proceeds of Prostitution; 1947, Assault and Battery, did two years at Ossining.'

'I never done no time,' Pete said.

'According to this, you did.'

'I never done no time,' he insisted.

'1950,' the Chief of Detectives went on, 'Carnal Abuse of a Child.' He paused. 'Want to tell us about that one, Pete?'

'I – uh . . .' Pete swallowed. 'I got nothing to say.'

'You're ashamed of *some* things, that it?'

Pete didn't answer.

'Get them out of here,' the Chief of Detectives said.

'See how long he kept them up there?' Skinner whispered. 'He knows what they are, wants every bull in the city to recognize them if they . . .'

'Come on,' a detective said, taking Skinner's arm.

Stevie watched as Skinner climbed the steps to the stage. Those two had really been something, all right. And just looking at them, you'd never know they were such operators. You'd never know they . . .

'Skinner, James, Manhattan two. Aged fifty-one. Threw a garbage-can through the plate-glass window of a clothing shop on Third Avenue. Arresting officer found him inside the shop with a bundle of overcoats. No statement. That right, James?'

'I don't remember,' Skinner said.

'Is it, or isn't it?'

'All I remember is waking up in jail this morning.'

'You don't remember throwing that ash can through the window?'

'No, sir.'

'You don't remember taking those overcoats?'

'No, sir.'

'Well, you must have done it, don't you think? The off-duty detective found you inside the store with the coats in your arms.'

'I got only his word for that, sir.'

'Well, his word is pretty good. Especially since he found you inside the store with your arms full of merchandise.'

'I don't remember, sir.'

'You've been here before, haven't you?'

'I don't remember, sir.'

'What do you do for a living, James?'

'I'm unemployed, sir.'

'When's the last time you worked?'

'I don't remember, sir.'

'You don't remember much of anything, do you?'

'I have a poor memory, sir.'

'Maybe the record has a better memory than you, James,' the Chief of Detectives said.

'Maybe so, sir. I couldn't say.'

'I hardly know where to start, James. You haven't been exactly an ideal citizen.'

'Haven't, I, sir?'

'Here's as good a place as any. 1948, Assault and Robbery; 1949, Indecent Exposure; 1951, Burglary; 1952, Assault and Robbery again. You're quite a guy, aren't you, James?'

'If you say so, sir.'

'I say so. Now how about that store?'

'I don't remember anything about a store, sir.'

'Why'd you break into it?'

'I don't remember breaking into any store, sir.'

'Hey, what's this?' the Chief of Detectives said suddenly.

'Sir?'

'Maybe we should've started back a little further, huh, James? Here, on your record. 1938, convicted of first-degree murder, sentenced to execution.'

The assembled bulls began murmuring among themselves. Stevie leaned forward eagerly, anxious to get a better look at this bum who'd offered him advice.

'What happened there, James?'

'What happened where, sir?'

'You were sentenced to death? How come you're still with us?'

'The case was appealed.'

'And never retried?'

'No, sir.'

'You're pretty lucky, aren't you?'

'I'm pretty unlucky, sir, if you ask me.'

'Is that right? You cheat the chair, and you call that unlucky. Well, the law won't slip up this time.'

'I don't know anything about law, sir.'

'You don't, huh?'

'No, sir. I only know that if you want to get a police station into action, all you have to do is buy a cheap bottle of wine and drink it quiet, minding your own business.'

'And that's what you did, huh, James?'

'That's what I did, sir.'

'And you don't remember breaking into that store?'

'I don't remember anything.'

'All right, next case.'

Skinner turned his head slowly, and his eyes met Stevie's squarely. Again there was the same mute pleading in his eyes, and then he turned his head away and shuffled off the stage and down the steps into the darkness.

The cop's hand closed around Stevie's biceps. For an instant he didn't know what was happening, and then he realized his case was the next one. He shook off the cop's hand, squared his shoulders, lifted his head and began climbing the steps.

He felt taller all at once. He felt like an actor coming on after his cue. There was an aura of unreality about the stage and the darkened room beyond it, the bulls sitting in that room.

The Chief of Detectives was reading off the information about him, but he didn't hear it. He kept looking at the lights, which were not really so bright, they didn't blind him at all. Didn't they have brighter lights? Couldn't they put more lights on him, so they could see him when he told his story?

He tried to make out the faces of the detectives, but he couldn't see them clearly, and he was aware of the Chief of Detectives' voice droning on and on, but he didn't hear what the man was saying, he heard only the hum of his voice. He glanced over his shoulder, trying to see how tall he was against the markers, and then he stood erect, his shoulders back, moving closer to the hanging microphone, wanting to be sure his voice was heard when he began speaking.

'. . . no statement,' the Chief of Detectives concluded. There was a long pause, and Stevie waited, holding his breath. 'This your first offense, Steve?' the Chief of Detectives asked.

'Don't you know?' Stevie answered.

'I'm asking you.'

'Yeah, it's my first offense.'

'You want to tell us all about it?'

'There's nothing to tell. You know the whole story, anyway.'

'Sure, but do you?'

'What are you talking about?'

'Tell us the story, Steve.'

'Whatya makin' a big federal case out of a lousy stick-up for? Ain't you got nothing better to do with your time?'

'We've got plenty of time, Steve.'

'Well, I'm in a hurry.'

'You're not going any place, kid. Tell us about it.'

'What's there to tell? There was a candy store stuck up, that's all.'

'Did you stick it up?'

'That's for me to know and you to find out.'

'We know you did.'

'Then don't ask me stupid questions.'

'Why'd you do it?'

'I ran out of butts.'

'Come on, kid.'

'I done it 'cause I wanted to.'

'Why?'

'Look, you caught me cold, so let's get this over with, huh? Whatya wastin' time with me for?'

'We want to hear what you've got to say. Why'd you pick this particular candy store?'

'I just picked it. I put slips in a hat and picked this one out.'

'You didn't really, did you, Steve?'

'No, I didn't really. I picked it 'cause there's an old crumb who runs it, and I figured it was a pushover.'

'What time did you enter the store, Steve?'

'The old guy told you all this already, didn't he? Look, I know I'm up here so you can get a good look at me. All right, take your good look, and let's get it over with.'

'What time, Steve?'

'I don't have to tell you nothing.'

'Except that we know it already.'

'Then why do you want to hear it again? Ten o'clock, all right? How does that fit?'

'A little early, isn't it?'

'How's eleven? Try that one for size.'

'Let's make it twelve, and we'll be closer.'

'Make it whatever you want to,' Stevie said, pleased with the way he was handling this. They knew all about it, anyway, so he might as well have himself a ball, show them they couldn't shove him around.

'You went into the store at twelve; is that right?'

'If you say so, Chief.'

'Did you have a gun?'

'No.'

'What, then?'

'Nothing.'

'Nothing at all?'

'Just me. I scared him with a dirty look, that's all.'

'You had a switch knife, didn't you?'

'You found one on me, so why ask?'

'Did you use the knife?'

'No.'

'You didn't tell the old man to open the cash register or you'd cut him up? Isn't that what you said?'

'I didn't make a tape recording of what I said.'

'But you did threaten him with the knife. You did force him to open the cash register, holding the knife on him.'

'I suppose so.'

'How much money did you get?'

'You've got the dough. Why don't you count it?'

'We already have. Twelve dollars; is that right?'

'I didn't get a chance to count it. The Law showed.'

'When did the Law show?'

'When I was leaving. Ask the cop who pinched me. He knows when.'

'Something happened before you left, though.'

'Nothing happened. I cleaned out the register and then blew. Period.'

'Your knife had blood on it.'

'Yeah? I was cleaning chickens last night.'

'You stabbed the owner of that store, didn't you?'

'Me? I never stabbed nobody in my whole life.'

'Why'd you stab him?'

'I didn't.'

'Where'd you stab him?'

'I didn't stab him.'

'Did he start yelling?'

'I don't know what you're talking about.'

'You stabbed him, Steve. We know you did.'

'You're full of crap.'

'Don't get smart, Steve.'

'Ain't you had your look yet? What the hell more do you want?'

'We want you to tell us why you stabbed the owner of that store.'

'And I told you I didn't stab him.'

'He was taken to the hospital last night with six knife-wounds in his chest and abdomen. Now how about that, Steve?'

'Save your questioning for the Detective Squad Room. I ain't saying another word.'

'You had your money. Why'd you stab him?'

Stevie did not answer.

'Were you afraid?'

'Afraid of what?' Stevie answered defiantly.

'I don't know. Afraid he'd tell who held him up? Afraid he'd start yelling? What were you afraid of, kid?'

'I wasn't afraid of nothing. I told the old crumb to keep his mouth shut. He shoulda listened to me.'

'He didn't keep his mouth shut?'

'Ask him.'

'I'm asking you!'

'No, he didn't keep his mouth shut. He started yelling. Right after I'd cleaned out the drawer. The damn jerk, for a lousy twelve bucks he starts yelling.'

'What'd you do?'

'I told him to shut up.'

'And he didn't.'

'No, he didn't. So I hit him, and he still kept yelling. So – I gave him the knife.'

'Six times?'

'I don't know how many times. I just – gave it to him. He shouldn't have yelled. You ask him if I did any harm to him before that. Go ahead, ask him. He'll tell you. I didn't even touch the crumb before he started yelling. Go to the hospital and ask him if I touched him. Go ahead, ask him.'

'We can't, Steve.'

'Wh . . .'

'He died this morning.'

'He . . .' For a moment, Stevie could not think clearly. Died? Is that what he'd said? The room was curiously still now. It had been silently attentive before, but this was something else, something different, and the stillness suddenly chilled him, and he looked down at his shoes.

'I – I didn't mean him to pass away,' he mumbled.

The police stenographer looked up. 'To what?'

'To pass away,' a uniformed cop repeated, whispering.

'What?' the stenographer asked again.

'He didn't mean him to pass away!' the cop shouted.

The cop's voice echoed in the silent room. The stenographer bent his head and began scribbling in his pad.

'Next case,' the Chief of Detectives said.

Stevie walked off the stage, his mind curiously blank, his feet strangely leaden. He followed the cop to the door, and then walked with him to the elevator. They were both silent as the doors closed.

'You picked an important one for your first one,' the cop said.

'He shouldn't have died on me,' Stevie answered.

'You shouldn't have stabbed him,' the cop said.

He tried to remember what Skinner had said to him before the lineup, but the noise of the elevator was loud in his ears, and he couldn't think clearly. He could only remember the word 'neighbors' as the elevator dropped to the basement to join them.

SOMEBODY'S TELLING THE TRUTH

Patricia McGerr

*In reading or writing mysteries, I get a special pleasure from the discovery of a new variation on an old theme. My first novel (*Pick Your Victim, *1946) reversed a classic formula by naming the murderer at the start of the book and keeping the identity of the victim secret until the end. This plot twist was repeated in my fifth book,* Follow as the Night, *which won France's* Grand Prix de Littérature Policière *in 1952. In other of my novels, the mystery was centered on both the murderer and the victim, or the detective, or the witness to the crime.*

My later mysteries, both long and short, have been more conventional. Most of my magazine stories chronicle the adventures of a female secret agent, Selena Mead, who, like me, lives in Washington, but roams the world in defense of peace and freedom.

Only a few of my stories have a policeman as hero; Captain Rogan and Sergeant Pringle have, to date, been teamed in three of them. I particularly enjoyed writing 'Somebody's Telling the Truth' because – though it fits the crime-and-detection mold – there is also a significant break with tradition. Most fictional murderers deny their guilt and try to escape conviction with contrived alibis, lies and misdirection. The crime-solver must try to disprove the lies and, in the end, force the villain to confess.

But this story begins *with a confession, and the murderer aims to deceive by telling the truth, the whole truth and nothing but the truth. Thus, he presents the detective with a new kind of challenge.*

'This one's a beauty,' Captain Rogan said cheerfully, as he climbed into the car beside Sergeant Pringle.

It was an odd term to apply to a murder, but the sergeant nodded agreement. By Homicide Squad definition it described any investigation that could be wrapped up without overtime. And the case they were headed toward on this crisp January evening was, it appeared, right at the top of that category. The desk man had recorded the call at 7:47.

'This is Horace Sanderson,' the authoritative voice at the other end had announced. 'I want to report a murder. I've shot a man in my office.'

So all they needed to do was visit the scene, hear his confession, and bring him in. As the captain said, 'This one's a beauty.'

'Sanderson,' Pringle ruminated while he eased the car away from the curb. 'Don't I know that name from somewhere?'

'You should,' Rogan returned. 'If he's never made a monkey of you on the witness stand, you're a lucky exception.'

'Oh, sure, the big defense lawyer. No, I haven't testified in any of his cases, but I've heard plenty from those who have. They say he gets an extra charge out of making our guys sweat.'

'Too right.' Rogan's lips twisted wryly in personal recollection. 'On cross-examination he can turn you around till you misspell your own name. But now it's our turn. I'm going to like seeing Mr Horace Sanderson in the dock.'

'Weird, isn't it, that after all the raps he's beaten for other people he'd turn himself in without a fight.'

'It has to mean the evidence against him is airtight,' Rogan said with satisfaction. 'Sanderson knows criminal law up and down, backwards and sideways. If he could've seen the smallest loophole he'd never have started off by admitting he did it.'

'Maybe he'll claim self-defense,' the sergeant suggested.

'On the phone he called it murder. He knows every meaning of that word and it doesn't include justifiable homicide.'

'How about not guilty because of temporary insanity?'

'That's one he might try,' Rogan conceded, 'but it won't affect our schedule. All we want are the facts. If he decides to take the psycho route it'll be the D.A.'s headache. Unless the lab boys slow us down, we'll be drinking squadroom coffee again before ten o'clock tonight.'

It was a short ride to the building that housed the Sanderson law offices. Pringle parked in front and the two men rode the elevator to the fourth floor. The only door that showed a light was lettered 'Sanderson, Sanderson & Sanderson, Attorneys-at-Law.' At Rogan's sharp rap it was opened by a tall, broad-shouldered man of 60-odd whose physique, grooming, and general air of affluence fitted him to intimidate the most hostile witness.

'You made fast time, gentlemen,' he complimented them. 'Captain Rogan, I believe.' He paused to nudge his recollection. 'Ah, yes, you were the arresting officer in the Hutchins murder, weren't you? A pity you got the wrong man. And your colleague – ' He looked questioningly at Pringle. 'I don't believe our paths have crossed before.'

'This is Sergeant Pringle,' Rogan snapped. Acquittal of the man he was sure had killed Tom Hutchins was still a rankling memory. 'It's my duty to inform you that you are not required to answer – '

'Skip the litany,' Sanderson cut him off. 'I'm well informed as to my rights and I'm already represented by counsel. If you'll come into the next room I'll show you the corpse and tell you what happened.'

A cool, cool customer, Rogan thought with reluctant admiration. His head's halfway in the noose, but he's the same take-charge guy as he is in the courtroom.

Sanderson crossed the reception room to open an inner door. He passed through it, then stepped aside to unblock the view. Sprawled on the dark green rug of what appeared to be a conference room was a man's body.

Rogan dropped to one knee beside it. Lifting the left wrist he felt for a pulse, though he was sure he wouldn't find one. The blood-matted hair at the back of the head indicated that a bullet must have entered the brain to bring instant death.

'D.O.A.,' he told Pringle. 'We'll want the technical unit and the morgue wagon.'

'Use the phone on the desk in the corner, Sergeant,' Sanderson said helpfully.

Rogan straightened and looked down at the dead man. He had fallen forward, but the face was turned to rest on one cheek. Rogan felt a glimmer of recognition.

'An old friend, Captain?' Sanderson asked. 'His name is – or was – Chet Tankersley.'

Gambler, confidence man, jack-of-many-crooked-trades. The computer in Rogan's head punched the appropriate slots. No loss to society. He liked the case even better.

'You shot him?' he asked.

'With this gun.' Sanderson stepped around the body to approach the long table that filled two-thirds the length of the room and pointed to the weapon that lay on its mirror-bright surface. 'I have a license for it, of course. A criminal practice can bring in some rough characters, so I keep it loaded and ready in my desk.'

Is he laying a basis for self-defense after all, Rogan wondered, then looked again at the victim and was reassured. The shot had come from behind and the position of the body showed that Tankersley had been on his way out of the office.

Pringle had finished telephoning. 'They're on the way, Captain,' he reported.

'Fine. Now we'd better hear your story, Mr Sanderson.'

'I'm waiting to tell it,' he assured him. 'I want my lawyers present, of course.'

Three private offices were connected to the conference room. On each was a name. Horace T. Sanderson, Sr. Horace T. Sanderson, Jr. Paul A. Sanderson. The lawyer walked to the center door – his own – and opened it to say, 'Come out, boys, I need you.'

'My sons and legal counsel,' he introduced the two young men who answered the summons. 'Horace, Junior and Paul.' Paul, the younger one, was a slim replica of his father, while Horace, Jr, slightly overweight, with narrow eyes and soft lips, showed no sign of the hard courage and sharp intelligence that marked the other two. Junior must favor the maternal line, Rogan decided. If the firm is to go on, it will be Paul who takes the old man's place.

'Sit down, gentlemen.' Sanderson took a seat at the end of the table farthest from the body, with one son on each side. Sergeant Pringle stayed at a desk near the door. Rogan turned one of the chairs round and straddled it to retain a sense of mobility.

'I'll get right to the point.' Sanderson, Sr's tone seemed more suited to chairing a board meeting than to confessing a crime. 'This afternoon, Sonny – that is, Horace, Junior – told me he was being blackmailed. Tankersley had a certain document bearing Horace, Junior's signature that could, if made public, lead to his disbarment. Tankersley asked $25,000 and was coming here today after office hours to collect.

'Sonny had managed to raise $15,000 on his own and asked me for the balance. I advised him not to give the man one cent and said that I would deal with him myself. My two sons, therefore, left the office at 5:30, the usual time, and drove home together. I stayed behind, and was alone when Tankersley arrived.

'I told him there would be no payoff, now or ever, and threatened him with arrest for blackmail unless he immediately gave me the incriminating document. It was, I admit, a bluff, and it failed. That paper, as Tankersley well knew, would not only end my son's career but cast doubt on the integrity of our law firm. He grew abusive and said I had until noon tomorrow to change my mind. If by that time he did not receive the entire sum, the document would be delivered to the secretary of the Bar Association.

'Well, gentlemen, what could I do? I looked at that miserable creature who held in his hand my family name, my son's future, the professional reputation I'd built with such care.' His voice rose to the dramatic height that had swayed so many juries. 'Something exploded in my brain.'

He paused and Rogan exchanged a quick glance with the sergeant. So it was to be a plea of temporary insanity.

'He walked out of my office. I took the gun from my drawer, followed him into this room, and shot him. Then I phoned my own house. Paul answered. I said I wanted them both here and they drove right back. I explained what had happened and, as my counsel, they advised me to notify the police and make a clean breast of it. Which I have just done.'

'And the document that Tankersley was holding?' Rogan asked.

'I took it from the dead man's pocket, tore it into small pieces, burned the pieces, and flushed away the ashes. I apologize for destroying evidence, but I believe my motive is clear enough without making public what I've killed a man to keep secret.'

Before Rogan could answer, a rap on the outer door signaled the arrival of the technical unit. Admitted by Pringle and instructed by Rogan, they set about their routines with camera and other equipment. The captain returned to the three Sandersons.

'I appreciate your giving us such a straightforward story,' Rogan told the father.

'I like to make your job easy when I can, Captain,' Sanderson, Sr returned with sham geniality. 'Besides, I really have no choice. The body is in my office. The bullet came from my gun. Tankersley may even have told someone about his appointment with Sonny. I know better than to try to buck those odds.'

'Then the next step is to go to Headquarters, get your statement typed and signed, and – '

'I'm familiar with the procedure,' Sanderson reminded him. 'And I'm sure you'll follow all the rules. We can't charge police brutality tonight, can we, boys?'

'No, we can't,' Paul answered for them both. His glance at Rogan held the same glint of mockery as his father's. 'Our client's statement was freely given and is correct in almost every detail.'

'Almost?' Rogan felt a stir of apprehension on the edge of his complacency.

'He's made one significant error,' Paul continued. 'Sonny didn't say anything to dad about being blackmailed. Sonny told me.'

'Oh? Then you passed it on to your father?'

'Certainly not. I agreed with my brother that we'd better keep it to ourselves. So I told dad I had some work to finish, and he and Sonny left together. After that everything happened just as my father reported it – except it was I who waited here for Tankersley. I'm the one who shot him.'

'You – ' Rogan left the sentence suspended.

'It's his word against mine, Captain,' Sanderson, Sr said. 'Which of us do you believe?'

'I'll get that answer from your other son.' Rogan's eyes moved to Horace, Jr. 'Did you tell your father or your brother about the blackmail? Which one rode home with you?'

Sonny's gaze stayed on the table top. His voice was low, with each word forced through stiff lips.

'I didn't tell anybody,' he answered. 'And I didn't go home. I said *I* had work to finish and let dad and Paul leave without me. When Tankersley came I told him I had only $15,000. He said it wasn't enough, he was sure my father would give me the rest sooner than see me disgraced. I said I didn't want dad to know and he laughed at me. He said I had until twelve o'clock tomorrow noon to raise the whole $25,000 or – as dad told you – he'd turn the paper over to the Bar Association. I couldn't let that happen. So when he started to go, I – I shot him.'

'Where did you get the gun?'

'Out of dad's drawer. I know where he keeps it.'

'Let's see if I have the picture straight. Tankersley left your office, you ran into your father's room, took his gun and – '

'No,' Sonny interrupted. 'I was already in dad's room when I talked to Tankersley. I'd put the money in his safe and wanted to be where I could get it out right away if he agreed to settle for what I had.'

'And you?' He turned to the younger brother. 'Where did you conduct the interview?'

'I'm the junior junior partner,' Paul returned smoothly. 'My room is small and my desk cluttered. When dad's away I take my visitors into his office.'

Very carefully arranged, Rogan thought glumly. Tankersley's fingerprints will show up only in the father's office – just as all three stories indicate.

'We're a close-knit family,' Sanderson explained. 'I told my two sons that I was guilty and that they shouldn't interfere. But you know how it is with young people nowadays. No respect.'

'One of you killed Tankersley.' Rogan organized his thinking out loud. 'Then he called the other two back to the office. The three of you talked it over and cooked up this round robin.'

'Exactly.' Sanderson beamed at him. 'So you have two confessions left over. Untidy, isn't it? If one of us is charged, each of the other two will swear he did it. You haven't a prayer of getting an indictment, much less a conviction.'

'Don't bet on it, Mr Sanderson,' Rogan said. 'You've wasted your time and mine with your phony confessions.'

'Only two are phony,' Paul murmured. 'One of us is telling the truth.'

Rogan ignored the interruption. 'Now we'll get on with our work, just as we would if all three of you had denied it. We solve a fair number of cases without anybody coming forward to say he did it.' He could not resist the sarcasm. 'Sometimes we even convict one of your clients.'

'Indeed you do,' Sanderson agreed heartily. 'The city has a very efficient force and I'll observe your work with great interest.' He looked beyond Rogan to watch the morgue men cover the body preparatory to its removal. 'I don't usually get to see the start of an investigation. But I'm afraid the evidence you'll collect here won't be very helpful. Fingerprints, for instance. I know how important they can be. But we were a bit nervous while we waited for you and we wandered about opening doors and drawers. As a result you'll find all three sets of prints in random order all over the place.'

'In other words,' Rogan interpreted, 'the one who committed the crime gave the other two a step-by-step account of his actions from the moment of Tankersley's arrival. Then the other two re-enacted the crime, taking care to touch all pertinent surfaces. No doubt all three of you handled the weapon.'

'Naturally.' Sanderson's face burlesqued repentance. 'I'm afraid we did something even more reprehensible. I call your attention to the holes in the wall near the ceiling. The two of us who aren't guilty both took a shot up there. Very bad for the panelling, but tests will show that all three of us recently fired a gun.'

The old sod's enjoying this, Rogan thought sourly. He's used to being called in to pick up the pieces after his client has made a mess of it and the police have all the evidence. For the first time he's been on the scene ahead of us, able to set the stage to show exactly what he wants us to see. He's handled more murder cases than most policemen and can anticipate all our moves, plus some we might not think of.

'Worried, Captain?' the senior Sanderson prodded.

'Just trying to work out a timetable.' Rogan left his chair and walked to the head of the table to place himself between father and older son. 'You said your sons left here at 5:30.' He focused on the father. 'How long does it usually take to get home?'

'In normal traffic, twenty-five minutes.'

'And what time did you phone them?'

'Six-fifteen. My interview with Tankersley was brief.'

'Then I can assume they got back here at 6:40. Right?'

'Give or take five minutes, that's correct.'

'That gave you a full hour to discuss the situation, make a plan, and arrange the – er – stage effects. I'm inclined to agree with you, Mr Sanderson, that we won't find evidence here to point to the one who actually committed the murder.' He waited for the other man's lips to curve into a satisfied smile before adding, 'It may be easier to discover which two went home.'

Rogan whirled to face Horace, Jr and leaned down till their noses were only inches apart. 'Tell me, Sonny,' he barked, 'who drove the car home?'

'Dad always – ' The young man broke off, gulped air. 'I mean, I don't know who drove tonight. I didn't go home. I told you, I stayed here. I – ' His eyes darted to his father, seeking rescue.

'Don't bully the boy,' Sanderson said softly. 'He's already told his story.'

'But he was about to tell a different one. He started to say that you drove home and he rode beside you. That places Paul in the office at the time of the murder.'

'So it does,' Paul agreed. 'You see, I was telling the truth all the time.'

'Don't talk nonsense, Captain,' Sanderson ordered. 'What Sonny started to say was, "Dad always drives." and that's true. When the three of us are together, I'm always the driver. But I wasn't in the car this evening, so I presume Paul took the wheel. That's how it usually is, isn't it, Sonny?'

'Yes, I – I don't care much for driving.'

And you don't care much for this game of bait-the-cop either, Rogan added mentally. Sanderson, Sr and Paul are riding every wave, but Sonny looks as if he's about to go under. Judging by the way he acts, he's guilty as hell, but that doesn't move me forward. Unquestionably he's guilty of falling into a blackmail trap – which makes him responsible for what happened tonight, even if someone else did the shooting.

Rogan walked down the table to confer with Sergeant Pringle, then returned to the Sandersons.

'Thought of some more questions, Captain?' the father asked.

'The same one,' Rogan answered. 'Which of you three killed him? We're going to look for the answer in places where you didn't have time to doctor the evidence. Your house and your car, for instance.'

'Good thinking,' Sanderson applauded. 'Since you can't find the guilty one, maybe you can pin down the two who are innocent. The car's parked in the garage under this building, but I doubt if it will yield any secrets. Will it, Paul?'

'No, dad,' the younger son answered confidently. 'You see,' Paul told Rogan, 'after I asked my father and brother to come back here, it occurred to us that you'd be curious about who drove and who was in the passenger seat. So I went down with a clean cloth and wiped off the wheel, the door handles – did a general cleanup job. Your fingerprint man is going to draw another blank.'

'But you didn't go all the way home with your clean cloth, did you?' Rogan asked. 'Or did you alert someone there to take care of it?'

'No,' Paul conceded. 'Mom's out of town and we're batching it this week. You'll get a fine collection of prints at home. But since that's where the three of us live, I don't know what you expect them to prove.'

'Don't underestimate the captain's intelligence,' his father advised. 'He's thinking of spots like doorknobs which might indicate who was the last man to go in or out.'

'How disappointing for you,' Paul said. 'There's an electric gadget in the car that opens the garage door. The stairs go right into the center hall with no need to turn any knobs.'

'Don't overlook the telephone,' Sanderson suggested. 'If it was Paul who answered my call, as I said he did, his prints will be on top. Unless he was in his own room at the time, in which case the prints won't prove anything.'

'No more,' Paul seconded, 'than can be proved if dad took my call on his bedside phone.'

'Just to complete the circle, Sonny,' Rogan asked without enthusiasm, 'who answered the phone when you called home?'

'Paul did. But I asked him to let me talk to dad.'

'You're not forgetting,' Sanderson put in, 'the possibility of witnesses?'

'I'm sure you didn't forget it, either,' Rogan returned.

'The boys assured me there was no one else in the elevator or in the garage when they left here and, of course, by the time they got back, the building was empty. If we weren't sure of that we wouldn't be taking this line.'

'But the streets and sidewalks weren't deserted,' Rogan reminded him. 'There's no way on earth you can be sure that someone won't come forward who saw you somewhere along the way.'

'No doubt many people saw the car,' Sanderson agreed. 'But it was dark by 5:30 and I challenge anybody to make positive identification in a moving vehicle under those conditions. Especially when there's such a strong family resemblance.'

So now, Rogan told himself, we're back to Go. Sanderson has foreseen every possible move. He reads my thoughts even before I think them.

Rogan left them to pace restlessly around the table. Since Sanderson is so knowledgeable about how the official mind works, I'd better stop thinking like a police officer and try to get inside the murderer. There must be some place he's slipped up.

He looked back at his antagonists. Sanderson, Sr and Paul were talking in low tones. Sonny watched them warily. Who scares Sonny most, Rogan wondered, his father or me? Is he shaking because he may be tagged for murder or because he may not be able to stick to the lie the old man's making him tell? Junior's getting closer and closer to the edge. If I could talk to him alone, he'd break. But the other two won't let that happen.

Rogan went into the office marked with the name of Horace, Jr and sat down at a desk whose bare top could indicate either extreme efficiency or that he was given very little to do. An inspection of the nearly empty drawers tended to support the second theory. Sergeant Pringle came in to report that the car, as predicted, showed no clue as to its most recent occupants.

'Tough going, Captain,' the sergeant commiserated. 'You got a favorite?'

'I like Sonny for it,' Rogan answered. 'His father and brother are the smart ones, the glib ones, the two who can stick to a lie and sidestep any trap that might give them away. If one of them had killed Tankersley, it's not likely they'd set up an escape route that would be shut off if Sonny broke under pressure. But with Sonny as the killer, the three-way confession lets him tell nothing but the truth. That way Sonny knows the answer to every question we ask and only the other two need to be quick-witted.'

'He looks like a very nervous boy,' Pringle said. 'Too bad you can't lean on him a little.'

'Maybe I can. I'm thinking about a breath test.'

'The kind the traffic squad uses on drunk drivers?'

'That's it. Can you get a machine up here in a hurry?'

'Right away.' Pringle looked puzzled, but he didn't ask any more questions. While he telephoned, Rogan moved on to the office of Sanderson, Sr, where the technicians were turning up an abundance of prints that pointed nowhere. Then he looked into Paul's room, which confirmed the younger son's statement about its smallness and clutter. When the sergeant announced the arrival of an officer with a breath machine, Rogan escorted all of them to the table.

'You don't seem to be making much progress, Captain,' Sanderson jibed.

'I'm still trying to eliminate the two who are lying,' Rogan answered. 'We've established that they arrived home about twenty minutes before the phone call that brought them back. The question is, how did they spend that time at home?'

'An intriguing question,' Sanderson said. 'Unfortunately, since none of us admits having gone home, there's no one to answer it.'

'So I'll have to guess. What does a successful lawyer do at the end of a hard day's work? I think he unwinds over a drink. Am I right?'

'Absolutely,' Sanderson agreed. 'My personal preference is a very dry martini. But I don't see how that's relevant.'

'I'm going to ask you to cooperate in an experiment. We have here a machine that measures blood alcohol content. If three of you blow into it and two register a recent intake of alcohol – well, you follow my reasoning, I'm sure.'

'You'll put it down that those two were relaxing at home while the third was committing murder. Very ingenious.' Sanderson's tone was indulgent. 'I've never seen one of these before. Always been curious about how they work.'

The officer placed the box-like machine in front of Sanderson, twisted a dial, and put a narrow tube into his hand.

'Just blow into it,' Rogan directed. 'The needle will tell us if you've had a drink.'

Sanderson followed instructions. The needle stayed at zero. The officer turned the machine to Paul, who provided a breath sample with the same result.

'Another good idea gone wrong,' Sanderson said in mock sympathy as the machine was moved in front of Sonny. 'There's one flaw in your reasoning, Captain. We're civilized people who treat our before-dinner drinks with ceremony. We don't rush from car to bar.' He looked at his older son who was regarding the machine with a suspicious scowl. 'Go ahead, Sonny. It won't bite.'

'This is stupid,' Sonny said.

'Play the game,' his father ordered. 'Give the captain his full quota of hot air.'

The officer lifted the tube to Sonny's mouth. His scowl deepened, but he gave a quick exhalation. The needle moved to the left.

'Alcoholic content point zero eight,' the officer read. 'At his weight that's about four ounces.'

'What?' Sanderson exploded. 'That's impossible. Sonny wasn't even – ' He broke off, clamped his lips shut.

'Go on,' Rogan prodded. 'Finish the sentence. "Sonny wasn't even at home tonight!" Of course he wasn't. You wouldn't have been so willing to take the test if you weren't sure there were no drinks taken at your house. What you didn't allow for was the possibility that Sonny gave you a censored account of his activities after you left the office. He probably has a habit of not telling you things you'd disapprove of.'

'I don't know what you're getting at,' Sanderson said. 'Your machine's obviously broken.'

'That can be checked,' Rogan said impassively. 'You've been a step ahead of me all the way, Mr Sanderson. Too bad you don't have as thorough an understanding of your older son. He had a twenty-five minute wait from the time he killed Tankersley until you two got back here. He was alone with a dead body, facing a murder charge and – maybe worst of all – about to have to explain it all to you. It should have occurred to you that he'd need a stiff drink to steady his nerves. Then you'd have found the vodka bottle he has hidden in his desk and fitted it into your triple confession. You see, Sonny, it doesn't pay to lie to your father.'

'Why, you – ' Sonny made a lunge toward Rogan.

'Shut up, you fool,' his father barked. 'Sit still and keep your mouth shut.'

'*You* told me to blow in his machine.' Sonny turned furiously on his father. 'I didn't want to do it, but you think you're so damn smart. I shouldn't have phoned you. I should have taken my $15,000 and headed for Mexico. I knew your fancy scheme would never work.'

'It came close,' Rogan said pleasantly. 'Do you and Paul want to withdraw your confessions now?' he asked Sanderson. 'Or will you wait until you're charged as accessories after the fact?'

BLACK SPIDER

Francis M. Nevins, Jr.

I was hooked on mysteries at the age of thirteen when, in rapid order, I discovered Sherlock Holmes, Charlie Chan and Perry Mason. Through high school and college I read and collected crime fiction, and kept on finding writers who were new to me – like Ellery Queen and Cornell Woolrich, who became the cornerstones of my fantasy cathedral.

In 1971, after fifteen years of reading mysteries and three or four years of writing occasional pieces of nonfiction about the genre and its practitioners, I yielded to the gentle nudging of Frederic Dannay (better known as Ellery Queen) and tried writing a mystery myself. Fred bought that story, and more than twenty subsequent tales, for Ellery Queen's Mystery Magazine, *and I still appear in that impossible-to-praise-too-highly publication a couple of times a year.*

My first series character was Loren Mensing, like myself a law professor, who has appeared in ten short stories and in my two novels: Publish and Perish *(1975) and* Corrupt and Ensnare *(1978). In 1976 I launched a new series, about Milo Turner – genial confidence man, devotee of multiple identities and detective-in-spite-of-himself – and am now at work on his ninth adventure.*

When I write a novel, I want it to combine the legal maneuverings of Erle Stanley Gardner, the plot convolutions and fair-play detection of Ellery Queen, and the anguished insight into relationships and life that one finds in the suspense stories of Cornell Woolrich. If attempting all this in a single book seems devilishly difficult, believe me it's damn near impossible in a short story of 5000—7500 words. But I keep trying, and I've selected 'Black Spider' for inclusion in this anthology because I think it works fairly well on all three of these levels.

And because, if I'd chosen anything else, the real *Tar Baby would have killed me.*

The first thing Loren Mensing saw as he swung off the Interstate that Sunday afternoon was a wreck. At the juncture of the off-ramp and

State Highway 47, two police cruisers huddled with blue roof-globes spinning. A tow-truck operator in an old infantry field-jacket was hooking his winch to the rear of a demolished Gremlin while the singsong keening of an ambulance died away in the white distance. One more casualty of the ice storm, Loren reflected sadly, and slowed his VW to a crawl as he passed. Along the six-mile stretch of 47 he counted eight more tow trucks, each struggling through the highway slush with a mangled auto mounted rear-end-up and whirling in reverse to an outrageously-priced appointment at some body shop. He almost wished he hadn't decided to make the detour.

Driving home through the sudden storm after the winter meeting of the Association of American Law Schools two states away, he'd been in a wretched mood. The Interstate was a sheet of ice, the filthy gray sky threatened, and the VW's heater had declared a holiday. Around 3:00 pm he had resolved to break early, stop for the night at the next intersection with a motel nearby. Then he saw the mileage sign CULVERTON 6, and he remembered Andra. He hadn't seen her in the ten years since he'd graduated from law school but, yes, that was the name of her home town, where she had planned eventually to set up her own practice. And she had been very lovely, and in the shivering bleakness of that afternoon he didn't want to be alone.

He stopped at a service station on 47 and checked the phone book, while an attendant in a red parka filled the VW's tank. The listing, *Hale Andra*, *atty*, with office and residence addresses, lifted his spirits. On a stormy Sunday afternoon she'd hardly be at her office and would most likely be home trying to keep warm. He thought of calling ahead, then decided to surprise her. The attendant gave him directions, and he turned east at the Brook Street stoplight.

It was a tall, old house, high-roofed and narrow-windowed, and as he maneuvered into the curb behind a bottle-green Catalina he saw lights in the curtained windows. He crunched up the icy path to the front door and pressed the bell button. As the chime sounded muffledly he heard a strange hollow chuckling noise from inside – *yuk-yuk-yuk yuk-yuk-yuk*. After a minute it died away and was replaced by the rap of heels on hardwood. The door opened the width of a chain bolt and Loren saw a wedge of female face, too old to be Andra's.

'Is Miss Hale home?' he asked. 'My name's Loren Mensing, I'm a law-school classmate of Andra's, just passing through.'

'Andra died last week,' the woman told him. Her voice was soft, but Loren sensed a steely tension beneath the words. She seemed to respond to the sudden grief she saw in his eyes, unlatching the chain bolt for him. 'Come in, please. I'm Mrs Boyd, Rose Boyd. I'm an attorney, too – in fact, I was the first woman to hang out a shingle in Culverton. Andra rented office space in my suite.'

She offered a firm, warm hand. Her face was lined and weary, her eyes were an alert milk-blue, her body was trim and straight. Loren guessed her age at 60. 'Andra mentioned you several times, Professor Mensing,' she said as she led him into a neat front room. 'She showed me some articles she'd clipped from newspapers about your – I guess I'd call them detective exploits.'

'I wish she'd called me,' Loren muttered unhappily. 'I wish I'd called her.' He forced himself not to think about lost chances, concentrating on the décor of the room. Chippendale sofa and chairs upholstered in blue, neat blue-green area rugs on a well-waxed hardwood floor marred by twin scratch marks at one corner of the room, heavy mahogany shelves holding sets of books in uniform bindings, and an assortment of massive-looking rocks. Andra had been a rockhound even in school, he remembered. 'May I ask why you're here on a wretched day like this?' he asked.

'I've come by for an hour or so every day since it happened to take care of Tar Baby.' She poured coffee for both of them from a glass carafe. Then, when she saw his puzzled look, her face crinkled into a smile. 'Tar is a black spider monkey, about nine years old. I suppose I'm responsible for Andra's becoming a monkey person. I've belonged to the Simian Society of America for ten years, ever since Mr Boyd died, and I own three myself, a golden spider and two capuchins. Part of Simian's work is finding new homes for mistreated monks. We rescued Tar three years ago from some fool downstate who was keeping her in an unheated outdoor shed. I taught Andra about monkey care and prevailed on her to adopt Tar. She was very lonely at the time, and the company was good for her. Tar grew to be a good companion, and usually was let out of her cage and given the run of the house when Andra was home.'

'I've never heard of people raising monkeys in their homes,' Loren said.

'I was just brushing Tar when you rang. Come, I'll show you.' Rose Boyd got to her feet and led him through a dining room and kitchen to a back bedroom furnished with a low table, a portable radio, and a huge locked cage of plywood and welded wire. Inside the cage Loren saw a coal-black monkey, about two feet tall, with a tiny pointed head, sad face, and protruding belly and hands much like a human's except for the absence of thumbs. Its ungainly arms and legs dangled as it swung by its long prehensile tail from a steel bar hanging on chains from the roof of the cage. When the animal perceived a staring stranger it leaped to the floor of the cage, cowered in a corner under a projecting shelf, and barked frenziedly.

'It takes a long time for a monk to trust a human,' Mrs Boyd said over the din. 'It's a wonder they ever trust us when you think how they're captured. Spiders come from southern Mexico and parts of South America – Brazil, Colombia, Bolivia. They live in the trees and stay up there full time, because there are snakes crawling along the jungle floor that will eat a monkey whole. The mother carries her baby on her abdomen the first four months and on her back for the next six.

'Professional animal catchers go through the jungles looking for mothers with newborn babies. They shoot the mother out of the trees and if the baby survives the fall it's captured. A few years ago Congress made it illegal to import monkeys into the States as pets, but at least 2000 monks are living in American homes right now, and Simian tries to see they're treated decently.'

'Fascinating,' Loren murmured, and knew that he'd heard enough monkey lore for the moment. 'How did Andra die?' he asked.

'She was murdered,' the older woman said as they returned to the front of the house. 'A week ago this evening, in this living room. Someone bludgeoned her to death with a geode.' She took down a heavy jagged piece of rock from a shelf and handed it to Loren, inner surface uppermost. Loren saw that the rock half was hollow-centered and glistened in the lamplight as if tiny diamonds were embedded in the stone. 'Quartz crystal,' Mrs Boyd said. 'The other half of this rock was the weapon. The police have it, of course. Sergeant Regas is in charge of the case. Everyone knows who the murderer is.'

'But I'm not sure we can convict him on the evidence we've got,' Regas told Loren an hour later as they sat at a scarred table in the chilly police interrogation room, an electric heater glowing near their feet. Loren had called headquarters from Andra's house, and finding Regas on duty, had identified himself with emphasis on his experience as deputy legal adviser to the department in his home city. He'd been lucky: Regas knew of him and had invited him down for a talk. The sergeant had thin gray hair, a tired stoop, and wore bifocals that made him resemble a kindly uncle; but the eyes behind those glasses were cop's eyes, harsh and alert and untrusting.

'Let me go over what Mrs Boyd told me so I can be sure I have it straight,' Loren said. 'Three years ago the court assigned Andra to defend this fellow Steve Heidler, who was charged with rape and aggravated assault on a 17-year-old girl. Heidler was convicted and sentenced to ten years. He found another lawyer and tried to get his conviction overturned on grounds of incompetence of counsel, or more precisely on the argument that Andra had deliberately thrown the case and let him be convicted because of her hatred of rapists. The conviction was affirmed and Heidler started serving his time.

'Last year Andra began to receive some nasty anonymous letters. Heidler was still locked up but she believed he'd gotten a friend on the outside to type and mail them. Naturally she couldn't prove it. Heidler was paroled two months ago and found a job as a maintenance man at Tri-County Airport, forty miles south of here. He rented a cheap apartment near where he worked and made no trouble for anyone. But those nasty letters kept coming to Andra, once a week like clockwork, until she was a nervous wreck.'

'And we couldn't trace them,' Regas grunted. 'No fingerprints, the cheapest dime-store stationery, and nothing helpful in the type face. And we couldn't spare the personnel to guard her twenty-four hours a day. Then, a week ago this morning, the ice storm hit and there was an accident or emergency every few minutes. Everyone on the force pulled thirty-six hours straight duty. The roads were in awful shape.

'Just before seven in the evening we got the call from Mrs Boyd. When she'd talked to Miss Hale, around eleven that morning, Miss Hale had said she'd be home all day studying some legal papers and taking care of her monkey. Mrs Boyd called her back around five, got no answer, and kept calling back every fifteen minutes until finally she got frightened and called us, saying she was afraid there'd been an accident.

'A patrol car went out to the Hale house and the officers discovered her body at 7:26. Her skull had been caved in by that half of a rock with the funny name. The monkey was in its cage and barking its head off. The autopsy showed that death had taken place between three and five that afternoon. Naturally we concentrated on Heidler as the top suspect.'

'And found,' Loren said, 'that he'd been called to the airport at nine that morning to work the snowplow and help keep the runways open, and that he'd stayed on duty till nine that night. It's a damned impressive alibi, Sergeant.'

'Oh, not all that impressive.' Regas sipped noisily from a cardboard coffee container. 'I talked to the other maintenance guys who were on the shift with Heidler. Most of them are weak witnesses. Sure, they say they yakked with him every now and then, but it was way below zero and they were all bundled up to the ears, so it could have been anyone posing as Heidler behind the protective clothing.'

Loren remembered the alleged friend on the outside who had mailed the threatening letters to Andra. The theory of an accomplice made a certain amount of sense, but Loren needed more. 'How about when they were indoors? On coffee breaks, trips to the john?'

'The place was on emergency status.' A note of annoyance crept into Regas' voice, as if Loren had mutated from ally to adversary. 'Breaks were staggered. Each man had ten minutes off every two hours. No congregating around the coffee machine. Two guys claim they saw Heidler in the break room but either the ice glare screwed up their eyesight or they were half asleep. But we can get around them all right.'

An alarm began to sound in Loren's head, and every additional word Regas said made him doubt Heidler's guilt the more. He made an effort to be neutral and objective. 'So Heidler took advantage of the storm, got someone to take his place on the job to give him an alibi, went to Culverton, killed Andra, then went back to his job?'

'That's it,' the sergeant grunted.

'What did he use for wheels?'

'Borrowed car, I guess. His own was stuck in the snow and ice at the airport employees' lot and was still there when we went out to question him Sunday night.' A subtle light gleamed in Regas' eyes and he adjusted his glasses on his broad nose. 'Want to help us break the alibi?' He leaned back in his wooden chair and studied Loren. 'After all, the girl was an old friend of yours, and you've helped the cops before, and you'd be a fool to drive on in this weather. Besides, you're on your Christmas vacation, and I want to nail Heidler to the wall before I retire next month.'

It was too tempting an offer to reject. If Heidler was innocent he needed an advocate desperately, and if he was guilty Loren wanted to help make him pay. 'You've just bought my services,' he said and offered his hand. 'And now that I'm an honorary member of the team, would you mind answering a question you'll probably think is ridiculous?'

'If I can,' the sergeant agreed puzzledly.

'Why couldn't Andra have been killed by her monkey? Either playfully or in anger, Tar Baby could have *thrown* that geode hard and hit her. Tar's got the strength and her hands are the same as ours except for the lack of a thumb, so she could have hurled it.'

'You forget,' Regas said, 'that the monk was locked in its cage when the officers found Miss Hale's body. You don't think it killed her and then locked itself in!'

'Mrs Boyd tells me that monkeys are incredibly clever animals,' Loren said.

'Not that clever,' the sergeant scoffed. 'Hell, you think I haven't checked that out myself? Last week I had Rose take Tar out of the cage and climbed in myself, and *I* couldn't twist a key in that lock from inside. Unless you think I'm not as smart as a monkey?'

It was a prudent moment to call it a night. At Regas' suggestion Loren used a police phone to reserve a room at the nearby Queen's Inn, and when he left the headquarters building and drove through snow-drifted streets to the hotel, a file with photocopies of all the police reports on the murder lay on the seat of the VW beside him.

That night, buried under two blankets in bed, he called Rose Boyd and told her he had taken a hand in the case. Then he began reading the reports. The only item that riveted his attention was the incident of the vacuum cleaner, and that was puzzling enough to make him call Regas at home and see if he'd understood the report correctly.

'Yeah,' the sergeant yawned. 'The prowl-car officers noticed two fresh-looking scratch marks on the living-room floor. You may have seen them yourself when you were out at the house. They were on a direct line with her hall closet. When I got there I opened the closet door and found her vacuum cleaner inside. It was the usual canister model with the long hose, and the distance between the wheels on the machine was a perfect match for the distance between the scratch marks. So what's the uproar? She'd taken the vacuum out to do some cleaning that afternoon.'

'Sergeant,' Loren pointed out, 'the file contains a signed statement by Andra's cleaning woman, who says she thoroughly vacuumed the house Saturday, the day before the murder, and replaced the machine's dust bag with a fresh one.'

'I remember,' Regas said through another yawn, 'and she put the vacuum back in the hall closet where it belonged. I still don't get your point.'

'The point is that there's also a technician's report buried in the file. And *that* report says that on laboratory examination the dust bag inside the vacuum was found to be perfectly clean!'

Softly and patiently, without a trace of resentment, Regas invited Loren to turn out his light and go to sleep. But it took Loren until two in the morning before he had expelled the puzzle from his mind and slipped into an exhausted half doze.

He woke at 7:30, unrested and besieged by a headache. After a painfully hot shower and shave and a breakfast of aspirin and tap water he dressed and went out into the frozen morning. A thin, dirty snowfall stung his ears, clung to his overcoat. He taxied to headquarters, found Regas at work, and asked him to arrange for an interview with Steve Heidler.

An hour later he sat gaunt-eyed on a three-legged stool in a cell, trying not to smell the jail odors that were beginning to make him feel queasy. The young man on the iron cot across from him exuded ruthlessness. His cold eyes, the chiseled planes of his unshaven face, the way he held his body coiled almost like a snake, everything about him made Loren want to drop the case and head home, taking his chances on the weather.

'I didn't kill the broad,' Heidler repeated in a grating monotone. 'Hell, I can prove I was forty miles away, what more do they want? Why hasn't that damn fool lawyer they assigned me got me out of this hole?'

'You know why.' Loren tried to keep the revulsion out of his voice. 'It's only in stories that a so-called perfect alibi takes a suspect off the hook. In real life it just draws the cops' attention, especially when the person who offers it has a yellow sheet as long as yours.'

'Yeah, man, but this time it's real.' Heidler shook his head from side to side like a punchdrunk boxer. 'If the other lawyer can't spring me maybe you can, I don't know. But I tell you this, Mensing.' He leaned forward and his eyes burned in the clammy dimness of the cell. 'I ain't goin' back to the stinkin' slam for nothin' I didn't do. I'd rather get shot trying to escape. Whatever you do or don't do, I swear I never give up and go peacefully with no cop nowhere again. Never.'

The stark determination in his face told Loren that he had only limited time to try and save this excuse for a man. Whenever Heidler saw a possibility of escape he would take the risk, and if he was killed in the attempt that would close the file on Andra's murder even if Heidler didn't do it.

Loren forced himself to be professional, and taking extensive notes as they talked, he made Heidler relive that icy Sunday eight days ago. Made him recall all the trivial incidents that happened while he was working the airport snowplow, which of his co-workers he'd seen, what he'd said to whom, what he ate and drank, what station the radio in the employees' break room was tuned to.

For almost two hours Loren combed through Heidler's story. Then he called the guard to let him out of the cell and left without shaking the prisoner's hand. After a coffee-shop breakfast across the street from the jail, he phoned a cab for the trip back through the gently falling snow to headquarters.

Regas stared gloomily out the window of his office cubicle. 'Hope the weatherman's right that it'll let up this afternoon,' he muttered. 'If it keeps up till dark the city'll be socked in again.' He had been changing the subject from the case to the weather at every opportunity for the last half hour, and at last Loren understood why.

'You're afraid he's innocent, too, aren't you? The same things that bug me about this murder have bugged you. That's why you invited me into the picture so readily. That's why you've been so generous with police reports, and why you didn't mind my calling you at home last night and poking a hole in your case.'

Regas let out a quiet sigh as if a burden had been lifted from him. 'He *may* be innocent and that's as far as I'll go. But I don't want the animal back on the streets even if he didn't kill the girl. These are my last three weeks on the force, Professor. I don't want the wrong man convicted and I don't want him loose either. Hell, I don't know what I want, except some good warm sun and peace of mind.' He pushed his glasses hard against the bridge of his nose. 'I thought you might be able to help sort it out.'

'I'm still trying,' Loren said. 'All right, if you've thought about the case that much you've probably formed some ideas about who might be guilty if Heidler isn't. Share them.'

Regas took a long sip from his coffee container. 'Three others might have done it,' he said. 'The three who were closest to her. Only there's something that rules each of them out. If it wasn't Heidler, it might have been George Wylie, the man she used to go with. Or if not him, maybe young Ernie Blount, the man she went with after Wylie.' He stopped and crumpled his coffee container.

'Or if not either of them, Rose Boyd?' Loren asked softly. 'Oh, don't look so surprised. You said three others and stopped after two, and I knew already that Mrs Boyd and Andra had been close.'

Regus very carefully said nothing, and Loren wondered why. 'All right,' he continued, 'what rules each of them out?'

The sergeant creaked wearily back in his chair. 'George Wylie,' he said, 'is the deputy mayor of Culverton – first-class reputation. Blount has an alibi a hell of a lot stronger than Heidler's. And Rose – well, way back before she married Henry Boyd I used to date Rose and I know –

the way a cop knows things – that she couldn't have committed a cold-blooded murder.'

'People change over the years,' Loren said. 'You might be thinking of a different Rose from the one who exists today.'

'I know,' Regas admitted. 'That's one of the things about this case that scares me.'

The temperature dropped and the falling snow turned to ice as they sat through the wretched day and dissected the problem. Every time the wall clock marked the beginning of a new hour Regas would switch on the office radio to a local station and they would listen to the news and weather. The news was dominated by storm-connected calamities – a four-car collision on 47, a tow-truck operator found dead in his wrecked vehicle at the foot of a steep slope west of town, several heart attacks among people shovelling their sidewalks – and it was almost a relief to return after ten minutes to dealing with a single deliberate death.

As Loren scrawled notes, Regas told what he knew about Andra's affair with George Wylie. The relationship had had little chance of growing into something permanent, Regas thought, because of Wylie's medical problem. The deputy mayor had an unfortunate tendency to break out into a rash in the presence of all animals, and Andra's philosophy had been love-me-love-my-monkey. She broke off with Wylie when Ernest Blount entered her life.

Blount, Regas said, was a West Point graduate who had lost his left foot to a Viet Cong booby trap and taken his disability pension into the civilian world. He could walk on his prosthetic foot but the only car he could handle was his own, specially-designed Toronado, a front-wheel-drive model with hand controls replacing the usual brake and clutch pedals. In 1976, when Blount's mother had died in a hit-and-run accident, he had retained Rose Boyd to handle the probate of her substantial estate, and Rose, who was exceptionally busy at the time, had with Blount's consent passed the file on to Andra. Within a month Ernie was not only Andra's client but her lover, and George Wylie was out of the picture.

'Which gives Wylie a motive of jealousy,' Loren said. 'And as for opportunity, you said before that he claims he was in and out of City Hall all that Sunday, working on storm crises, so he could have slipped away and killed her. The house is only a ten-minute drive from downtown. And as a former lover and no doubt frequent visitor to her house, he'd know that those heavy geodes were on the shelves and he'd also have learned something about monkeys. But' – Loren tried not to make his sarcasm too blatant – 'but he's the Deputy Mayor with an excellent reputation, so of course he must be innocent.'

'If I had to pick one of the three it would be Blount,' Regas said. 'He killed a lot of people over in Asia, I hear, and you can't just shake off that way of handling a problem when you hang up your uniform. I don't know of any motive he had, but anything can happen between lovers. And as her current boy friend he'd know about the geodes, too, plus he'd have learned some monkey stuff. If only he didn't have that damn alibi! It sounds so hokey I almost have to buy it.'

'Run it past me again.' Loren squeezed his eyes shut tight.

'One gimmick on that car of his,' Regas began, 'is that it's impossible to tamper with the mileage reading. The car has a new protective device that the manufacturer started offering a few years ago, when there was all that publicity about used-car dealers routinely setting back the mileage on the autos they sold. I've checked with Consumers Union and this baby is tamperproof.'

'At this point enter the Jergens kid,' Loren said. 'The 10-year-old with the wacky hobby, who lives in the same townhouse complex with Blount. He likes to peer into parked cars and record the mileage figures and guess from the daily increases where each car was driven.'

'He read Blount's meter a week ago Saturday afternoon,' Regas continued. 'You saw the penciled note in the file. As of 4:00 pm that day the mileage was exactly 21,472. And Blount saw the kid take down the figure and told us about it late Sunday night when we paid him a visit to break the news and question him. He went out to his parking slot with us, unlocked his car, and showed us the mileage – and, by damn, it still read 21,472.'

'And no one in the townhouses remembers the car being out of its slot at any time Sunday,' Loren added, 'although considering the weather I doubt that anyone really would have noticed. All right, how about Rose Boyd?'

'Rose is a mighty sharp lawyer,' Regas said slowly. 'Maybe too sharp. Maybe that's one reason why I, ah, don't date her now. Since her husband died her life has revolved around three things – money, monkeys, and clout. Being in the same office suite with her, maybe Miss Hale found out something she shouldn't have. Rose doesn't have an alibi, but she's the one who called headquarters and precipitated the finding of the body.'

'She could have done that just to make herself look innocent,' Loren pointed out. 'You know, it's too bad monkeys can't talk. Her golden spiders and her capuchin could tell us whether she was home all Sunday as she claimed.'

'Hell,' Regas grunted, 'if monks could talk, we could just ask Tar Baby who killed Miss Hale.'

Loren thought about that remark, and about other things, and closed his eyes, retreating deep into himself. Then he emerged into the stuffy cubicle again, and blinked, and came close to grinning stupidly.

'Who says we can't do just that?' he asked.

The storm had mercifully blown away before dusk, and a little after eight that evening Loren paused in his analysis of the case and, standing before the mahogany shelves in what had been Andra Hale's living room, scanned his audience. Sergeant Regas, eyes hooded behind his bifocals, rubbed his palms together as if his hands were cold. Rose Boyd sat stiffly in a high-backed armchair, her face carefully empty of expression. Deputy Mayor George Wylie, a tall, lean, fortyish man with pouched eyes, sprawled at one end of the Chippendale sofa. At the other end sat the Vietnam veteran, Ernest Blount, round-faced and stoic-looking, tapping his fingers against his thick cane.

From the back bedroom the harsh yapping continued, keeping nerves on edge. Loren would have identified the sound as a dog barking if he hadn't known it was the monkey. Tar Baby had begun the outcry when the first strangers had unlocked the house that evening – Loren, Regas, and the two plainclothesmen who now stood warily near the front door – and Mrs Boyd had excused herself several times during Loren's presentation and gone back to try and calm Tar, but nothing had worked. It was almost as if the black spider knew that the fate of its mistress's murderer was being sealed.

'Back to business,' Loren said. 'Now that we've gone over the basic facts of Andra's murder, let's eliminate the least likely suspect.' Blount and Wylie and Mrs Boyd stirred and glanced at each other. 'None of you,' he went on. 'I meant the monkey. Monks are known to be quite strong, and except for lacking thumbs Tar's hands are just like a human's. One of the first thoughts that crossed my mind was that Tar could have hurled that geode, playfully or in anger, and killed Andra. Sergeant Regas disproved that theory by pointing out that, when the officers found Andra's body, Tar was securely locked in her cage, and that there was no way she could have locked herself in.

'Now my original assumption, and the sergeant's too, was that Tar had been locked in her cage before Andra's killer came here and stayed locked in throughout the crime. However, there's nothing that compels us to believe this. And the fresh vacuum-cleaner scratch marks found in this living room suggest the opposite theory.' He pointed toward the twin scratches defacing the polished floorboards. 'They suggest that, as Mrs Boyd told me was often the case when Andra was home, Tar was free and loose at the time of Andra's death!'

Rose Boyd's eyes widened with a sort of horror, then blinked shut as if the woman had retreated into herself. A glint of puzzlement showed on the deputy mayor's face. 'You'd better explain what that means. I never learned too much about monkeys when Andra and I were going together.'

'Glad to oblige, Mr Wylie. Please remember that Andra's vacuum cleaner was a canister model, on wheels, and with a long hose. Now her cleaning woman had thoroughly vacuumed the house on Saturday, the day before the murder, and had replaced the dirt-filled dust bag with a clean fresh one – which was still immaculate and empty when the police found the machine the next day. Therefore the vacuum cleaner, when it was removed from its customary place in the hall closet, was not taken out for use as a sweeping instrument.

'Why, then, *was* it taken out? This afternoon, Mrs Boyd, I remembered something you told me yesterday, namely that in the jungle monkeys are preyed on by snakes that can swallow them whole. Now, think of that long vacuum-cleaner hose, which, I submit, resembles nothing so much as a snake! If you were a monkey, wouldn't you run like hell if that hose were being brandished at you?

'Therefore I concluded that Tar was free in this house at the time of the murder, actually witnessed the death of Andra, and was herded back into her cage afterwards by the killer with the help of the vacuum-cleaner hose. That nerve-wracking barking we've heard all evening must have been exactly how Tar reacted to Andra's death. No wonder the killer felt he had to get the monkey out of the way and possibly quieted down!

'Now, this conclusion tells us who the murderer was *not*. First, it wasn't Steve Heidler, because it had to be someone Andra identified as familiar enough with monkeys so that Tar could be left free during his visit. If confirmation of the point is needed, it's provided by the killer's choice of an implement to force Tar into her cage later. Second, it wasn't George Wylie, because he is known to break out into an allergic rash whenever he's near an animal, and it's most unlikely Andra would have left Tar out while he was in the house. Third, it wasn't Rose Boyd, because if Tar indeed witnessed her killing Andra it's hardly plausible that she would have voluntarily come back here every day since the murder, as she has, to feed and brush Tar and take care of her.

'So you see that once the true meaning of those scratch marks and the vacuum cleaner is understood, and all the deductions teased out of them, we can pretty much eliminate all our suspects. Except one.'

Ernest Blount tightened his grip on his walking stick but his face retained its mandarin calm. 'So I'm to be the patsy?' he asked pleasantly. 'Well, unfortunately, Professor, I just don't fit your little frame. By the grace of God and the National Liberation Front, I happen to be a cripple. The only way I can get around is in a car specially fitted with hand controls.'

'Sergeant Regas told me about your car,' Loren said. 'A front-wheel-drive model, a Toronado.'

'Then did he tell you that a disinterested, incorruptible witness noted down the mileage on my car Saturday afternoon?' Blount's voice rose almost to a snarl. 'Did he tell you that it registered the exact same mileage Sunday evening when the police came to question me?'

'He told me,' Loren replied slowly. 'That was a bad mistake on your part. I'm amazed that a hard-nosed professional soldier would gamble on such a theatrical alibi gimmick. All I had to do to puncture it was to think back to the traffic conditions I observed yesterday as I drove into this town. The major arteries were choked with tow trucks. And several of them had disabled cars mounted on them, rear-end-up.

'Now I've had my Volkswagen towed that way once, and it cost me a small fortune, but it taught me something I hadn't known before. In automobiles with front-wheel drive, like my VW and your Toronado, the speedometer cable runs through the left axle. When such a car is mounted rear-end-up on a tow truck, *the speedometer runs backwards*. And this is true even on cars equipped, like yours, with a device to keep the mileage from being manually tampered with. The loophole in the device is of no use to a crooked used-car dealer, of course, because no one is going to have a car towed in reverse for 5000 miles just to get the mileage to read that many miles less. But it's of fantastic use to an overly-clever murderer who thought it would give him a perfect alibi.

'Blount, you planned this murder in advance. You waited until a storm hit the city to carry it out. But you'd arranged in advance with an accomplice to mount your Toronado on a tow truck rear-end-up and drive it around after the murder until the mileage was back where you wanted it, probably a few miles less than the mileage the Jergens boy noted, so you could drive back to your townhouse in the normal way and have it read 21,472 when you parked it. In that ice storm Sunday, one more tow truck working the streets would never be noticed.'

Blount's facial muscles seemed frozen in a cadaver's grimace as Loren's courtroom voice filled the house. Wylie and Mrs Boyd stared at the ex-officer with horror, as if they were watching someone die. His hand on the walking stick had turned the color of ice.

'Your accomplice,' Loren went on, 'was named Joe Sutton. He owned a towing garage in town. He was the man who killed your mother for you in that fake hit-and-run two years ago, so you could inherit. He helped you kill Andra a week ago Sunday. And this morning you killed him, either because he was blackmailing you or just to protect yourself.'

Loren remembered how he'd heard the news report of a tow-truck operator's death on Regas' office radio an hour or so before the sergeant had described Blount's alibi, and how he'd made another connection and insisted that Regas take him out to the scene of the man's death that afternoon. But even if he hadn't made the connection, even if he'd never stopped off in Culverton yesterday, everything would have happened pretty much the same way. That thought made Loren feel ancient and useless.

Sergeant Regas motioned the two plainclothesmen to come forward. 'Sutton left a letter in his office safe, Ernie,' the sergeant said. 'To be opened in the event of his death. He confessed to your mother's murder, to helping with your alibi last week. He spilled it all. I've gotta give you your rights, son.' He fumbled in a cracked cowhide wallet for his Miranda card and began to read the litany in an emotionless monotone. At the other end of the sofa George Wylie shuddered a little, and Rose Boyd wept silently in her chair. In the distance, the barking of the monkey went on and on.

Loren left Culverton early the next morning, before another storm had a chance to break. A week later, halfway through the night, the bedside phone rang in his apartment. He jerked upright, reached for the receiver, and heard Regas' voice crackling with static.

'Thought you'd want to know why Ernie killed the girl,' the voice said. 'We went through the paperwork on his mother's estate and found a check for $3500 he'd made out to Joe – oh, what the hell was his name? The tow operator. That must have been the payoff for killing his mother. Miss Hale noticed the check stub while she was working on the estate, I guess, and started wondering out loud, and he knew he'd have to get rid of her, too.'

'Has he confessed yet?'

'The war hero's still hanging tough, but we'll nail him. By the way, I had to release Heidler today. We know he was responsible for those threatening letters to Miss Hale, but we can't prove it.'

'I bet it made you glow to see Heidler on the streets again, Sergeant.'

'Just Regas from now on. Today was my last day on the force. You mean you can't tell? Man, I'm drunk as a skunk!'

'Enjoy the peace and sunshine when you sober up,' Loren said quietly. 'You've paid your dues.'

Six months later he picked up a paper and read the report of the Loop Shootout. A lone gunman had been interrupted by two policemen during a Chicago jewelry store holdup, and the bloody running gunfight through the Loop district had ended with one officer dead, another critically wounded, and the gunman riddled with more than a dozen bullets. He had been identified at the morgue as one Stephen Heidler.

Loren remembered that interview in the chilly Culverton jail, Heidler's vow never to go peacefully with a cop again. He wondered whether saving Heidler from the one charge of which he'd been innocent had been worth it. He wondered if anything was worth it.

That night he drank more than was good for him.

INVITATION TO A MURDER

Josh Pachter

'Invitation to a Murder' is the only short story I ever dreamed. *I dreamed it one night when I was 19, woke up at 3 am with the whole story complete in my mind and wrote it down right then and there so I wouldn't forget it. When I read it over in the morning I wasn't very happy with the* way *I had written it, but I was clear that the* idea *was a good one. Over the next eight months I produced six or seven revised drafts, but I never did get the story exactly the way I wanted it; finally I gave up and sent what I had off to Frederic Dannay, figuring he'd tell me what was wrong with it and make some suggestions about improving it. He didn't, though: he bought it as it was, dammit, and published it in the August 1972 issue of* Ellery Queen's Mystery Magazine.

With its controversial theme and open ending, the story drew a lot of attention. In fact, EQMM *received more letters from readers about 'Invitation to a Murder' than they'd ever received about any other story they've published – most of them asking, 'What the hell* happens *at the end of that story?'*

In 1979 I did one more rewrite, for the Mystery Writers of America's Women's Wiles *anthology; this time, I finally managed to work the story into a state where I was satisfied with it. A shortened version of the* Women's Wiles *draft appeared in* Libelle *in 1981; that was a big event for me, as I'd been living in The Netherlands for several years by that time, and this was my first publication in Dutch. In 1983, 'Invitation' was the title piece in my first short-story collection, also published in Dutch.*

On top of all that, I like *'Invitation to a Murder'. I think it stands up as an effective, well-plotted and well-written mystery, and I'm proud of it.*

For those reasons, I've selected it as my own contribution to this volume.

The envelope was edged in black.

Curious, Branigan set the rest of his stack of mail aside and reached for the jeweled souvenir dagger he used as a letter opener. He slit the envelope open carefully, and slid out a square of heavy, cream-colored notepaper.

It, too, was black-rimmed.

It was a formal, embossed announcement, and the raised letters read:

ELEANOR MADELINE ABBOTT
ANNOUNCES THE IMPENDING

MURDER

OF HER HUSBAND, GREGORY ELIOT ABBOTT,
AT THEIR HOME,
217A WEST 86TH STREET, NEW YORK CITY, NEW YORK,
BETWEEN THE HOURS OF
NINE-THIRTY AND ELEVEN O'CLOCK
ON THE EVENING OF DECEMBER 16, 1971.
YOU ARE CORDIALLY INVITED TO ATTEND.

Branigan read through the invitation twice, then set it down on his desk and picked up the envelope it had arrived in. Heavy, cream-colored, black-bordered. Addressed in a precise feminine hand to *Chief Inspector Lawrence A. Branigan, New York Police Department, 240 Center Street, New York, New York*. No zip code. No return address. Postmarked New York City.

Branigan picked up the announcement and read it again.

Eleanor Abbott, he mused. Mrs Eleanor Madeline Abbott . . .

He reached for his telephone and began dialing.

It was still snowing when Branigan walked up the brownstone's eight steps and rang the bell. The door was opened almost immediately by a large man in butler's livery, black from head to toe except for the thin white triangle of his shirtfront.

'Inspector Branigan?' he asked, his voice surprisingly soft.

Branigan, nodding, pulled the black-rimmed invitation from his overcoat pocket and handed it over. Behind the butler, all he could see was a dimly-lit corridor stretching back into darkness.

'Thank you, sir,' the man said. 'All the others have already arrived. Would you follow me, please?'

The others? Branigan thought, as he stepped into the house. *All the others?*

Halfway down the corridor, before a large wooden door, they stopped. The butler twisted the ornate brass knob and pushed the door open. 'In here, sir,' he said. 'Mrs Abbott is expecting you. May I take your coat?'

The room was dim, too. Like the corridor, like the butler, like the night. Thick damask curtains hid what might have been windows; subdued lighting trickled down from small panels set into the ceiling.

It was a large, plain room. No rugs or carpeting on the simple parquet floor, no paintings, nothing personal hanging from the dark, gloomy walls. There was nothing extra in the room, nothing decorative. Every item, every piece of furniture, was there because it was functional, because it was needed.

Like the double bed standing with its head flush to the far wall.

There was a man on the bed, propped up almost to a sitting position. His body was invisible, swathed to the neck in heavy blankets, but his wrinkled white face almost shone through the dimness.

Gregory Abbott.

At first Branigan thought he was too late, thought Abbott was already dead: the pale grey eyes, half-covered by deeply creased lids, stared emptily across the room; the ravaged face, wreathed by wisps of snowy hair, was perfectly still. No smile of welcome, no frown of disapproval crossed the old man's thin, bloodless lips.

Then he noticed the slight rise and fall of the blankets, and separated the faint sound of labored breathing from the steady ticking of the clock that hung on the wall several feet above Abbott's head.

Branigan sighed with relief, and looked away.

To his right, a high-backed chair stood against the side wall. A young woman was poised lightly on the edge of the chair, her hands folded delicately in her lap. She wore a long black gown, simple and yet striking, set off by a single strand of pearls around her neck and a sparkling diamond on the fourth finger of her left hand. Branigan had learned that Eleanor Abbott was an attractive woman. He saw now that she was beautiful: as beautiful and, somehow, as cold as the December night outside.

Across the room from her, a dozen identical chairs stood side by side. The seat closest to Branigan was empty, obviously his, but each of the others was occupied. And, even in the dimness of the room, he recognized the eleven faces that were turned toward him, waiting.

Ryan was there, from the Los Angeles Police Department, and

DiNapoli from San Francisco, both officers he had worked with in the past. There was Coszyck, who ran a local detective agency; Huber, an insurance investigator from Boston he had worked with once before; Braun, a private eye based in Cleveland, whose picture he had recently seen featured in a national news magazine. There was Devereaux, a Federal District Court justice from New Orleans; Gould, a St Louis appellate court judge; even Walter Fox, 'the old Fox,' as he was known, just retired from the bench of the United States Supreme Court. Maunders, Detroit's crusading District Attorney, was there, and Szambel from Pittsburgh, and Carpenter, who had left Szambel's staff to become D.A. of Baltimore.

The eleven men looked at him closely, and Branigan could see that most of them recognized him, too.

They were fourteen people in all, lining the walls of the nearly dark, nearly quiet room, the silence broken only by Gregory Abbott's uneven breathing and by the inexorable ticking of the clock.

Finally, Branigan's eyes rested on the plain deal table in the center of the room, and on the five objects that sat on its surface: a long-bladed kitchen knife, a thin strand of wire with a wooden grip attached to each end, a length of iron pipe, an amber bottle labelled with a grinning skull and crossbones, and a revolver that glinted dully in the dim light of the room.

It was Miss Scarlet, Branigan found himself thinking. *In the conservatory, with the candelabra.*

The image should have been funny, but it wasn't. It frightened him, frightened him deeply, and he was not sure why.

He looked back at the woman in the black gown.

She was smiling at him, and Branigan saw that she knew what he was thinking.

She's playing with us, he thought. *She set it up like this, and now she's playing with us. It's just a game to her.*

A game with the highest stakes imaginable. A game where the life of the old man in the double bed goes to the winner.

Okay, Branigan thought. *Okay, I'm ready.*

He took a step forward, into the room, and eased the door shut behind him.

Eleanor Abbott stood up. A lock of hair drifted down across her eyes as she rose, and she carelessly brushed it back with the tips of her fingers.

'Good evening, Inspector Branigan,' she said. 'If you'll take your seat, we can get started.' She spoke softly, pleasantly, almost in a whisper, yet her voice carried firmly across the room.

It was a good voice, Branigan decided. It suited her.

He moved to the empty chair at the end of the row of twelve, and sat.

'Thank you,' she said. 'And thank you for coming. I want to thank *all* of you for being here tonight. I knew that *you* would come, Inspector, and you, Mr Coszyck, since both of you live and work right here in New York. And I was confident that my invitation would pique your curiosities, Mr Huber and Mr Carpenter, enough to get you to make the trip to town. But most of the rest of you, though, I have to admit that your presence comes as a very welcome surprise. Some of you had to travel great distances to get here; your dedication to the protection of human life impresses me. And especially you, Mr Justice Fox, I want to – '

'Come off it, young lady!' Fox said hoarsely. 'Why I showed up here tonight doesn't make a damn bit of difference. What I want to know is why you sent me that – that incredible invitation!'

'Why did I invite you?' She smiled at him, the same warm smile she had already used once on Branigan. 'I'm not a liar, sir. I invited you here – I invited all twelve of you gentlemen, twelve of this country's most eminent and respected legal and law-enforcement minds – I invited you here to witness a murder.'

She paused, then – paused dramatically, Branigan realized with a start. He glanced down the row of his colleagues' faces and saw eleven pairs of eyes fixed, unwavering, on Eleanor Abbott. Only the old man in the bed was not looking at her; his blank eyes never moved from an invisible spot on the door across the room.

'But first,' the woman went on, 'I want to give you just a little bit of personal history. I was born in Philadelphia in 1945, and – '

'You were born on *Thursday*, September the thirteenth, 1945,' Braun broke in, 'and not in Philadelphia but in Essington, which is a few miles outside the city limits. I guarantee that every one of us has looked very carefully into your personal history, Mrs Abbott, so why don't you cut the crap and get to the point?'

'The point,' she said slowly. 'I *am* getting to the point, Mr Braun. I know that you've all done your homework, and I hope you'll all be willing to let me tell this in my own way.'

She looked around her and smiled again. 'You can see that this means quite a lot to me. I'll try not to take up more of your time than I have to.'

That's one for her, Branigan thought. *This is her party*, *and she knows it*.

'Go ahead, Mrs Abbott,' he said. 'Do it your way.'

She turned to him and nodded and said 'Thank you.' Her leaving off the 'Inspector' at the end of it made it a personal statement, and he thought for a moment that he would like to call her Eleanor.

And then she turned again, faced the old man in the bed and looked through him.

'I came to New York about five years ago,' she said, 'when I was twenty-one. The first two years I was here, I must have lived in half a dozen different tiny little apartments around town, and worked at three or four different silly little jobs. I made sandwiches in a delicatessen. I was a secretary for a few weeks, and not a very good one. I worked in a record store. One time I applied to a couple of the airlines, trying to get into stewardess school, but none of them were hiring.

'Three years ago, I was waiting tables at a little Indian restaurant down in the Village; Greenwich Village. One night – I can tell you what night it was; it was October nineteenth, 1968 – that night, Gregory came in for dinner with some woman he'd been going out with and another couple.'

She closed her eyes, and it was a moment before she went on. 'I served them their dinner, they ate, they left, I never really noticed them. Then, a few hours later, I got off work, and Gregory was waiting for me outside. I don't know what he did with his girlfriend, but there he was. It was just like a movie: Gregory Abbott's got six million dollars in the bank, and he's leaning up against a parking meter with his grubby old hat on the back of his head and a beautiful bunch of flowers he'd picked up somewhere, at that hour, in his arms, and he's waiting for *me*. That was Gregory. That was the way he was.

'We got married six months later, a year and a half ago. It turned out he loved me.' She opened her eyes and faced them. 'It turned out I loved him, too.'

'He was thirty-five years older than you were!'

'He still *is* thirty-five years older than I am. I thought it didn't matter.' She let her eyes close again before going on. 'I was wrong,' she said. 'It does matter. One year ago today, Gregory and I were staying with some friends in Aspen. I ski very badly, Gregory hadn't skied before at all, but they were very good friends and we were having a wonderful time. Late in the afternoon, Gregory said he felt practised enough to try a run down one of the more advanced slopes. I – I remember thinking it wasn't a very good idea, but he was so full of energy, so full of life . . .'

The room seemed subtly brighter, Branigan thought, and before he could wonder why he knew it was her face. *She looks as white as the snow must have been*, he told himself, and then was irritated by the thought.

'He fell,' Eleanor Abbott said. 'He lost his balance half-way down and fell. I was coming down behind him, I saw it happen, and there was nothing I could do. We got the ski patrol to bring him down the rest of the way. They had an ambulance waiting, and I rode to the hospital with him. The doctors said he had a massive coronary. He was in critical condition for more than a week.

'He pulled through, though. He survived.' The color flushed back into her face, a violent red. 'If you can call the way it left him survival. He's totally paralysed. He can't see or hear. After it happened, I spent two hysterical months trying to get him to blink an *eye* for me, to show me it's just something gone wrong with his body, to tell me that somewhere in there *he* is still okay. There was no response. The doctors tell me he is no longer able to think.'

'Mrs Abbott,' Maunders said, softly.

She looked up. 'It's been a year, now. He doesn't get any better or any worse. The doctors tell me there is no chance that he will ever recover, they hold out no hope at all. They *do* think, though, that with the proper medical care and treatment they can keep his *body* alive for ten more years, or even longer.'

She said it bitterly, angrily, and for an instant Branigan found that he shared her anger.

'I'm not going to let them do that,' she said. 'Gregory Abbott is dead. That – that *thing* in the bed there is not my husband. My husband died a year ago today.'

There was something new in her voice now, layered over the bitterness: something insistent, almost hypnotic. They stared at her, all of them, as motionless as the empty old man in the double bed.

'I loved my husband,' she told them. 'Out of my love for him, I feel that there's one last thing I have to do for him. I have to put an end to that horror the doctors say is still alive, that terrible thing that *I* know is Gregory's corpse. I want to give him what the doctors have refused to let him have, this last year. I want to let him rest.'

'And of course you don't give a damn about the six million dollars,' Gould snapped at her. It was, somehow, a shocking statement, and it seemed natural for her just to gaze at him in silence, until he backed away from it and said, 'No. No, I guess you don't. I'm sorry.'

'The money is already mine, Mr Gould,' she said. 'Gregory can't use it any more. And you're right, I don't give a damn about it. The only thing I give a damn about right now is my husband. That's why I'm going to kill him.'

There, Branigan thought. *That's it. That's what I came to hear her say*. And then he frowned, asking himself why, now that he had heard her say it, the words surprised him.

'Just a minute, now,' Ryan began, but she smiled at him and cut him off. 'I know, Captain,' she said gently. 'I'm talking about murder, and murder is against the law. That's the *second* reason I invited the twelve of you here tonight: I wanted to give the law a fair chance to stop me. If you can, if you can keep what I intend to happen here from happening, then I give you my word that I'll never try anything like this again; I'll leave Gregory's body to his doctors and let them do what they like with it. But I want to warn you: you are not going to stop me. I am going to murder the minuscule amount of my husband the doctors have succeeded in keeping alive, tonight, in this room, within the next hour. It's now' – she turned her head to glance at the clock on the wall – 'It is now ten o'clock. By eleven, in one hour, even the doctors will agree that Gregory Abbott is dead.'

No one spoke. The woman in the long black gown sat down to silence, except for the whisper of her husband's breathing and the steady ticking of the clock hanging over his bed.

The twelve men looked at each other, at Eleanor Abbott, at the old man. They sat without speaking, spellbound, waiting, not quite sure what it was they should be doing, not at all sure there was anything they *could* do to prevent the murder they had been invited to witness.

They sat until ten minutes had passed, until Eleanor Abbott rose, walked quickly to the table of weapons in the center of the room, and picked up the amber bottle of poison.

Then they moved, and strong hands grabbed her from both sides before she could step away from the table. Branigan pulled the bottle away from her, and he and Coszyck led her back to her chair. She sat willingly, and they went back to their own seats without a word.

What the hell is she up to? Branigan thought. *She can't possibly imagine we'll let her get near him. What does she think is going on?*

At 10:20, she rose again. She was halfway to the table when Branigan and Coszyck stopped her, turned her around, and put her back in her chair.

This time they stayed with her, one on either side.

And still the old man's breathing and the ticking of the clock were the only sounds in the room. There was a moment when Carpenter put a hand to his mouth and coughed softly: Eleanor Abbott seemed not to notice and Gregory Abbott stared ahead vacantly; most of the rest of them glared at Carpenter, and he turned away, embarrassed.

At 10:30, Huber jumped up and moved impatiently to the old man's bedside. He went down to his hands and knees and carefully examined the floor beneath the bed and the bed itself. As he straightened up, dusting off the legs of his trousers, Braun and Devereaux looked at each other and got up and joined him. They ranged themselves around the three open sides of the bed, watching Abbott and his wife and the clock uneasily.

At 10:40, Eleanor Abbott suddenly stood, but Branigan and Coszyck clamped firm hands on her shoulders and forced her back into her chair.

Again, not a word was said.

The thin red second hand of the clock swept around and around as the minute hand labored slowly up the numbered face. DiNapoli glanced from the clock to his wrist, then quickly back at the clock. He scowled impatiently and adjusted his watch so the two timepieces were synchronized.

At 10:50 Maunders and Fox stood up together, grim-faced, and stepped to the table of weapons. The old Fox, his arthritic fingers quivering slightly, picked up the revolver. He broke open the cylinder, emptied out the cartridges and pocketed them, snapped the cylinder shut and placed the gun back on the table.

At 10:55, Branigan and Coszyck rested their hands lightly on Mrs Abbott's shoulders.

Devereaux, at Abbott's bedside, pulled a handkerchief from his hip pocket and wiped beads of moisture from his forehead.

The old man on the bed breathed weakly, in and out, in and out, and the blankets piled over him rose and fell almost imperceptibly.

At 10:57 Gould stood up fitfully. He peered around the room and saw that there was nowhere left for him to go, and flung himself back into his chair.

It was 10:58. They tensed.

Huber and Braun and Devereaux inched closer to the old man's bed. Branigan and Coszyck tightened their grips on Eleanor Abbott's shoulders. Maunders and Fox braced themselves, leaning towards her as if defying her to seize one of the weapons on the table. Even the five men still seated – Szembel and Carpenter, DiNapoli, Gould, and Ryan – found themselves on the edge of their chairs, ready to spring into action.

But as the clock on the wall ticked loudly and its minute hand crawled closer and closer to the twelve, Eleanor Abbott sat calmly on her high-backed chair, and did not move.

Just before 10:59, Gregory Eliot Abbott's wrinkled eyelids flickered and closed, and his shallow breathing stopped.

'Gentlemen!' Eleanor Abbott's voice shot through the uproar. 'If you'll go back to your seats and calm down, I'll explain.'

They obeyed her.

She stood by the side of her chair, watching them, her full lips turned slightly upward.

'I warned you,' she said. 'I told you I was going to kill him, and I did.'

'*How?*' Huber demanded.

Her smile broadened.

'Gregory's accident did serious damage to his heart, Mr Huber, weakened it to a point where it was no longer strong enough to function normally by itself. What's kept it going all year has been medication, a heart stimulant that has to be administered at *very* regular intervals.'

Branigan's eyes went wide. She waited, though, until Maunders saw it, and Szambel, and DiNapoli.

'The stimulant,' she went on, pointing to the table of weapons, 'is in that bottle. It's an incredibly powerful drug, which makes it incredibly dangerous if taken by a person with a normal heart. That's why the bottle is labeled with a skull and crossbones: even a small dose would make a healthy heart speed up so enormously that it could actually burn itself out. But Gregory needed that stimulant to make *his* heart beat normally, and he needed it frequently. He was due for a dose of it at ten minutes past ten this evening. I got up and tried to give it to him, but *you* stopped me.'

'You said it was poison!' Coszyck rasped.

'I said no such thing. You *assumed* it was poison, and it *would* have been if *you* had swallowed it – but it was medicine for Gregory, and it was keeping him alive. I tried to give it to him. I tried three times, and each time I tried, you and Inspector Branigan chose to stop me. Without it, Gregory's heart just wasn't strong enough to go on beating, and so he died.'

And so he died, Branigan thought. *I took the bottle out of her hands myself, and so he died.*

The twelve criminologists were silent.

Until, 'Well?' Ryan said, his voice thick.

'Well,' Eleanor Abbott told them, 'you've got two choices. You can arrest me and accuse me of murdering my husband, but I'd like you to stop and think about that for a second. After all, gentlemen, *I* tried to give Gregory his medicine. *You* are the ones who stopped me, and caused his death. If you look at it that way, then *you* killed him, not me. I might get slapped on the wrist for not telling you what was in the bottle an hour ago, but once it gets out that you all sat back and let this happen, you men will be ruined. Your careers will be over.'

'She's right,' Braun said heavily. 'With a story like this, there isn't a jury in the country that would convict her of murder.'

'And we'd be sunk,' Carpenter added. 'I don't think anyone would *dare* to try and make out any kind of a case against us, but the publicity would rip us to pieces. It would destroy us.'

The old Fox cleared his throat nervously.

'You said we had *two* possible choices,' he reminded her.

'Yes, I did. I've gotten what I wanted, now: a release for Gregory. Is that such a terrible thing to have done? Do you really think he was better off the way he was, in that empty state that medicine and the law agreed was "alive"? You can turn me in and see where it gets you, gentlemen – or you can work with me, and help me to get away with it.'

'You're asking us to help you get away with murder!' Szambel protested.

She held up a hand.

'No, Mr Szambel, I'm not *asking* you for anything. Arrest me and ruin yourselves, or help to protect me. The choice is entirely yours.'

'I can't!' Devereaux cried. 'I've spent forty years *upholding* the law. How can I turn around now and make a mockery of it?'

'We've got to,' DiNapoli muttered. 'She's got us over a barrel. There's no other way out.'

'Forget it,' Maunders grumbled. 'Even if we wanted to, it'd be impossible. We'd never get away with it.'

'The twelve of *us*?' Judge Gould chuckled grimly. 'Don't be ridiculous! Who'd ever even *think* of challenging us?'

Branigan made the decision for them. 'We'll *all* have to discuss it,' he said.

She waved a hand at them and turned away.

They gathered in together and talked. Across the room, Eleanor Abbott was unable to make out individual voices or words, but she listened absently, confidently, to the meaningless hum, smiled at explosions of obvious protest, grinned at the eventual murmurs of agreement.

When they finally became silent, she turned to face them.

They were staring at her.

'Gentlemen of the jury,' she said, mocking them in her triumph, 'have you reached a verdict?'

And Branigan stood up. There was a strange light in his eyes, a light that Eleanor Abbott could not have known, a light that had never been there before.

'We have,' he said clearly.

And stopped, waiting.

For a moment she was confused, and then she realized what he wanted and completed the ritual: 'How do you find?'

'We find the defendant guilty of murder in the first degree, as charged.'

Her smile faded.

'What?' she asked him, not understanding it at first. 'What do you mean?'

But when Branigan moved to the table of weapons in the center of the room and picked up the amber bottle and came toward her, she understood.

PROOF OF GUILT

Bill Pronzini

*I was born in California in 1943, made my first professional writing sale in 1966 and became a full-time writer in 1969. Since that first sale, I've published 26 novels, 250 short stories, articles and essays, one short-story collection and one nonfiction book (*Gun in Cheek, *a humorous history of* bad *mystery fiction); I've also edited or co-edited 16 anthologies in a variety of categories.*

I've selected 'Proof of Guilt' for this anthology for a number of reasons: it was my first non-collaborative sale to Ellery Queen's Mystery Magazine, *the best of the American crime digests;* EQMM *editor Fred Dannay liked it well enough to also include it in two of his own anthologies, including his* Masterpieces of Mystery *series; it was filmed in England for the* Tales of the Unexpected *television series (the first screen adaptation of any of my stories or novels); and I'm rather proud of the central gimmick of the story, which has been called unique among impossible-crime ideas by writers and aficionados of that type of mystery.*

The story was written in 1973, while I was living in Europe (I was based in Spain and West Germany for three years in the early '70s). The idea came one morning when I was toying with various possibilities for locked-room crimes. I asked myself, 'How could someone shoot someone else in a locked room and then get rid of the weapon without himself leaving the room?' The answer that immediately popped into my mind – the last three words of 'Proof of Guilt,' in fact – made me laugh because, at first, it seemed a pretty facetious notion. But then I realized that, with the right set of circumstances and the right cast of characters, it could be made to work rather nicely. And like all writers who have latched onto a good idea, I stopped laughing and got to work . . .

I've been a city cop for 32 years now, and during that time I've heard of and been involved in some of the weirdest, most audacious crimes imaginable – on and off public record. But as far as I'm concerned, the murder of an attorney named Adam Chillingham is *the* damnedest case in my experience, if not in the entire annals of crime.

You think I'm exaggerating? Well, listen to the way it was.

My partner Jack Sherrard and I were in the Detective Squadroom one morning last summer when this call came in from a man named Charles Hearn. He said he was Adam Chillingham's law clerk, and that his employer had just been shot to death; he also said he had the killer trapped in the lawyer's private office.

It seemed like a fairly routine case at that point. Sherrard and I drove out to the Dawes Building, a skyscraper in a new business development on the city's south side, and rode the elevator up to Chillingham's suite of offices on the 16th floor. Hearn, and a woman named Clarisse Tower, who told us she had been the dead man's secretary, were waiting in the anteroom with two uniformed patrolmen who had arrived minutes earlier.

According to Hearn, a man named George Dillon had made a 10:30 appointment with Chillingham, had kept it punctually, and had been escorted by the attorney into his private office at that exact time. At 10:40 Hearn thought he heard a muffled explosion from inside the office, but he couldn't be sure because the walls were partially soundproofed.

Hearn got up from his desk in the anteroom and knocked on the door, and there was no response; then he tried the knob and found that the door was locked from the inside. Miss Tower confirmed all this, although she said she hadn't heard any sound; her desk was farther away from the office door than was Hearn's.

A couple of minutes later the door had opened and George Dillon had looked out and calmly said that Chillingham had been murdered. He had not tried to leave the office after the announcement; instead, he'd seated himself in a chair near the desk and lighted a cigarette. Hearn satisfied himself that his employer was dead, made a hasty exit, but had the presence of mind to lock the door from the outside by the simple expediency of transferring the key from the inside to the outside – thus sealing Dillon in the office with the body. After which Hearn put in his call to Headquarters.

So Sherrard and I drew our guns, unlocked the door, and burst into the private office. This George Dillon was sitting in the chair across the desk, very casual, both his hands up in plain sight. He gave us a relieved look and said he was glad the police had arrived so quickly.

I went over and looked at the body, which was sprawled on the floor behind the desk; a pair of French windows were open in the wall just beyond, letting in a warm summer breeze. Chillingham had been shot once in the right side of the neck, with what appeared by the size of the wound to have been a small-caliber bullet; there was no exit wound, and there were no powder burns.

I straightened up, glanced around the office, and saw that the only door was the one which we had just come through. There was no balcony or ledge outside the open windows – just a sheer drop of 16 stories to a parklike, well-landscaped lawn which stretched away for several hundred yards. The nearest building was a hundred yards distant, angled well to the right. Its roof was about on a level with Chillingham's office, it being a lower structure than the Dawes Building; not much of the roof was visible unless you peered out and around.

Sherrard and I then questioned George Dillon – and he claimed he hadn't killed Chillingham. He said the attorney had been standing at the open windows, leaning out a little and that all of a sudden he had cried out and fallen down with the bullet in his neck. Dillon said he'd taken a look out the windows, hadn't seen anything, checked that Chillingham was dead, then unlocked the door and summoned Hearn and Miss Tower.

When the coroner and the lab crew finally got there, and the doc had made his preliminary examination, I asked him about the wound. He confirmed my earlier guess – a small-caliber bullet, probably a .22 or .25. He couldn't be absolutely sure, of course, until he took out the slug at the post-mortem.

I talked things over with Sherrard and we both agreed that it was pretty much improbable for somebody with a .22 or .25 caliber weapon to have shot Chillingham from the roof of the nearest building; a small caliber like that just doesn't have a range of a hundred yards and the angle was almost too sharp. There was nowhere else the shot could have come from – except from inside the office. And that left us with George Dillon, whose story was obviously false and who just as obviously had killed the attorney while the two of them were locked inside his office.

You'd think it was pretty cut and dried then, wouldn't you? You'd think all we had to do was arrest Dillon and charge him with homicide, and our job was finished. Right?'

Wrong.

Because we couldn't find the gun.

Remember, now, Dillon had been locked in that office – except for the minute or two it took Hearn to examine the body and slip out and relock the door – from the time Chillingham died until the time we came in. And both Hearn and Miss Tower swore that Dillon hadn't stepped outside the office during that minute or two. We'd already searched Dillon and he had nothing on him. We searched the office – I mean, we *searched* that office – and there was no gun there.

We sent officers over to the roof of the nearest building and down onto the landscaped lawn; they went over every square inch of ground and rooftop, and they didn't find anything. Dillon hadn't thrown the gun out the open windows, then, and there was no place on the face of the sheer wall of the building where a gun could have been hidden.

So where was the murder weapon? What had Dillon done with it? Unless we found that out, we had no evidence against him that would stand up in a court of law; his word that he *hadn't* killed Chillingham, despite the circumstantial evidence of the locked room, was as good as money in the bank. It was up to us to prove him guilty, not up to him to prove himself innocent. You see the problem?

We took him into a large book-filled room that was part of the Chillingham suite – what Hearn called the 'archives' – and sat him down in a chair and began to question him extensively. He was a big husky guy with blondish hair and these perfectly guileless eyes; he just sat there and looked at us and answered in a polite voice, maintaining right along that he hadn't killed the lawyer.

We made him tell his story of what had happened in the office a dozen times, and he explained it the same way each time – no variations. Chillingham had locked the door after they entered, and then they sat down and talked over some business. Pretty soon Chillingham complained that it was stuffy in the room, got up, and opened the French windows; the next thing Dillon knew, he said, the attorney collapsed with the bullet in him. He hadn't heard any shot, he said; Hearn must be mistaken about a muffled explosion.

I said finally, 'All right, Dillon, suppose you tell us why you came to see Chillingham. What was this business you discussed?'

'He was my father's lawyer,' Dillon said, 'and the executor of my father's estate. He was also a thief. He stole $350,000 of my father's money.'

Sherrard and I stared at him. Jack said, 'That gives you one hell of a motive for murder, if it's true.'

'It's true,' Dillon said flatly. 'And yes, I suppose it does give me a strong motive for killing him. I admit I hated the man, I hated him passionately.'

'You admit that, do you?'

'Why not? I have nothing to hide.'

'What did you expect to gain by coming here to see Chillingham?' I asked. 'Assuming you didn't come here to kill him.'

'I wanted to tell him I knew what he'd done, and that I was going to expose him for the thief he was.'

'You tell him that?'

'I was leading up to it when he was shot.'

'Suppose you go into a little more detail about this alleged theft from your father's estate.'

'All right.' Dillon lit a cigarette. 'My father was a hard-nosed businessman, a self-made type who acquired a considerable fortune in textiles; as far as he was concerned, all of life revolved around money. But I've never seen it that way; I've always been something of a free spirit and to hell with negotiable assets. Inevitably, my father and I had a falling-out about fifteen years ago, when I was twenty-three, and I left home with the idea of seeing some of the big wide world – which is exactly what I did.

'I traveled from one end of this country to the other, working at different jobs, and then I went to South America for a while. Some of the wanderlust finally began to wear off, and I decided to come back to this city and settle down – maybe even patch things up with my father. I arrived several days ago and learned then that he had been dead for more than two years.'

'You had no contact with your father during the fifteen years you were drifting around?'

'None whatsoever. I told you, we had a falling-out. And we'd never been close to begin with.'

Sherrard asked, 'So what made you suspect Chillingham had stolen money from your father's estate?'

'I am the only surviving member of the Dillon family; there are no other relatives, not even a distant cousin. I knew my father wouldn't have left me a cent, not after all these years, and I didn't particularly care; but I *was* curious to find out to whom he had willed his estate.'

'And what did you find out?'

'Well, I happen to know that my father had three favorite charities,' Dillon said. 'Before I left, he used to tell me that if I didn't "shape-up," as he put it, he would leave every cent of his money to those three institutions.'

'He didn't, is that it?'

'Not exactly. According to the will, he left $200,000 to each of two of them – the Cancer Society and the Children's Hospital. He also, according to the will, left $350,000 to the Association for Medical Research.'

'All right,' Sherrard said, 'so what does that have to do with Chillingham?'

'Everything,' Dillon told him. 'My father died of a heart attack – he'd had a heart condition for many years. Not severe, but he fully expected to die as a result of it one day. And so he did. And because of this heart condition his third favorite charity – the one he felt the most strongly about – was the Heart Fund.'

'Go on,' I said, frowning.

Dillon put out his cigarette and gave me a humorless smile. 'I looked into the Association for Medical Research and I did quite a thorough bit of checking. It doesn't exist; there *isn't* any Association for Medical Research. And the only person who could have invented it is or was my father's lawyer and executor, Adam Chillingham.'

Sherrard and I thought that over and came to the same conclusion. I said, 'So even though you never got along with your father, and you don't care about money for yourself, you decided to expose Chillingham.'

'That's right. My father worked hard all his life to build his fortune, and admirably enough he decided to give it to charity at his death. I believe in worthwhile causes, I believe in the work being done by the Heart Fund, and it sent me into a rage to realize they had been cheated out of a substantial fortune which could have gone toward valuable research.'

'A murderous rage?' Sherrard asked softly.

Dillon showed us his humorless smile again. 'I didn't kill Adam Chillingham,' he said. 'But you'll have to admit, he deserved killing – and that the world is better off without the likes of him.'

I might have admitted that to myself, if Dillon's accusations were valid, but I didn't admit it to Dillon. I'm a cop, and my job is to uphold the law; murder is murder, whatever the reasons for it, and it can't be gotten away with.

Sherrard and I hammered at Dillon a while longer, but we couldn't shake him at all. I left Jack to continue the field questioning and took a couple of men and re-searched Chillingham's private office. No gun. I went up onto the roof of the nearest building and searched that personally. No gun. I took my men down into the lawn area and supervised another minute search. No gun.

I went back to Chillingham's suite and talked to Charles Hearn and

Miss Tower again, and they had nothing to add to what they'd already told us; Hearn was 'almost positive' he had heard a muffled explosion inside the office, but, from the legal point of view, that was the same as not having heard anything at all.

We took Dillon down to Headquarters finally, because we knew damned well he had killed Adam Chillingham, and advised him of his rights and printed him and booked him on suspicion. He asked for counsel, and we called a public defender for him, and then we grilled him again in earnest. It got us nowhere.

The F.B.I. and state check we ran on his fingerprints got us nowhere either; he wasn't wanted, he had never been arrested, he had never even been printed before. Unless something turned up soon in the way of evidence – specifically, the missing murder weapon – we knew we couldn't hold him very long.

The next day I received the lab report and the coroner's report and the ballistics report on the bullet taken from Chillingham's neck – .22 caliber, all right. The lab's and coroner's findings combined to tell me something I'd already guessed: the wound and the calculated angle of trajectory of the bullet did not entirely rule out the remote possibility that Chillingham had been shot from the roof of the nearest building. The ballistics report, however, told me something I hadn't guessed – something which surprised me a little.

The bullet had no rifling marks.

Sherrard blinked at this when I related the information to him. 'No rifling marks?' he said. 'Hell, that means the slug wasn't fired from a gun at all, at least not a lawfully manufactured one. A homemade weapon, you think, Walt?'

'That's how it figures,' I agreed. 'A kind of zipgun probably. Anybody can make one; all you need is a length of tubing or the like and a bullet and a grip of some sort and a detonating cap.'

'But there was no zipgun, either, in or around Chillingham's office. We'd have found it if there was.'

I worried my lower lip meditatively. 'Well, you can make one of those zips from a dozen or more small component parts, you know; even the tubing could be soft aluminium, the kind you can break apart with your hands. When you're done using it, you can knock it down again into its components. Dillon had enough time to have done that, before opening the locked door.'

'Sure,' Sherrard said. 'But then what? We *still* didn't find anything – not a single thing – that could have been used as part of a homemade zip.'

I suggested we go back and make another search, and so we drove once more to the Dawes Building. We re-combed Chillingham's private office – we'd had a police seal on it to make sure nothing could be disturbed – and we re-combed the surrounding area. We didn't find so much as an iron filing. Then we went to the city jail and had another talk with George Dillon.

When I told him our zipgun theory, I thought I saw a light flicker in his eyes; but it was the briefest of reactions, and I couldn't be sure. We told him it was highly unlikely a zipgun using a .22 caliber bullet could kill anybody from a distance of a hundred yards, and he said he couldn't help that, *he* didn't know anything about such a weapon. Further questioning got us nowhere.

And the following day we were forced to release him, with a warning not to leave the city.

But Sherrard and I continued to work doggedly on the case; it was one of those cases that preys on your mind constantly, keeps you from sleeping well at night, because you know there has to be an answer and you just can't figure out what it is. We ran checks into Chillingham's records and found that he had made some large private investments a year ago, right after the Dillon will had been probated. And as George Dillon had claimed, there was no Association for Medical Research; it was a dummy charity, apparently set up by Chillingham for the explicit purpose of stealing old man Dillon's $350,000. But there was no definite proof of this, not enough to have convicted Chillingham of theft in a court of law; he'd covered himself pretty neatly.

As an intelligent man, George Dillon had no doubt realized that a public exposure of Chillingham would have resulted in nothing more than adverse publicity and the slim possibility of disbarment – hardly sufficient punishment in Dillon's eyes. So he had decided on what, to him, was a morally justifiable homicide. From the law's point of view, however, it was nonetheless Murder One.

But the law still had no idea what he'd done with the weapon and, therefore, as in the case of Chillingham's theft, the law had no proof of guilt.

As I said, though, we had our teeth into this one and we weren't about to let go. So we paid another call on Dillon, this time at the hotel where he was staying, and asked him some questions about his background. There was nothing more immediate we could investigate, and we thought that maybe there was an angle in his past which would give us a clue toward solving the riddle.

He told us, readily enough, some of what he'd done during the fifteen years since he'd left home, and it was a typical drifter's life: lobster packer in Maine, ranch hand in Montana, oil worker in Texas, road construction in South America. But there was a gap of about four years which he sort of skimmed over without saying anything specific. I jumped on that and asked him some direct questions, but he wouldn't talk about it.

His reluctance made Sherrard and me more than a little curious; we both had that cop's feeling it was important, that maybe it was the key we needed to unlock the mystery. Unobtrusively we had the department photographer take some pictures of Dillon; then we sent them out, along with a request for information as to his whereabouts during the four blank years, to various law enforcement agencies in Florida – where he'd admitted to being just prior to the gap, working as a deckhand on a Key West charter-fishing boat.

Time dragged on, and nothing turned up, and we were reluctantly forced by sheer volume of other work to abandon the Chillingham case; officially, it was now buried in the Unsolved File. Then, three months later, we had a wire from the Chief of Police of a town not far from Fort Lauderdale. It said they had tentatively identified George Dillon from the pictures we'd sent and were forwarding by airmail special delivery something which might conceivably prove the nature of Dillon's activities during at least part of the specified period.

Sherrard and I fidgeted around waiting for the special delivery to arrive, and when it finally came I happened to be the only one of us in the squadroom. I tore the envelope open and what was inside was a multicolored and well-aged poster, with a picture of a man who was undeniably George Dillon depicted on it. I looked at the picture and read what was written on the poster at least a dozen times.

It told me a lot of things all right, that poster did. It told me exactly what Dillon had done with the homemade zipgun he had used to kill Adam Chillingham – an answer that was at once fantastic and yet so simple you'd never even consider it. And it told me there wasn't a damned thing we could do about it now, that we couldn't touch him, that George Dillon actually had committed a perfect murder.

I was brooding over this when Jack Sherrard returned to the squadroom. He said, 'Why so glum, Walt?'

'The special delivery from Florida finally showed up,' I said, and watched instant excitement animate his face. Then I saw some of it fade while I told him what I'd been brooding about, finishing with, 'We simply can't arrest him now, Jack. There's no evidence, it doesn't exist any more; we can't prove a thing. And maybe it's just as well in one respect, since I kind of liked Dillon and would have hated to see him convicted for killing a crook like Chillingham. Anyway, we'll be able to sleep nights now.'

'Damn it, Walt, will you tell me what you're talking about!'

'All right. Remember when we got the ballistics report and we talked over how easy it would be for Dillon to have made a zipgun? And how he could make the whole thing out of a dozen or so small component parts, so that afterward he could break it down again into those small parts?'

'Sure, sure. But I don't care if Dillon used a hundred components, we didn't find a single one of them. Not one. So what, if that's part of the answer, did he do with them? There's not even a connecting bathroom where he could have flushed them down. What did he do with the damned zipgun?'

I sighed and slid the poster – the old carnival side-show poster – around on my desk, so he could see Dillon's picture and read the words printed below it: STEAK AND POTATOES AND APPLE PIE IS OUR DISH; NUTS, BOLTS, PIECES OF WOOD, BITS OF METAL IS HIS! YOU HAVE TO SEE IT TO BELIEVE IT: THE AMAZING MR GEORGE, THE MAN WITH THE CAST-IRON STOMACH.

Sherrard's head jerked up and he stared at me open-mouthed.

'That's right,' I said wearily. 'He *ate* it.'

THE ADVENTURE OF ABRAHAM LINCOLN'S CLUE

Ellery Queen

'As you read through the introductions to the stories in this volume, you will notice one name which appears with much greater frequency than any other: the name of Frederic Dannay, whose insight and encouragement sparked and nurtured and inspired the careers of many dozens of writers.

In addition to his enormously influential work as an editor, Fred Dannay was, with his cousin, Manfred B. Lee, Ellery Queen. And Ellery Queen, according to the late, great mystery critic Anthony Boucher, "is *the American detective story".*

The large body of Ellery Queen novels and short stories – brilliantly, intricately and fairly plotted, wonderfully written, refreshingly real – will surely live forever. But Manny Lee passed on in April of 1971 and, now, a decade later, Fred Dannay is also gone.

Shortly before his death in the autumn of 1982, I asked him to select his favorite Ellery Queen story for inclusion in this collection. Without hesitation, he chose 'The Adventure of Abraham Lincoln's Clue'. Why? "It combines certain passions that Mr Lee and I shared," he told me; 'our love and devotion for Abraham Lincoln and for Edgar Allan Poe, and our lifelong hobby of stamp-collecting."

For those who remember Frederic Dannay and Manfred B. Lee with respect, with admiration, and with thanks – and for those whose passions include the writings of Ellery Queen – the story which follows may perhaps serve as a small but fitting memorial.'

Fourscore and eighteen years ago, Abraham Lincoln brought forth (in this account) a new notion, conceived in secrecy and dedicated to the proposition that even an Honest Abe may borrow a leaf from Edgar A. Poe.

It is altogether fitting and proper that Mr Lincoln's venture into the detective story should come to its final resting place in the files of a man named Queen. For all his life Ellery has consecrated Father Abraham as the noblest projection of the American dream; and, insofar as it has been within his poor power to add or detract, he has given full measure of devotion, testing whether that notion, or any notion so conceived and so dedicated, deserves to endure.

Ellery's service in running the Lincoln clue to earth is one the world has little noted nor, perhaps, will long remember. That he shall not have served in vain, this account:

The case began on the outskirts of an upstate-New York city with the dreadful name of Eulalia, behind the flaking shutters of a fat and curlicued house with architectural dandruff, recalling for all the world some blowsy ex-Bloomer Girl from the Gay Nineties of its origin.

The owner, a formerly wealthy man named DiCampo, possessed a grandeur not shared by his property, although it was no less fallen into ruin. His falcon's face, more Florentine than Victorian, was – like the house – ravaged by time and the inclemencies of fortune; but haughtily so, and indeed DiCampo wore his scruffy purple velvet house jacket like the prince he was entitled to call himself, but did not. He was proud, and stubborn, and useless; and he had a lovely daughter named Bianca, who taught at a Eulalia grade school and, through marvels of economy, supported them both.

How Lorenzo San Marco Borghese-Ruffo DiCampo came to this decayed estate is no concern of ours. The presence there this day of a man named Harbidger and a man named Tungston, however, is to the point: they had come, Harbidger from Chicago, Tungston from Philadelphia, to buy something each wanted very much, and DiCampo had summoned them in order to sell it. The two visitors were collectors, Harbidger's passion being Lincoln, Tungston's Poe.

The Lincoln collector, an elderly man who looked like a migrant fruit picker, had plucked his fruits well: Harbidger was worth about $40,000,000, every dollar of which was at the beck of his mania for Lincolniana. Tungston, who was almost as rich, had the aging body of a poet and the eyes of a starving panther, armament that had served him well in the wars of Poeana.

'I must say, Mr DiCampo,' remarked Harbidger, 'that your letter surprised me.' He paused to savor the wine his host had poured from an ancient and honorable bottle (DiCampo had filled it with California claret before their arrival). 'May I ask what has finally induced you to offer the book and document for sale?'

'To quote Lincoln in another context, Mr Harbidger,' said DiCampo, with a shrug of his wasted shoulders, ' "the dogmas of the quiet past are inadequate to the stormy present." In short, a hungry man sells his blood.'

'Only if it's of the right type,' said old Tungston, unmoved. 'You've made that book and document less accessible to collectors and historians, DiCampo, than the gold in Fort Knox. Have you got them here? I'd like to examine them.'

'No other hand will ever touch them except by right of ownership,' Lorenzo DiCampo replied bitterly. He had taken a miser's glee in his lucky finds, vowing never to part with them; now forced by his need to sell them, he was like a suspicion-caked old prospector who, stumbling at last on pay dirt, draws cryptic maps to keep the world from stealing the secret of its location. 'As I informed you gentlemen, I represent the book as bearing the signatures of Poe and Lincoln, and the document as being in Lincoln's hand; I am offering them with the customary proviso that they are returnable if they should prove to be not as represented; and if this does not satisfy you,' and the old prince actually rose, 'let us terminate our business here and now.'

'Sit down, sit down, Mr DiCampo,' Harbidger said.

'No one is questioning your integrity,' snapped old Tungston. 'It's just that I'm not used to buying sight unseen. If there's a money-back guarantee, we'll do it your way.'

Lorenzo DiCampo reseated himself stiffly. 'Very well, gentlemen. Then I take it you are both prepared to buy?'

'Oh, yes!' said Harbidger. 'What is your price?'

'Oh, no,' said DiCampo. 'What is your bid?'

The Lincoln collector cleared his throat, which was full of slaver. 'If the book and document are as represented, Mr DiCampo, you might hope to get from a dealer or realize at auction – oh – $50,000. I offer you $55,000.'

'$56,000,' said Tungston.

'$57,000,' said Harbidger.

'$58,000,' said Tungston.

'$59,000,' said Harbidger.

Tungston showed his fangs. '$60,000,' he said.

Harbidger fell silent, and DiCampo waited. He did not expect miracles. To these men, five times $60,000 was of less moment than the undistinguished wine they were smacking their lips over; but they were veterans of many a hard auction-room campaign, and a collector's victory tasted very nearly as sweet for the price as for the prize.

So the impoverished prince was not surprised when the Lincoln collector suddenly said, 'Would you be good enough to allow Mr Tungston and me to talk privately for a moment?'

DiCampo rose and strolled out of the room, to gaze somberly through a cracked window at the jungle growth that had once been his Italian formal gardens.

It was the Poe collector who summoned him back. 'Harbidger has convinced me that for the two of us to try to outbid each other would simply run the price up out of all reason. We're going to make you a sporting proposition.'

'I've proposed to Mr Tungston, and he has agreed,' nodded Harbidger, 'that our bid for the book and document be $65,000. Each of us is prepared to pay that sum, and not a penny more.'

'So that is how the screws are turned,' said DiCampo, smiling. 'But I do not understand. If each of you makes the identical bid, which of you gets the book and document?'

'Ah,' grinned the Poe man, 'that's where the sporting proposition comes in.'

'You see, Mr DiCampo,' said the Lincoln man, 'we are going to leave that decision to you.'

Even the old prince, who had seen more than his share of the astonishing, was astonished. He looked at the two rich men really for the first time. 'I must confess,' he murmured, 'that your compact is an amusement. Permit me?' He sank into thought while the two collectors sat expectantly. When the old man looked up he was smiling like a fox. 'The very thing, gentleman! From the typewritten copies of the document I sent you, you both know that Lincoln himself left a clue to a theoretical hiding place for the book which he never explained. Some time ago I arrived at a possible solution to the President's little mystery. I propose to hide the book and document in accordance with it.'

'You mean whichever of us figures out your interpretation of the Lincoln clue and finds the book and document where you will hide them, Mr DiCampo, gets both for the agreed price?'

'That is it exactly.'

The Lincoln collector looked dubious. 'I don't know . . .'

'Oh, come, Harbidger,' said Tungston, eyes glittering. 'A deal is a deal. We accept, DiCampo! Now what?'

'You gentlemen will of course have to give me a little time. Shall we say three days?'

Ellery let himself into the Queen apartment, tossed his suitcase aside, and set about opening windows. He had been out of town for a week on a case, and Inspector Queen was in Atlantic City attending a police convention.

Breathable air having been restored, Ellery sat down to the week's accumulation of mail. One envelope made him pause. It had come by airmail special delivery, it was postmarked four days earlier, and in the lower left corner, in red, flamed the word *URGENT*. The printed return address on the flap said: *L.S.M.B.R. DiCampo, Post Office Box 69, Southern District, Eulalia, N.Y.* The initials of the name had been crossed out and 'Bianca' written above them.

The enclosure, in a large agitated female hand on inexpensive notepaper, said:

> Dear Mr Queen,
> The most important detective book in the world has disappeared. Will you please find it for me?
> Phone me on arrival at the Eulalia RR station or airport and I will pick you up.
>
> Bianca DiCampo

A yellow envelope then caught his eye. It was a telegram, dated the previous day:

> WHY HAVE I NOT HEARD FROM YOU STOP AM IN DESPERATE NEED YOUR SERVICES
>
> BIANCA DICAMPO

He had no sooner finished reading the telegram than the telephone on his desk trilled. It was a long-distance call.

'Mr Queen?' throbbed a contralto voice. 'Thank heaven I've finally got through to you! I've been calling all day – '

'I've been away,' said Ellery, 'and you would be Miss Bianca DiCampo of Eulalia. In two words, Miss DiCampo: Why me?'

'In two words, Mr Queen: Abraham Lincoln.'

Ellery was startled. 'You plead a persuasive case,' he chuckled. 'It's true, I'm an incurable Lincoln addict. How did you find out? Well, never mind. Your letter refers to a book, Miss DiCampo. Which book?'

The husky voice told him, and certain other provocative things as well. 'So will you come, Mr Queen?'

'Tonight if I could! Suppose I drive up first thing in the morning. I ought to make Eulalia by noon. Harbidger and Tungston are still around, I take it?'

'Oh, yes. They're staying at a motel downtown.'

'Would you ask them to be there?'

The moment he hung up, Ellery leaped to his bookshelves. He snatched out his volume of *Murder for Pleasure*, the historical work on detective stories by his good friend Howard Haycraft, and found what he was looking for on page 26:

> And . . . young William Dean Howells thought it significant praise to assert of a nominee for President of the United States:
>
> > The bent of his mind is mathematical and metaphysical, and he is therefore pleased with the absolute and logical method of Poe's tales and sketches, in which the problem of mystery is given, and wrought out into everyday facts by processes of cunning analysis. It is said that he suffers no year to pass without a perusal of this author.
>
> Abraham Lincoln subsequently confirmed this statement, which appeared in his little known 'campaign biography' by Howells in 1860 . . . The instance is chiefly notable, of course, for its revelation of a little suspected affinity between two great Americans. . . .

Very early the next morning Ellery gathered some papers from his files, stuffed them into his briefcase, scribbled a note for his father, and ran for his car, Eulalia-bound . . .

He was enchanted by the DiCampo house, which looked like something out of Poe by Charles Addams; and, for other reasons, by Bianca, who turned out to be a genetic product supreme of northern Italy, with Titian hair and Mediterranean blue eyes and a figure that needed only some solid steaks to qualify her for Miss Universe competition. Also, she was in deep mourning; so her conquest of the Queen heart was immediate and complete.

'He died of a cerebral hemorrhage, Mr Queen,' Bianca said, dabbing at her absurd little nose. 'In the middle of the second night after his session with Mr Harbidger and Mr Tungston.'

So Lorenzo San Marco Borghese-Ruffo DiCampo was unexpectedly dead, bequeathing the lovely Bianca near-destitution and a mystery.

'The only things of value father really left me are that book and the Lincoln document. The $65,000 they now represent would pay off father's debts and give me a fresh start. But I can't find them, Mr Queen, and neither can Mr Harbidger and Mr Tungston – who'll be here soon, by the way. Father hid the two things, as he told them he would; but where? We've ransacked the place.'

'Tell me more about the book, Miss DiCampo.'

'As I said over the phone, it's called *The Gift: 1845*. The Christmas annual that contained the earliest appearance of Edgar Allan Poe's *The Purloined Letter*.'

'Published in Philadelphia by Carey & Hart? Bound in red?' At

Bianca's nod, Ellery said, 'You understand that an ordinary copy of *The Gift: 1845* isn't worth more than about $50. What makes your father's copy unique is that double autograph you mentioned.'

'That's what he said, Mr Queen. I wish I had the book here to show you – that beautifully handwritten *Edgar Allan Poe* on the flyleaf, and under Poe's signature the signature *Abraham Lincoln*.'

'Poe's own copy, once owned, signed, and read by Lincoln,' Ellery said slowly. 'Yes, that would be a collector's item for the ages. By the way, Miss DiCampo, what's the story behind the other piece – the Lincoln document?'

Bianca told him what her father had told her.

One morning in the spring of 1865, Abraham Lincoln opened the rosewood door of his bedroom in the southwest corner of the second floor of the White House and stepped out into the red-carpeted hall at the unusually late hour – for him – of 7:00 am; he was more accustomed to beginning his work day at six.

But (as Lorenzo DiCampo had reconstructed events) Mr Lincoln that morning had lingered in his bedchamber. He had awakened at his usual hour but, instead of leaving immediately on dressing for his office, he had pulled one of the cane chairs over to the round table, with its gas-fed reading lamp, and sat down to reread Poe's *The Purloined Letter* in his copy of the 1845 annual; it was a dreary morning, and the natural light was poor. The President was alone; the folding doors to Mrs Lincoln's bedroom remained closed.

Impressed as always with Poe's tale, Mr Lincoln on this occasion was struck by a whimsical thought; and, apparently finding no paper handy, he took an envelope from his pocket, discarded its enclosure, slit the two short edges so that the envelope opened out into a single sheet, and began to write on the blank side.

'Describe it to me, please.'

'It's a long envelope, one that must have contained a bulky letter. It is addressed to the White House, but there is no return address, and father was never able to identify the sender from the handwriting. We do know that the letter came through the regular mails, because there are two Lincoln stamps on it, lightly but unmistakably cancelled.'

'May I see your father's transcript of what Lincoln wrote out that morning on the inside of the envelope?'

Bianca handed him a typewritten copy and, in spite of himself, Ellery felt goose-flesh rise as he read:

Apr. 14, 1865

Mr Poe's The Purloined Letter is a work of singular originality. Its

> simplicity is a master-stroke of cunning, which never fails to arouse my wonder.
>
> Reading the tale over this morning has given me a 'notion.' Suppose I wished to hide a book, this very book, perhaps? Where best to do so? Well, as Mr Poe in his tale hid a letter *among letters*, might not a book be hidden *among books*? Why, if this very copy of the tale were to be deposited in a library and on purpose not recorded – would not the Library of Congress make a prime depository! – well might it repose there, undiscovered, for a generation.
>
> On the other hand, let us regard Mr Poe's 'notion' turn-about: suppose the book were to be placed, not amongst other books, but *where no book would reasonably be expected*? (I may follow the example of Mr Poe, and, myself, compose a tale of 'ratiocination'!)
>
> The 'notion' beguiles me, it is nearly seven o'clock. Later to-day, if the vultures and my appointments leave me a few moments of leisure, I may write further of my imagined hiding-place.
>
> In self-reminder: the hiding-place of the book is in 30d, which

Ellery looked up. 'The document ends there?'

'Father said that Mr Lincoln must have glanced again at his watch, and shamefacedly jumped up to go to his office, leaving the sentence unfinished. Evidently he never found the time to get back to it.'

Ellery brooded. Evidently indeed. From the moment when Abraham Lincoln stepped out of his bedroom that Good Friday morning, fingering his thick gold watch on its vest chain, to bid the still-unrelieved night guard his customary courteous 'Good morning,' and make for his office at the other end of the hall, his day was spoken for. The usual patient push through the clutching crowd of favor-seekers, many of whom had bedded down all night on the hall carpet; sanctuary in his sprawling office, where he read official correspondence; by 8:00 am having breakfast with his family – Mrs Lincoln chattering away about plans for the evening, 12-year-old Tad of the cleft palate lisping a complaint that 'nobody asked me to go,' and young Robert Lincoln, just returned from duty, bubbling with stories about his hero Ulysses Grant and the last days of the war; then back to the presidential office to look over the morning newspapers (which Lincoln had once remarked he 'never' read, but these were happy days, with good news everywhere), sign two documents, and signal the soldier at the door to admit the morning's first caller, Speaker of the House Schuyler Colfax (who was angling for a Cabinet post and had to be tactfully handled); and so on throughout the day – the historic Cabinet meeting at 11:00 am, attended by General Grant himself, that stretched well into the afternoon; a hurried lunch at almost half-past two with Mrs Lincoln (had this 45-pounds underweight man eaten his usual midday meal of a biscuit, a glass of milk, and an apple?); more visitors to see in his office (including the unscheduled Mrs Nancy Bushrod, escaped slave and wife of an escaped slave and mother of three small children, weeping that Tom, a soldier in the Army of the Potomac, was no longer getting his pay: 'You are entitled to your husband's pay. Come this time tomorrow,' and the tall President escorted her to the door, bowing her out 'like I was a natural-born lady'); the late afternoon drive in the barouche to the Navy Yard and back with Mrs Lincoln; more work, more visitors, into the evening . . . until finally, at five minutes past 8:00 pm, Abraham Lincoln stepped into the White House formal coach after his wife, waved, and sank back to be driven off to see a play he did not much want to see, *Our American Cousin*, at Ford's Theatre . . .

Ellery mused over that black day in silence. And, like a relative hanging on the specialist's yet undelivered diagnosis, Bianca DiCampo sat watching him with anxiety.

Harbidger and Tungston arrived in a taxi, to greet Ellery with the fervor of castaways grasping at a smudge of smoke on the horizon.

'As I understand it, gentlemen,' Ellery said when he had calmed them down, 'neither of you has been able to solve Mr DiCampo's interpretation of the Lincoln clue. If I succeed in finding the book and paper where DiCampo hid them, which of you gets them?'

'We intend to split the $65,000 payment to Miss DiCampo,' said Harbidger, 'and take joint ownership of the two pieces.'

'An arrangement,' growled old Tungston, 'I'm against on principle, in practice, and by plain horse sense.'

'So am I,' sighed the Lincoln collector, 'but what else can we do?'

'Well,' and the Poe man regarded Bianca DiCampo with the icy intimacy of the cat that long ago marked the bird as its prey, 'Miss DiCampo, who now owns the two pieces, is quite free to renegotiate a sale on her own terms.'

'Miss DiCampo,' said Miss DiCampo, giving Tungston stare for stare, 'considers herself bound by her father's wishes. His terms stand.'

'In all likelihood, then,' said the other millionaire, 'one of us will retain the book, the other the document, and we'll exchange them every year, or some such thing.' Harbidger sounded unhappy.

'Only practical arrangement under the circumstances,' grunted Tungston, and *he* sounded unhappy. 'But all this is academic, Queen, unless and until the book and document are found.'

Ellery nodded. 'The problem, then, is to fathom DiCampo's interpretation of that *30d* in the document. 30d . . . I notice, Miss DiCampo – or, may I? Bianca? – that your father's typewritten copy of the Lincoln holograph text runs the *3* and *0* and *d* together – no spacing in between. Is that the way it occurs in the longhand?'

'Yes.'

'Hmm. Still . . . 30d . . . Could *d* stand for *days* . . . or the British *pence* . . . or *died*, as used in obituaries? Does any of these make sense to you, Bianca?'

'No.'

'Did your father have any special interest in, say, pharmacology? chemistry? physics? algebra? electricity? Small *d* is an abbreviation used in all those.' But Bianca shook her splendid head. 'Banking? Small *d* for *dollars, dividends*?'

'Hardly,' the girl said with a sad smile.

'How about theatricals? Was your father ever involved in a play production? Small *d* stands for *door* in playscript stage directions.'

'Mr Queen, I've gone through every darned abbreviation my dictionary lists, and I haven't found one that has a point of contact with any interest of my father's.'

Ellery scowled. 'At that – I assume the typewritten copy is accurate – the manuscript shows no period after the *d*, making an abbreviation unlikely. 30d . . . let's concentrate on the number. Does the number 30 have any significance for you?'

'Yes, indeed,' said Bianca, making all three men sit up. But then they sank back. 'In a few years it will represent my age, and that has enormous significance. But only for me, I'm afraid.'

'You'll be drawing wolf whistles at twice thirty,' quoth Ellery warmly. 'However! Could the number have cross-referred to anything in your father's life or habits?'

'None that I can think of, Mr Queen. And,' Bianca said, having grown roses in her cheeks, 'thank you.'

'I think,' said old Tungston testily, 'we had better stick to the subject.'

'Just the same, Bianca, let me run over some "thirty" associations as they come to mind. Stop me if one of them hits a nerve. The Thirty Tyrants – was your father interested in classical Athens? The Thirty Years War – in seventeenth-century European history? Thirty-all – did he play or follow tennis? Or . . . did he ever live at an address that included the number 30?'

Ellery went on and on, but to each suggestion Bianca DiCampo could only shake her head.

'The lack of spacing, come to think of it, doesn't necessarily mean that Mr DiCampo chose to view the clue that way,' said Ellery thoughtfully. 'He might have interpreted it arbitrarily as *3*-space-*0*-*d*.'

'Three od?' echoed old Tungston. 'What the devil could that mean?'

'Od? Od is the hypothetical force or power claimed by Baron von Reichenbach – in 1850, wasn't it? – to pervade the whole of nature. Manifests itself in magnets, crystals and such, which according to the excited Baron explained animal magnetism and mesmerism. Was your father by any chance interested in hypnosis, Bianca? Or the occult?'

'Not in the slightest.'

'Mr Queen,' exclaimed Harbidger, 'are you serious about all this – this semantic sludge?'

'Why, I don't know,' said Ellery. 'I never know till I stumble over something. Od . . . the word was used with prefixes, too – *biod*, the force of animal life; *elod*, the force of electricity; and so forth. *Three* od . . . or *triod*, the triune force – it's all right, Mr Harbidger, it's not ignorance on your part, I just coined the word. But it does rather suggest the Trinity, doesn't it? Bianca, did your father tie up to the Church in a personal, scholarly, or any other way? No? That's too bad, really, because Od – capitalized – has been a minced form of the word God since the sixteenth-century. Or . . . you wouldn't happen to have three Bibles on the premises, would you? Because – '

Ellery stopped with the smashing abruptness of an ordinary force meeting an absolutely immovable object. The girl and the two collectors gawped. Bianca had idly picked up the typewritten copy of the Lincoln document. She was not reading it, she was simply holding it on her knees; but Ellery, sitting opposite her, had shot forward in a crouch, rather like a pointer, and he was regarding the paper in her lap with a glare of pure discovery.

'That's it!' he cried.

'What's it, Mr Queen?' the girl asked, bewildered.

'Please – the transcript!' He plucked the paper from her. 'Of course. Hear this: "On the other hand, let us regard Mr Poe's 'notion' turn about." *Turn-about*. Look at the 30d "turn-about" – as I just saw it!'

He turned the Lincoln message upside down for their inspection. In that position the 30d became:

POƐ

'*Poe!*' exploded Tungston.

'Yes, crude but recognizable,' Ellery said swiftly. 'So now we read the Lincoln clue as: "The hiding-place of the book is in *Poe*"!'

There was a silence.

'In Poe,' said Harbidger blankly.

'In Poe?' muttered Tungston. 'There are only a couple of trade editions of Poe in DiCampo's library, Harbidger, and we went through those. We looked in every book here.'

'He might have meant among the Poe books in the *public* library. Miss DiCampo – '

'Wait.' Bianca sped away. But when she came back she was drooping. 'It isn't. We have two public libraries in Eulalia, and I know the head librarian in both. I just called them. Father didn't visit either library.'

Ellery gnawed a fingernail. 'Is there a bust of Poe in the house, Bianca? Or any other Poe-associated object, aside from books?'

'I'm afraid not.'

'Queer,' he mumbled. 'Yet I'm positive your father interpreted "the hiding-place of the book" as being "in Poe." So he'd have hidden it "in Poe" . . .'

Ellery's mumbling dribbled away into a tormented sort of silence: his eyebrows worked up and down, Groucho Marx-fashion; he pinched the tip of his nose until it was scarlet; he yanked at his unoffending ears; he munched on his lip . . . until, all at once, his face cleared and he sprang to his feet. 'Bianca, may I use your phone?'

The girl could only nod, and Ellery dashed. They heard him telephoning in the entrance hall, although they could not make out the words. He was back in two minutes.

'One thing more,' he said briskly, 'and we're out of the woods. I suppose your father had a key ring or a key case, Bianca? May I have it, please?'

She fetched a key case. To the two millionaires it seemed the sorriest of objects, a scuffed and dirty tan leatherette case. But Ellery received it from the girl as if it were an artifact of historic importance from a newly discovered IV Dynasty tomb. He unsnapped it with concentrated love; he fingered its contents like a scientist. Finally he decided on a certain key.

'Wait here!' Thus Mr Queen; and exit, running.

'I can't decide,' old Tungston said after a while, 'whether that fellow is a genius or an escaped lunatic.'

Neither Harbidger nor Bianca replied. Apparently they could not decide, either.

They waited through twenty elongated minutes; at the twenty-first they heard his car, champing. All three were in the front doorway as Ellery strode up the walk.

He was carrying a book with a red cover, and smiling. It was a compassionate smile, but none of them noticed.

'You – ' said Bianca. ' – found – ' said Tungston. ' – the book!' shouted Harbidger. 'Is the Lincoln holograph in it?'

'It is,' said Ellery. 'Shall we all go into the house, where we may mourn in decent privacy?'

'Because,' Ellery said to Bianca and the two quivering collectors as they sat across a refectory table from him, 'I have foul news. Mr Tungston, I believe you have never actually seen Mr DiCampo's book. Will you now look at the Poe signature on the flyleaf?'

The panther claws leaped. There, toward the top of the flyleaf, in faded inkscript, was the signature *Edgar Allan Poe*.

The claws curled, and old Tungston looked up sharply. 'DiCampo never mentioned that it's a full autograph – he kept referring to it as "the Poe signature." Edgar *Allan* Poe . . . Why, I don't know of a single instance after his West Point days when Poe wrote out his middle name in an autograph! And the earliest he could have signed this 1845 edition is obviously when it was published, which was around the fall of 1844. In 1844 he'd surely have abbreviated the "Allan," signing "Edgar *A*. Poe," the way he signed everything! This is a forgery.'

'My God,' murmured Bianca, clearly intending no impiety; she was as pale as Poe's Lenore. 'Is that true, Mr Queen?'

'I'm afraid it is,' Ellery said sadly. 'I was suspicious the moment you told me the Poe signature on the flyleaf contained the "Allan". And if the Poe signature is a forgery, the book itself can hardly be considered Poe's own copy.'

Harbidger was moaning. 'And the Lincoln signature underneath the Poe, Mr Queen! DiCampo never told me it reads *Abraham* Lincoln – the full Christian name. Except on official documents, Lincoln practically always signed his name "*A*. Lincoln." Don't tell me this Lincoln autograph is a forgery, too?'

Ellery forbore to look at poor Bianca. 'I was struck by the "Abraham" as well, Mr Harbidger, when Miss DiCampo mentioned it to me, and I came equipped to test it. I have here – ' and Ellery tapped the pile of documents he had taken from his briefcase ' – facsimiles of Lincoln signatures from the most frequently reproduced of the historic documents he signed. Now I'm going to make a precise tracing of the Lincoln signature on the flyleaf of the book – ' he proceeded to do so

' – and I shall superimpose the tracing on the various signatures of the authentic Lincoln documents. So.'

He worked rapidly. On his third superimposition Ellery looked up. 'Yes. See here. The tracing of the purported Lincoln signature from the flyleaf fits in minutest detail over the authentic Lincoln signature on this facsimile of the Emancipation Proclamation. It's a fact of life that's tripped many a forger that *nobody ever writes his name exactly the same way twice*. There are always variations. If two signatures are identical, then one must be a tracing of the other. So the "Abraham Lincoln" signed on this flyleaf can be dismissed without further consideration as a forgery also. It's a tracing of the Emancipation Proclamation signature. Not only was this book not Poe's own copy; it was never signed – and therefore probably never owned – by Lincoln. However your father came into possession of the book, Bianca, he was swindled.'

It was the measure of Bianca DiCampo's quality that she said quietly, 'Poor, poor father,' nothing more.

Harbidger was poring over the worn old envelope on whose inside appeared the dearly beloved handscript of the Martyr President. 'At least,' he muttered, 'we have *this*.'

'Do we?' asked Ellery gently. 'Turn it over, Mr Harbidger.'

Harbidger looked up, scowling. 'No! You're not going to deprive me of this, too!'

'Turn it over,' Ellery repeated in the same gentle way. The Lincoln collector obeyed reluctantly. 'What do you see?'

'An authentic envelope of the period! With two authentic Lincoln stamps!'

'Exactly. And the United States has never issued postage stamps depicting living Americans; you have to be dead to qualify. The earliest U.S. stamp showing a portrait of Lincoln went on sale April 15, 1866 – a year to the day after his death. Then a living Lincoln could scarcely have used this envelope, with these stamps on it, as writing paper. The document is spurious, too. I am so very sorry, Bianca.'

Incredibly, Lorenzo DiCampo's daughter managed a smile with her '*Non importa, signor*.' He could have wept for her. As for the two collectors, Harbidger was in shock; but old Tungston managed to croak, 'Where the devil did DiCampo hide the book, Queen? And how did you know?'

'Oh, that,' said Ellery, wishing the two old men would go away so that he might comfort this admirable creature. 'I was convinced that DiCampo interpreted what we now know was the forger's, not

Lincoln's, clue, as *30d* read upside-down; or, crudely, *Poe*. But "the hiding-place of the book is in Poe" led nowhere. So I reconsidered. *P, o, e*. If those three letters of the alphabet didn't mean Poe, what could they mean? Then I remembered something about the letter you wrote me, Bianca. You'd used one of your father's envelopes, on the flap of which appeared his address: *Post Office Box 69, Southern District, Eulalia, N.Y.* If there was a Southern District in Eulalia, it seemed reasonable to conclude that there were post offices for other points of the compass, too. As, for instance, an Eastern District. Post Office Eastern, P.O. East. P.O.E.'

'Poe!' cried Bianca.

'To answer your question, Mr Tungston: I phoned the main post office, confirmed the existence of a Post Office East, got directions as to how to get there, looked for a postal box key in Mr DiCampo's key case, found the right one, located the box DiCampo had rented especially for the occasion, unlocked it – and there was the book.' He added, hopefully, 'And that is that.'

'And that *is* that,' Bianca said when she returned from seeing the two collectors off. 'I'm not going to cry over an empty milk bottle, Mr Queen. I'll straighten out father's affairs somehow. Right now all I can think of is how glad I am he didn't live to see the signatures and documents declared forgeries publicly, as they would surely have been when they were expertized.'

'I think you'll find there's still some milk in the bottle, Bianca.'

'I beg your pardon?' said Bianca.

Ellery tapped the pseudo-Lincolnian envelope. 'You know, you didn't do a very good job describing this envelope to me. All you said was that there were two cancelled Lincoln stamps on it.'

'Well, there are.'

'I can see you misspent your childhood. No, little girls don't collect things, do they? Why, if you'll examine these "two cancelled Lincoln stamps", you'll see that they're a great deal more than that. In the first place, they're not separate stamps. They're a vertical pair – that is, one stamp is joined to the other at the horizontal edges. Now look at this upper stamp of the pair.'

The Mediterranean eyes widened. 'It's upside-down, isn't it?'

'Yes, it's upside-down,' said Ellery, 'and what's more, while the pair have perforations all around, there are no perforations between them, where they're joined.

'What you have here, young lady – and what our unknown forger didn't realize when he fished around for an authentic White House cover of the period on which to perpetrate the Lincoln forgery – is what stamp collectors might call a double printing error: a pair of 1866 black 15-cent Lincolns imperforate horizontally, with one of the pair printed upside down. No such error of the Lincoln issue has ever been reported. You're the owner, Bianca, of what may well be the rarest item in U.S. philately, and the most valuable.'

The world will little note, nor long remember.

But don't try to prove it by Bianco DiCampo.

SEVEN LITTLE CROSSES IN A NOTEBOOK

Georges Simenon

'Georges Simenon was born in Belgium on 13 February 1903. By the age of twenty-six, he had already published some 500 pulp novels and short stories, under a total of 17 different pseudonyms. In 1929 he wrote the first of what was to be a long series of novels about that implacable policeman, Inspector Maigret; this was also the first book to be signed with the author's real name.

In the half-century since the appearance of that first of Maigret's cases, Simenon has published 211 more novels under his own name, 79 of them about Maigret. Every one of those books is currently in print in French; they have been translated into 55 other languages and have sold well over half a billion copies world-wide. In addition to his incredible output of fiction, M. Simenon has also published 21 volumes of daily dictations, a collection of his letters to his mother, and a long autobiography, Mémoires Intimes, *which appeared in France in November 1981.*

Georges Simenon himself writes: "I believe it can be said that my most successful short story is the one entitled in French 'Sept petites Croix dans un Carnet,' which is to be found in a volume entitled Un Noël de Maigret *(Maigret's Christmas). It is certainly the most widely translated and reproduced in magazines, and it has been adapted to the cinema, to radio and, frequently, to television." It has a charmingly original "angle", and despite being the longest story in the book, holds the reader's attention to the very end.'*

1

'At home,' said Sommer, who was making coffee on an electric ring, 'we used to go to midnight Mass all together, and the village was half an hour from the farm. There were five of us boys. Winters were colder in those days, for I remember going to church in a sleigh.'

Lecoeur, sitting at his switchboard with its hundreds of plugs, had pushed back the headphones from his ears in order to follow the conversation.

'In what part of the country?'

'In Lorraine.'

'Winters weren't any colder in Lorraine forty years ago, but the peasants had no cars. How many times did you go to midnight Mass in a sleigh?'

'I don't know . . .'

'Twice? Three times? Perhaps only once? But it impressed you because you were only a kid.'

'In any case when we got home we had a splendid blood sausage, the like of which I've never tasted since. And that's not fancy. We never discovered how my mother made it, or what she put into it, to make it different from all other blood sausages. My wife has tried. She asked my elder sister, who claimed to have mother's recipe.'

He went up to one of the great curtainless windows behind which lay nothing but darkness, and scratched the glass with his finger-nail.

'Why, it's all frosted up. And that again reminds me of when I was little. In the mornings when I wanted to wash I often had to break the ice in my jug, although it was standing in my bedroom.'

'Because they didn't have central heating,' Lecoeur objected calmly.

There were three of them on night duty, and they had been shut up in the huge room since 11 pm the previous evening. Now they were limp with 6 am fatigue. Remains of food lay about on the tables, with three or four empty bottles.

A light as big as an aspirin tablet appeared on one of the walls.

'Thirteenth arrondissement,' muttered Lecoeur, putting back his headphones. 'Croulebarbe district.'

He seized a plug and thrust it into one of the holes.

'Croulebarbe district? Your van's just gone out. What's up?'

'Officer calling, Boulevard Masséna. A scuffle between two drunks.'

Lecoeur carefully made a little cross in one of the columns in his notebook.

'What are you chaps doing?'

'There are only four of us in the station. Two of them are playing dominoes.'

'Have you been eating black pudding?'

'No. Why?'

'Oh, no reason. I must hang up; something's happening in the sixteenth.'

A gigantic map of Paris was painted on the wall in front of him, and the little lights that flashed on represented police stations. As soon as one of these received a warning for one reason or another, the light went on and Lecoeur pushed in the plug.

'Hello! Chaillot district? Your van's just gone out.'

In each of the twenty arrondissements in Paris, in front of the blue lamp of every police station, one or more vans stood ready to rush off at the first warning.

'What is it?'

'Veronal.'

A woman, obviously. It was the third that night, the second in the fashionable Passy district.

Lecoeur marked a cross in another column while Mambret, at his desk, filled in official forms.

'Hello! Odéon? What's happening your way? Stolen car?'

That concerned Mambret, who took notes, picked up another phone, dictated the description of the car to Piedboeuf the telegraphist, the drone of whose voice could be heard immediately overhead. It was the forty-eighth stolen car that Piedboeuf had reported since eleven o'clock.

For other people, Christmas Eve must have a special flavour. Hundreds of thousands of Parisians had flocked to cinemas and theatres. Thousands more had been shopping until a late hour in the big stores where weary-legged assistants were bustling about, as though in some nightmare, in front of their almost denuded shelves.

There were family gatherings behind drawn curtains, with turkeys roasting and blood sausages probably prepared, like Sommer's, from some private recipe carefully handed down from mother to daughter.

There were children sleeping restlessly, while their parents were quietly setting out presents round the Christmas tree.

There were restaurants and night-clubs where all the tables had been reserved days in advance. There was the Salvation Army's barge on the Seine, where dossers queued up, hungrily sniffing the good smells.

Sommer had a wife and children. Piedboeuf, the telegraphist on the floor above, had become a father a week ago.

Except for the ice on the windows, they would not have realized that it was cold outside. Christmas Eve, for them, wore the drab yellow colour of their big office facing the Palais de Justice, in the now deserted buildings of the Préfecture of Police, where in two days' time, and not before, crowds would pour in with requests for aliens' cards, driving licences, passport visas, demands of every sort.

Down below in the courtyard vans were waiting for urgent calls, with their drivers dozing on the seats.

But there had been no urgent calls. The little crosses in Lecoeur's notebook were eloquent. He did not trouble to count them. He knew that there were some two hundred in the drunks' column.

The police were being indulgent that night. They tried to persuade people to go home quietly, and only intervened when some drunks turned nasty and began to smash glasses or threaten peaceful fellow-customers.

Two hundred individuals, some of them women, were sound asleep on the floor in various police stations, behind bars.

There had been five knifings, two at the Porte d'Italie and three at the summit of Montmartre, not the Montmartre of the night-clubs but the outer zone, among the shanties built of old wooden boxes and tarred felt, inhabited by over a hundred thousand North Africans.

A few children reported missing – they were found again soon after – in the throng attending Mass.

'Hello! Chaillot? How's your veronal case?'

She had not died. They seldom do. They usually manage things so as not to die. They've made their gesture.

'Talking of blood sausages,' began Randon, who was smoking a big meerschaum pipe, 'that reminds me . . .'

They never learnt what it reminded him of. They heard hesitant footsteps in the unlighted staircase, a hand fumbled at the door and they saw the knob turn. The four of them stared in surprise that anyone should come to visit them at six o'clock in the morning.

'*Salut!*' said the man, throwing his hat down on a chair.

'What are you doing here, Janvier?'

Janvier was a young detective from the Homicide Squad, who went first of all to warm his hands over the radiator.

'I was bored, all alone over there,' he said. 'If the killer gets going I'll get the information here soonest.'

He, too, had spent the night on the job, but across the street, in the offices of the Police Judiciaire.

'May I?' he asked, lifting the coffee-pot. 'The wind's icy.'

He was blinking and scarlet-eared from the cold.

'We shan't know anything before 8 am or later,' said Lecoeur.

For the past fifteen years he had spent all his nights here in front of the map with its little lights and the telephone switchboard. He knew most of the Parisian police by name, at any rate those on night duty, he was even knowledgeable about their private affairs, since on quiet nights, when long intervals elapsed between the flashing of the lights, they could gossip together across space.

'How are things going with you?'

In this way he knew most of the police stations, too, although not all of them. He could imagine the atmosphere, as the policemen sat around with loosened belts and open-necked shirts, making coffee, just as they were doing here. But he had never seen them. He would not have recognized them in the street, any more than he had set foot in the hospitals whose names he knew as well as other people know the names of their uncles and aunts.

'Hello! Bichat? How's the injured man they brought in twenty minutes ago? Dead?'

A little cross in his notebook. You could ask him difficult questions:

'How many crimes are committed for money each year in Paris?'

He would reply unhesitatingly: 'Sixty-seven.'

'How many murders committed by foreigners?'

'Forty-two.'

'How many . . .'

He did not pride himself on it; he was meticulous, that was all. It was his job. He was not obliged to inscribe the little crosses in his notebook, but it helped to pass the time and it gave him as much satisfaction as collecting stamps.

He was unmarried. Nobody knew where he lived or what he did once he had left that office where he spent every night. Actually, one could scarcely imagine him outside in the street, like anybody else.

'For important happenings, you have to wait till people get up, till the concierge brings up the mail and the maids prepare breakfast and wake up their employers.'

His knowledge did him no particular credit, since things always happened that way. Earlier in summer, later in winter. And today it would be even later than usual, because a large proportion of the population was still sleeping off the wine and champagne drunk at last night's *réveillon* suppers. There were still some people about in the streets, and restaurant doors opened to let out the last customers.

More stolen cars would be reported, and probably two or three drunks overcome by the cold.

'Hello! Saint-Gervais?'

His Paris was a peculiar Paris, whose monuments were not the Eiffel Tower, the Opéra or the Louvre, but sombre administrative buildings with a police van standing under the blue lamp and policemen's bicycles propped up against the wall.

'The Chief's convinced,' Janvier was saying, 'that the man will do something tonight. It's the sort of night for those people. Holidays get them excited.'

No name was mentioned, because no name was known. One couldn't even say 'the man in the brown overcoat' or 'the man in the grey hat', because nobody had seen him. Some newspapers had called him 'Monsieur Dimanche', because three of the murders had been committed on a Sunday, but since then there had been five more, committed on weekdays, one per week on an average, only there was no regular pattern about that either.

'Is it on his account you've been kept up?'

For the same reason, an extra close watch was being kept throughout Paris, which meant that constables and detectives had to work overtime.

'You'll see,' said Sommer, 'when we lay hands on him, he'll turn out to be a lunatic.'

'A lunatic, but a killer,' sighed Janvier, as he drank his coffee. 'Say, one of your lights has gone on.'

'Hello! Bercy? Your van's gone out? What's that? Half a minute. Drowned?'

They could see Lecoeur hesitating into which column he should put his cross. There was one for suicide by hanging, another for people who, for lack of a weapon, threw themselves out of windows. There were columns for drownings, for shootings, for . . .

'Listen, you fellows! Do you know what a chap's just done on the Pont d'Austerlitz? Who was talking about lunatics just now? This man tied a stone to his ankles and a rope round his neck, climbed on to the parapet and shot himself through the head.'

Come to think of it, there was a column for that too: mentally disturbed.

It was the time now when people who had not been celebrating last night were going to early Mass, with damp noses, hands thrust deep into pockets, walking bent double against the cold wind that drove a sort of powdery rime along the pavements. It was the time, too, when children were beginning to wake up, switch on the light and rush, barefooted and nightgowned, towards the wonderful tree.

'If our chap were really a crackpot, according to the pathologist, he would always kill in the same way, whether with a knife or a revolver or whatever.'

'What weapon did he use last time?'

'A hammer.'

'And the time before?'

'A dagger.'

'What proof is there that it's always the same man?'

'In the first place, the fact that the eight crimes were committed almost immediately one after another. It would be surprising if eight new murderers suddenly went to work in Paris.'

Inspector Janvier had obviously heard the matter discussed at length at Police Headquarters.

'Moreover there's a sort of family resemblance about these murders. Each time the victim has been somebody living alone, whether old or young, somebody without friends or relations.'

Sommer looked at Lecoeur, whom he could not forgive for being a bachelor and above all for having no children. He himself had five and his wife was expecting a sixth.

'Like you, Lecoeur! Take care!'

'Another clue is the areas in which he operates. Not one of the murders has been committed in wealthy or even middle-class districts.'

'And yet he steals.'

'He steals, but never much at a time. Small sums. Hoards hidden in mattresses or old clothes. He doesn't go in for housebreaking, he doesn't seem to be specially well equipped for burglary, and yet he leaves no trace.'

A small light flashed on. A stolen car, at the door of a restaurant in the Place des Ternes, not far from the Etoile.

'What must particularly infuriate people who can't find their car is having to go home in the métro.'

Another hour, an hour and a half, and they would be relieved, all except Lecoeur; he had promised to replace a colleague who was spending Christmas with his family near Rouen.

This often happened. It had become so usual that people no longer hesitated to ask him.

'Say, Lecoeur, couldn't you take my place tomorrow?'

In the beginning they used to find some sentimental pretext, a sick mother, a funeral, a child's first communion. They used to bring him a cake, something from a delicatessen or a bottle of wine.

In fact, if he had been able to, Lecoeur would have spent twenty-four hours out of the twenty-four in that room, with an occasional rest on a camp bed, and his meals simmering on the electric ring. Oddly enough, although he was as well-groomed as the rest, more so than some, more than Sommer for instance, whose trousers seldom looked pressed, there was something drab about him which betrayed his bachelordom.

He wore glasses with heavy lenses which made his eyes look round and staring, and it came as a surprise, when he took off his spectacles to wipe them with the chamois leather he always carried in his pocket, to discover his evasive, almost timid glance.

'Hello! Javel?'

One of the lights of the fifteenth arrondissement, in the industrial zone near the Quai de Javel, had just flashed on.

'Your van's gone out?'

'We don't know what's happened yet. Someone's broken the glass of an emergency call-box in the Rue Leblanc.'

'Did anybody speak?'

'Not a word. The van's gone to investigate. I'll call you back.'

All along the streets of Paris there are hundreds of these red call-boxes, of which one has only to break the glass to be in telephonic communication with the nearest police station. Might a passer-by have broken this one by accident?

'Hello! Central? Our van's just back. There was nobody there. All quiet in the neighbourhood. We're going to patrol the district.'

Not to miss out altogether Lecoeur inscribed a little cross in the last column, devoted to the unclassified.

'Any more coffee?' he asked.

'I'll make some more.'

The same light came on again on the board. It was not ten minutes since the last signal.

'Javel? What's up?'

'Another emergency call.'

'And nobody spoke?'

'Not a word. A practical joker. Somebody who thinks it's fun to disturb us. This time we're going to try and get hold of him.'

'Where was it?'

'Pont Mirabeau.'

'I say, your friend's a fast walker!'

It was in fact quite a distance between the two red alarm call-boxes. But these calls were not yet being taken seriously. Three days earlier, somebody had broken the glass of a call-box and shouted defiantly: 'Death to the pigs!'

Janvier, with his feet up on one of the radiators, was starting to doze off, and when once again he heard Lecoeur's voice at the telephone he opened his eyes, noticed that one of the little lights was on and asked sleepily:

'Is it him again?'

'A glass broken in the Versailles area.'

'How idiotic!' he muttered, sinking back into comfortable drowsiness.

Daylight would come late, not before half-past seven or eight. From time to time the church bells sounded dimly, as though from another world. The poor police officers down below in the stand-by cars must be frozen.

'Talking of blood sausages . . .'

'What blood sausages?' muttered Janvier, who, drowsy and rosy-cheeked, looked like a small boy.

'The sausages that my mother . . .'

'Hello! You're not going to tell me someone's broken the glass of one of your emergency call-boxes? . . . What? . . . It's true . . . He's just broken two in the fifteenth . . . No, they've not managed to get hold of him . . . I say, he can run, that chap . . . He crossed the Seine by the Pont Mirabeau . . . He seems to be making for the city centre . . . Yes, try . . .'

That made another little cross, and by half-past seven, half an hour before relief time, there were five of them in the same column.

Maniac or not, the fellow was going at a good pace. It's true that it was hardly the temperature for lounging about. At one point he had seemed to be keeping to the banks of the Seine. He did not follow a straight line; he had made a detour through the wealthy streets of Auteuil and broken a glass in the Rue Fontaine.

'He's only five minutes away from the Bois de Boulogne,' Lecoeur announced. 'If that's where he's going we shall lose track of him.'

But the unknown person had made a virtual about turn and come back towards the river, breaking a glass in the Rue Berton, close by the Quai de Passy.

The first calls had come from the poor, working-class districts of Grenelle. The stranger had only had to cross the Seine to be in a different setting, wandering through spacious streets that were certainly deserted at this time of day. Everything must be shut; his footsteps would echo on the hard, frozen pavement.

A sixth call: he had skirted the Trocadéro and was now in the Rue de Longchamp.

'He must think he's Hop o' my Thumb,' commented Mambret. 'Failing breadcrumbs and white pebbles, he marks his trail with broken glass.'

Other messages came through, at rapid intervals: more stolen cars, a shot fired in the Rue de Flandre region, where the injured man denied all knowledge of his assailant, although he'd been seen drinking all night with a companion.

'Well, well! It's Javel again! Hello, Javel! I assume it's your glass-breaker again; he's not had time to get back to his starting-point. What? Yes indeed, he's been carrying on. He must be somewhere near the Champs-Elysées by now. What's that? . . . Wait a minute . . . Tell us . . . What street? Michat? . . . *chat* like cat, yes . . . Between the Rue Lecourbe and the Boulevard Félix-Faure . . . Yes . . . There's a railway bridge near . . . Yes . . . I'm with you, No. 17 . . . Who called? . . . The concierge? . . . She was up at this hour? . . . Shut up, you lot!

'No, I didn't mean you. I was talking to Sommer, who's boring us stiff with his blood sausage . . .

'So then the concierge . . . I can picture it . . . A big shabby block . . . seven floors . . . Okay . . .'

That district was full of buildings that were not old, but so badly built that they seemed decrepit as soon as they were lived in. They stood in the midst of waste ground, with their bare gloomy walls, their gable-ends bedizened with advertisements, towering above the suburban houses and bungalows.

'You say she heard someone running down the stairs and then slamming the door? . . . It had been open? . . . The concierge didn't know why? . . . On which floor? . . . The mezzanine, overlooking the courtyard . . . Go on . . . I see the van of the eighth arrondissement has just gone out and I bet it's my pane-smasher . . . An old woman . . . What did you say? . . . Old Madame Fayet? . . . She used to go out charring . . . Dead? . . . A blunt instrument . . . Is the doctor there? . . . You're quite sure she's dead? . . . Have her savings been pinched? . . . I ask that because I presume she had savings . . . Yes . . . Call me back . . . Otherwise I'll ring you . . .'

He turned towards the sleeping detective.

'Janvier! Hey, Janvier! I think this is something for you.'

'Who? What is it?'

'The killer.'

'Where?'

'At Javel. I've written the name on this bit of paper. This time he's attacked an old charlady, Madame Fayet.'

Janvier was putting on his overcoat and hunting for his hat; he swallowed the remaining drop of coffee in his cup.

'Who's in charge of the fifteenth?'

'Gonesse.'

'Let them know at Headquarters that I'm down there.'

A moment later Lecoeur was able to inscribe another little cross, the seventh, in the last column in his notebook. Someone had broken the glass of an emergency call-box in the Avenue d'Iéna, a hundred and fifty metres from the Arc de Triomphe.

'Among the fragments of glass they've found a blood-stained handkerchief. It's a child's handkerchief.'

'No initials?'

'No, it's a blue and white checked handkerchief, rather grubby. Whoever it was must have wrapped it round his fist when he broke the pane.'

Steps sounded in the stairway. It was their relief, the day shift. The men had shaved, and their cheeks had a raw pink look that came from washing in cold water and facing the icy wind.

'Had a good party, you chaps?'

Sommer was closing the little tin box in which he had brought his meal. Lecoeur alone did not bestir himself, since he was going to stay behind with the new team.

Godin, a big stout fellow, was pulling on the denim overall that he wore for working; as soon as he arrived he put some water on to boil for a hot toddy. His invariable cold dragged on all winter, and he dosed it, or coddled it, with copious toddies.

'Hello! Yes . . . No, I'm not leaving . . . I'm replacing Potier who's gone to visit his family . . . So what . . . Yes, I'm personally interested . . . Janvier has gone, but I'll pass on the message to Headquarters . . . A cripple? . . . What sort of cripple?'

It always takes patience to begin with, to get the hang of things, because people talk to you about the case they're dealing with as if the whole world knew all about it.

'The bungalow at the back, yes . . . So not in the Rue Michat . . . Which street? . . . Rue Vasco de Gama? . . . Yes, I know it . . . The little house with a garden and a railing . . . I didn't know he was a cripple . . . Right . . . So he doesn't sleep much . . . A small boy climbing up the drain-pipe . . . How old? . . . He doesn't know? . . . True, of course it was dark . . . How does he know it was a small boy? . . . Listen, be kind enough to call me back . . . You're going off too? . . . Who's replacing you? . . . Big Jules? . . . The one who . . . Yes . . . Okay . . . Say hello to him from me and ask him to call me.'

'What's all that about?' asked one of the newcomers.

'An old woman who's got herself bumped off at Javel.'

'By whom?'

'A crippled fellow who lives in a house behind the block of flats says he saw a small boy climbing up the wall towards her window.'

'Could the boy have killed her?'

'At any rate it was a child's handkerchief that they picked up beside one of the alarm boxes.'

They were listening to him inattentively. The lights were still on, but bleak daylight was coming through the frost-patterned panes. Once again somebody went to scratch the crisp surface; an instinctive gesture, perhaps a childhood memory recalled, like Sommer's blood sausage?

The night shift had left. The others were getting organized, settling down for the day, leafing through reports.

A stolen car, Square La Bruyère.

Lecoeur looked at his seven little crosses with a preoccupied air, and got up with a sigh to stand in front of the huge mural map.

'Are you learning your map of Paris by heart?'

'I know it already. But there's one detail that's struck me. In about an hour and a half seven emergency call-boxes have had their glass broken. Now I've noticed that the person who's been playing this game not only didn't go straight ahead, or take a definite route from one place to the next, but he zigzagged about to a considerable extent.'

'Perhaps he doesn't know Paris well?'

'Or else he knows it too well. He didn't once go past a police station, whereas if he'd taken the shortest way he would have passed several of them. And which are the crossroads where one is likely to meet a policeman?'

He pointed them out.

'He didn't go past these either. He skirted them. The only risk he ran was when he crossed over the Pont Mirabeau, but it would have been just the same if he'd crossed the Seine anywhere else.'

'He's probably tight,' said Godin jokingly, as he sipped his hot rum after cooling it with his breath.

'What I'm wondering is why he's stopped breaking panes of glass?'

'The chap's probably gone home by now.'

'A fellow who turns up in the Javel district at six in the morning isn't likely to be living near the Etoile.'

'Are you interested?'

'I'm frightened.'

'You don't mean it?'

Such signs of uneasiness were in fact surprising in the case of Lecoeur, for whom the most dramatic nocturnal happenings of Paris were usually summed up by a few little crosses in a notebook.

'Hello! Javel? . . . Big Jules? . . . Lecoeur here, yes . . . Tell me . . . Behind the block of flats in the Rue Michat, there's the cripple's house . . . Yes . . . But beside it there's another block, a red brick building with a grocer's shop on the ground floor . . . Yes . . . Has anything happened in that house? . . . The concierge didn't say? . . . I don't know . . . No, I know nothing . . . Perhaps it would be as well to go and ask her, yes . . .'

He suddenly felt very warm, and he stubbed out a half-smoked cigarette.

'Hello! Les Ternes? You've had no emergency calls in your district? Nothing? Only drunks? Thanks. By the way, has the cyclist patrol gone out? . . . They're just going out? . . . Ask them to look out in case they happen to see a small boy . . . A boy who's looking tired and whose right hand is bleeding . . . No, it's not a missing person . . . I'll explain another time . . .'

His eyes never left the mural map, where for at least ten minutes no light appeared; and then it was to report a case of accidental gassing in the eighteenth arrondissement, right at the top of Montmartre.

The cold streets of Paris were empty save for the dark figures of people returning from early Mass, shivering with cold.

2

Among the sharpest impressions that André Lecoeur retained from his childhood was one of stillness. His world, then, had been a large kitchen on the outskirts of Orléans. He must have spent winters there as well as summers, but he remembered it chiefly as flooded with sunlight, its door wide open, with a barred gate which his father had put up one Sunday to prevent him from wandering alone into the garden, where hens were clucking and rabbits nibbling all day behind their netting.

At half-past eight his father used to go off on his bicycle to the gas works where he was employed, at the other end of the town. His mother did the housework, always following the same routine, going up into the bedrooms and laying the mattresses on the window sill.

And then almost at once the greengrocer's bell, as he pushed his barrow along the street, told that it was ten o'clock. At eleven, twice a week, the bearded doctor came to see his small brother, who was always ill and whose room he was not allowed to visit.

That was all. Nothing else ever happened. He barely had time to play and drink his glass of milk before his father was back for lunch.

Now his father had been round several districts collecting payments and had met lots of people, about whom he talked at table, while here time had scarcely moved. And the afternoon, maybe because he had to take a rest, passed even more quickly.

'No sooner have I got down to my housework than it's time to eat,' his mother used to sigh.

It was somewhat the same here, in the big room at the Central Office where even the air never stirred, where the men on duty seemed to grow numb, until they heard voices and telephone calls as though through a thin layer of sleep.

A few little things flashed on against the wall, a few little crosses were put down – a bus had run into a car in the Rue de Clignancourt – and then there came a call from the Javel police station.

It was not big Jules this time. It was Inspector Gonesse, the one who had gone to visit the spot. They had had time to contact him and tell him about the house in the Rue Vasco de Gama. He had been there, and had just got back, highly excited.

'Is that you, Lecoeur?'

There was a special note of annoyance or suspicion in his voice.

'Say, how did you come to think of that house? Did you know old Madame Fayet?'

'I never saw her, but I know who she is.'

What was happening this Christmas morning was something André Lecoeur had been anticipating for ten years at least. More precisely, when he let his eyes wander over the map of Paris where the electric lights flashed on, he sometimes said to himself:

'One of these days, inevitably, it'll be somebody I know.'

Occasionally something had happened in his own district, not far from his own street, but never actually in it, moving nearer or further away like a thunderstorm without ever striking the exact spot where he lived.

Now it had happened.

'Have you questioned the concierge?' he asked. 'Was she up?'

He could imagine the ambiguous expression of Inspector Gonesse at the other end of the line, and he went on:

'Is the boy at home?'

And Gonesse growled: 'You know him too?'

'He's my nephew. Didn't they tell you his name is Lecoeur, François Lecoeur?'

'They told me.'

'Well then?'

'He's not at home.'

'And his father?'

'He came back soon after seven this morning.'

'As usual, I know. He's a night worker too.'

'The concierge heard him go up to his flat, third floor at the back.'

'I know it.'

'He came down again almost immediately and knocked at the door of the concierge's lodge. He looked very upset, quite wild, she said.'

'Has the boy disappeared?'

'Yes. His father asked if anyone had seen him go out, and if so, when. The concierge didn't know. Then he asked if a telegram had been delivered during the evening, or early this morning.'

'Had there been a telegram?'

'No. Do you understand anything about it? Don't you think, since you're a relative and in the picture, you'd better come over here?'

'It wouldn't be any use. Where's Janvier?'

'In Mère Fayet's room. The fingerprints people have just come and have set to work. The first thing they found was a child's prints on the handle of the door. Why don't you come along?'

Lecoeur replied half-heartedly:

'There's nobody to take my place here.'

It was true: at a pinch, by telephoning here and there, he might have found a colleague prepared to spend an hour or two at the Central Office. The truth was that he had no desire to be on the spot, that it would have served no useful purpose.

'Listen, Gonesse, I've got to find that boy, do you understand? Half an hour ago he must have been wandering about near the Etoile. Tell Janvier I'm stopping here, and that Mère Fayet probably had a good sum of money hidden in her place.'

Somewhat hectically, he transferred his plug to another hole and rang up the various police stations of the eighth arrondissement.

'Look for a small boy, ten or eleven years old, rather poorly dressed, and keep a special watch on emergency call-boxes.'

His two colleagues stared at him with some curiosity.

'Do you think it's the kid who did the job?'

He did not bother to reply. He was calling the telphone exchange overhead.

'Justin! Why, so it's you on duty? Will you ask the radio cars to look out for a ten-year-old boy wandering somewhere in the Etoile region? No, I don't know where he's making for. He seems to be avoiding the streets where there's a police station and the main crossroads where he might come across a traffic cop.'

He knew his brother's flat in the Rue Vasco de Gama, a couple of dark rooms and a minute kitchen, where the boy spent all his nights alone while his father was out at work. The windows looked on to the back of the Rue Michat, where there were lines of washing hanging out, pots of geraniums, and behind the windows, many of them curtainless, there lived a motley assortment of human beings.

Incidentally, there too the panes must be frosted over. This detail struck him. He put it away in a corner of his memory, for he felt it might be of some importance.

'Do you think it's a child who's been smashing the panes of the call-boxes?'

'A child's handkerchief has been picked up,' he said briefly.

And he stayed there in suspense, wondering into which hole he should push his plug.

Outside, people seemed to be doing things at a breathless speed. No sooner had Lecoeur answered a call than the doctor was on the spot, then the Deputy Public Prosecutor and an examining magistrate who must have been torn from his slumbers.

What was the point of going to the spot, since from where he sat he could see the streets and houses as clearly as the men who were there, with the railway bridge cutting across the landscape in a great black line?

Only the poor lived in that district, young people who hoped to get out of it some day, others less young who were beginning to lose heart, and those, even less young, almost old or really old, who were trying to come to terms with their lot.

He called Javel once again.

'Is Inspector Gonesse still there?'

'He's writing up his report. Shall I get him?'

'Yes, please . . . Hello, Gonesse? Lecoeur here . . . I'm sorry to bother you . . . Did you go up into my brother's flat? . . . Good! Was the child's bed unmade? That reassures me a little . . . Wait a minute . . . Were there any parcels? . . . That's right . . . What? A chicken, a blood sausage, a cream cake and . . . I don't understand the rest . . . A radio set? . . . It hadn't been unwrapped? . . Obviously! . . . Is Janvier with you? . . . He's already rung up Headquarters? . . . Thank you . . .'

He was quite surprised to see that it was already half-past nine. There was no longer any point in watching the Etoile district on the map of Paris. If the boy had gone on walking at the same pace, he'd have had time to reach one of the city suburbs by now.

'Hello! Police Judiciaire? Is Superintendent Saillard in his office?'

He, too, must have been dragged out of his warm home by Janvier's call. How many people were having their Christmas spoilt by this business?

'Excuse me for calling you, Superintendent. It's about the Lecoeur boy.'

'Do you know anything? Is he a relative of yours?'

'He's my brother's son. He's probably responsible for smashing the glass of seven emergency call-boxes. I don't know if they've had time to inform you that after the Etoile we've lost track of him. I'd like to ask your permission to send out a general message.'

'Couldn't you come and see me?'

'I've nobody available to replace me here.'

'Send out the message. I'll come round.'

Lecoeur remained calm, but his hand shook a little as he manipulated the plug.

'Is that you, Justin? A general message. Give the boy's description. I don't know how he's dressed, but he's probably wearing his khaki jacket cut down from an American wind-cheater. He's tall for his age, and thinnish. No, no cap, he's always bare-headed, with hair hanging over his forehead. Perhaps you'd better give his father's description too. That's rather harder for me. You know me, of course? Well, he's like me, only paler. He looks timid and rather sickly, the sort of man who dares not walk in the middle of the pavement but slinks along beside the walls of houses. He walks a bit awkwardly, because he was wounded in the foot during the last war. No, I haven't the least idea where they are going. I don't believe they are together. What's more than likely is that the kid's in danger. Why? That would take too long to explain. Send out your message. Let me know here if there's anything new.'

By the time that phone call was over Superintendent Saillard had appeared, having had time to leave the Quai des Orfèvres and walk across the street and through the empty buildings of the Préfecture of Police. He was an imposing figure in a huge overcoat. To greet the company he merely touched the rim of his hat, then he picked up a chair as if it were a straw and sat down astride it.

'The kid?' he asked at last, staring at Lecoeur.

'I wonder why he's stopped calling us.'

'Calling us?'

'Why should he break the glass of emergency call-boxes if not to draw our attention to himself?'

'And why, having taken the trouble to break them, doesn't he speak into the telephone?'

'Suppose he's being followed? Or that he's following somebody?'

'I thought of that. Tell me, Lecoeur, isn't your brother in low water financially?'

'Yes, he's a poor man.'

'Only a poor man?'

'He lost his job three months ago.'

'What job?'

'He was a linotype operator at La Presse in the Rue du Croissant, where he worked nights. He always worked nights. It seems to run in the family.'

'Why did he lose his job?'

'He probably quarrelled with somebody.'

'Was that a habit of his?'

A call interrupted them. It came from the eighteenth arrondissement, where a small boy had just been picked up in the street, at the corner of the Rue Lepic. He was selling sprigs of holly. He was Polish and could not speak a word of French.

'You were asking me if quarrelling was a habit of his? I don't know quite how to answer that. My brother had been a sick person for most of his life. When we were young he lived almost entirely in his bedroom, all alone, reading. He's read tons of books. But he never had any regular schooling.'

'Is he married?'

'His wife died after two years of marriage, leaving him alone with a ten-month-old baby.'

'He brought up the child himself?'

'Yes. I can still see him bathing it, changing its nappies, preparing its bottles.'

'That doesn't explain why he was quarrelsome.'

Of course, words hadn't the same meaning in the Superintendent's big head as they had in Lecoeur's heart.

'Was he embittered?'

'Not particularly. He was used to it.'

'Used to what?'

'To not living like other people. Maybe Olivier (that's my brother's name) isn't very intelligent. Perhaps he knows too much about some subjects, owing to his reading, and not enough about others.'

'Do you think he'd have been capable of killing the old Fayet woman?'

The Superintendent was puffing at his pipe. Upstairs the telegraphist could be heard walking about, and the other two policemen in the room were pretending not to listen.

'She was his mother-in-law,' Lecoeur said with a sigh. 'You were bound to find out sooner or later.'

'He didn't get on with her?'

'She hated him.'

'Why?'

'Because she held him responsible for what happened to her daughter. There was some business about an operation that wasn't done in time. It was not my brother's fault but the hospital's; they refused to take her in because her papers were not in order. None the less the old woman has always held it against my brother.'

'Did they ever see one another?'

'They must have met in the street sometimes, since they lived in the same district.'

'Did the boy know?'

'That Mère Fayet was his grandmother? I don't think so.'

'Hadn't his father told him?'

Lecoeur's eyes remained fixed on the map with its little lights, but this was the slack time of day; they seldom came on, and almost always, now, for traffic accidents. Somebody's pocket had been picked in the métro, somebody's luggage had been stolen at the Gare de l'Est.

No news of the boy. And yet the streets of Paris were half empty. In the more densely populated districts a few children were trying out their new toys on the pavements, but most houses seemed shut up and most windows were clouded with steam from the warmth of the rooms. Shops were closed, and small bars deserted save for a few regular customers. Only the pealing bells rang out over the roof tops, while families in their Sunday best made their way to churches from which the boom of great organs flowed out in waves.

'Will you excuse me a moment, Superintendent? I'm still thinking about the boy. It's obviously harder for him now to smash panes of glass without attracting attention. But perhaps we could have a look in the churches? In a bar or a café he could not pass unnoticed. In a church, on the other hand . . .'

He rang up Justin again.

'The churches, old man! Get them to watch the churches. And the stations. I hadn't thought of the stations either.'

He took off his glasses and revealed reddened eyelids, possibly from lack of sleep.

'Hello! Yes, Central Office here. What? Yes, the Superintendent's here.'

He handed the receiver to Saillard.

'It's Janvier wanting to speak to you.'

The north wind was still blowing outside and the light was harsh and bleak, although behind the massed clouds a faint yellowness gave a promise of sunlight.

As the Superintendent hung up again, he commented gruffly:

'Dr Paul says the crime must have been committed between five and six o'clock this morning. The old woman was not killed immediately. She must have been lying down when she heard a noise; she got up to confront her attacker, and probably hit him with a shoe.'

'Was the weapon found?'

'No. It looks as if it was a piece of lead piping or a rounded instrument, such as a hammer.'

'Was her money taken?'

'Only her purse, containing notes of small amounts and her identity card. Tell me, Lecoeur, did you know that woman lent money at high rates of interest?'

'Yes, I knew.'

'Didn't you tell me just now that your brother lost his job about three months ago?'

'That's correct.'

'The concierge didn't know.'

'Nor did his son. It was on his son's account that he said nothing about it.'

The Superintendent sat uneasily crossing and uncrossing his legs, and glanced at the other two men, who could not help hearing. At last he stared at Lecoeur with a baffled air.

'Do you realize, old man, what . . .'

'Yes, I realize.'

'Have you thought of that?'

'No.'

'Because he's your brother?'

'No.'

'How long has the killer been at it? Nine weeks, isn't that so?'

Lecoeur deliberately consulted his little notebook and looked for a certain cross in a certain column.

'Nine and a half weeks. The first crime took place in the Epinettes district at the other end of Paris.'

'You've just told me that your brother did not admit to his son that he was out of a job. He therefore went on leaving home and coming back at the usual time. Why?'

'So as not to lose face.'

'What do you mean?'

'It's hard to explain. He's not an ordinary sort of father. He brought up the child entirely on his own. They live together, they're a sort of little household, don't you see? During the day my brother prepares the meals and does the housework. He puts his son to bed before going out, wakes him up when he gets back . . .'

'That doesn't explain . . .'

'Do you think such a man would consent to appear in his son's eyes as a poor sort of chap who finds every door shut against him because he's incapable of adapting himself?'

'And what's he been doing at night over the past few months?'

'For a couple of weeks he had a job as night watchman in a factory at Billancourt. It was only temporary. Most often he washed cars in garages. When he couldn't find any other work he carried vegetables in Les Halles. When he had one of his attacks . . .'

'Attacks of what?'

'Asthma . . . He got them from time to time . . . He'd go and lie down in a railway station waiting-room. Once he came to spend the night here, gossiping with me . . .'

'Suppose the boy had looked out early this morning and seen his father at old Madame Fayet's!'

'There was frost on the window panes.'

'Not if the window had been left ajar. Many people sleep with open windows, even in winter.'

'That's not the case with my brother. He feels the cold, and they are too poor to waste heat.'

'The child might have scratched the frost with his finger-nails. When I was little I used to . . .'

'So did I. We'd have to find out whether the old woman's window was found open.'

'The window was open and the light was on.'

'I wonder where François can be.'

'The kid?'

It was surprising and somewhat embarrassing to find him thinking solely of the child. It was even more embarrassing to hear him calmly saying such devastating things about his brother.

'When he came back this morning his arms were full of parcels; have you thought about that?'

'It's Christmas.'

'He'd have needed money to buy a chicken, cakes, a radio set. Has he borrowed any from you lately?'

'Not for the past month. I wish he had, for I'd have told him not to buy a radio for François. I've got one here in the cloakroom which I was going to take him when I went off duty.'

'Would Mère Fayet have been willing to lend her son-in-law money?'

'It's not likely. She's a queer sort of woman. She must have enough savings to live on and she still goes out charring from morning till night. She often lends money at a high rate of interest to the people she works for. The whole district knows about it. People go to her when they're hard up at the end of the month.'

The Superintendent rose, still feeling ill at ease.

'I'm going round there,' he said.

'To the old woman's?'

'To the old woman's and to the Rue Vasco de Gama. If anything fresh turns up, give me a ring.'

'There's no telephone in either of the buildings. I'll send a message to the police station.'

The Superintendent was on his way down and the door had closed behind him when the telephone bell rang. No light had flashed on. The call came from the Gare d'Austerlitz.

'Lecoeur? Inspector on special duty speaking. We've got your chap.'

'Which chap?'

'The one whose description we were given. His name's Lecoeur, like yours. Olivier Lecoeur. I've checked his identity card.'

'One moment.'

He ran to the door and rushed downstairs into the courtyard, catching Saillard just as the latter was getting into a small police car.

'Gare d'Austerlitz on the line. They've found my brother.'

The Superintendent, who was a stout man, sighed as he climbed up the stairs again. He took up the receiver.

'Hello, yes . . . Where was he? . . . What was he doing? . . . What does he say? . . . What? . . . No, it's not worth your questioning him now . . . You're sure he doesn't know? . . . Keep up your watch at the station . . . That may very well be . . . As for him, send him here right away . . .'

He hesitated, with an eye on Lecoeur.

'Yes, send somebody with him. It's safer.'

He took time to fill and light his pipe before explaining, as though he were addressing nobody in particular:

'When they picked him up he'd been prowling for over an hour about the waiting-rooms and platforms. He seems to be in a very excited state. He's talking about a message from his son; he was waiting for the boy there.'

'Has he been told of the old woman's death?'

'Yes. It seems to have terrified him. They're bringing him along.'

He added, hesitantly:

'I thought it was best to have him come here. Seeing you're his relative, I didn't want you to think . . .'

'I'm grateful to you.'

Lecoeur had been sitting on the same chair in the same office since 11 pm the previous evening, and he felt just as he used to as a child in his mother's kitchen. Nothing stirred around him. Little lights came on, he thrust plugs into holes, time flowed by smoothly without one's noticing it, and yet, outside, Paris had lived through another Christmas; thousands of people had attended midnight Mass, others had supped noisily in restaurants, drunks had spent the night in the police station and were waking up now in the presence of an inspector; later, children had rushed towards the bright lights on the tree.

What had his brother Olivier been doing all this while? An old woman had died, and before dawn a small boy had walked the empty streets of Paris to the point of exhaustion, and thrust his fist, wrapped in a handkerchief, through the glass panes of a number of emergency call-boxes.

What had Olivier been waiting for, with such tense excitement, in the overheated waiting-rooms and on the draughty platforms of the Gare d'Austerlitz?

Less than ten minutes elapsed, just time enough for Godin, whose nose was really running by now, to brew himself another toddy.

'Would you like one, Superintendent?'

'No, thanks.'

Saillard whispered anxiously to Lecoeur: 'Would you rather we went into the other room to question him?'

But Lecoeur had no intention of leaving his little lights and his switchboard that connected him with every corner of Paris. Footsteps came up the stairs. Olivier was flanked by two policemen, but he had not been handcuffed.

He looked like a bad, faded photograph of André. His eyes turned to his brother immediately.

'François?'

'We don't know yet. They're looking for him.'

'Where?'

And Lecoeur could only point to the map and his switchboard with its innumerable holes.

'Everywhere.'

The two policemen had been dismissed, and the Superintendent said:

'Sit down. You've heard that the old Fayet woman is dead, haven't you?'

Olivier wore no spectacles, but he had the same pale, evasive eyes that his brother revealed when he took off his glasses, so that he always looked as if he had been weeping. He glanced briefly at the Superintendent, taking little notice of him.

'He left me a note,' he said, hunting in the pockets of his old raincoat. 'Can *you* understand it?'

He finally held out a scrap of paper torn from a schoolboy's exercise book. The writing was not very steady. The lad was probably not one of the best pupils in his class. He had used a purple pencil, moistening the tip, which had doubtless left a stain on his lip.

> Uncle Gédéon arriving this morning Gare d'Austerlitz. Come quick meet us there. Love. Bib.

Without saying a word, André Lecoeur handed the paper to the Superintendent, who turned it round several times in his thick fingers.

'Why Bib?'

'It was my pet name for him. Not in front of people, because it would have embarrassed him. It goes back to the time when I used to feed him as a baby.'

He spoke in a neutral, unemphatic voice, probably seeing nothing around him but a sort of fog in which figures were moving.

'Who is Uncle Gédéon?'

'He doesn't exist.'

Did he even realize that he was speaking to the chief of the Homicide Squad, in charge of a criminal investigation?

His brother explained:

'Or rather he no longer exists. A brother of our mother's, whose name was Gédéon, left for America when he was very young.'

Olivier was looking at him as though to say: 'What's the good of telling them all that?'

'It had become a family joke; we used to say: "Some day we shall inherit from Uncle Gédéon." '

'Was he a rich man?'

'We didn't know. He never sent us news of himself. Just a New Year's card signed Gédéon.'

'Is he dead?'

'He died when Bib was four years old.'

'Do you think there's any point, André?'

'We're trying to find out. Leave it to me. My brother carried on the family tradition by talking to his son about Uncle Gédéon. He'd become a sort of legendary figure. Every night before going to sleep the boy demanded a story about Uncle Gédéon, and we made up all sorts of adventures about him. Of course he was fabulously wealthy, and when he came back . . .'

'I think I understand. And he died?'

'In hospital. At Cleveland, where he washed dishes in a restaurant. We never told the boy. We kept up the story.'

'Did he believe it?'

The father put in a timid word, almost raising his hand like a schoolboy.

'My brother says he didn't, that he had guessed, that it was just a game for him. But I'm practically sure, myself, that he still believed it. When his friends told him Father Christmas didn't exist he went on contradicting them for two whole years.'

When he spoke of his son he came to life again; he was transformed.

'I can't understand why he wrote me that note. I asked the concierge if there had been a telegram. For one moment I thought André had played a trick on us. Why did François leave home at six in the morning, telling me to meet him at the Gare d'Austerlitz? I rushed there like a madman. I looked everywhere, I kept expecting him to appear. Look here, André, are you sure that . . .'

He was looking at the map on the wall and telephone switchboard. He knew that all the disasters, all the accidents in Paris were inevitably recorded here in the end.

'He hasn't been found,' said Lecoeur. 'They're still looking. At eight o'clock or thereabouts he was in the Etoile district.'

'How do you know? Did anyone see him?'

'It's hard to explain. All along the way from your house to the Arc de Triomphe someone has broken the panes of glass in the emergency call-boxes. A child's blue and white checked handkerchief was picked up beside the last of them.'

'He had handkerchiefs with blue checks.'

'Since eight o'clock there has been nothing.'

'But then I must go back to the station at once. That's where he's sure to go, since he told me to meet him there.'

Surprised at the silence that seemed suddenly to gather oppressively around him, he stared at each of them in turn, puzzled and then anxious.

'What . . .'

His brother lowered his head, while the Superintendent, after a slight cough, finally asked in a reluctant tone:

'Did you pay a visit to your mother-in-law last night?'

Perhaps, as his brother had implied, his intelligence was not quite normal. Words took a long time to reach his brain. And one could practically follow the slow progress of his thought by watching his face.

He stopped looking at the Superintendent and turned to his brother, suddenly flushed, his eyes glittering, and cried:

'André! You dared to . . .'

Without any transition his excitement lapsed, he leaned forward on his chair, buried his head in his hands and started weeping with great hoarse sobs.

3

Superintendent Saillard looked at André uneasily, surprised to find him so calm, and possibly a little shocked at what he must have taken for indifference. Perhaps Saillard had no brother. Lecoeur had been used to his since early childhood. He had seen Olivier subject to such attacks when he was quite small, and in the present circumstances he was almost relieved, for things might have been worse; instead of tears, of exhausted resignation, of this sort of numbness, Olivier might have embarrassed them by bursting forth in declamatory indignation, giving them all a piece of his mind.

Wasn't that how he had lost most of his jobs? For weeks, for months at a time he would be meek and subservient, brooding over his humiliation, nursing his pain; then suddenly, when it was least expected, almost invariably for some trivial reason, for a casual word, a smile, an unimportant contradiction, he would flare up.

'What shall I do?' the Superintendent's glance questioned.

And André Lecoeur's eyes replied:

'Wait.'

It did not take long. The sobs, like a child's, grew less violent, almost dying away, then broke out again for a moment with increased intensity. Then Olivier sniffed, ventured to glance around, but seemed to sulk a little longer, hiding his face.

At last he drew himself up in bitter resignation, and said with a certain pride:

'Ask your questions, I'll answer them.'

'At what time during the night did you go to Mère Fayet's? One minute. Tell me first at what time you left home.'

'At eight o'clock as usual, after putting my boy to bed.'

'And did nothing unusual happen?'

'No. We had supper together. He helped me wash the dishes.'

'Did you talk about Christmas?'

'Yes. I'd hinted that there'd be a surprise for him when he woke up.'

'Was he expecting a radio set?'

'He'd been wanting one for a long time. He doesn't play in the street, he's got no friends, he spends all his spare time at home.'

'Did you never think that your son might perhaps know that you'd lost your job at La Presse? Did he never ring you up there?'

'Never. He's always asleep when I'm at work.'

'Could nobody have told him?'

'Nobody knows about it in the neighbourhood.'

'Is he observant?'

'He misses nothing of what goes on around us.'

'You put him to bed and you went off. Didn't you take a snack with you?'

The Superintendent had just thought of that on seeing Godin unwrap a ham sandwich. Then Olivier Lecoeur suddenly looked at his empty hands and muttered:

'My tin!'

'The tin in which you carried something to eat?'

'Yes. I had it last night, I'm sure. There's only one place where I could have left it . . .'

'At Mère Fayet's?'

'Yes.'

'One minute . . . Lecoeur, pass me the phone . . . Hello! Who am I speaking to? Is Janvier there? . . . Call him, will you? . . . Is that you, Janvier? . . . Have you searched the old woman's lodging? Did you notice a tin containing some food? . . . Nothing of the sort? . . . You're sure? . . . Yes, I'd rather you did . . . Call me back as soon as you've checked . . . It's important . . .'

And turning to Olivier, he asked:

'Was your son asleep when you left?'

'He was just going to sleep. We kissed each other goodnight. I began by walking in the neighbourhood. I went as far as the Seine and sat down on the parapet to wait.'

'To wait for what?'

'For the boy to be sound asleep. From our flat we can see Madame Fayet's windows.'

'You'd decided to call on her?'

'It was the only way. I couldn't even afford to take the métro.'

'What about your brother?'

The two Lecoeurs looked at one another.

'I've asked him for so much money lately that he can't have any to spare.'

'You rang at the door of the block of flats? What time was it?'

'A little after nine o'clock. The concierge saw me go in. I wasn't hiding, except from my son.'

'Had your mother-in-law not gone to bed?'

'No. She opened the door to me and said: "So here you are, you bastard!" '

'Did you know that she would let you have some money none the less?'

'I was practically certain of it.'

'Why was that?'

'I only had to promise her that she'd make a big profit. She could never resist that. I signed a paper saying I owed her double the sum.'

'To be paid back when?'

'In a fortnight.'

'And when it fell due, how would you have paid it?'

'I don't know. I'd have managed somehow. I wanted my son to have his Christmas treat.'

André Lecoeur longed to interrupt his brother to tell the astonished Superintendent:

'He's always been like that!'

'Did you find it easy to get what you wanted?'

'No. We argued for a long time.'

'About how long?'

'Half an hour. She reminded me that I was a good-for-nothing, that I'd brought her daughter nothing but misery and that it was my fault she had died. I didn't say anything. I wanted the money.'

'Did you threaten her?'

He flushed and hung his head, mumbling: 'I told her that if I didn't get the money I would kill myself.'

'Would you have done so?'

'I don't think so. I don't know. I was very tired, very disheartened.'

'And once you'd got the money?'

'I went on foot as far as Beaugrenelle station, where I took the métro. I got out at the Palais-Royal and went into the Grands Magasins du Louvre. The place was very crowded. People were queuing up at the counters.'

'What time was it?'

'Maybe eleven o'clock. I was in no hurry. I knew the store would stay open all night. It was hot there. There was an electric train running.'

His brother looked at the Superintendent with a slight smile.

'Didn't you notice that you had mislaid the tin with your supper in it?'

'I was only thinking of Bib's Christmas.'

'In short, you were very much excited at having cash in your pocket?'

The Superintendent was beginning to understand, even though he had not known Olivier as a child. Whereas when his pockets were empty he was dim and depressed and would slink along timidly, crouching against the walls, when he had a little money on him he became self-confident and almost reckless.

'You've told me you signed a paper for your mother-in-law. What did she do with it?'

'She slipped it into an old wallet she always carried about with her, in a pocket she wore fastened to her belt, underneath her skirt.'

'You're familiar with that wallet?'

'Yes. Everybody is.'

The Superintendent turned to André Lecoeur.

'It hasn't been found.'

Then he said to Olivier: 'You bought the radio, then the chicken and the cake. Where?'

'In a shop I know in the Rue Montmartre, next to a shoe-shop.'

'What did you do the rest of the night? What time was it when you left the shop in the Rue Montmartre?'

'It was close on midnight. Crowds were leaving the theatres and cinemas and hurrying into the restaurants. There were some very lively gangs of people and a great many couples.'

His brother, at that time, had already been sitting here at his switchboard.

'I was on the Grands Boulevards, near the Crédit Lyonnais bank, carrying my parcels, when the bells began to ring. People were kissing one another in the street.'

Why did Saillard feel impelled to ask a preposterous, cruel question: 'Did anybody kiss you?'

'No.'

'Did you know where you were going?'

'Yes. At the corner of the Boulevard des Italiens there's a cinema that stays open all night.'

'Had you been there before?'

Somewhat embarrassed, and avoiding his brother's eye, he replied:

'Two or three times. It doesn't cost more than a cup of coffee in a bar, and you can stay there as long as you want to. It's warm there. Some people go there to sleep.'

'When did you decide to spend the rest of the night in the cinema?'

'As soon as I'd got the money.'

And the other Lecoeur, the calm, meticulous switchboard operator, longed to explain to the Superintendent:

'You see, these poor wretches aren't always as miserable as you think. Otherwise they wouldn't hold out. They have their own world, too, and in the corners of it they have a certain number of small joys.'

It was so typical of his brother that, having borrowed a few notes – and heaven knows how he'd ever repay them – he had forgotten his troubles and thought only of making his son happy next morning, and then, none the less, had given himself a little treat!

He had gone to the cinema all alone, while family parties were gathering round loaded tables, crowds were dancing in night-clubs and other people were finding spiritual exaltation in dark, candle-lit churches.

In short he'd had his own Christmas, a Christmas cut down to size.

'What time did you leave the cinema?'

'Shortly before six o'clock, to take the métro.'

'What film did you see?'

'*Burning Hearts*. And there was a documentary about the Eskimos.'

'Did you see the programme only once?'

'Twice, except for the news, which was just being shown again when I left.'

André Lecoeur knew that this would be checked, if only as a matter of routine. But this proved unnecessary. His brother fumbled in his pockets and pulled out a scrap of torn cardboard, his cinema ticket, and at the same time another bit of pink cardboard.

'Here you are! Here's my métro ticket too.'

It bore the time and date and the stamp of the Opéra station where it had been issued.

Olivier had told the truth. He could not have been in the old woman's room between five and half-past six that morning.

Now there was a flash of slightly scornful defiance in his eyes. He seemed to be saying to them all, including his brother:

'Because I'm a poor specimen, you suspected me. It's the rule. I don't bear you ill-will for it.'

And curiously enough a sudden chill seemed to fall over that great room where one of the clerks was having a telephone discussion with a suburban inspector about a stolen car.

It was probably due to the fact that, now Lecoeur had been cleared, everyone's thoughts were once more concentrated on the child. This was so true that all eyes now turned instinctively to the map of Paris; for quite a while now, the lights had stopped coming on.

It was the slack period. On any other day there would have been, from time to time, some traffic accident, some old lady run over at a busy crossroads in Montmartre or some other densely crowded area.

Today the streets remained almost empty, just as they are in August when most Parisians are in the country or at the seaside.

It was half-past eleven. For three hours now they had had no news of the little boy, had received no signal from him.

'Hello! Yes . . . Go on, Janvier . . . You say there's no sign of a tin in the flat? . . . Okay . . . You searched the dead woman's clothes yourself? . . . Gonesse had already done so? . . . You're sure she wasn't wearing an old wallet under her skirt? You'd heard about that? . . . The concierge saw somebody go up last night about half-past nine? . . . I know who that was . . . And then? There were comings and goings in the house all night . . . Of course . . . Will you go over to the other house, the one behind? . . . I'd like to know if anyone heard a noise during the night, particularly on the third floor . . . Call me back, that's right . . .'

He turned towards the father, who was sitting motionless on his chair, as meek again as though he were in a doctor's waiting-room.

'Do you see why I asked that question? Does your son often wake up during the night?'

'He sometimes calls out in his sleep.'

'Does he get up and walk about?'

'No. He sits up in bed and screams. It's always the same thing. He thinks the house is on fire. His eyes are open but he sees nothing. Then, gradually, he looks at you with a normal expression and he lies down again with a deep sigh. Next day he remembers nothing about it.'

'Is he always asleep when you get back in the morning?'

'Not always. But even if he's not asleep he pretends to be, so that I should go and wake him up by kissing him and tweaking his nose. It's a gesture of affection, don't you see?'

'The neighbours are likely to have been noisier than usual last night. Who lives on the same floor as you?'

'A Czech who works at the car factory.'

'Is he married?'

'I don't know. There are so many people in our block of flats and the tenants change so frequently that one scarcely knows them. On Saturdays the Czech usually gets together half a dozen of his friends to drink and sing their own popular songs.'

'Janvier is going to let us know if that was the case last night. If so, it may have woken up your son. In any case he was probably over-excited at the thought of the surprise you'd promised him. If he got up he may have automatically gone to the window and seen you with old Madame Fayet. Did he have any suspicion that she was your mother-in-law?'

'No. He didn't like her. He called her the bed-bug. He often met her in the street and he used to say she smelt like a squashed bed-bug.'

The child must have known what he was talking about, for there was probably no lack of such creatures in the great tenement where they lived.

'Would he have been surprised to see you in her room?'

'Certainly.'

'Did he know that she was a money-lender?'

'Everybody knew that.'

The Superintendent turned to the other Lecoeur.

'Do you think there'd be anyone at La Presse today?'

The former typographer replied for him:

'There's always someone there.'

'Ring them up then. Try to find out whether anyone has ever asked for Olivier Lecoeur.'

The latter, once again, averted his head. Before his brother had opened the telephone directory he gave them the number of the printing press.

While the call was going on, there was no alternative for them but to stare at one another and then to stare at the little lamps which obstinately refused to light up.

'It's very important, Mademoiselle. It may be a question of life or death . . . Yes, please take the trouble to put the question to anybody who's there at the moment . . . What did you say? I can't help that! It's Christmas for me too and yet I'm ringing you up . . .'

'Little bitch!' he muttered between his teeth.

And they waited again, while the clatter of the linotypes could be heard down the telephone.

'Hello! . . . What . . . three weeks ago? A child, yes . . .'

The father had turned very pale and was staring at his hands.

'He didn't ring up? He came himself? About what time? On a Thursday? And then? . . . He asked whether Olivier Lecoeur was working at the press . . . What? . . . What did they tell him? . . .'

His brother looked up and saw him flush and hang up the receiver with a furious gesture.

'Your son went there one Thursday afternoon . . . He must have suspected something . . . They told him you'd stopped working at La Presse some weeks before.'

What was the point of repeating the words he had just heard? What the boy had been told was: 'That fool was fired some time ago!'

It may not have been meant cruelly. They probably never imagined that the visitor might be his son.

'Are you beginning to understand, Olivier?'

Every evening the father went off, carrying his sandwiches and talking about his work-place in the Rue du Croissant, and the son knew that he was lying.

One might surely draw the conclusion that he knew the truth, too, about the mythical Uncle Gédéon.

He had played the game.

'And I'd promised him his radio . . .'

They scarcely dared speak to one another, because words might call up terrifying pictures.

Even those who had never been to the Rue Vasco de Gama could now visualize the shabby dwelling, the ten-year-old boy who spent long hours there alone, the strange household of father and son who told each other lies for fear of hurting one another.

One had to imagine things as they appeared to the child: his father leaving after a goodnight kiss, and Christmas everywhere around, neighbours drinking and singing at the tops of their voices.

'Tomorrow morning you shall have a surprise.'

It could only be the longed-for radio, and Bib knew how much that cost.

Did he know, that evening, that his father's wallet was empty?

The man went off as though he were going to his work, and that work did not exist.

Had the boy tried to go to sleep? Opposite his room, on the other side of the courtyard, rose a huge dark wall with lighted windows, behind which lived a motley crowd of people.

Had he leaned on the window-sill, in his night-shirt, to look out?

His father, who had no money, was going to buy him a radio.

The Superintendent gave a sigh as he knocked his pipe out against his heel and emptied it on to the floor.

'It's more than likely that he saw you in the old woman's room.'

'Yes.'

'I'll check up on one point presently. You live on the third floor and she lives on the mezzanine. It's probable that only part of the room is visible from your windows.'

'That's correct.'

'Could your son have seen you leave?'

'No! The door is at the back of the room.'

'Did you go up to the window?'

'I sat down on the window-sill.'

'One detail, which may be important. Was the window ajar?'

'Yes, it was. I remember it struck cold down my back. My mother-in-law always sleeps with her window open, winter and summer. She was a country woman. She lived with us for a while, when we were first married.'

The Superintendent turned to the switchboard operator.

'Did you think of that, Lecoeur?'

'The frost on the window? I've been thinking about it ever since this morning. If the window was partly open the difference between the temperature of the air outside and that of the room would not be great enough to produce frost.'

A call. The plug was thrust into one of the holes.

'Yes . . . What did you say? . . . A boy? . . .'

They stood watching him, tensely.

'Yes . . . Yes . . . What? . . . Yes, send all police cyclists to search the district . . . I'll deal with the station . . . How long ago was it? . . . Half an hour? . . . Couldn't he have informed us sooner?'

Without giving himself time to explain things to those around him, Lecoeur thrust his plug into another hole.

'Gare du Nord? . . . Who am I speaking to? . . . It's you, Lambert? . . . Listen, this is very urgent . . . Have the station thoroughly searched . . . Keep an eye on all the premises and on the railway lines . . . Ask the staff whether they've seen a boy of about ten years old wandering around the ticket offices or elsewhere . . . What? . . . Is there anybody with him? . . . That doesn't matter . . . There may well be . . . Quickly! . . . Keep me informed . . . Of course, get hold of him . . .'

'Somebody with him?' his brother repeated in bewilderment.

'Why not? Anything's possible. It may perhaps not be him, but if it is we've wasted half an hour . . . It's a grocer in the Rue de Maubeuge, close by the station, who has an open-air stall . . . He saw a kid take a couple of oranges from his display and run off . . . He didn't chase him . . . Some time later, however, as a policeman happened to pass he mentioned the fact.'

'Had your son any money in his pocket?' asked the Superintendent. 'No? None at all? Didn't he have a money-box?'

'He had one. But I'd taken the little it contained two days ago, on the pretext that I didn't want to change a big note.'

All these details seemed to have become so important now!

'Don't you think I'd better go to the Gare du Nord myself?'

'I think it would be pointless, and we may need you here.'

They felt imprisoned in this room, held captive by the great map with its lamps, the switchboard that connected them with every corner of Paris. Whatever happened, this was where they would get the first news of it. The Superintendent was so well aware of this that he did not return to his office, and had finally resigned himself to taking off his big overcoat, as though he now belonged to the Central Office.

'So he can't have taken the métro or a bus. Nor can he have gone into a café or a public call-box to telephone. He's had nothing to eat since six o'clock this morning.'

'But what's he doing?' exclaimed the father, his agitation reviving. 'And why did he send me to the Gare d'Austerlitz?'

'Probably to help you to escape,' Saillard said in a low voice.

'To escape, me?'

'Listen, my lad . . .' The Superintendent had forgotten that this was the brother of Inspector Lecoeur and spoke to him as though to one of his 'clients'.

'The kid knows that you've lost your job, that you're broke and yet you've promised him a splendid Christmas . . .'

'My mother used to stint herself for months to give us Christmas treats . . .'

'I'm not blaming you. I'm just stating a fact. He leans at the window and sees you visiting an old harridan who lends money at high interest. What does he conclude from that?'

'I understand.'

'He says to himself that you've gone to borrow from her. All right.

He may have been touched, or sorry, I don't know. He gets back into bed and goes to sleep.'

'D'you think so?'

'I'm practically certain. If he had discovered at half-past nine last night what he discovered at six o'clock this morning he'd not have stayed put quietly in his room.'

'I understand.'

'He goes back to sleep. Perhaps he's thinking more about his radio than about what you may have done to get the money for it. Didn't you yourself go to the cinema? He sleeps restlessly, as all children do on Christmas Eve. He wakes earlier than usual, while it's still dark, and the first thing he sees is that the windows are covered with frost-flowers. Don't forget that it's the first frost of the winter. He wants to look at it close, to touch it . . .'

The other Lecoeur, the man at the switchboard, the man who made little crosses in his notebook, gave a faint smile when he observed that the big Superintendent was not as remote from his childhood as one might have expected.

'He scratched it with his nails . . .'

'As I saw Biguet doing right here this morning,' broke in André Lecoeur.

'We shall have proof of that, if need be, through the fingerprints people, since the prints will show once the frost has thawed. What is the first thing that strikes the child? Whereas it's all dark in the neighbourhood, there's a light on in one single window; and it happens to be that of the room where he last saw his father. I shall get all these details checked. I'm willing to bet, however, that he caught sight of the body, at any rate of part of it. Even if he'd only seen the feet on the floor, this, combined with the fact that the light was on, would have been enough.'

'Did he believe? . . .' Olivier began, his eyes starting out of his head.

'He believed you had killed her, yes, as I was inclined to believe myself. Think, Lecoeur. The man who for a number of weeks now has been killing people in the outlying parts of the city is a night bird like yourself. It may be somebody who has suffered a grave shock, like yourself, since one doesn't become a killer overnight for no good reason. Does the child know what you've been doing every night since you lost your job?

'You told us just now that you sat down on the window-sill. Where did you put your sandwich tin?'

'On the ledge, I'm practically certain.'

'So he must have seen it . . . And he didn't know at what time you left your mother-in-law's . . . He didn't know if, after you'd gone, she was still alive . . . He must have imagined the light staying on all night . . . What would have struck you most, in his place?'

'The tin . . .'

'Exactly. The tin which would enable the police to identify you. Was your name on it?'

'I'd scratched it on with a pen-knife.'

'You see! Your son assumed that you'd be coming home at your usual time, that's to say between seven and eight. He did not know whether his venture would be successful. In any case he decided not to come home. He wanted to keep you out of danger.'

'Was that why he left me a note?'

'He remembered Uncle Gédéon, and wrote to tell you that his uncle was arriving at the Gare d'Austerlitz. He knew that you'd go, even though Uncle Gédéon didn't exist. The message couldn't possibly compromise you . . .'

'He's ten and a half!' the father protested.

'Do you think a lad of ten and a half doesn't know quite as much about such matters as yourself? Doesn't he read detective stories?'

'Yes . . .'

'If he's so keen on a radio, perhaps it's less for the sake of the music or broadcast plays than for the police thriller serials . . .'

'That's true.'

'Before anything else he had to get back the incriminating evidence, the tin. He knew the courtyard very well. He must have played there often.'

'He's spent days playing there with the concierge's daughter.'

'He knew, then, that he could use the drain-pipe. He may have climbed up it before.'

'And now?' asked Olivier with striking quietness. 'He retrieved the tin, okay. He left my mother-in-law's house without difficulty, for the front door can be opened from inside without summoning the concierge. You say it must have been a little after six in the morning.'

The Superintendent grunted. 'I follow,' he said. 'Even without hurrying, he could have reached the Gare d'Austerlitz in under two hours. He'd told you to meet him there, but he didn't go there.'

Oblivious of these arguments, the other Lecoeur was thrusting in his plugs, saying with a sigh: 'Still nothing, old man?'

And the answer came from the Gare du Nord: 'We've questioned about twenty people accompanying children, but none of them answer to the description we've been given.'

Any child, obviously, might have stolen oranges from a stall. But not every child would have smashed in the glass of seven emergency call-boxes in succession. Lecoeur kept reverting to his little crosses. He had never thought himself much cleverer than his brother, but he had patience and obstinacy in his favour.

'I'm sure,' he said, 'that we shall find the sandwich tin in the Seine, close to the Pont Mirabeau.'

Footsteps sounded on the stair. On ordinary days one would not have noticed them, but on a Christmas morning one listened involuntarily.

It was a police cyclist bringing the bloodstained handkerchief that had been picked up beside the seventh call-box. This was shown to the boy's father.

'Yes, that's Bib's.'

'So he's being followed,' the Superintendent declared. 'If he were not being followed, if he'd had time, he wouldn't confine himself to breaking glass. He would speak.'

'Excuse me,' said Olivier, the only one who had not understood. 'Followed by whom? And why should he call the police?'

They were all reluctant to enlighten him. His brother took on the job.

'Because, if when he went into the old woman's room he believed you were the murderer, when he left her house he no longer believed it. *He knew*.'

'He knew what?'

'He knew *who*! D'you understand now? He had discovered something, we don't know what, and that's what we've been hunting for for hours. Only he's not being given a chance to tell us.'

'You mean . . .'

'I mean that your son is on the murderer's heels, or else the murderer is on his. One of them's following the other, I don't know which, and won't let go. Tell me, Superintendent, has a reward been offered?'

'A big reward, since the third murder. It was doubled last week. All the papers have talked about it.'

'Then,' said André Lecoeur, 'it's not necessarily Bib who is being followed. It may be he who is following. Only in that case . . .'

It was twelve o'clock, and it was four hours since the child had given any sign of life, unless it was he who had stolen the oranges in the Rue de Maubeuge.

4

Perhaps, after all, his day had dawned? André Lecoeur had read somewhere or other that any human being, however dim and unfortunate he may be, has at least one glorious hour in his life during which he is able to fulfil himself.

He had never had a high opinion of himself or of his potentialities. When he was asked why he had chosen a sedentary and monotonous job instead of putting his name down, for instance, for the Homicide Squad, he would reply: 'I'm so lazy!'

And sometimes he would add: 'And perhaps I'm scared of getting hurt!'

That was untrue. But he knew he was slow-witted.

Everything he had learned at school had cost him a lot of effort. The police examinations, which are child's play to some people, had given him great trouble.

Was it because of this self-knowledge that he had never married? It might well be so. It seemed to him that whatever wife he chose, he would feel himself her inferior and let himself be dominated by her.

He was not thinking of all that today. He did not know that his hour, if there were such a thing, was at hand.

The morning's team had now been replaced by another lot, looking spruce and smart, who had had time to celebrate Christmas with their families and whose breath was redolent of cake and liqueurs.

Old Bedeau had taken up his position at the switchboard, but Lecoeur had not gone away; he had simply remarked:

'I'm staying a bit longer.'

Superintendent Saillard had gone for a quick lunch at the nearby Brasserie Dauphine, asking to be called if anything fresh turned up. Janvier had returned to the Quai des Orfèvres, where he was writing up his report.

Lecoeur did not feel like going to bed. He was not sleepy. In the past, he had once spent thirty-six hours at his post, during the riots in the Place de la Concorde, and on another occasion, during the general strike, the men from the Central Office had camped out in their room for four days and four nights.

His brother was more impatient.

'I want to go and find Bib,' he had declared.

'Where?'

'I don't know. Somewhere near the Gare du Nord.'

'And suppose it wasn't he who stole the oranges? Suppose he's in a quite different district? Suppose we get news of him in a few minutes or in a couple of hours?'

'I want to do something.'

They had made him sit on a chair, in one corner, since he refused to lie down. His eyelids were red with fatigue and anguish and he had begun to twist his fingers as he used to when, as a child, he'd been put in the corner.

André Lecoeur had tried to rest, by way of self-discipline. Adjoining the main room there was a sort of closet with a wash-basin, two camp beds and a coat-rack, where the men on night duty sometimes took a nap when things were quiet.

Lecoeur had closed his eyes. Then he happened to lay his hand on the notebook which he always kept in his pocket, and lying on his back, he began to turn its pages.

It contained crosses, nothing but columns of minute crosses which for years he had persisted in inscribing of his own free will, without knowing exactly what purpose they might serve some day. Some people keep a journal, others note down their most trivial expenses or their losses at bridge.

Those crosses in their narrow columns represented years of the city's nightly existence.

'Coffee, Lecoeur?'

'Yes, please.'

But since he felt too remote, in that closet from which he could not see his illuminated board, he pulled the camp bed into the office, and after that spent his time alternately consulting the crosses in his notebook and shutting his eyes. Sometimes, between half closed lids, he watched his brother hunched up on his chair, his shoulders bent, his head drooping, the only sign of his inner tension being the occasional convulsive clenching of his long pale fingers.

Hundreds of policemen now, in the suburbs as well as in the city, had been given the child's description. From time to time a police call brought a ray of hope; but the child in question turned out to be a little girl, or if a boy was either too young or too old.

Lecoeur had closed his eyes again and then suddenly he reopened them, as though he had just dozed off, looked at the time and glanced round in search of the Superintendent.

'Has Saillard not come back?'

'He's probably gone round by the Quai des Orfèvres.'

Olivier looked at his brother, surprised to see him striding up and down the great room; Lecoeur scarcely noticed that, outside, the sun had finally pierced through the white dome of clouds, and that Paris, on this Christmas afternoon, had a bright, almost springlike air.

He was watching out for a step in the stairway.

'You should go and buy a few sandwiches,' he said to his brother.

'What sort?'

'Ham, or whatever you like. Whatever you can find.'

Olivier left the office after a glance at the map on the wall, relieved in spite of his anxiety to be getting a breath of fresh air.

The men who had replaced the morning team knew scarcely anything about the affair, except that it concerned the killer and that somewhere in Paris a small boy was in danger. For those who had not spent the night here, it wore a different complexion; it was, as it were, decanted, reduced to a few cold, precise data. Old Bedeau, sitting in Lecoeur's place and wearing his headphones, was doing a crossword, barely breaking off for the traditional: 'Hello! Austerlitz? Your van's gone out?'

A drowned woman had just been fished out of the Seine. This, too, formed part of the Christmas tradition.

'Could I speak to you a moment, Superintendent?'

The camp bed had been replaced in the closet, and this was where Lecoeur now took the head of the Homicide Squad. The Superintendent was smoking his pipe; he shed his overcoat, and looked at his companion in some surprise.

'Please forgive me for interfering in what's not my business, but it's about the killer . . .'

He had his little notebook in his hand, but he appeared to know it by heart and to consult it only so as to keep himself in countenance.

'Forgive me if I tell you rather confusedly what's in my mind, but I've been thinking about it so much since this morning that . . .'

A short while ago, while he was lying down, it had all seemed dazzlingly clear to him. Now he was searching for words, and his ideas had become less precise.

'It's like this. I noticed first of all that the eight crimes were committed after 2 am and most of them after 3 am.'

From the Superintendent's expression he realized that this observation implied nothing particularly disturbing for other people.

'Out of curiosity, I investigated the time at which most crimes of this sort have been committed during the last three years. It was almost always between 10 pm and 2 am.'

He must be on the wrong track, for he got no reaction. Why not say openly how the idea had occurred to him? This was not the time to be held back by embarrassment.

'Just now, while looking at my brother, I thought that the man you're looking for must be somebody like him. For a moment I even wondered if it could be him. Wait a minute . . .'

He was on the right track after all. He had seen the Superintendent's eyes expressing something more than merely polite but bored attention.

'If I'd had time I'd have set my thoughts in order. But you'll see . . . A man who kills eight times, almost in quick succession, is a maniac, surely? A person whose brain has been disturbed suddenly, for some reason or another . . .

'My brother lost his job, and in order not to admit it to his son, not to lose face in his eyes, he went on for weeks leaving home at the same time, behaving exactly as if he were going to work . . .'

The idea, translated into words and phrases, lost some of its force. He was well aware that, in spite of an obvious effort, Saillard could not see light there.

'A man who finds himself suddenly deprived of everything he had, everything that made up his life . . .'

'And who goes off his head?'

'I don't know if he goes off his head. Perhaps you could call it that. Somebody who thinks he has reasons for hating the whole world, for needing to be revenged on all men . . .

'You know, of course, Superintendent, that the other sort, the real murderers, always kill in the same way.

'This one used a knife, then a hammer, then a spanner. He strangled one woman.

'And nowhere did he let himself be seen. Nowhere did he leave a single trace. Wherever he lives, he must have covered miles in Paris at a time of night when there are no taxis or underground trains. Now, although the police have been on the watch ever since the man's first crimes, although they scrutinize passers-by and challenge all suspicious characters, he never attracted their attention on a single occasion.'

So sure did he feel that he was on the right track at last, so anxious was he that his hearer should not tire of his argument, that he felt like murmuring: 'Please listen to me to the end . . .'

The closet was a constricted place, and he was walking three steps forward and three back, in front of the Superintendent who sat on the edge of the camp bed.

'These are not logical arguments, believe me. I'm not capable of any remarkable arguments. But it's because of my little crosses, the little facts I've noted . . . This morning, for instance, he crossed half Paris without passing in front of a single police station or going over a crossing where there's an officer on duty.'

'Do you mean that he knows the fifteenth arrondissement well?'

'Not only the fifteenth, but two others at least, to judge by the earlier crimes: the twentieth and the twelfth. He did not choose his victims at random. In every case he knew that they were lonely people, living in circumstances where he could attack them without much risk.'

He almost lost heart when he heard his brother's melancholy voice.

'The sandwiches, André!'

'Yes, thanks. You have some. Go and sit down . . .'

He dared not close the door, out of a sort of humility. He was not a sufficiently important person to be closeted with the Superintendent!

'If he took a different weapon each time, it's because he knows that this will confuse people's minds, he knows that murderers generally stick to a single method.'

'Look here, Lecoeur . . .'

The Superintendent had stood up and was now staring at him abstractedly, as though following out his own thoughts.

'Do you mean that . . .'

'I don't know. But it occurred to me that it might be one of our own people. At any rate, somebody who had worked with us.'

He dropped his voice.

'Somebody to whom the same thing had happened as to my brother, don't you see? A fireman who's been sacked would readily think of arson. That happened twice in the last three years. Somebody from the police . . .'

'But why steal?'

'My brother needed money, too, to make his son believe he was still earning his living, that he'd still got his job at La Presse. If the man's a night worker and wants to make out that he's still employed, he's bound to stay out all night, and that explains why he commits his crimes after three in the morning. He can't go home till daybreak. The earlier hours of the night are easy. There are bars and cafés open. After that he's alone in the streets . . .'

Saillard grunted, as though talking to himself: 'There's no one in the Personnel office today.'

'Perhaps we could contact the Personnel manager himself? Perhaps he might remember?'

Lecoeur was still unsatisfied. There were many things he would have liked to say but which escaped him. Perhaps the whole thing was merely fantasy. At times he thought so, and at other times he felt that what he had discovered was as clear as daylight.

'Hello! . . . Can I speak to Monsieur Guillaume, please? He's not at home? Do you happen to know where I'm likely to find him? At his daughter's, at Auteuil? Do you know her telephone number?'

There, too, they'd been enjoying a pleasant family lunch party, and must now be sipping their coffee and liqueurs.

'Hello, Monsieur Guillaume? Saillard here, yes: I hope I'm not disturbing you too much? You weren't still at table? It's about the killer. There's something new. Nothing definite yet. I'd like to check a hypothesis and it's urgent. Don't be too surprised at my question. Has any member of the force, of whatever grade, been dismissed during these last months? What did you say? Not one this year?'

Lecoeur felt his heart sink as though a disaster were overtaking him and cast a despairing glance at the map of Paris. He'd lost the game. From now on he'd give up; but to his surprise his chief persisted.

'It might be earlier than that, I don't know. The person involved would have been a man on night duty, working in several arrondissements, including the fifteenth, the twentieth and the twelfth. Somebody who strongly resented his dismissal. What did you say?'

Saillard's voice as he uttered these last words renewed Lecoeur's hopes, while those around them were nonplussed by the conversation.

'Sergeant Loubet? Yes, I've heard speak of him, but I wasn't on the disciplinary committee at that time. Three years, yes. You don't know where he lived. Somewhere near Les Halles?'

Three years, however, was too big a gap, and Lecoeur lost heart once more. It was unlikely that a man would nurse his humiliation and his rancour for three years before taking action.

'You don't know what's become of him? Obviously. Yes. It won't be easy today . . .'

He hung up again, and looked at Lecoeur attentively, speaking to him as though to an equal.

'Did you hear? There was Sergeant Loubet, who was given a whole series of warnings and moved from one station to another three or four times before finally being dismissed. He took it very badly. He used to drink. Guillaume believes he joined some private detective agency. If you'd like to try . . .'

Lecoeur did so without conviction, but after all it meant taking action instead of waiting in front of that map of his. He began with the most dubious agencies, assuming that a man like Loubet would not have been taken on by a reliable firm. Most of the offices were closed. He called people at their homes.

Often he heard children's voices.

'Never heard of him. Try Tisserand in the Boulevard Saint-Martin. He collects all the riff-raff.'

But he drew a blank at Tisserand's, whose speciality was shadowing. For three quarters of an hour Lecoeur stayed glued to the telephone, and finally he heard an angry voice protesting:

'Don't talk to me about that swine. Over two months ago I fired him and he's threatened to blackmail me, though he hasn't lifted a finger yet. If I meet him I'll punch his nose.'

'What work did he do for you?'

'Watching blocks of flats by night.'

André Lecoeur was once again transfigured.

'Was he a heavy drinker?'

'The fact is he was always drunk after an hour on duty. I don't know how he set about it, but he always managed to be given free drinks.'

'Have you got his correct address?'

'27 bis Rue du Pas-de-la-Mule.'

'Is he on the telephone?'

'He may be. I've no desire to ring him up. Is that all? Can I get back to my bridge?'

As he hung up, the man could be heard explaining things to his friends.

The Superintendent had already seized a telephone directory and found Loubet's name. He rang the number. There was now a tacit understanding between himself and André Lecoeur. They shared the same hope. Now that their goal was within sight they were both tremulous with excitement, while the other Lecoeur, Olivier, sensing that something important was happening, was standing up and looking at each of them in turn.

Without being asked to, André Lecoeur took a liberty which, only that morning, he would never have dared allow himself: he seized the second receiver. The bell could be heard ringing down there in the Rue du Pas-de-la-Mule; it rang a long time, as though the place were empty, and Lecoeur's heart was beginning to sink again when someone lifted the receiver.

Thank heaven! It was a woman's voice, an elderly-sounding woman's voice, that replied:

'Is that you at last? Where are you?'

'Madame, this is not your husband speaking.'

'Has something happened to him?'

She sounded almost pleased at the idea, as though she had been expecting such news for a long time.

'Am I speaking to Madame Loubet?'

'Of course.'

'Is your husband not at home?'

'In the first place, who is speaking?'

'Superintendent Saillard . . .'

'What d'you want him for?'

The Superintendent briefly held his hand over the receiver and whispered to Lecoeur:

'Ring up Janvier and tell him to go there immediately.'

There was a call from a local station at the same time, so that three telephones were in use simultaneously in the room.

'Has your husband not come home this morning?'

'If you policemen did your job properly, you'd know.'

'Does this often happen?'

'That's his business, isn't it?'

She probably detested her drunken sot of a husband, but since he was being attacked she took his side.

'You know he's no longer in the Force?'

'I suppose he's not enough of a bastard for that!'

'When did he stop working for the Argus agency?'

'What's that? . . . One moment, please . . . What are you saying? . . . You're trying to worm things out of me, aren't you?'

'I'm sorry, Madame. It's over two months since your husband was fired from the agency.'

'You're lying!'

'In other words, for the past two months he's been going to work each evening?'

'Where else would he have gone? To the Folies Bergère?'

'Why hasn't he come back this morning? Hasn't he rung you up?'

She was probably afraid of being caught out, for she simply hung up.

When the Superintendent himself replaced the receiver and turned round, he found Lecoeur standing close behind him, averting his head as he said:

'Janvier has gone over there . . .'

And with his finger he wiped away a trace of moisture at the corner of his eye.

5

He was being treated as an equal. He knew that it would not last, that tomorrow he would be merely an insignificant clerk at his switchboard, obsessively putting down little crosses in a futile notebook.

The others did not count. Even his brother stood unnoticed, staring at them each in turn like a timid rabbit, listening to them without understanding, wondering why, when his son's life was at stake, they were talking so much instead of taking action.

Twice he had tugged André by the sleeve.

'Let me go and look . . .' he had begged.

Look where? Look for whom? The description of ex-Sergeant Loubet had already been circulated to all police stations, railway stations and patrols.

Now the search was on not only for a child but for a man of fifty-eight, who was probably drunk, who knew Paris and the Parisian police like the back of his hand, and who was wearing a black overcoat with a velvet collar and an old grey felt hat.

Janvier had returned, bringing in a breath of fresh air. An aura of freshness invariably lingered for a while round those who had just come in from outside; then, gradually, they became submerged in the drab atmosphere in which life seemed to be lived in slow motion.

'She tried to shut the door in my face, but I took care to put my foot in the doorway. She doesn't know anything. She claims that he's brought back his pay these last months as usual.'

'That's why he was obliged to steal. He didn't need large sums, he'd not have known what to do with them. What's she like?'

'Small, swarthy, with very bright eyes and dyed hair, almost blue. She must have eczema or some skin eruption, for she wears mittens.'

'Did you get a photo of him?'

'I took one practically by force, off the sideboard in the dining-room. She didn't want me to.'

It showed a thickset, full-blooded man with protuberant eyes, who must have been a lady-killer in his youth and still wore a look of stupid arrogance. Moreover the photo was several years old, and today Loubet had probably gone to pieces, become flabbily fleshy, with a shifty look instead of one of self-confidence.

'Were you able to discover what places he frequents?'

'As far as I can see she keeps him on a tight rein, except at night when he's at work, or supposed to be. I questioned the concierge. He's very much afraid of his wife. In the mornings, the concierge often sees him come staggering along, but he pulls himself together as soon as he puts his hand on the stair rail. His wife takes him shopping with her, he never goes out in the daytime except with her. When he's asleep and she has to leave the house, she locks him in and takes away the key.'

'What d'you think about it, Lecoeur?'

'I'm wondering whether he and my nephew are together.'

'What do you mean?'

'They weren't together to begin with, at half-past six this morning, for Loubet would have prevented the boy from smashing the glass of the call-boxes. They were some distance apart. One of them was following the other . . .'

'Which, do you think?'

It was disconcerting to be listened to thus, as though he had on the spur of the moment become a sort of oracle. Such was his fear of making a mistake that he had never felt so small in his life.

'When the boy climbed up the drain-pipe he must have believed his father was guilty, since he used the note about the legendary Uncle Gédéon to send him to the Gare d'Austerlitz, where he probably planned to join him after getting rid of the sandwich tin.'

'That seems likely . . .'

'Bib can't have believed . . .' Olivier attempted to protest.

'Shut up! . . . At that point the crime had just been committed. The child wouldn't have ventured on his climb if he had not caught sight of the body . . .'

'He did see it,' Janvier asserted. 'From his window he could see the body from feet to mid-thigh.'

'What we don't know is whether the man was still in the room.'

'No,' put in the Superintendent. 'No, for if he had been, he'd have stayed hidden while the boy came in through the window, and then done away with such a dangerous witness, as he'd just done away with the old woman.'

It was essential, however, to get the whole thing clear, reconstructing it down to the slightest detail, if they were to find young Lecoeur, for whom a Christmas present of not one but two radios was waiting.

'Tell me, Olivier, when you got home this morning was the light on?'

'It was.'

'In the boy's room?'

'Yes. It gave me a shock. I thought he must be ill.'

'So the killer must have seen the light. He was afraid of having a witness. He certainly never expected anyone to get into the room by way of the drain-pipe. He rushed out of the house.'

'And waited outside to see what would happen.'

That was all they could do: put forward hypotheses, trying to be as logical as possible. The rest was up to the police patrols and the hundreds of policemen scattered about Paris; in the last resort it was a matter of chance.

'Rather than go back the way he'd come, the child left the old woman's house by the front door . . .'

'One minute, sir. By that time he probably knew that his father was not the murderer.'

'Why?'

'I heard someone say just now, I think it was Janvier, that the old woman had lost a great deal of blood. If the crime had just been committed, the blood would scarcely be dry and the body would still be warm. Now it was the previous evening, about nine o'clock, that Bib had seen his father in the room.'

Each fresh piece of evidence brought fresh hope. They felt they were getting somewhere; the rest looked easier. Sometimes the two men spoke at once, struck by an identical idea.

'It was when he went out that the boy must have discovered the man, Loubet or someone else, probably Loubet. And the man couldn't know whether his face had been seen. The child was frightened and rushed straight forward . . .'

This time the boy's father interrupted to contradict them, explaining in a monotonous tone of voice:

'Not if Bib knew there was a big reward. Not if he knew I'd lost my job. Not if he'd seen me borrowing money from my mother-in-law . . .'

The Superintendent and André looked at one another, and because they felt that the other Lecoeur was right, they both felt frightened.

It was a nightmare picture. An empty street in one of the loneliest parts of Paris, while it was still dark, two hours before dawn. And here was a man with an obsession, who had just committed his eighth murder in a few weeks, out of hatred and resentment as well as from need, possibly to prove heaven knows what to himself, a man who put his ultimate pride into defying the whole world through the police.

Was he drunk, as usual? No doubt, on Christmas Eve when the bars stay open all night, he had been drinking more than usual and saw the world through an alcoholic haze; there, in that street, in that wilderness of stone, behind the blind house-fronts, he saw a child, a small boy who knew, and who was going to get him arrested, to put an end to his frantic adventures.

'I'd like to know if he had a revolver,' the Superintendent sighed.

He did not have to wait for an answer; it came promptly from Janvier.

'I put that question to his wife. He always carries an automatic, but it was unloaded.'

'Why?'

'His wife is afraid of him. When he was in a certain condition, instead of submitting meekly he sometimes threatened her. She had shut away the cartridges, on the grounds that in case of need the sight of the weapon would be enough to frighten anyone without his having to fire it.'

Had the pair of them, the old maniac and the child, really been playing cat and mouse in the streets of Paris? The ex-policeman could not hope to run faster than a ten-year-old boy; the child, on the other hand, could not hope to overcome a man of that bulk.

Now that man, for the child, represented wealth, the end of all their miseries. His father would no longer have to wander through the town at night, pretending that he was still working in the Rue du Croissant, nor to carry vegetables in the market, nor finally to go crawling to an old woman like Mère Fayet to obtain a loan which he could scarcely hope to repay.

Words were scarcely needed now. They stared at the map, at the names of streets. No doubt the child was keeping at a prudent distance from the murderer and no doubt, too, the man had shown his weapon to frighten the child.

The houses of the city were honeycombed with rooms where thousands of people were sleeping who could be no help to either of them.

Loubet could not stop for ever in the street watching the child, who kept warily away from him, and he had begun walking, avoiding dangerous streets, the blue lamps of police stations and the crossroads where policemen were on duty.

In two or three hours there would be people on the pavements, and the boy would probably rush at the first he met, calling for help.

'Loubet was walking in front,' the Superintendent said slowly.

'And my nephew smashed the glass of the call-boxes because I'd told him how they worked,' added André Lecoeur.

The little crosses were coming to life. What had seemed a mystery to begin with was now acquiring a kind of tragic simplicity.

The most tragic aspect of it was possibly the question of hard cash, the reward for the sake of which a child of ten was deliberately undergoing such terrors and risking his life.

The boy's father had begun to weep, quite gently, without sobbing or gasping, and he did not attempt to hide his tears. His nervous tension had dropped and he had ceased to react in any way. He was surrounded by strange objects and barbarous instruments, by men who talked about him as though he were someone else or were not there, and his brother was one of these men, a brother whom he scarcely recognized and at whom he looked with involuntary awe.

Their sentences were becoming briefer, for Lecoeur and the Superintendent understood one another's slightest word.

'Loubet couldn't go home.'

'Nor enter a bar with the child at his heels.'

André Lecoeur gave a sudden smile.

'It can't have occurred to the man that the boy hadn't a centime in his pockets and that he could have escaped by taking the métro.'

That would not have worked, though; Bib had seen him and would give an exact description of him.

The Trocadéro. The Etoile district. Time had elapsed. It was nearly daylight. People came out of houses; steps sounded on the pavements. It was no longer possible, for a man without a weapon, to kill a child in the street without attracting attention.

The Superintendent pulled himself together, as though awakening from a nightmare. 'Well, however it happened, they must have made contact with one another,' he decided.

At that moment a light came on. As though he knew that it concerned their problem, Lecoeur took the phone instead of his colleagues.

'Yes . . . I guessed as much . . . Thank you . . .'

He explained: 'It was about the two oranges. They've just found a North-African boy asleep in the third class waiting-room at the Gare du Nord. He still had one of the two oranges in his pocket. He had run away from his home in the eighteenth arrondissement this morning, because he'd been given a beating.'

'Do you think Bib's dead?'

Olivier Lecoeur was twisting his fingers as though to break them.

'If he were dead Loubet would have gone home, because, after all, he'd have nothing more to be afraid of.'

So the contest was still going on, in the Paris streets where the sun was shining at last and family parties with children in their Sunday best were out walking.

'Probably Bib was afraid of losing track of him in the crowd. He edged up closer . . .'

Loubet must have spoken to him and threatened him with his gun:

'If you call out, I shall shoot . . .'

And thus each of them pursued a separate aim: the man hoping to get rid of the child, by leading him on to some lonely spot where murder could be done; the child trying to give the alarm before his companion had time to shoot.

Each was wary of the other. For each of them, life was at stake.

'Loubet won't have made for the centre of the city, where there are too many policemen about. Particularly since most of them know him.'

From the Etoile they must have gone up towards Montmartre, not the Montmartre of the night-clubs but the working-class district, towards drab streets which on a day like this must be looking particularly provincial.

It was half-past two. Had they had anything to eat? Had Loubet, despite the threat hanging over him, been able to last out so long without a drink?

'Tell me, Superintendent . . .'

In spite of himself, André Lecoeur could not bring himself to speak self-confidently; he still felt as though he was usurping a function to which he was not entitled.

'There are hundreds of small bars in Paris, I know. But if we began by the most likely ones, and put a great many men on the job . . .'

Not only did those present settle down to it, but Saillard contacted the Quai des Orfèvres, where six detectives on duty each took up his post at a telephone.

'Hello! *Le Bar des Amis*? Has a middle-aged man in a black overcoat, accompanied by a ten-year-old boy, been in at any time since this morning?'

Lecoeur was once more marking crosses, not in his notebook now but in the telephone directory. Here there were ten pages of bars, with more or less fanciful names. Some were closed. In others the sound of music could be heard.

On a map which had been spread out on the table he ticked off the streets with a blue pencil one by one, and it was somewhere behind the Place Clichy, in a passage with a somewhat unsavoury reputation, that the first red mark was made.

'A chap like that came in about noon. He drank three calvadoses and ordered a glass of white wine for the boy. The kid didn't want to drink it but did so in the end, and ate a couple of hard-boiled eggs.'

Olivier Lecoeur looked as if he were hearing his son's voice.

'You don't know where they went?'

'Towards the Batignolles . . . The man was pretty well soused already . . .'

The boy's father would have liked to seize hold of a telephone himself, but there was none available and he walked about from one to another, with knitted brows.

'Hello! The *Zanzi Bar*? Has a middle-aged man . . .'

It had become a regular refrain, and when one of the men had ceased uttering it another took it up at the far end of the room.

Rue Damrémont. Right at the top of Montmartre. At half-past one; the man's movements were becoming uncertain and he had broken a glass. The boy had made as though to go to the lavatory and his companion had followed him. Then the kid had given up the attempt, as if he'd been frightened.

'A queer sort of chap. He kept on sniggering as though he were having a good joke.'

'You hear, Olivier? Bib was still there, an hour and forty minutes ago.'

André Lecoeur, by now, was afraid to say what he thought. The struggle was nearing its end. Since Loubet had started drinking he'd go on doing so. Would this be the boy's opportunity?

In a way, yes, if he had the patience to wait and did not embark on any futile venture.

But suppose he was mistaken, suppose he believed his companion to be more drunk than he really was, suppose . . .

André Lecoeur's eyes fell on his brother, and he had a sudden vision of what Olivier might have become if his asthma had not, by some miracle, prevented him from drinking.

'Yes . . . What did you say? . . . Boulevard Ney?'

That meant the outer limits of Paris, and implied that the ex-policeman was not as drunk as he appeared. He was making his way along quietly, leading the child out of the city gradually and almost imperceptibly, towards the waste ground on the outskirts.

Three police vans had already left for that district. All available police cyclists had been sent there, and Janvier himself rushed off in the Superintendent's little car; they had great difficulty in restraining the child's father from accompanying him.

'I've told you, this is where you'll have the first news of him . . .'

Nobody had time to make coffee. They could not help being over-excited; their words came in nervous jerks.

'Hello! The *Orient Bar*? Hello! Who's speaking?'

André Lecoeur, at the telephone, stood up as he listened, made peculiar signals and was practically dancing with excitement.

'What? . . . Not so close to the phone . . .'

Then the others caught the sound of a high-pitched voice like a woman's.

'Whoever you are, tell the police that . . . Hello! Tell the police that I've got him . . . the killer . . . Hello! What? Uncle André?'

The voice dropped a tone lower, took on an anguished note. 'I tell you I'm going to shoot . . . Uncle André! . . . '

Lecoeur had no idea to whom he handed the receiver. He rushed up the stair and nearly broke in the door of the telegraphist's room.

'Quick! The *Orient Bar*, Porte de Clignancourt . . . Every available man . . .'

He did not wait to hear the call put through, but leapt down the stairs four at a time, then halted on the threshold of the big room, where to his stupefaction everyone was standing motionless, with the tension relaxed.

Saillard was holding the receiver, listening to a hearty working-class voice saying:

'It's okay . . . Don't worry . . . I hit him on the head with a bottle . . . He's out now . . . I don't know what he was trying to do to the boy, but . . . What's that? You want to talk to him? . . . Come here, kid . . . Give me your popgun . . . I don't much like that sort of toy . . . But say, it isn't loaded . . .'

Another voice: 'Is that you, Uncle André?'

The Superintendent, holding the receiver, looked about him, and it was not to André Lecoeur but to Olivier that he handed it.

'Uncle André? . . . I've got him . . . The killer! . . . I've got the re . . .'

'Hello, Bib!'

'What?'

'Hello, Bib, it's . . .'

'What are you doing there, dad?'

'Nothing . . . I was waiting . . . I . . .'

'I'm happy, you know . . . Wait . . . Here are some police cyclists who want to talk to me . . . And a car's stopped . . .'

There were confused sounds, a buzz of voices, the clink of glasses. Olivier Lecoeur held the telephone receiver awkwardly and stared at the map, probably without seeing it. It was happening a long way off, right up in the northern part of the city, in a great windswept open square.

'I'm going off with them . . .'

Another voice. 'Is that you, Chief? Janvier here . . .'

Olivier Lecoeur looked as if he was the one who had been knocked on the head, the way he held out the receiver into empty space.

'He's completely sozzled, Chief. When the kid heard the phone ring, he realized it was his opportunity; he managed to snatch the gun from Loubet's pocket and took a leap . . . Thanks to the *patron*, a tough guy who knocked the man out on the spot . . .'

A little light flashed out on the board, up in the Clignancourt district. Stretching his hand over his colleague's shoulder, André Lecoeur thrust the plug into a hole.

'Hello! Your van's gone out?'

'Someone's broken the glass of the emergency call-box in the Place Clignancourt to say there's trouble in a bar there . . . Hello! . . . Shall I call you back?'

There was no need to this time.

Nor was there any need to mark a little cross in his notebook.

A very proud small boy was being driven across Paris in a police car.

THE RIGHT KIND OF A HOUSE

Henry Slesar

Writing takes many forms, and I've had the opportunity to indulge in most of them. But after 500 works of fiction, seven novels, four screenplays, 100 teleplays, 50 radio scripts, more than 3000 daytime serial episodes and countless chunks of advertising copy, I still feel that there is nothing so uniquely satisfying as a short story.

'The Right Kind of a House' was written at a time in my career when the short story was my only *effort, since the joys (and financial lure) of TV hadn't yet beckoned. I was still hungry for the large thrills and small checks that accompanied sales to the mystery and science-fiction magazines, then the most accessible target for budding mystery writers. I wrote at least one story a week, and woke up every morning with my mind unconsciously baited for the short-story idea that would start my idle typewriter moving that evening.*

This one came in a donut restaurant. I was big on donuts at the time, since I was earning a smallish salary in a smallish advertising agency. There was a woman sitting at the counter, complaining to her companion about her aging mother, who persisted in living alone in a large, empty house, and who had (deliberately, she thought) placed a much-too-high price on the place in order to discourage its sale.

The trap sprung. All I had to do was answer the question: what other *reason (besides love of an established home) would an old lady have for putting too high a price on a house?*

I had 'The Right Kind of a House' completely written in my mind by the time I dunked my last donut. I sold it for $30. Since then, it's earned enough to buy several thousand donuts, including a Reader's Digest *sale and a television adaptation.*

I think it's my favorite story, because it was such a clear demonstration to me of the possibilities of the mind.

The automobile that was stopping in front of Aaron Hacker's real-estate office had a New York license plate. Aaron didn't need to see the yellow rectangle to know that its owner was new to the elm-shaded streets of Ivy Corners. It was a red convertible; there was nothing else like it in town.

The man got out of the car.

'Sally,' Hacker said to the bored young lady at the only other desk. There was a paperbound book propped in her typewriter, and she was chewing something dreamily.

'Yes, Mr Hacker?'

'Seems to be a customer. Think we oughta look busy?' He put the question mildly.

'Sure, Mr Hacker!' She smiled brightly, removed the book, and slipped a blank sheet of paper into the machine. 'What shall I type?'

'Anything, anything!' Aaron scowled.

It looked like a customer, all right. The man was heading straight for the glass door, and there was a folded newspaper in his right hand. Aaron described him later as heavy-set. Actually, he was fat. He wore a colorless suit of lightweight material, and the perspiration had soaked clean through the fabric to leave large, damp circles around his arms. He might have been fifty, but he had all his hair, and it was dark and curly. The skin of his face was flushed and hot, but the narrow eyes remained clear and frosty-cold.

He came through the doorway, glanced toward the rattling sound of the office typewriter, and then nodded at Aaron.

'Mr Hacker?'

'Yes, sir,' Aaron smiled. 'What can I do for you?'

The fat man waved the newspaper. 'I looked you up in the real-estate section.'

'Yep. Take an ad every week. I use the *Times*, too, now and then. Lot of city people interested in a town like ours, Mr – '

'Waterbury,' the man said. He plucked a white cloth out of his pocket and mopped his face. 'Hot today.'

'Unusually hot,' Aaron answered. 'Doesn't often get so hot in our town. Mean temperature's around 78° in the summer. We got the lake, you know. Isn't that right, Sally?' The girl was too absorbed to hear him. 'Well. Won't you sit down, Mr Waterbury?'

'Thank you.' The fat man took the proffered chair, and sighed. 'I've been driving around. Thought I'd look the place over before I came here. Nice little town.'

'Yes, we like it. Cigar?' He opened a box on his desk.

'No, thank you. I really don't have much time, Mr Hacker. Suppose we get right down to business.'

'Suits me, Mr Waterbury.' He looked toward the clacking noise and frowned. '*Sally!*'

'Yes, Mr Hacker?'

'Cut out the darn racket.'

'Yes, Mr Hacker.' She put her hands in her lap, and stared at the meaningless jumble of letters she had drummed on the paper.

'Now, then,' Aaron said. 'Was there any place in particular you were interested in, Mr Waterbury?'

'As a matter of fact, yes. There was a house at the edge of town, across the way from an old building. Don't know what kind of building – deserted.'

'Ice-house,' Aaron said. 'Was it a house with pillars?'

'Yes. That's the place. Do you have it listed? I thought I saw a "for sale" sign, but I wasn't sure.'

Aaron shook his head, and chuckled dryly. 'Yep, we got it listed all right.' He flipped over a loose-leaf book, and pointed to a typewritten sheet. 'You won't be interested for long.'

'Why not?'

He turned the book around. 'Read it for yourself.'

The fat man did so:

> AUTHENTIC COLONIAL. Eight rooms, two baths, automatic oil furnace, large porches, trees and shrubbery. Near shopping, schools. $75,000.

'Still interested?'

The man stirred uncomfortably. 'Why not? Something wrong with it?'

'Well.' Aaron scratched his temple. 'If you really like this town, Mr Waterbury – I mean, if you really want to settle here, I got any number of places that'd suit you better.'

'Now, just a minute!' The fat man looked indignant. 'What do you call this? I'm asking you about this colonial house. You want to sell it, or don't you?'

'Do I?' Aaron chuckled. 'Mister, I've had that property on my hands for five years. There's nothing I'd rather collect a commission on. Only my luck just ain't that good.'

'What do you mean?'

'I mean, you won't buy. That's what I mean. I keep the listing on my books just for the sake of old Sadie Grimes. Otherwise, I wouldn't waste the space. Believe me.'

'I don't get you.'

'Then let me explain.' He took out a cigar, but just to roll it in his fingers. 'Old Mrs Grimes put her place up for sale five years ago, when her son died. She gave me the job of selling it. I didn't want the job – no, sir. I told her that to her face. The old place just ain't worth the kind of money she's asking. I mean, heck! The old place ain't even worth $10,000!'

The fat man swallowed. 'Ten? And she wants $75,000?'

'That's right. Don't ask me why. It's a real old house. Oh, I don't mean one of those solid-as-a-rock old houses. I mean *old*. Never been de-termited. Some of the beams will be going in the next couple of years. Basement's full of water half the time. Upper floor leans to the right about nine inches. And the grounds are a mess.'

'Then why does she ask so much?'

Aaron shrugged. 'Don't ask me. Sentiment, maybe. Been in her family since the Revolution, something like that.'

The fat man studied the floor. 'That's too bad,' he said. 'Too bad!' He looked up at Aaron, and smiled sheepishly. 'And I kinda liked the place. It was – I don't know how to explain it – the *right* kind of house.'

'I know what you mean. It's a friendly old place. A good buy at $10,000. But $75,000?' He laughed. 'I think I know Sadie's reasoning, though. You see, she doesn't have much money. Her son was supporting her, doing well in the city. Then he died, and she knew that it was sensible to sell. But she couldn't bring herself to part with the old place. So she set a price tag so big that *nobody* would come near it. That eased her conscience.' He shook his head sadly. 'It's a strange world, ain't it?'

'Yes,' Waterbury said distantly.

Then he stood up. 'Tell you what, Mr Hacker. Suppose I drive out to see Mrs Grimes? Suppose I talk to her about it, get her to change her price.'

'You're fooling yourself, Mr Waterbury. I've been trying for five years.'

'Who knows? Maybe if somebody *else* tried – '

Aaron Hacker spread his palms. 'Who knows, is right. It's a strange world, Mr Waterbury. If you're willing to go to the trouble, I'll be only too happy to lend a hand.'

'Good. Then I'll leave now . . .'

'Fine! You just let me ring Sadie Grimes, I'll tell her you're on your way.'

Waterbury drove slowly through the quiet streets. The shade trees that lined the avenues cast peaceful dappled shadows on the hood of the convertible. The powerful motor beneath it operated in whispers, so he could hear the fitful chirpings of the birds overhead.

He reached the home of Sadie Grimes without once passing another moving vehicle. He parked his car beside the rotted picket fence that faced the house like a row of disorderly sentries.

The lawn was a jungle of weeds and crabgrass, and the columns that rose from the front porch were entwined with creepers.

There was a hand knocker on the door. He pumped it twice.

The woman who responded was short and plump. Her white hair was vaguely purple in spots, and the lines in her face descended downward toward her small, stubborn chin. She wore a heavy wool cardigan, despite the heat.

'You must be Mr Waterbury,' she said. 'Aaron Hacker said you were coming.'

'Yes.' The fat man smiled. 'How do you do, Mrs Grimes?'

'Well as I can expect. I suppose you want to come in?'

'Awfully hot out here.' He chuckled.

'Mm. Well, come in then. I've put some lemonade in the ice-box. Only don't expect me to bargain with you, Mr Waterbury. I'm not that kind of person.'

'Of course not,' the man said winningly, and followed her inside.

It was dark and cool. The window shades were opaque, and they had been drawn. They entered a square parlor with heavy, baroque furniture shoved unimaginatively against every wall. The only color in the room was in the faded hues of the tasseled rug that lay in the center of the bare floor.

The old woman headed straight for a rocker, and sat motionless, her wrinkled hands folded sternly.

'Well?' she said. 'If you have anything to say, Mr Waterbury, I suggest you say it.'

The fat man cleared his throat. 'Mrs Grimes, I've just spoken with your real-estate agent – '

'I know all that,' she snapped. 'Aaron's a fool. All the more for letting you come here with the notion of changing my mind. I'm too old for changing my mind, Mr Waterbury.'

'Er – well, I don't know if that was my intention, Mrs Grimes. I thought we'd just – talk a little.'

She leaned back, and the rocker groaned. 'Talk's free. Say what you like.'

'Yes.' He mopped his face again, and shoved the handkerchief only halfway back into his pocket. 'Well, let me put it this way, Mrs Grimes.

I'm a business man – a bachelor. I've worked for a long time, and I've made a fair amount of money. Now I'm ready to retire – preferably, somewhere quiet. I like Ivy Corners. I passed through here some years back, on my way to – er, Albany. I thought, one day, I might like to settle here.'

'So?'

'So, when I drove through your town today, and saw this house – I was enthused. It just seemed – right for me.'

'I like it too, Mr Waterbury. That's why I'm asking a fair price for it.'

Waterbury blinked. 'Fair price? You'll have to admit, Mrs Grimes, these days a house like this shouldn't cost more than – '

'That's enough!' the old woman cried. 'I told you, Mr Waterbury – I don't want to sit here all day and argue with you. If you won't pay my price, then we can forget all about it.'

'But, Mrs Grimes – '

'Good *day*, Mr Waterbury!'

She stood up, indicating that he was expected to do the same.

But he didn't. 'Wait a moment, Mrs Grimes,' he said, 'just a moment. I know it's crazy, but – all right. I'll pay what you want.'

She looked at him for a long moment. 'Are you sure, Mr Waterbury?'

'Positive! I've enough money. If that's the only way you'll have it, that's the way it'll be.'

She smiled thinly. 'I think that lemonade'll be cold enough. I'll bring you some – and then I'll tell you something about this house.'

He was mopping his brow when she returned with the tray. He gulped at the frosty yellow beverage greedily.

'This house,' she said, easing back in her rocker, 'has been in my family since 1802. It was built some fifteen years before that. Every member of the family, except my son, Michael, was born in the bedroom upstairs. I was the only rebel,' she added raffishly. 'I had new-fangled ideas about hospitals.' Her eyes twinkled.

'I know it's not the most solid house in Ivy Corners. After I brought Michael home, there was a flood in the basement, and we never seemed to get it dry since. Aaron tells me that there are termites, too, but I've never seen the pesky things. I love the old place, though; you understand.'

'Of course,' Waterbury said.

'Michael's father died when Michael was nine. It was hard lines on us then. I did some needlework, and my own father had left me the small annuity which supports me today. Not in very grand style, but I manage. Michael missed his father, perhaps even more than I. He grew up to be – well, wild is the only word that comes to mind.'

The fat man clucked, sympathetically.

'When he graduated from high school, Michael left Ivy Corners and went to the city. Against my wishes, make no mistake. But he was like so many young men; full of ambition, undirected ambition. I don't know what he did in the city. But he must have been successful – he sent me money regularly.' Her eyes concluded. 'I didn't see him for nine years.'

'Ah,' the man sighed, sadly.

'Yes, it wasn't easy for me. But it was even worse when Michael came home because, when he did, he was in trouble.'

'Oh?'

'I didn't know how bad the trouble was. He showed up in the middle of the night, looking thinner and older than I could have believed possible. He had no luggage with him, only a small black suitcase. When I tried to take it from him, he almost struck me. Struck *me* – his own mother!

'I put him to bed myself, as if he was a little boy again. I could hear him crying out during the night.

'The next day, he told me to leave the house. Just for a few hours – he wanted to do something, he said. He didn't explain what. But when I returned that evening, I noticed that the little black suitcase was gone.'

The fat man's eyes widened over the lemonade glass.

'What did it mean?' he asked.

'I didn't know then. But I found out soon – too terribly soon. That night, a man came to our house. I don't even know how he got in. I first knew when I heard voices in Michael's room. I went to the door, and tried to listen, tried to find out what sort of trouble my boy was in. But I heard only shouts and threats, and then . . .'

She paused, and her shoulders sagged.

'And a shot,' she continued, 'a gunshot. When I went into the room, I found the bedroom window open, and the stranger gone. And Michael – he was on the floor. He was dead.'

The chair creaked.

'That was five years ago,' she said. 'Five long years. It was a while before I realized what had happened. The police told me the story. Michael and this other man had been involved in a crime, a serious crime. They had stolen many, many thousands of dollars.

'Michael had taken that money, and run off with it, wanting to keep it all for himself. He hid it somewhere in this house – to this very day I don't know where. Then the other man came looking for my son, came to collect his share. When he found the money gone, he – he killed my boy.'

She looked up. 'That's when I put the house up for sale, at $75,000. I knew that, someday, my son's killer would return. Someday, he would want this house at any price. All I had to do was wait until I found the man willing to pay much too much for an old lady's house.'

She rocked gently.

Waterbury put down the empty glass and licked his lips, his eyes no longer focusing, his head rolling loosely on his shoulders.

'*Ugh!*' he said. 'This lemonade is bitter.'

A THEME FOR HYACINTH
Julian Symons

This story has two points of origin. One is Wallace Stevens's marvellous poem, 'Le Monocle de Mon Oncle', much of which has stayed in my mind ever since I first read it many years ago. When a vague idea of a story about a middle-aged man's love affair, an affair which should involve some sort of disillusionment and betrayal, occurred to me, the poem with its idealism about love came flooding back.

If sex were all, then every trembling hand
Could make us squeak, like dolls, the wished-for words.

My story would be about a love affair basically sexual, yet, as in the poem, sex, at least for one of the partners, emphatically wouldn't be all.

The setting for the story was provided by Lokrum, that attractive little island very near to Dubrovnik. 'Very fertile and heavily wooded, and an excellent spot for a walk and a picnic', as one guide book accurately says. The other islands in the story, near to Lokrum, certainly exist, although I've never landed on one of them.

These two elements, Stevens's poem and the little islands outside Dubrovnik, certainly shaped the story, and could even be said to bear responsibility for it. I just wrote it down.

Happiness, Robin Edgley thought as he felt the sun on his chest and stomach and legs, seeping through the epidermis to irradiate the blood and sinew and, yes, heart beneath; it is by pure chance that I have discovered happiness for the first time in my life. If Felix had not been laid low by influenza and been delayed leaving England for a week, Gerda would never have spoken to me and this would have been simply another holiday. Instead, it was a revelation to himself of his inmost nature.

Happiness, happiness! It was a golden body that you held in your hands on a green island beside a blue sea, but it was also – to move beyond that rather seaside-posterish conception – the inward reassurance given by his love for Gerda, the feeling of merging his identity with that of another human being, something that went beyond the possibilities of words.

Pleasurable warmth was turning into heat. Perhaps his front had been cooked sufficiently. He removed the bandage from his eyes, glanced round, and saw that he shared the terrace beside the sea with half a dozen old men and women; he turned onto his stomach and picked up the poetry anthology he had been reading. One poem, *Le Monocle de Mon Oncle* by Wallace Stevens, fascinated him. It was a middle-aged man's reflections on love:

> In the high west there burns a furious star.
> It is for fiery boys that star was set
> And for sweet-smelling virgins close to them.
> The measure of the intensity of love
> Is measure, also, of the verve of earth.

True, he thought. He felt in himself a sharpening of the senses, a deepened awareness of everything about him. But the next verse provoked disagreement.

> When amorists grow bald, then armours shrink
> Into the compass and curriculum
> Of introspective exiles lecturing.
> It is a theme for Hyacinth alone.

No, no, he cried silently. His head was silvered and not bald, but the point was that love between a mature man and a young woman could contain everything felt by those 'fiery boys' – and more, much more. Was the poem not proved untrue by almost the first words Gerda had spoken to him?

He was wondering at that time, three days ago, why he had ever come. He had succumbed to the boyish eagerness of his cousin Felix, and had regretted it almost immediately. Looking sideways at him out of those dark eyes that were absurdly long-lashed for a man's, Felix had said he was going away and asked why Nunky – which was his name for Robin, although they were not blood relations – didn't come too.

'I'm fed up with bloody agents, bloody producers, bloody theatre. Getting out of it, Nunky, going to look for the sun. Let them bloody ring my flat and not find me, they'll be keener when I come back. Since you're a man of leisure, why not make it a twosome?' Where was he going? He didn't know but it turned out to be Yugoslavia, the Adriatic coast. Dubrovnik. 'Boiling hot, wonderful swimming, fishing, and cheap. Not that that matters to you, but it does to me. And we might find a couple of birds. If you're so inclined.'

Again that sideways glance from the fine eyes that – he could admit it frankly now – always disturbed him. The disturbance came from the doubts about himself raised by such glances and by the impulse he felt at times to put an arm round the young man's shoulders, to push him playfully over onto a sofa when they had an argument. It was five years since Mary's death and he had neither remarried nor even engaged in a love affair since then. Was there something wrong with him?

Thinking of his own fastidiousness, of the care he took about the colour and fit of clothes, of his liking for picking up nice little pieces of bric-à-brac and of putting them in just the right spot in his flat, he wondered whether he could possibly be (a word he disliked using, disliked even the thought of) queer? Or was it just that the rackety life Felix lived fascinated him, shifting quarterly from flat to flat, often out of work and sometimes tremendously hard up? Occasionally Robin had lent him small sums of money which had always been returned, but he had worried even about these. Was he trying to buy affection?

He could admit all this now, since Gerda had proved that there was nothing queer about him.

So much for Felix, who had done him the best turn of his life by contracting influenza and by telephoning, in a woebegone voice about which there was as always a hint of self-mockery, to say that he would come out as soon as he felt better. But these had not been Robin's thoughts as he took a hot bath, changed into a dashing maroon dinner jacket, and sat down to dinner alone on that first night in the hotel. Afterward he stood on the terrace leaning on his silver-headed malacca cane, and stared gloomily at the lights of the old city. He felt a touch on his arm.

'You will forgive me if I speak to you,' the girl said. 'But I could not help looking at you in the restaurant. You were the most attractive man in the room.' She paused and made a careful amendment. 'That is not quite right. I should have said the most *interesting* man.'

That made it easier for him to say, 'Thank you.'

'My name is Gerda.'

'Robin Edgley.' She was young, blonde, beautiful. He felt a moment's panic. 'Shall we sit down? Would you like a drink?'

When they were sitting in chairs that overlooked the bay, drinks by their sides, he felt a little more comfortable. 'You took my breath away. Do you often say that kind of thing to a strange man?'

'Never before. Please believe me.' She spoke gravely, and he did believe her. She was not, he now saw, quite the dazzling beauty he had thought. Her hair was silky and her features fine, but the large mouth turned down sulkily at the corners and her blue eyes were very wide apart under their thick blonde brows. The eyes looked cold, but a kind of warmth came from her, almost as if some fire burned within her. Her English was perfect, but accented.

He asked if she was a German and she nodded. 'You're a very unusual girl.'

'Don't talk like that. As if you were my uncle.' She spoke sharply. 'We are the same age, you and I.'

'What nonsense. I might be your uncle. I am forty-five.' In fact, he was four years older.

'I did not mean in that way. We feel the same emotions. When you look at this landscape what do you feel?'

He looked into gathering darkness and she said impatiently, 'Not now. When you came.'

'Romantic, I suppose.'

'And subtle.'

'Yes, romantic in a subtle way,' he said, although he had not felt this at all.

'Young men do not feel such things. They bore me.' Without taking breath she asked, 'Shall we go for a walk?'

They walked in the Gradac Park, among old cypress and pine trees, above the sea. He found himself talking with unusual freedom, telling her that he had been a partner in a small firm manufacturing a new kind of air vent for kitchens, and that he had retired from it a couple of years ago. He tried to explain something of his feeling.

'Suddenly it seemed ridiculous, going in to an office every day. I thought, is this all I'm going to do with my life? Of course when Mary was alive it was different, but she died five years ago.'

'Mary?'

'My wife. I forgot you didn't know her. Isn't that silly?'

'Nothing about you is silly. Yes, there is one thing.' She pointed to the stick. 'Why use that? It is for lame men.'

'Ah, but you don't realize – ' With a twist and a flourish he drew the sword from its sheath. 'If I am attacked.'

'I think it is foolish.' In her precise English it sounded very definite. 'What else have you found in life?'

'I don't know. Places – all the places I haven't seen. Poetry – I always liked reading poetry. Meeting people, not just English people.'

'Have you found what you hoped?'

'I don't know. Enough to be glad that I gave up business.'

But as he spoke it seemed to him that something was terribly missing. He asked what she did, and she laughed deep in her throat.

'You will see.' She would say nothing more. On the way back he was very conscious of her physical presence at his side. There was something animal, assured yet stealthy, about the movements of her body. Once he touched her arm and felt an almost irresistible desire to grip her shoulders and turn her to him. Then the moment was over and they were walking along again.

In the hotel lobby he was uncertain whether to suggest a drink in his room. Then that moment also passed. She said good night and was walking away, the golden hair like a cap at the back of her head.

On the following morning he woke in excellent spirits. He ate breakfast on the balcony outside his room and watched tourists going off in coaches to Mostar, the bay of Kotor, and on the Grand Tour of Montenegro. The holiday makers, mostly brawny Germans and unbecomingly sunburned English, stood about chatting until they were shepherded by energetic guides into the coaches. The voices of the guides rang out like those of schoolteachers gathering children to cross the road.

'Hurry, please. We are already five minutes late.'

There was something familiar about the precision of the tone even as it floated up to him, and he identified her in a blue and white sleeveless dress, with a dark-blue peaked cap on the side of her head. She looked up, saw him, touched her fingers to her lips, then jumped into the coach and was gone.

He was in the sun lounge when the travellers returned in the early evening. He assured himself that he was not waiting for her, but the thrill that went through his body at the sight of her golden hair under the peaked cap was something he had not felt for years.

She came up to him at once. Beads of moisture marked her upper lip. He asked if she wanted a drink. She shook her head. 'I am not presentable. Those coaches are hot. But in ten minutes I should like a large, *large* gin and tonic.'

He had it waiting for her in the bar.

'So you're a guide.'

'Only for a few days, with this one party. On Sunday my husband comes out. Then we shall be on holiday.' Her petulant mouth turned down. 'His name is Porter, so that I am Gerda Porter. It sounds ridiculous. He is a travel agent. I thought it would be amusing to play the part of a guide, for just one party, so he arranged it.'

'He sounds nice.'

'Don't let us talk about him. Shall I come to your room now or after dinner?' He stared at her. 'I have shocked you? You do not like women to be frank?'

He went on staring and she looked back with one thick eyebrow raised, half-smiling. 'Now,' he said and then added, with what he felt at the time to be wretched pusillanimity, 'in separate lifts. We must be careful.'

They went up in separate lifts. They did not come down to dinner.

Two days later her party went home. He watched her with them, talking to the men who asked about playing at the casino where only foreign currency was permitted and about making special trips to see what they called 'something of the way people really live here' (as though the Yugoslavs were another species), and with the women who engaged her in endless chats about what they could buy and what they could take home.

She handled all their queries with efficiency, courtesy and an apparently endless patience. After seeing them off at the airport she came back and sat in a chair beside him.

'I'm glad that's over. What a boring lot!'

'You handled them perfectly.'

'Why not? I used to be a travel courier. I was enjoying it. But after meeting you – ' She left the sentence unfinished. 'We have three days.'

'Three days?'

'Before my husband arrives.' Her eyes were like blue marbles.

That day they explored Dubrovnik, intoxicated by the pleasure of being in a city sacred to walkers. They wandered from side to side of the Placa looking in the windows of shops that all seemed to sell the same goods, priced head scarfs and rugs in the Gundulic Square market, ate unidentifiable fish at a little restaurant in Ul Siroka, made a circuit of the ramparts. After lunch they drank coffee on the terrace of the Gradska Kafana by the harbour. Then they hired a motorboat with surprising ease, and in the motorboat discovered the island.

The Dalmatian coast is full of islands, including Lokrum, less than half a mile from the walled city, which appears to be covered with pine woods but in fact contains a park filled with subtropical vegetation and twenty small coves for bathers. Lokrum is a 'trippers' haunt', but a little beyond it there are a dozen tiny islands, no more than a few hundred yards long, some almost pure rock, others covered by shrubs and dwarf trees, and with natural landing places.

It was one of these that they found, rowing in the last few yards and pulling up the boat into a tiny bay. They took off their clothes, swam naked in the clear blue water, then walked back a few yards from the beach and made love on the grass. The walls of Dubrovnik were visible less than a mile away, yet they were completely alone. This is unreal, he told himself; it has nothing to do with any life I have ever known. These thoughts were interrupted by Gerda.

Look at me. I smell like a pig.' There was moisture on her brow and on her body. 'Disgusting. Not like you – your body is dry.'

'Dry with old age.'

'Don't talk like that, it's stupid. My husband is an old man.'

'Gerda – '

'And I do not wish you to call me Gerda, it is the name he uses. I tell you my secret name – it is Hella. You call me Hel.'

'Hel, you have shown me heaven,' he said inanely. 'Does he look like me, your husband?'

She snorted with laughter. 'You'll see.' With her face half buried in grass she told him about her life. Her parents had escaped from East to West Germany, and she had gone from West Germany to England, where she worked as an *au pair* girl. She had no intention of remaining with the family, but she could not get a job without a labour permit. So she forged one and was engaged as a courier by Porter Travel Limited.

'And then you married the boss.' He said it lightly, to hide the fact that her calm talk of forgery had shocked him.

'Yes.'

'You say he is – my age. Did he attract you?'

'Yes, but that was not important. He found out that my permit was no good, so it was the only thing to do. When I see something must be done I do it.'

'You're ruthless.'

'When it is necessary. But if I had known what it would be like – ' Again she did not finish the sentence but stared at him with her brilliant marble eyes. Then she turned and ran down again to the sea. He got up and followed her.

It was on the island, the following day, that he told her he loved her. This was something he had not said to any woman, except to Mary in the early days of their marriage. She made no reply. 'But you don't love me, Hel, do you?'

'I am not sure. Anyway it does not matter. It is Friday. On Sunday afternoon my husband will arrive.'

'Felix too. I've had a cable.' He had told her about Felix.

'When he is here it will be all over.'

'I want to marry you.' He had not known that he was going to say these words, but as soon as they were uttered he knew them to be true. She remained silent. 'Did you hear me?'

'I heard you. It is impossible.'

'Why?'

'My husband is a Catholic. He would not divorce me.'

'If you left him we could live together.' He was astonished to hear himself suggest it.

'He would bring a law case, drag you through the Courts. Would you like that, respectable Robin? There is only one way we could be together.'

'How?'

'If he were dead.'

He had closed his eyes. Now he opened them. She had a towel wrapped round her, and she was leaning on one arm looking at him. He realized at once that she meant they should kill her husband in some way. He was not even surprised, for he understood by now the total ruthlessness of her character. But he was a conventional man, and conventional words accurately expressed his reaction. 'You must be mad.'

She made no reply, but began to dress. They went down to the boat in silence. Then she put her arms round him. 'I love you, Robin, but how can I permit myself to do so? What would be the use?'

'If you loved me you wouldn't talk like that.'

'I love like a German. If I want something I try to get it. If I cannot get it I do without and don't complain. You do not have the courage to help me, so we have till Sunday. We can enjoy that much.'

But Robin did not enjoy it, or not in the same way. The sensual grip she exerted on him was very powerful. He had always thought of himself as a less than average sensual man, for he had never experienced with Mary anything like the feelings that Gerda inspired in him. The intensity of his actions and reactions during lovemaking frightened him, just as in a different way he was frightened by the feeling that he existed as an instrument for her satisfaction. He told himself that he loved her, but did he feel anything more than a sexual itch? Lines from another poem came into his head:

> But at my back from time to time I hear
> The sound of horns and motors which shall bring
> Sweeney to Mrs Porter in the spring.

To think of himself as apeneck Sweeney, the image of mindless sensuality, distressed and worried him. But over-riding such feelings was the longing he felt for her that made another part of himself say, 'This is the first happiness you have had in your long dreary life. Are you going to throw it away?'

He held out until Sunday morning. On Saturday they went to the island but it was not a success, and on Sunday morning neither of them suggested a visit. When they found that two places were vacant on a coach expedition to Cilipi, a few miles away, to see the peasants come to church in local costume, they got in.

The scene as they approached was farcical. Dozens of coaches were drawn up along the roadside. They parked half a mile from the church square. When they reached it, the place was packed with camera-carrying tourists, taking shots of everything in sight. A few locals moved in and out of the throng, the women wearing white nunlike coifs, embroidered blouses, and long black skirts. Tourists snapped cameras within inches of their faces, asked them to hold still, climbed onto cars to get angled shots. A scrawny American with white knees showing below baggy shorts aimed his camera at a fezzed village elder who sat placidly smoking a long clay pipe.

'Excuse it, please.' The American pushed Robin and Gerda aside, dropped to one knee, then suddenly flung himself flat onto the ground and squinted up at the Cilipian who stared into the distance with imperturbable dignity. Robin looked at Gerda. They both burst out laughing, then walked out of the square and the village down a rough path that led through scrub to nowhere.

'You do not have your cane.' He had left it in his room ever since that first evening. He said curtly she had been right, he did not need it. She glanced at him, said nothing.

'Did you ever see anything so awful as those tourists? The Yugoslavs must think we're all barbarians.'

'But I am a barbarian. You think so.' Her words were like an accusation.

She leaned against a rock. 'You are afraid of everything. If I said to you take me into that field, make love to me, would you do it?'

'Hel, it wouldn't be – ' Two coiffed women came up the stony path. '*Dobar dan*,' he said.

'*Dobar dan*.' They passed on.

She said ironically, as he stumbled on a rock. 'You need your cane. I think you should carry it.' She wore dark glasses, but he knew that behind them her blue eyes would be cold. He could not bear the thought of losing her. 'Hel, tell me what you want.'

'It must be what *we* want.'

'What we want.' When he put his hand on her arm it seemed to burn him.

She told him in her precise English, speaking in a rapid low voice. She used sleeping tablets and would put two of them into her husband's coffee one day after lunch. Robin would take him out in the boat. In half an hour her husband would be asleep. Near the island the boat would overturn and the sleeping man would drown. Robin was a strong swimmer, he could easily reach the island. There he would wait until a boat saw him, or an expedition came looking for them from Dubrovnik.

'It would be murder.'

'He would know nothing.'

'I should be suspected. People have seen us together.'

'Do you think the Yugoslav police will trouble about that? They are peasants, like the people here. It is obviously an accident. Probably they do not find the body. And if they do – ' The sulky mouth curved upward in a smile. 'I will tell you something. He cannot swim.'

'*La Belle Dame sans Merci*,' he said.

'What is that?'

'A poem. It means you are ruthless. And I am in thrall to you.'

'I do not understand.'

'Yes. It means that I say yes.'

She did not reply, did not take off the dark glasses, merely looked at him and nodded. Then she took his hand and led him into the field. The pleasure that followed was intense, and almost painful.

'You're looking uncommonly fit, Nunky,' Felix said. 'A fine bronzed figure of an Englishman. You bear every sign of not having missed me. Discovered any female talent?'

'Don't be absurd.'

'Most of them look over the age of consent to me.'

'I have been out once or twice with Mrs Porter. Her husband was on your plane. They're staying at this hotel.'

'Little fat chap – I remember meeting her. A blonde piece, a bit too Nordic for me.'

'She is of German origin,' he said with what he knew to be ridiculous stiffness.

Felix looked at him and whistled. 'You sound as if you've fallen for the fair Nordic lady. I shall have to look after you, Nunky, I can see that.'

He went out with Felix in the boat that afternoon, and landed on the island. They both swam and then Felix put on his skindiving equipment and disappeared for three-quarters of an hour while Robin lay on the beach and thought about Hel. Her absence ached in him like a tooth, and when Felix reappeared and talked enthusiastically about the marvellous clarity of the water so that he could see fish swimming fifty feet below him, and said it would be quite easy to swim from the island to Dubrovnik, he heard himself becoming unreasonably snappish.

The old relationship with Felix, in which he had responded eagerly to his young cousin's coquettish facetiousness, had been replaced by a feeling of irritation. He no longer wished to be called Nunky and felt no inclination to indulge in pseudoboyish horseplay. When the young man took out a mirror and began carefully to comb his hair he felt a faint stirring of distaste.

Closing his eyes he immediately saw Hel in bed with her fat stumpy husband, forced to accept his lovemaking or – worse still – welcoming it. He got up, walked to the water's edge, began to throw stones into the sea. Felix watched him with a smiling mouth and inquisitive eyes.

She introduced him to Porter that evening. Good heavens, Robin thought as he looked at the squat paunchy little man who shook hands with him, he's *old*! However did she bring herself to marry him? It was a shock to remember that Porter was no more than two or three years older than himself, but then there was the difference between them of a man who had kept his body in trim and one who had let it go to seed.

'Hear you've been squiring Gerda around, Mr Edgley. I appreciate that. Not that she's had much spare time, with this crazy idea she had of being guide to one of my parties. Had to indulge her – I'm an indulgent man, isn't that so, my dear?' He patted her hand.

'From what I saw she was a most efficient guide.'

'Should be. Used to do it for a living, now it's for fun. I tell you what I'd like, Robin – don't mind if I call you that, I know Gerda does – what I'd like is for you and your friend to be my guests this evening. Let's go and paint this little old Communist town red.'

'Norman knows all the best places,' Gerda said without smiling.

'I should, my dear, I should. The food at this place is – well, it's hotel food and that's all you can say for it. But I know a little place where – just you leave it to me.' He winked one eye.

It was a terrible evening. They ate a special Montenegrin dinner which began with smoked ham, followed by red mullet and *raznici*, which proved to be brother to *kebab*, meat grilled on a skewer. The restaurant was set in a garden, just outside the city walls.

Porter – or as he insisted on being called, Norman – talked Serbo-Croat to waiters who responded in English. They drank slivovitz to begin with, continued with several bottles of full red Yugoslav wine, and ended with more slivovitz. Norman sent back one bottle of slivovitz with what sounded like a flow of objectionable remarks in Serbo-Croat. When the waiter shrugged and brought a bottle of another make he said triumphantly, 'You see. You have to know to get the right stuff.'

There was a band, and all three of them danced with Gerda. When Robin moved round, feeling the hard warmth of her body beneath his hand, he found the sensation almost intolerable. 'You see what he is like,' she said. 'An old man. Disgusting.'

'Not much older than I am.'

'Do not be stupid. It is not at all the same.'

'Hel, I have to see you, talk to you.'

'We cannot,' she said crisply. 'This I told you.'

'I just have to see you alone.'

'Impossible. Besides, what is there to talk about? Today is Sunday. Tomorrow after lunch.'

The dance was almost finished before he said, 'Yes.'

Felix danced with Gerda, holding her as lightly as possible, his arched nostrils slightly distended, his head held high in the manner of a horse ready to shy at what he may meet round the next corner. They seemed to exchange little conversation. Norman drank another glass of slivovitz, belched slightly.

'After this I want you to be my guests at the casino.'

'Very kind of you, but – ' Robin protested.

'Won't take but for an answer. Beautiful, isn't she?'

An alarming remark. Robin did not know what to say. 'Very charming.'

'Some men would be jealous. Not me. I like it, like her to have other friends. I understand.' He drummed with his fingers on the table. Robin realized that his host was drunk. 'I've never regretted anything – want you to know that. No regrets, no heel taps. Loveliest girl I ever saw, married her. What d'you say to that?'

Robin had no desire to say anything to it. When Gerda and Felix came back, Porter rose a little unsteadily. 'May I have the pleasure?'

She said nothing, but moved into his arms. Felix seemed about to speak, then did not. Robin watched them dancing. Porter's arm was on her bare back, and he seemed to be talking continuously.

Felix, like a man who has come to a decision, said, 'Nunky.'

Irritation spilled over. 'Once and for all, will you please understand that I do not want to be called by that ridiculous name!'

'Sorry.'

There was a disturbance among the dancers. Gerda emerged from it, half supporting her husband. Porter sat down heavily, closed his eyes, and opened them again. He insisted they must all go on to the casino, but with the headwaiter's help they got a taxi and returned to the hotel. During the taxi ride Porter began to snore. At the hotel Felix and Robin each took an arm to get him into the lift. In the bedroom Gerda removed his jacket and waved them away.

'I can put him to bed, thank you. I have done it before.'

Alone in his room Robin looked at himself in the glass. Below the abundant white hair his face was youthful. Calves and thighs were slightly withered but his body was supple, his stomach flat.

'With this body I thee worship,' he said aloud. He picked up the malacca walking stick, drew the sword from it, made a few passes at an imaginary enemy. Perhaps he too was a little drunk, he thought, as he carried on a dialogue with himself while staring into the glass.

Robin Edgley, he said, retired director of a firm manufacturing fan ventilators, you are reaching out for happiness, and there is only one way to obtain it. Make up your mind to that. But what you are about to do is crazy, another part of himself said; you are thinking of forever but she is thinking of today and tomorrow and perhaps next year. And not only is it crazy but it is wrong, opposed to all the instincts you have lived by since youth. How can you imagine that after doing wrong you will be happy? What does that matter, the first voice said, when I have been given a glimpse of eternity . . .

It was a long time before he fell asleep, and when he slept he dreamed. He was in the sea and Porter was with him, the boat overturned; he was holding Porter under the water, but instead of submitting quietly the man flailed and twisted like a fish. Then Robin gripped a throat which was smooth, young, and white instead of the swollen wrinkled column he was expecting, and it was Hel's throat he was squeezing, her face that was gaspingly lifted to his own before he too started to gasp and thrash about, conscious that life was being pressed out of him . . .

He woke with the sheet twisted round his body. The dream disturbed him. There was some element in it that he could not recall;

something had happened that his conscious mind refused to register. He looked at his watch and saw that it was only two o'clock. He did not sleep again until four . . .

In the morning Porter looked pale but cheerful. At eleven o'clock he was drinking a champagne cocktail on the terrace. 'Hear you put me to bed last night, old man, very nice of you. Sort of thing that's liable to happen, you know, first night.' He spoke like the victim of some natural disaster.

'How do you feel now?'

'I'm okay. Champagne with cognac always puts me right. Though mind you, it's got to be cognac, not this filthy local brandy. You're a fisherman, Gerda tells me.'

'I do fish, yes.'

'How about taking a boat after lunch, the two of us, eh?'

'I'm really not at all expert.'

'That's all right, neither am I. We'll just trawl for mullet and bream – what do they call 'em here, *dentex*? That's a hell of a name to give a fish.'

'What about your wife?'

'She wants to go to Lokrum, going to show it to that cousin of yours. I've been out half a dozen times myself, sooner do a bit of fishing. Bores Gerda, I know it does. Anyway, I want to have a quiet natter.'

'All right, let's go fishing.'

Later, walking round Dubrovnik with Felix, he learned a little more about the intended expedition to Lokrum. Sitting between the coupled columns in the elegant cloister of the Franciscan monastery, swinging a leg clad in tight sky-blue slacks, Felix calmly admitted that he had deliberately arranged it.

'Let's be frank about it, Porter's a slob but Hel's poison. You don't want to be mixed up with her.'

'I am not mixed up, as you put it.'

'Oh, come *on*.' Felix could not help posing, whatever his surroundings, and now he turned away from Robin so that his fine profile was outlined against the grey stone like the head on a coin. 'You follow her with your eyes wherever she goes, you treat her as though she were made of china. And believe me she's not, she's tough as old boots. I know her kind.' Robin made no reply. Felix went on. 'Even old slob Porter must spot it soon. So I thought I'd remove you from temptation this afternoon. And for the rest of the time we're here – well, they tell me there are lots of perfectly fascinating places to see on guided tours.'

'Thank you.' He knew how much Felix disliked guided tours.

'Think nothing of it. And now shall we go and look at the Museum of the Socialist Revolution? You know I've been longing to do that ever since I got here.'

They visited the museum and then went round the ramparts. Coming away from them down the narrow steps Felix slipped and fell. He got up and grimaced. He had twisted his ankle. After hobbling back to the hotel he borrowed Robin's stick. 'If I'm going to hobble I'll do it in style, look like a man of distinction.'

He was with Gerda alone for a few minutes before lunch. She wore an op art dress in zigzags that drew a great many eyes to her. Catching a brief glimpse of them both in a glass and admiring his own dark-blue linen shirt and pale trousers, he could not help thinking they made a handsome couple. She let him buy her a drink in the bar. She spoke rapidly.

'This afternoon your cousin takes me to Lokrum, so I shall be out of the way. You will drink coffee with us after lunch.'

'Hel, I don't know.'

'What?' she said sharply. 'What do you not know?'

'Whether I can go through with it.'

She finished her drink, turned on her heel, and left him.

After lunch it was Porter who stopped by their table and suggested that they all have coffee together. Really, Robin thought, if ever a man could be called the architect of his own destruction it was Porter – but no doubt Hel had put him up to it. She smiled briefly as she waited for them at the table, with coffee already poured. Porter was jovial.

'You know what made me marry Gerda? Because she's the most honest woman I ever met.'

'Is that so?' Felix made the question sound like an insult.

'You know she worked for me as a courier and I found she had a phony work permit. So when I said marry me she said, "I might consider it; this way at least I won't have to worry about a permit." '

'The kind of thing that other people think I am prepared to say.' Gerda spoke with a touch of complacency.

'And would you believe it, she made another condition. A girl in her position, making conditions with me!' He roared with laughter. ' "You're more than twice my age," she says, "you'll have the best years of my life. So what happens to me when you die?" She actually *said* that, mind you. So I told her I'd look after her, and I have.'

'Very rash.' Felix murmured the words so that Porter did not hear them, but Gerda did.

'I am a German, and Germans are realistic.' Her glance at Felix was hostile. It seemed likely to be an uncomfortable afternoon for them both on Lokrum. 'We will walk down to the boat with you. If you can manage that,' she said to Felix.

'I'm improving rapidly.' Certainly he limped much less as they went down to the harbour. Porter was carrying some fishing tackle in case, as he said, he had a chance to use it. Robin changed into clean shorts. The crisp elegance of his appearance contrasted favourably, he thought, with Porter's sweatstained shirt and general grubbiness.

The slick young man who rented the boat indicated with a slightly contemptuous air the trawling lines fixed to it, and Porter nodded and waved his hand to indicate that he did not need to be told. He climbed in, complete with fishing tackle. Robin in the stern started the outboard, and they were away. Felix and Gerda waved from the harbour.

They skirted Lokrum and moved into the open water beyond. Porter dropped his lines, lighted a pipe, and sat back. He looked what he was – a prosperous businessman carrying too much weight. Robin stared at him, unable to believe what he was going to do.

'Tell me something.' Porter's next words were inaudible. Robin almost closed the throttle, so that the boat jogged up and down on the blue water.

'What's that?'

'I like you, Robin, so I thought I ought to – ' His next words were again inaudible. 'Gerda,' he ended.

'I can't hear properly.' He closed the throttle completely, so that the motor cut out. They drifted slowly toward the island, his island, only a few hundred yards away. Porter's voice came through the stillness.

'Gerda likes to be with me. I don't say she's happy, because she's not a contented person, never would be. But don't get the wrong idea.'

'I don't know what you mean.'

'She likes me. She thinks of crazy things, does them sometimes. Ran away from me once, came back after a couple of weeks, no money. She needs money, that's her motive power, like the engine that runs this boat. So she always comes back.'

'Why are you telling me this?' There was something wrong in the boat.

'Just wanted you to understand. I'm not a fool, Robin – I may look it but I'm not. Why do you think I let her do this crazy little job out here? Think I haven't got other couriers? I knew she wanted an affair, wanted to let off steam.'

With a feeling of disbelief he saw that his cane lay just below Porter's fishing tackle. 'How did that get there?' he cried.

'What? Oh, the cane. Your cousin asked me to slip it in with my tackle, thought you might need it. In case the rocks were slippery, he said. He's a bit of a joker, that boy.'

'I don't understand.'

'About Gerda now, don't get the wrong idea, that's all. You were just a pebble who happened to be on the beach. She doesn't like men of our age. I ought to know.' Porter knocked out his pipe. 'Okay, start her up again.'

Robin tugged savagely at the cord and the outboard sprang to life. They roared through the water with the throttle wide open. When will it happen, he thought, when are the pills going to work? I can't stand much more of this. He felt weary himself, a weariness that sprang from the bad dreams and restlessness of the night.

Porter's voice seemed to come from far away and he ignored it. The island loomed larger, and momentarily he lost his grip on the tiller. Porter was scrambling toward him, his face alarmed. The boat rocked. Robin began to laugh.

'Better not upset the boat when you can't swim,' Robin warned.

'Who the hell told you I couldn't swim? All fat men can swim. Here, give me the tiller, I'll take the boat in. Are you ill?'

He wanted to say that he had the situation under control and that Porter's own wife had said he was a non-swimmer; but suddenly he was too tired to speak. *She's* made a mess of it, he thought as Porter leaned over him, pushing him to the bottom of the boat in his anxiety to steer. *She put the pills in the wrong cup*. Then he could no longer keep his eyes open.

He was in the middle of a dream which was both pleasurable and disturbing. Pleasurable because he was not fighting for breath as he had been last night, nor involved in any kind of struggle. He lay on the island beach, just a few yards from the sea, the sun burning down. Concern about the boat was removed by the sight of it carefully drawn up onto the beach.

Good old Porter! All that nonsense about the boat overturning – it must have been nonsense because Porter could swim. It had been a figment of his imagination. 'Figment,' he said happily, but could not hear the word. When he felt more energetic he would go into the sea.

Why was he disturbed then? Well, first of all, was he dreaming or not? 'Do I wake or sleep?' he asked, but again could hear no words spoken. But that was not the main thing. The main thing was that in his dream he had heard a cry. Perhaps the cry of a bird, but no bird was visible. Had the cry wakened him, or was he still dreaming?

He found it difficult to focus. The boat, like everything else, looked hazy. And now a monster appeared in the sea, vanished, reappeared briefly, then sank under the waves. What kind of monster? Dark and with nothing very distinguishable in the way of a head, a strange dark monster that writhed and splashed and vanished. The sea snake of Dubrovnik?

But surely sea snakes did not exist. I refuse to believe in you, monster, he thought, you are part of my dream. And sure enough the monster had gone – he *was* dreaming. He closed his eyes again.

When they reopened the sun was low in the sky and had lost its power. He felt cold, he knew that he was awake, and his uneasiness had increased. Where was Porter? Asleep somewhere else? It was still an effort to move, and a greater effort to think.

Had Porter gone back to Dubrovnik? There was something wrong with this idea, and he worked out what it was. Porter could not have gone to Dubrovnik or the boat would not still be on the beach.

Something else worried him, something done or said which he must try to remember. Was it perhaps that he had never even attempted what he had set out to do, that whether through his fault or hers he had failed? Oh, hell, he thought, oh, hell, oh, Hel, what is there left for us now?

And then he traced the origin of this particular uneasiness. Hel, she had said, was a special name, one that even her husband never used, and that he himself must never use in public. He had not done so. How did it happen that Felix knew the name? He remembered the conversation, which seemed long ago although it was only this morning; he even remembered the words: 'Porter's just a slob but Hel's poison.'

Desperately, like a man submerged trying to reach the surface, he strove to understand this but failed.

At the far end of the beach, jewels glittered. Were they diamonds? Through the haze of his mind came the thought that jewels are not found on beaches. If he was lying on jewels it would be proof that he was dreaming. He picked up a handful of sand, looked at it, saw that it was the characteristic powdery shingle of the coast. It did not shine, so why were diamonds flashing less than a hundred yards away?

Collect them, he thought, sell them, and he would be rich. He tried to get up, dropped on his knees again dizzily, and then managed it. Tottering like an invalid he approached the thing that shone. Half a dozen yards away he identified it. His swordstick, removed from its walking-stick sheath, was what glittered in the setting sun.

That was not surprising, for the sun always glittered on metal. But what was it doing here, and why did one end of it look dull? At the same time he noticed dark smears on his shirt.

He ran down to the sea, dipped the blade in the water. The stick itself lay a little farther back up the beach. He stared at it, stared again at the blade, began to shiver. The putt-putt of an engine came into his consciousness, and looking out to sea he saw a motor launch making for the island. A man in uniform stood in the bow, blasts sounded on a hooter.

Robin Edgley dropped to his knees and prayed that what he saw and felt might still be a dream . . .

The young Yugoslav Lieutenant of police and his assistant found the woman's husband without difficulty. The body lay a few yards back from the beach in a hollow, with stab wounds through the chest. The weapon was present, the swordstick which the man Edgley had been cleaning in the water.

As for the motive, the woman herself had admitted behaving badly with Edgley when she called on them to ask for police help because she was worried that the boat had not returned. The Lieutenant found the situation both ridiculous and disgusting. One would not have supposed – this was the only surprise – that so fussy a man as this Englishman would have been capable of so vigorous a reaction.

He offered no resistance when the Lieutenant handcuffed him. They put the dead man into the other boat, and his assistant brought it back. On the return journey the Lieutenant, who was proud of the English he had learned as a second language at school, tried without success to make conversation. The Englishman said almost nothing, except when they passed Lokrum. Then he made the suggestion that a man wearing skindiving equipment could have swum from Lokrum to the island.

'It would be possible,' said the Lieutenant. 'But what man? And my dear Mr Edgley, how would he have obtained your sword? And why were you cleaning the sword when we came?'

'It is hopeless,' Edgley said, and then after a pause, 'It was all planned, of course.'

Was this a kind of religious determinism, a reference to the God in whom Edgley no doubt believed? The Lieutenant decided to make the situation clear. 'It is hopeless to attempt to deceive. But it was a crime of passion. You will find that we understand such things. You will perhaps be only five years in prison.'

The Englishman made no reply. He said only one more thing, just before they tied up in Dubrovnik harbour. The woman waited there, her gold hair visible in the dusk. A man whom the Lieutenant knew to be Edgley's cousin waited with her. Edgley then said something which the Lieutenant, in spite of his excellent English, did not understand. 'Will you please repeat that?' he asked, a little annoyed.

'A theme for Hyacinth,' Edgley said. 'It is a theme for Hyacinth alone.'

It made no better sense the second time.

L AS IN LOOT

Lawrence Treat

I am always a bit flustered when asked for the best of anything – I don't believe that, ordinarily, there is a Number One of anything. Occasionally, yes, but in general there are a number of top stories, paintings, people, whatever. I have a few favorites of my own, and 'L as in Loot' is one of them. But to call it the *best, or my Number One favorite? Maybe. I think it's a good Mitch Taylor story, and* one *of the best. I hope you like it.*

It was the middle of the morning when Mitch Taylor drove the patrol car through the archway and into the big courtyard in the center of the municipal building. He parked in the space reserved for police, picked up the hub cap with the bullet hole – if it was a bullet hole – and stuck it under his arm.

Mitch Taylor was a stocky guy, of medium height, chesty, with a small-featured face that had enough flesh on it to take an occasional sock without getting hurt. He always looked cheerful enough but you could never tell what he was thinking, because usually it was nothing. Or anyhow, nothing you ought to know.

What he was thinking now was, he should have left the thing back in the junk yard where he'd spotted it. Because he was going on vacation tomorrow – three weeks of it up at the lake – and no new business was going to mess up that vacation.

A couple of hours ago he'd had everything figured out. He still had those summonses to serve, and he'd string those out till afternoon. Then he'd stop in at the garage and tell them there was something wrong with the steering, he didn't know exactly what, they'd better look it over. He'd hang around while they found nothing, and, when it was time to quit, they'd stop kidding themselves and he could go home and start packing.

That's what life was for. Vacations. Him and Amy and the kids, taking it easy, having a good time. A girl like Amy, she came ahead of everything else. She always had and always would.

Still, when a hub cap starts telling you stuff, you can't pass it up. You take it up to the lab and find out – from Jub Freeman, who was a wizard at things like that.

Jub, perched on a stool and hunched over a work bench, was studying something under a microscope when Mitch marched into the lab. At the sound of the door Jub swung around, grinned, and ran his hand through what was left of his hair, which was pretty well thinned out from brain-work.

'Hi,' he said energetically. 'All set to go?'

'Right after breakfast tomorrow. Bought me a hub cap, too, on account I had one missing.'

Jub glanced at the disk in Mitch's hand. 'That's the new one?' Jub asked.

Mitch shook his head. 'No, I got mine outside. Thought maybe you'd want to look this one over.'

Jub took it and examined it carefully. He tilted it so that the light caught it at an angle, then he bent down and squinted at the hole. He ran his finger along the rim, turned the cap around, and studied the inside. After a couple of minutes he put it down on his work bench.

'Chevy,' he said. 'Almost brand-new. Not driven in the winter because there's no corrosion from the salt. No wrench marks, either. Where'd you get it, Mitch?'

'Junk yard,' Mitch answered. He didn't give any details and Jub didn't ask for them. Jub merely tapped the disk as if he wanted to test the ring it gave out.

'Brand-new Chevy,' Jub said again. 'Are you thinking the same thing I am?'

'Rogan,' Mitch said promptly.

Jub nodded. Rogan was a bank robber who'd broken out of jail the month before and was still on the loose. His picture, on Wanted sheets, was all over the place and showed a squat, heavy-set guy with bulging eyes, a broad bulging forehead, and spread ears. A teller at the Farmers' Bank had identified him as one of the pair that had held up the bank a week ago and got away with $14,000, after exchanging shots with the guard. They'd been driving a brand-new, stolen Chevy; but they'd ditched it somewhere, switched cars, and smashed their way through a road block, where they'd killed a State Trooper in a gun battle and then escaped in his car. The state car had been found the next day, with the body of one of the bandits in it. But neither Rogan nor the money had showed up.

Jub fingered the hub cap. 'Didn't notice a new Chevy in that junk yard, did you?'

'When I got a vacation coming up?'

Jub got the point. 'Look,' he said. 'Why don't you go back there while I check this over? If it's a bullet, I'll know it from the trace metals, and I can drive over later and try to spot the Chevy. That way, I'll turn in the report, not you. Okay?'

Mitch nodded. 'Just so I don't get tagged with a case,' he said.

But out at the junk yard again, Mitch saw he'd taken on too much. There were acres of cars – rusty jalopies, smashed-up wrecks, cars without motors, cars without wheels, cars upside-down or lying on their sides. Killer cars – and over-age cars that had been towed here to die a natural death. They were stacked up everywhere and they overflowed into a marshy hollow wild with sumac or something . . . Easy to run a hot car in here, bust it up with an ax, and then seem to abandon it. And, maybe, with $14,000 in cash locked up in the trunk . . . It was possible – a graveyard of old cars was a pretty safe hiding place for loot.

Nevertheless Mitch realized he had pulled a boner coming back. Because after a while this Jackson fellow who ran the place would come over and ask Mitch what he was doing. Mitch would say he was just looking, or else he'd say he was doing calisthenics or something, and the guy would get nasty about it and the whole thing would end up with an arrest. Then Mitch would have to hang around tomorrow so he could show up in court.

This Jackson fellow was built like a tackling dummy, except he had muscles instead of cotton wadding inside him. An hour ago he'd told Mitch to fork over 50 cents and go out and find his own hub cap. Tough cookie, this Jackson.

Any other time Mitch would have taken it all in stride and walked in without any worries, except maybe was there any poison ivy around. But now he stared at the shack that was supposed to be an office, over there at the other end of the lot. There was no sign of Jackson, so the hell with him.

Mitch had gone about 20 or 30 feet, watching his step so he didn't trip over the rusty springs and fenders and stuff, when the kid's voice sounded out. 'Boom-boom – you're dead!'

Mitch swung around and saw this brat with the toy gun. He was maybe six years old, but for a second or two that mug of his had wrinkles and the gun was real, so Mitch froze.

There couldn't be two faces like that – the same bulging eyes and spread ears and oversized forehead. For that second Mitch felt as if he were seeing Rogan cut down to size. Then the kid's eyes seemed to get a little smaller, the ears weren't quite so spread out, and the forehead looked almost normal. Mitch wasn't sure now, except the impression stuck.

Yes, this was Rogan's kid. He was sure of it.

Mitch let out a smile, lifted his hands and said, hamming it up, 'You got me, kid. Now what?'

The kid stared, bug-eyed. Mitch, real friendly-like, said, 'What's your name, huh?'

The kid didn't answer.

You can chase a kid in the open and catch him easy, but six-year-olds are slippery and they get through narrow spaces where a grown man can trip and land flat on his puss. And by the time Mitch could get hold of the kid and drag him off, he would have Jackson on his neck, and then what?

So Mitch said, 'You know what?'

The kid didn't move.

Mitch lowered his hands and said, 'I give up. Now you take me to jail and lock me up.' And, trying to make like a crook caught with the goods, he approached the kid.

'Pretend that's your car over there,' Mitch said softly. 'You bring me over there and make me drive, see? You just keep your gun on me, and I can't do a thing about it.'

The kid still stood his ground, still didn't say anything. Maybe he was scared or maybe they'd left the brains out of him and he didn't have enough sense to scram. Anyhow, all he did was say 'Boom-boom' again, but in a frightened kind of a whisper.

So Mitch put his arm around him, and when the kid tried to pull back, Mitch picked him up and said, 'What's your name, huh? What are you doing here?'

The kid shook his head and dropped the toy gun. Mitch picked it up, stuck it in his pocket, and brought the kid over to the squad car and settled him down on the front seat. Mitch chattered all the way back to headquarters, but the kid didn't say a word. His vocabulary was *boom-boom*, and that was it.

He took Mitch's hand when they got out of the car, and he kept hanging on tight while they walked down the corridor and through the door marked Homicide Squad. There, a couple of the boys were kidding around with the blonde who did secretarial work for the lieutenant.

They stopped talking at the sight of Mitch and the kid. Bankhart said, 'Holy hell – did you make a pinch?'

The blonde smiled and bent down and said to the kid in a soft, sugary voice, 'Hello. What's your name?'

Junior's face puckered up like a walnut and he burst out crying. Mitch, still holding his hand, said, 'He don't talk much. Lieutenant in?'

The girl nodded. Mitch, dragging this yowling brat along with him, crossed the room, knocked on the lieutenant's door, and went in.

Lieutenant Decker had the smallest office and the biggest collection of junk in the Police Department. He went in for souvenirs of his cases and for magazines on criminology, and he stacked them up on the filing cabinets and the shelves and the window sill and the extra chair, along with the official reports he was always in the middle of reading. He swung around and looked at Mitch and the kid as if they both belonged in the loony bin, which maybe they did.

'Well?' – Decker said. But the kid let out a blast and kept pumping it out, and Decker put his hands over his ears. When the kid finally stopped for breath, Mitch had a chance to say something.

'Take a gander at him,' Mitch said. 'What does he look like?'

'Like a damn nuisance,' Decker said. 'What's the idea?'

Things weren't working out exactly the way Mitch had intended. He'd figured the gang outside might be a little slow on the trigger, but the lieutenant ought to be sharper. Still, Mitch had to admit that a six-year-old, with his face screwed up and his heart in shreds on account maybe he wanted his mother, didn't look much like Public Enemy Number One.

All Mitch said was, 'He got lost.'

'Brother!' the lieutenant exclaimed. 'You've pulled some screwy ones, but this time – wow! Listen, Taylor. In case nobody ever told you, the Homicide Squad handles crimes of violence against the person, but there's a Lost and Found Department and a Juvenile Bureau, and you can classify the kid either way. Use your own judgment.' Decker grinned. 'What's really on your mind?'

Mitch came straight out with it. 'He's Rogan's kid.'

Decker flipped back in his chair and almost dumped over. 'Did he tell you that?'

'No. But when he quits crying, he looks like Rogan.'

'And when does that happen?' Decker asked.

'Lieutenant,' Mitch said, 'this looks like a lead. I could be wrong, but do you want to bet on it?'

Decker nodded. 'Yes,' he said. 'How much?'

Mitch didn't take the bait. 'What I want,' he said, 'is we should put the kid's description on the teletype and on the municipal radio. A kind of appeal. Then somebody comes and picks him up, and we tail whoever it is.'

Decker frowned, searched his soul, and decided to give Mitch a break. 'All right,' Decker said. 'You're going on vacation tomorrow, you'll be out of my hair. Tell the girl to send it out.'

'Thanks,' Mitch said, and went outside.

The kid quieted down a little, but he wasn't happy. He needed somebody to blow his nose and tie his left shoelace, which the blonde proceeded to do. Meanwhile, Mitch pulled a form from the supply shelf behind the door and began filling out the description: age, color of eyes, color of hair, height, weight, clothing worn, where found, identifying scars or marks, if any, and so on.

He handed the sheets to the blonde and told her what the lieutenant had said. Then Mitch took the kid upstairs to Jub.

Jub turned out to be no smarter than the others. He frowned at the kid and said, 'Who's he?'

'Rogan,' Mitch said.

'Doesn't look like him.'

'You know how kids are,' Mitch said. 'They change. They look like one thing one minute, and a couple of minutes later they're different.'

'All right,' Jub said, smiling. 'Make him look like Rogan.'

Mitch perched the kid on a stool, gave it a spin, and turned his back. 'What about the hub cap?' he asked.

'A .38 slug, and the car was moving fairly fast when it was hit. What about that Chevy?'

'I found the kid, instead,' Mitch said. 'I figure Rogan was hiding out back there and used the kid for a lookout. All the kid had to do was make a nuisance of himself, which he's good at, and that would warn Rogan so he could beat it. I picked up Junior on account somebody has to come around and claim him.'

'Sure,' Jub said. 'His mother.'

For the next couple of hours Mitch hung around kind of nursemaiding the kid. Word spread that Taylor had come up with a lulu, and guys from other parts of the building dropped in to see.

Mitch explained cheerfully. 'He's a child prodigy. Going to grow up and be a mental defective. No work, no trouble. State'll take care of him.'

The kid sat in a corner and played with a busted pinball machine. Mitch almost got to like him, because he was a guarantee against a last-minute assignment. So Mitch was figuring on staying put until five, and then he could blow.

But the kid's mother walked in, and she had brown, bulging eyes. Her forehead was sort of wide and her ears almost stuck out of her hairdo. She was a dead ringer for the kid.

She gave her name as Mrs Leonard Jackson and she said her husband ran an automobile junk yard and her child had been playing there when he'd disappeared. And she thought something ought to be done about it.

She was nervous and scared and determined, all at the same time. She threatened to bring a kidnaping charge, but she wouldn't sign a complaint and nobody could figure out exactly what she was after.

Finally the lieutenant got fed up and gave her a lecture on how she shouldn't let a six-year-old run around loose in a junk yard where he could hurt himself or get lost or something and she was lucky they didn't bring charges against her and her husband for not taking proper care of their child.

She said they wouldn't dare say that to her husband, they were taking advantage of her because she was a woman, and she up and left. As soon as she was gone, the lieutenant burst out laughing. And the ribbing that Mitch got after that was just a beginning. He figured these wisecracks, they'd still be coming at him three weeks from now, when he got back from the lake.

Mitch let them ride him – there was nothing he could do about it; but he kept remembering that hub cap and how the kid had looked like Rogan when he aimed the toy gun. And how maybe that Chevy and the $14,000 in loot *were* in the junk yard. And finally, if a kid looked like his mother, why couldn't he look like his old man, too?

So Mitch, partly because he had this idea in the back of his head and partly because he was sick of being kidded, wanted an excuse to beat it. When he felt the toy gun still there in his pocket, he took the thing out and said maybe he ought to return it. The lieutenant said sure, go ahead, why not?

Before Mitch left, he went upstairs to the lab and told Jub what the score was and asked him to take a trip down to the junk yard. Because, even if Mitch had made a mistake about the kid, that bullet hole was real and there was still a chance of locating the Chevy. So Mitch arranged to meet Jub there and help him look.

The Jackson address was in the west end of town, not too far from the yard. The house was in a fairly good residential section and there were two cars in the driveway, one of them the jalopy Mrs Jackson had driven down to headquarters and the other a brand-new job.

Because of the new car and because nobody who ran a broken-down junk yard could afford to live in a house like this, Mitch had a funny feeling as he walked up the short path to the front door and rang the bell. The Jackson female opened the door, and she looked just as scared and nervous as she had been at headquarters.

She kind of shrank back from Mitch and then she said, 'We just phoned and asked to have you come and bring it, and they said you were on your way.' She raised her voice and called out, 'Len, he's here.'

Jackson came from somewhere in the rear of the house. 'Come on in,' he said. He'd been sullen and itching for a scrap when Mitch had bought that hub cap this morning, but now the guy was all smiles and tail-wagging. So he wanted something, and the question was what.

Mitch stepped inside and took the imitation gun out of his pocket. 'Junior forgot his toy,' he said.

'That's what we wanted, that's what we called about,' Jackson said. He grabbed it, and Mitch wondered if maybe the thing meant something and he'd missed out on it.

He asked directly. 'What's so important about it?'

Mrs Jackson answered. 'It's Junior's favorite toy, and he's unhappy without it. He just can't bear to lose it.'

'Yeah,' Mitch said, thinking how Junior had forgotten all about it ever since Mitch had stuck it in his pocket, and how neither of the Jacksons bothered to give it to the kid now.

So the toy gun was a handle to get Mitch here; they wanted to talk to him and now they were tense and edgy, but Mitch still couldn't figure out what the play was.

Jackson said, 'How about a drink?'

And Mrs Jackson said, 'Yes, what would you like?'

'Make it a beer,' Mitch said. He kept looking around the room, but he found nothing out of the ordinary, except that the place didn't look used – no personal stuff lying around, as if they'd just got here and hadn't had time to get settled.

The Jackson dame went out to the kitchen for the beer. Jackson and Mitch sat down and Mitch said, 'How come you're not working? Yard closed up?'

'Too worried about the kid to bother with business,' Jackson said. 'I been sitting here and stewing around, wondering what happened to him.'

'Must have been tough,' Mitch said. But if the guy had been worried, why hadn't he gone up to headquarters instead of sending his wife?

'What was the idea of you grabbing him?' Jackson asked.

Mitch shrugged off the question with the gesture of a guy who had nothing but innocence inside him. 'He was lost,' Mitch said. 'I felt sorry for the little fella.'

'How'd you get along with him?' Jackson asked.

'Okay.'

'I mean, did he talk much? Kids are funny sometimes. What did he say?'

'A little of this and a little of that,' Mitch said, and he began to understand. Jackson was worried whether the kid had given something away – so worried that he had to find out.

The guy made some remark about the weather and about the neighborhood, and Mitch asked Jackson how long he'd lived here and Jackson switched the subject without answering direct. And all the time Mitch's mind was churning, trying to figure out the real reason Jackson had phoned for him. Besides wanting to know if the kid had said anything, Jackson hoped Mitch would go back and say the Jacksons were nice normal people, that they had nothing to hide, had even invited Mitch in and given him a beer.

Which meant they weren't normal and had plenty to hide.

Then it hit Mitch with a jolt that they were covering up – covering up for Rogan.

The kid was Rogan's, and Rogan wasn't far away. He'd come back for the loot. Jackson was a stand-in for him and was putting on an act to fool the police, and maybe the dame was Rogan's wife and maybe she wasn't, but sure as hell Jackson wasn't the kid's father. So if Mitch could slip in a question to show it one way or the other, he'd be on first base, anyhow.

He leaned back in his chair, as if he had nothing in mind except a little small talk. 'That kid of yours,' he said. 'He go to school?'

'Sure. What about it?'

'I was wondering what grade he's in.'

'What do you think?' Jackson snapped. Obviously the subject was a touchy one and he forgot about being polite. 'He's six years old. Think he's in high school?'

'Naah,' Mitch said. 'I thought he was in college, maybe.'

Jackson picked up the toy gun and kind of hefted it, balancing it and fingering it as if he were plenty used to guns. 'You got a real sense of humor,' he said.

'Yeah,' Mitch said. 'What school's he in?'

'Public school,' Jackson said, spitting the words out.

'Sure. Which one?'

It was the key question. Any father knew what school his kid went to. So if the kid was Jackson's and everything was on the up-and-up, he'd rattle it off without even thinking. But if he couldn't, then Mitch was right all the way.

Jackson turned around and called out to the kitchen. 'Hey, Betty – our friend wants to know what school Junior goes to.'

She came out of the kitchen to answer. 'P.S. 45,' she said. 'And we don't have any beer.'

'That's okay,' Mitch said. He looked at his watch and stood up. 'Time for me to blow, anyhow.' And he left.

But outside, sitting in the car, he saw he had a problem.

He couldn't let this ride – not when there was a chance he had a lead on a cop killer. On the other hand, if Mitch told the lieutenant that this was nothing but a theory on Mitch's part, the lieutenant would either laugh it off or else tell Mitch to stay with it until he got something – which meant goodbye tomorrow.

So Mitch was hooked, and he knew it. His only hope was that Jub would dig up something at the junk yard that would blow the case wide open today . . . or else that Jackson would scare and lead the way straight to Rogan.

Mitch started the car, drove to the corner, and parked on the side street where he had a full view of the Jackson house.

He waited about 10 minutes, and then he saw Jackson come out and get in the new car, nose it out the driveway, and head up the street, past Mitch. Mitch followed, staying maybe 50 feet behind and letting himself be seen. After a couple of blocks Jackson pulled up at the curb and got out of his car. Mitch stopped directly behind and waited for Jackson to step alongside.

'What's the big idea?' Jackson said. Being polite hadn't worked; it hadn't fooled Mitch, so Jackson was going to be nasty again. 'You tailin' me?' he demanded.

Mitch shrugged. 'Maybe.'

'What for?'

'You guess.'

'Look, copper – I got a right to go where I want to.'

'Sure,' Mitch said. 'Anybody stopping you?'

'Just lay off. Turn around and beat it.'

Mitch tapped his hand on the steering wheel, and Jackson had sense enough to see there was nothing he could do.

'Okay,' the big guy mumbled. 'Meet me in my office, we can talk there. I'll be waiting inside.' And Jackson wheeled, marched back to his car, and took off. Mitch stayed behind, still at a 50-foot distance.

It didn't take much brain power to dope things out. Rogan was hiding in the office, and when Mitch stepped inside, they'd gun him down and take their chances. Because the way things stood, what did they have to lose?

Jackson kept going, nice and easy, and Mitch kept tagging along behind. He'd find Jub at the yard and pick him up. And what to do then was a tricky business. They couldn't take the chance of going into that shack, they had no grounds for an arrest, and at the same time they couldn't just kiss the thing off and go home.

If it wasn't for that vacation of Mitch's he'd have hung around and kept an eye on Jackson while Lieutenant Decker ordered an investigation. At the school, from neighbors. Check Mrs Jackson, check the files. And after a while they'd know. Except that Mitch was planning to go up to the lake tomorrow, and how could you tell how long an investigation like that would take?

So he rolled along and tried to cook up an angle. And all he drew was a blank.

The road was deserted out here, a long stretch with the marsh on one side and the junk yard and its wrecked cars strung along the other. Jub's police car – its insignia plainly marked – was parked on the macadam, and a couple of hundred feet away Jub was hard at work. He had a crowbar and was forcing open the trunk of a car – a Chevy.

What happened next took Mitch by surprise.

He was expecting Jackson to turn into the dirt road that led to the office-shack, but the guy went right on past, still going slow. Maybe he expected Mitch to stop and talk to Jub, but Mitch didn't. Mitch gave a blast on his horn, blinked his lights, then touched the siren button to attract Jub's attention. When Jub turned around, Mitch waved for him to come over.

Jackson reacted to that siren as if he were wired for sound. His car seemed to jerk and leap forward, and he had a hundred-yard lead by the time Mitch realized it.

Mitch gave his car the gun, locked the siren button in the On position, and picked up his radio phone. He spoke crisply.

'Signal Nine-Nine,' he said. 'Gray Mercury going west on Lincoln.' Then he slapped the phone back in its cradle and concentrated on driving. Signal Nine-Nine would bring out every radio car and every State Trooper on patrol, and Lincoln Avenue would be blocked off. But how soon?

Mitch, with the wail of the siren and the roar of air and the scream of tires in his ears, drove like a speed demon. Four miles to the turnpike. Jackson would cover it in three minutes maybe. Three minutes wasn't long enough to mobilize and set up a road block, and Mitch had to hang on until help arrived.

Jackson, with that head-start he'd got by speeding up first, was now a couple of hundred yards ahead, and gaining. He swung out to the left abruptly, whizzed past a green car, then careened back to the right. Mitch saw a truck coming toward him, filling the opposite lane.

Mitch realized immediately that he was in a helpless position. Braking easy wouldn't do any good, and braking hard would probably throw him into a skid – and he'd lose Jackson, besides. So the green car ahead of him or the truck coming toward him had to save his hide – but what the hell was the matter with them? They could see him, they could hear his siren. Didn't they know they were supposed to pull over and give a cop room?

He gritted his teeth, thought of Amy, of Jackson, of the lake, of everything, of nothing. A green car and a truck, a couple of damn fools who'd lost their head or didn't know the rules. Mitch tensed; maybe he prayed and maybe he didn't. He had no idea. And then the green car ahead of him started doing tricks in slow motion.

The tail lights went red, the turning signal blinked, but for a left turn. The guy at the wheel was rattled and doing everything wrong. The left blinker went off and the right blinker came on. Mitch was practically on top of the car when the driver finally edged over to the right and slipped onto the shoulder of the road.

Mitch whizzed by, but he never knew how he made it. He felt the sweat pouring down into his eyes and he wanted to wipe it off. But his hands wouldn't move, they were locked tight on the wheel. Up ahead Jackson was still gaining.

Mitch came out of it slow, and in a funny way he was able to relax a little, to think, to move his fingers again. He brushed off the sweat, decided the hell with this, he'd slow down, save his own life, and let the other boys close in on Jackson. The guy was trapped, wasn't he?

Then Mitch saw the turnpike overpass ahead, saw Jackson's brake lights flash on. Jackson's car seemed to sway, flutter, almost go off the road as it careened into the approach to the turnpike.

Mitch applied his brakes gradually. He didn't want to go shooting into turnpike traffic at 80 – or at 60 or 40 either. And once Jackson was out there, the State Troopers could worry. Mitch didn't even have jurisdiction.

Above the dull roar of wind and tires Mitch heard the crash. He had a sick, empty feeling in the pit of his stomach, and he hoped nobody else was involved in the smash-up. He slowed up, and was doing a modest 30 when he sighted the smoldering wreckage where Jackson had rammed almost head-on into a retaining wall . . .

Mitch got home around seven. Amy was giving the kids supper, and the hallway of the apartment was jammed with suitcases and bundles. Amy came flying into his arms as he opened the door.

'Mitchell,' she said, holding on tight, 'I was getting worried. I couldn't imagine what kept you so late.'

'We got that bank robber,' he said. 'Jub found the loot in an old car in the junk yard, and the guy killed himself trying to get away.'

'Rogan?' she said.

Mitch shook his head. 'Naah. That's what we thought at first. But this bank teller had Rogan on the brain, like lots of other people did. I don't want to blame the guy for making a mistake.'

'Of course not,' Amy said.

'Well, when somebody held up that bank, the teller thought he recognized Rogan. Only Rogan had nothing to do with it. We just got word they nabbed him out west.'

'Then who did it?'

'Guy named Jackson. We caught up with him this afternoon. He got rattled when he was followed and when he saw Jub searching cars for the money. He knew we were closing in, so he tried a getaway and ran into a stone wall.'

'Well, you can tell me all about it later. Do you know you forgot to write that note to Joey's school? The one the PTA wants everybody to send, asking for better lunches. I promised you'd write. As a policeman, what you say carries weight.'

'Sure,' he said. 'I'll take care of it right away. Amy, does Joey look like me?'

She laughed at the question. 'Sometimes,' she said. 'Some people think so and others don't. Why?'

'Nothing,' he said. 'I better go write that note. Only – look, Amy, what's the name of the school? I mean, what's the number?'

A GREAT SIGHT

Janwillem van de Wetering

'Send me your best story,' I was asked, 'and explain why you think it is your best.' Giving orders, though, is often easier than following them. I've written a lot of stories, about love and horror and policework; I've even imagined tales, sneaking across the borders of imagination and bringing back stuff that, perhaps, should never be told. They could all have been better, I think, when I read them again, and I blush when I see how they could have been improved.

Making a choice is always difficult, so I solved the problem by writing a new story, using for its plot a tale I heard two rough characters sharing at the bar in town. They were whispering and grinning, and banging their glasses on the counter. Maybe their tale was true; it could have been, for it's odd country out here, much of it beyond the reach of the law.

The theme of their story stunned me, and I had to write various versions before I came up with something that I thought might do. The general drift of the story fits in with my own ideas about justice. As you'll see, it all ends happily. I believe that all tales should have happy endings, for there has to be a light at the end of the tunnel. Otherwise, the creation wouldn't be so beautiful.

No, it wasn't easy. It took a great deal of effortful dreaming to get where I am now. Where I am now is Moose Bay, on the Maine coast, which is on the east of the United States of America, in case you haven't been looking at maps lately. Moose Bay is long and narrow, bordered by two peninsulas and holding some twenty square miles of water. I've lived on the south shore for almost thirty years now, always alone – if you don't count a couple of old cats – and badly crippled. Lost the use of my legs I have, thirty years ago, and that was my release and my ticket to Moose Bay. I've often wondered whether the mishap was really an accident. Sure enough, the fall was due to faulty equipment (a new strap that broke) and quite beyond my will. The telephone company that employed me acknowledged their responsibility easily enough, paying me handsomely so that I could be comfortably out of work for the rest of my life. But didn't I, perhaps, dream myself into that fall? You see, I wasn't exactly happy being a telephone repairman. Up one post and down another, climbing or slithering up and down forever, day after day, and not in the best of climates. For years I did that and there was no way I could see in which the ordeal would ever end. So I began to dream of a way out, and of where I would go. To be able to dream is a gift. My father didn't have the talent. No imagination the old man had, in Holland he lived, where I was born, and he had a similar job to what I would have later. He was a window-cleaner and I guess he could only visualize death, for when *he* fell it was the last thing he ever did. I survived, with mashed legs. I never dreamed of death, I dreamed of the great sights I would still see, whisking myself to a life on a rocky coast, where I would be alone, maybe with a few old cats, in a cedar logcabin with a view of the water, the sky, and a line of trees on the other shore. I would see, I dreamed, rippling waves or the mirror-like surface of a great expanse of liquid beauty on a windless day. I never gave that up, the possibility of seeing great sights, and I dreamed myself up here, where everything is as I thought it might be, only better.

Now don't get me wrong, I'm not your dreamy type. No long hair and beads for me, no debts unpaid or useless things just lying about in the house. Everything is spic-and-span with me; the kitchen works, there's an ample supply of staples, each in their own jar, I have good vegetables from the garden, an occasional bird I get with the shotgun, and fish caught off my dock. I can't walk so well, but I get about on my crutches and the pick-up has been changed so that I can drive it with my hands. No fleas on the cats, either, and no smell from the outhouse. I have all I need and all within easy reach. There must be richer people in the world (don't I see them sometimes, sailing along in their hundred-foot skyscrapers?), but I don't have to envy them. May they live happily for as long as it takes; I'll just sit here and watch the sights from my porch.

Or I watch them from the water. I have an eight-foot dory and it rows quite well in the bay if the waves aren't too high, for it *will* ship water when the weather gets rough. There's much to see when I go rowing. A herd of harbor seals lives just out of my cove and they know me well, coming to play around my boat as soon as I sing out to them. I bring them a rubber ball that they push about for a bit, and throw even, until they want to go about their own business again and bring it back.

I've named them all and can identify the individuals when they frolic in the spring, or raise their tails and heads, lolling in the summer sun.

I go out most good days, for I've taken it upon myself to keep this coast clean. Garbage drifts in, thrown in by the careless, off ships I suppose, and by the city people, the unfortunates who never look at the sights. I get beer cans to pick up in my net, and every variety of plastic container, boards with rusty nails in them and occasionally a complete vessel, made out of crumbly foam. I drag it all to the same spot and burn the rubbish. Rodney, the fellow I share Moose Bay with – he lives a mile down from me in a tarpapered shack – makes fun of me when I perform my duty. He'll come by in his smart powerboat, flat on the water and sharply pointed, with a loud engine pushing it that looks like three regular outboards stacked on top of each other. Rodney can really zip about in that thing. He's a thin ugly fellow with a scraggly black beard and big slanted eyes above his crooked nose. He's from here, of course, and he won't let me forget his lawful nativity. Much higher up the scale than me, he claims, for what am I but some itinerant, an alien washed up from nowhere, tolerated by the locals? If I didn't happen to be an old codger, and lame, Rodney says, he would drown me like he does his kittens. Hop, into the sack, weighed down with a good boulder, and away with the mess. But being what I am, sort of human in a way, he puts up with my presence for a while, provided I don't trespass on his bit of the shore, crossing the high tide line, for then he'll have to shoot me, with the deer rifle he now uses for poaching. Rodney has a vegetable garden, too, even though he doesn't care for greens. The garden is a trap for deer so that he can shoot them from his shack, preferably at night, after he has frozen them with a flashlight.

There are reasons for me not to like Rodney too much. He shot my friend, the killer whale that used to come here some summers ago. Killer whales are a rare sight on this coast, but they do pop up from time to time. They're supposed to be wicked animals, that will push your boat over and gobble you up when you're thrashing about, weighed down by your boots and your oilskins. Maybe they do that, but my friend didn't do it to me. He used to float alongside my dory, that he could have tipped with a single flap of his great triangular tail. He would roll over on his side, all thirty feet of him, and grin lazily from the corner of his huge curved mouth. I could see his big gleaming teeth and mirror my face in his calm humorous eye, and I would sing to him. I haven't got a good loud voice, but I would hum away, making up a few words here and there, and he'd lift a flipper in appreciation and snort if my song wasn't long enough for his liking. Every day that killer whale came to me; I swear he was waiting for me out in the bay, for as soon as I'd splash my oars I'd see his six-foot fin cut through the waves, and a moment later his black and white head, always with that welcoming grin.

Now we don't have any electricity down here, and kerosene isn't as cheap as it used to be, so maybe Rodney was right when he said that he shot the whale because he needed the blubber. Blubber makes good fuel, Rodney says. Me, I think he was wrong, for he never got the blubber anyway. When he'd shot the whale, zipping past it in the powerboat, and got the animal between the eyes with his deer rifle, the whale just sank. I never saw its vast body wash up. Perhaps it didn't die straight away and could make it to the depth of the ocean, to die there in peace.

He's a thief, too, Rodney is. He'll steal anything he can get his hands on, to begin with his welfare. There's nothing wrong with Rodney's back but he's stuffed a lot of complaints into it, enough so that the doctors pay attention. He collects his check and his food stamps, and he gets his supplies for free. There's a town, some fifty miles further along, and they employ special people there to give money to the poor, and counsellors to listen to pathetic homemade tales, and there's a society that distributes gifts on holidays. Rodney even gets his firewood every year, brought by young religious men on a truck; they stack it right where Rodney points – no fee.

'Me against the world,' Rodney says, 'for the world owes me a living. I never asked to be born but here I am, and my hands are out.' He'll be drinking when he talks like that, guzzling my Sunday bourbon on my porch, and he'll point his long finger at me. 'You some sort of Kraut?'

I say I'm Dutch. The Dutch fought the Krauts during the war; I fought a bit myself until they caught me and put me in a camp. They were going to kill me, but then the Americans came. 'Saved you, did we?' Rodney will say, and fill up his glass again. 'So you owe us now, right? So how come you're living off the fat of this land, you with the crummy legs?' He'll raise his glass and I'll raise mine.

Rodney lost his wife. He still had her when I settled in my cabin, I got to talk to her at times and liked her fine. She would talk to Rodney, about his ways, and he would leer at her, and he was still leering when she was found at the bottom of a cliff. 'Never watched where she was going,' Rodney said to the sheriff, who took the corpse away. The couple had a dog, who was fond of Rodney's wife and unhappy when she was gone. The dog would howl at night and keep Rodney awake, but the dog happened to fall off the cliff, too. Same cliff. Maybe I should have reported the coincidence to the authorities, but it wasn't much more than a coincidence and, as Rodney says, accidents will happen. Look at me, I fell down a telephone post, nobody pushed *me*, right? It was a brand-new strap that snapped when it shouldn't have; a small event, quite beyond my control.

No, I never went to the sheriff and I've never stood up to Rodney. There's just the two of us on Moose Bay. He's the bad guy who'll tip his garbage into the bay and I'm the in-between guy who's silly enough to pick it up. We also have a good guy, who lives at the end of the north peninsula, at the tip, facing the ocean. Michael his name is, Michael the lobsterman. A giant of a man, Michael is, with a golden beard and flashing teeth. I can see his smile when his lobster boat enters the bay. The boat is one of these old-fashioned jobs, sturdy and white and square, puttering along at a steady ten knots in every sort of weather. Michael's got a big winch on it, for hauling up the heavy traps, and I can see him taking the lobsters out and putting the bait in and throwing them back. Michael has some thousand traps, all along the coast, but his best fishing is here in Moose Bay. Over the years we've got to know each other and I sometimes go out with him, much further than the dory can take me. Then we see the old squaws flock in, the diver ducks that look as if they've flown in from a Chinese painting, with their thin curved tailfeathers and delicately-drawn wings and necks. Or we watch the big whales, snorting and spouting, and the haze on the horizon where the sun dips, causing undefinably soft colors, or we just smell the clear air together, coming to cool the forests in summer. Michael knows Rodney, too, but he isn't the gossipy kind. He'll frown when he sees the power boat lurking in Moose Bay and gnaw his pipe before he turns away. When Michael doesn't stop at my dock he'll wave and make some gesture, in lieu of conversation – maybe he'll hold his hands close together to show me how far he could see when he cut through the fog, or he'll point at a bird flying over us, a heron in slow flight, or a jay, hurrying from shore to shore, gawking and screeching, and I'll know what he means.

This Michael is a good guy, I knew it the first time I saw his silhouette on the lobster boat, and I've heard good stories about him, too. A knight in shining armor who has saved people about to drown in storms, or marooned and sick on the islands. A giant and a genius, for he's built his own boat, and his gear – even his house, a big sprawling structure out of driftwood on pegged beams. And he'll fight when he has to, for it isn't always cosy here. He'll be out in six-foot waves and I've seen him when the bay is frozen up, excepting the channel where the current rages, with icicles on his beard and snow driving against his bow – but he'll still haul up his traps.

I heard he was out in the last war, too, flying an airplane low above the jungle, and he still flies now, on Sundays, for the National Guard.

Rodney got worse. I don't know what devil lives in that man but the fiend must have been thrown out of the lowest hells. Rodney likes new games and he thought it would be fun to chase me a bit. My dory sits pretty low in the water, but there are enough good days here and I can get out quite a bit. When I do Rodney will wait for me, hidden behind the big rocks east of my cove, and he'll suddenly appear, revving his engine, trailing a high wake. When his curly waves hit me I have to bail for my life, and as soon as I'm done the fear will be back, for he'll be after me again.

I didn't quite know what to do then. Get a bigger boat? But then he would think of something else. There are enough games he can play. He knows my fondness for the seals, he could get them one by one, as target practice. There's my vegetable garden, too, close to the track; he could back his truck into it and get my cats as an afterthought, flattening them into the gravel, for they're slow these days, careless with old age. The fear grabbed me by the throat at night, as I watched my ceiling, remembering his dislike of my cabin and thinking how easily it would burn, being made of old cedar with a roof of shingles. I knew it was him who took the battery out of my truck, making me hitchhike to town for a new one. He was also sucking my gas, but I keep a drum of energy near the house. Oh, I'm vulnerable here all right, with the sheriff coming down only once a year. Suppose I talk to the law, suppose the law talks to Rodney, suppose *I* fall down that cliff, too?

I began to dream again, like I had done before, when I was still climbing the telephone posts like a demented monkey. I was bored then, hopelessly bored, and now I was hopelessly afraid. Hadn't I dreamed my way out once before? Tricks can be repeated.

My dream gained strength; it had to, for Rodney was getting rougher. His powerboat kept less distance, went faster. I couldn't see myself sticking to the land. I need to get out on the bay, to listen to the waves lapping the rocks, to hear the seals blow when they clear their nostrils, to hear the kingfishers and the squirrels whirr in the trees on shore, to spot the little ringnecked ducks, busily investigating the shallows, peering eagerly out of their tufted heads. There are the quiet herons stalking the mudflats and the ospreys whirling slowly; there are eagles, even, diving and splashing when the alewives run from the brooks. Would I have to potter about in the vegetable patch all the time, leaning on a crutch while pushing a hoe with my free hand?

I dreamed up a bay free of Rodney. There was a strange edge to the dream – some kind of quality there that I couldn't quite see, but it was splendid, a great sight and part of my imagination although I couldn't quite make it out.

One day, fishing off my dock, I saw Michael's lobster boat nosing into the cove: I waved and smiled and he waved back, but he didn't smile.

He moored the boat and jumped onto the jetty, light as a great cat, touching my arm. We walked up to my porch and I made some strong coffee.

'There's a thief,' Michael said, 'stealing my lobsters. He used to take a few, few enough to ignore maybe, but now he's taking too many.'

'Oho,' I said, holding my mug. Michael wouldn't be referring to me. Me? Steal lobsters? How could I ever haul up a trap? The channel is deep in the bay. A hundred feet of cable and a heavy trap at the end of it, never. I would need a winch, like Rodney has on his power boat.

Besides, doesn't Michael leave me a lobster every now and then? Lying on my dock in the morning, its claws neatly tied with a bit of yellow string?

'Any idea?' he asked.

'Same as yours,' I said, 'but he's hard to catch. The power boat is fast. He nips out of the bay before he does his work, to make sure you aren't around.'

'Might get the warden,' Michael said, 'and then he might go to jail, and come out again, and do something bad.'

I agreed. 'Hard to prove, it would be,' I said. 'A house burns down, yours or mine. An accident maybe.'

Michael left. I stayed on the porch, dreaming away, expending some power. A little power goes a long way in a dream.

It happened the next day, a Sunday it was. I was walking to the shore, for it was low tide and I wanted to see the seals on their rocks. It came about early, just after sunrise. I heard an airplane. A lot of airplanes come by here. There's the regular commuter plane from the town to the big city, and the little ones the tourists fly in summer, and the flying club. There are also big planes, dirtying up the sky, high up, some of them are Russians, they say; the National Guard has to be about, to push them back. The big planes rumble, but this sound was different, light but deadly, far away still. I couldn't see the plane, but when I did it was coming silently, ahead of its own sound, it was that fast. Then it slowed down, surveying the bay.

I've seen fighter planes during World War II, Germans and Englishmen flew them, propeller jobs that would spin around each other above the small Dutch lakes, until one of the planes came down, trailing smoke. Jet planes I only saw later, here in America. They looked dangerous enough, even while they gambolled about, and I felt happy watching them, for I was in the States and they were protecting me from the bad guys lurking in the east.

This airplane was a much advanced version of what I had seen in the late '40s. Much longer it was, and sleek and quiet as it lost height, aiming for the channel. A baby-blue killer, with twin rudders, sticking up elegantly far behind the large gleaming canopy up front, reflecting the low sunlight. I guessed her to be seventy feet long, easily the size of the splendid yachts of the rich summer people, but there was no pleasure in her; she was all functional, programmed for swift pursuit and destruction only. I grinned when I saw her American stars, set in circles, with a striped bar sticking out at each side. When she was closer I thought I could see the pilot, all wrapped up in his tight suit and helmet, the living brain controlling this deadly superfast vessel of the sky.

I saw that the plane was armed, with white missiles attached to its slender streamlined belly. I had read about those missiles. Costly little mothers they are. Too costly to fire at Rodney's boat, busily stealing away right in front of my cove. Wouldn't the pilot have to explain the loss of one of his slick rockets? He'd surely be in terrible trouble if he returned to base incomplete.

Rodney was thinking the same way for he was jumping up and down in his power boat, grinning and sticking two fingers at the airplane hovering above the bay.

Then the plane roared and shot away, picking up speed at an incredible rate. I was mightily impressed and grateful, visualizing the enemy confronted with such force, banking, diving, rising again at speeds much faster than sound.

The plane had gone and I was alone again, with Rodney misbehaving in the bay, taking the lobsters out as fast as he could – one trap shooting up after another, yanked up by his nastily whining little winch.

The plane came back, silently, with the roar of its twin engines well behind it. It came in low, twenty-five feet above the short choppy waves. Rodney, unaware, busy, didn't even glance over his shoulder. I was leaning on the railing of my porch, gaping stupidly. Was the good guy going to ram the bad guy? Would they go down together? This had to be the great sight I had been dreaming up. Perhaps I should have felt guilty.

Seconds it took, maybe less than one second. Is there still time at five thousand miles an hour?

Then there was the flame, just after the plane passed the power boat. A tremendous cloud of fire, billowing, deep orange with fiery red tongues, blotting out the other shore, frayed with black smoke at the edges. The flame shot out of the rear of the plane and hung sizzling around Rodney's boat. The boat must have dissolved instantly, for I never found any debris. Fried to a cinder. Did Rodney's body whizz away inside that hellish fire? It must have, bones, teeth and all.

I didn't see where the plane went. There are low hills at the end of the bay, so it must have zoomed up immediately once the afterburners spat out the huge flame.

Michael smiled sadly when he visited me a few days later and we were having coffee on my porch again.

'You saw it happen?'

'Oh yes,' I said. 'A great sight indeed.'

'Did he leave any animals that need taking care of?'

'Just the cat,' I said. The cat was on my porch, a big marmalade tom that had settled in already.

Time has passed again since then. The bay is quiet now. We're having a crisp autumn and I'm enjoying the cool days, rowing about on the bay, watching the geese gather, honking majestically as they get ready to go south.